THE *Games* WE PLAY

THE *Games* WE PLAY

M. HARTLEY

Page & Vine
An Imprint of Meredith Wild LLC

Paperback ISBN: 978-1-964264-55-4

For my Mimi,
Thank you for always being my girl.
One day, my books will be in audio, just like you always wished. I hope you're listening
from somewhere soft and golden.

And for anyone missing someone who helped shape your life…
This one's for you, too.

PROLOGUE

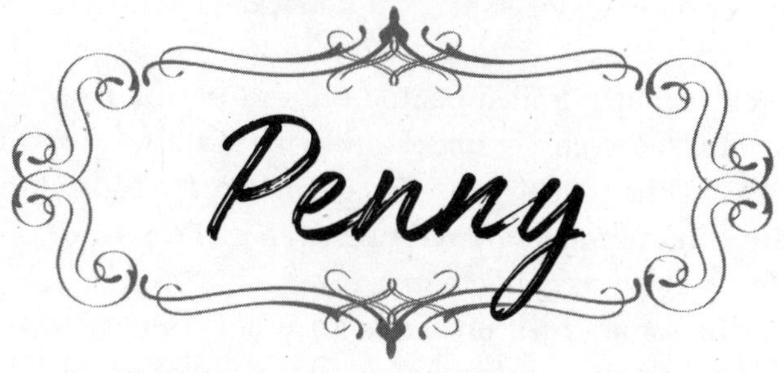

APRIL. ONE MONTH AGO.

"Are you going to tell us why we are sneaking up to The Tequila Cowboy... and why you're holding a bag of pink glitter?" Aspen whispered, her voice low and laced with suspicion as the three of us crouched in the narrow alleyway beside the bar. The brick walls towered above us, casting long shadows, and the faint bass from the music inside vibrated through the pavement.

"I told you, the less you know, the better," I hissed, clutching the glitter like a sacred artifact.

I glanced over my shoulder to make sure the door hadn't opened and then pulled Theo and Aspen closer, my hands gripping their shoulders like we were planning a high-stakes heist. In a way, we were.

"You two need to go inside and make sure no one comes out back. Can you do that?"

Theo and Aspen exchanged a quick look—one of those unspoken best-friend-conversations—and then nodded in perfect sync, eyes wide with mischief and loyalty.

"Good," I said with a slow grin. "I need three minutes. That's it. Whatever chaos you have to cause to buy me that time? I accept all consequences."

"We've got just the idea," Theo said with a wicked grin, holding her palm up for Aspen, who smacked it with a crisp high-five.

Their laughter trailed behind me as I peeled away, the bag of glitter tucked securely under my arm. My boots were nearly silent against the pavement as I crept toward the back of the bar, adrenaline humming in my veins like a shot of espresso.

Mac Ridley was going to pay.

Not in some cruel, break-his-kneecaps kind of way. No, I wasn't a woman of violence, but I *was* a woman of statements. And this? This was going to be *loud and sparkly.*

The moment I saw his truck, my heart thudded in satisfaction. That rusted-out heap of metal was unmistakable. The faded paint had given up years ago, and the left mirror hung on by pure faith.

I let out a quiet, gleeful cackle as I rounded the front and tugged on the driver's side door.

Click.

Bingo.

The door creaked open with almost no resistance. Mac chose to trust the world to not mess with his stuff. Bad call today.

Sliding into the driver's seat, I left the door wide open. If I had to bolt, I wasn't going to get stuck fumbling with it. I pulled out the bag, the plastic crinkling softly, and opened it with a flick of my wrist.

The pink glitter glimmered like fairy dust in the dusk sun, and with one sweep of my arm, it rained down onto the back seat like a sparkly snowstorm. It floated through the air, settling into the carpet, the cushions, every crease and crevice.

Mac was going to find glitter for *months.* In his boots, his jeans, his steering wheel. And every time he did? He'd think of *me.*

He broke my heart.

Sprinkle.

He hadn't called.

Sprinkle.

He hadn't texted.

Sprinkle again.

Did he ever even care?

I poured a little extra into the cup holder for good measure.

I made sure the passenger side got the same treatment, a generous pile in the center. Then the dashboard, because that would be the real kicker. Pink glitter would wedge into the vents and *never* come out.

And in a final, glittery flourish, I dragged my finger through the layer of pink on the surface and drew a big, swooping P, followed by a cheeky xo.

Let him know who.

I checked my imaginary stopwatch. Three minutes, or damn near it.

With my heart racing and laughter bubbling in my chest, I pushed myself out of the truck and slammed the door with dramatic flair. I didn't care who heard. In fact, I hoped someone did.

I took off running toward Main Street, boots pounding the pavement, adrenaline fueling every step. I was breathless from laughing before I even spotted them—Theo and Aspen tearing out of the bar, grinning like they'd just robbed a bank.

Without a word, we fell into step, sprinting down the street toward my apartment, a block and a half away. We didn't talk. We just ran, giggling like teenagers skipping school, the thrill of rebellion stitched into every breath.

When we burst through the vestibule door of my apartment, we collapsed against the wall in a heap of gasps and laughter, our chests heaving, cheeks flushed.

None of us could even speak.

The bell above the flower shop door rang, and we all turned, panting.

Sandy, my landlord, stood in the doorway of Petal Pusher, arms crossed, one eyebrow arched with what could only be described as suspicious amusement.

The smirk tugging at her lips said it all: *I know you're up to no good.*

Sandy leaned against the frame of her flower shop, the door half-open behind her, the scent of lavender and roses wafting into the vestibule.

"Well, well, well," she drawled, that knowing smirk deepening. "Odd time of day for cardio, don't you think, girls?"

I straightened, trying to act casual, though the laughter was still bubbling in my throat and my hair was sticking to my face in all the wrong places. Theo nudged me in the ribs. Aspen was bent over, hands on her knees, wheezing out a laugh.

"We're just... really into fitness now," I said, breathless, trying to wipe the smile off my face and failing miserably.

"Sure you are," Sandy replied, her eyes twinkling. "Fitness... or fleeing the scene of a crime?"

She stepped out onto the sidewalk, arms crossed over her faded green Petal Pusher apron, and looked each of us up and down like a detective solving her favorite mystery. "You wouldn't happen to know anything about a certain trail of pink glitter leading down the sidewalk, would you?"

Aspen snorted.

Theo wheezed, "Coincidence."

Sandy knew something was up; she always did. I'd tell her, just not right now, because I didn't want my friends to hear the real reason I'd roped them into glittering Mac's truck on a random Sunday.

I was lucky for the kind of friends I had, willing to show up and commit some questionable acts because I needed them.

That was what mattered most, not some bartender who used my heart like a cat toy and then didn't have the balls to even apologize for it.

CHAPTER 1

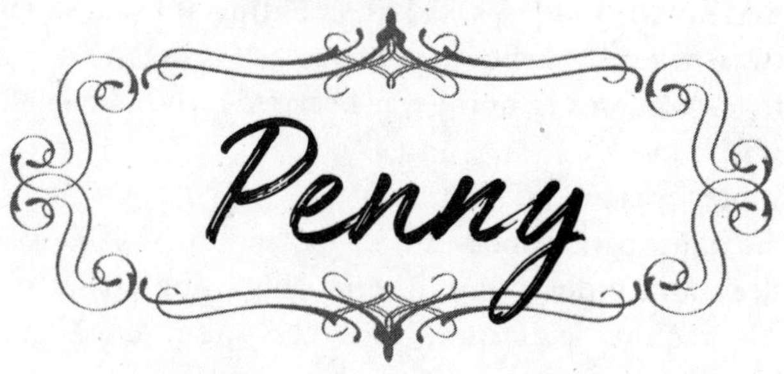

OCTOBER. SEVEN MONTHS AGO.

I pressed my lips together, smoothing out the soft pink lipstick before parting them slightly. With a practiced motion, I ran a fingertip along the edges, wiping away any color that might have bled past the lines. I let out a slow breath and took one last lingering glance in the mirror.

From the bathroom speaker, the familiar twang of "Why Don't We Just Dance" by Josh Turner filled the space—a staple in my getting-ready playlist.

Music had always been woven into my routine, a constant in the background of my life. Whether I was showering, getting dressed, cooking—hell or even cleaning—there was always a melody playing, filling the silence and keeping me company.

I lived alone, which meant the quiet could be deafening if I let it settle too long. I hated the stillness, the way it made the world feel too big, too empty. So, I filled it with music and conversation, even if it was just me talking to myself.

Some might call me a chatterbox, maybe even annoying, but I'd long since let go of the need to change myself for anyone. I liked who I was, and if that meant filling a quiet house with sound, then so be it.

Tonight, I was heading to Cassidy Ranch for a Halloween party, and my costume? A sexy kitten. Fitting, if I said so myself.

I was never shy when it came to self-expression. Whether through fashion, words, or the way I carried myself, I owned every piece of who I was.

Tonight was no different.

The tight spandex bodysuit hugged my curves like a second skin, sleek and unforgiving. Peeling this thing off later would definitely require assistance, preferably from one person in particular.

I ran my hands down my body, the smooth fabric between my fingertips. Hair swept into a high ponytail, cat ears perched perfectly, eyeliner sharp enough to cut. The finishing touch? A spritz of my signature perfume and a pair of knee-high black heeled boots that added the right amount of edge.

With the music still humming in my veins, I turned off the speaker, flicked off the bathroom light, and stepped into my living room—a space as bold and vibrant as I was. Bright colors and playful patterns filled every corner, each piece a reflection of me. My passion for color—for chaos—was woven into everything I touched.

Flopping onto the couch, I reached for my first boot, slipping it on with ease before zipping up the next. My main goal tonight? Finally breaking this tension-filled energy that had been simmering between me and Mac Ridley, the infuriatingly good-looking bartender living in my head rent-free.

I'd spent my time finding ways to tease him, to pull him in, but nothing ever stuck. Mac had this effortless charm, a mix of brazen and rebellious, that made my insides twist in ways I was willing to admit to anyone who listened.

Mac thrived on being playful, untamed, the kind of man who could turn any moment into an adventure. The two of us together? The chaos we'd cause, the energy we'd ignite, was undeniable.

And I wanted all of that.

I wasn't too proud to beg. Hell, I'd drop to my damn hands and knees and crawl to that man if it meant getting what I wanted—though, that wasn't something I did often.

Tonight, I wasn't leaving without a taste of cigarettes and beer straight from Mac's lips.

Tossing my purse over my shoulder, I headed for my car. She wasn't anything fancy, but she was mine, and that's what mattered. Rideshares didn't exist in Faircloud—too small, too quiet—so I already knew I'd be crashing at Aspen's.

Aspen had been my best friend since grade school. We grew up in Faircloud, a town so small you could probably fit the entire population on the main lawn of the Community Park. One stoplight. Everybody knew everybody. If you sneezed in the morning, by noon, Mrs. Winchester from the diner was offering you a home remedy.

Aspen and I had always been inseparable, bonded by our love of books and an almost identical taste in fashion. Lately, though, things had changed. She'd fallen hard for Boone Cassidy, the former chaos creator, now reformed gentleman. That meant I hadn't just gained a future brother-in-law, but a whole new circle of friends.

What started as three friends —Aspen, Theo, and me—expanded to seven. Funny enough, we'd all grown up together, but our worlds had never fully meshed. Not until now, when circumstances changed.

I was eager to see them all. However, one person in particular was on my radar.

Mac wanted me just as badly as I wanted him, and tonight, I planned to finally do something about it.

"A LITTLE TO the left!" Aspen called out, her voice carrying through the barn as I balanced precariously on Boone's broad shoulders. My arms burned from holding up yet another fake bat, the last in a long line of decorations I'd been wrestling with since I arrived.

Why was I the one up here instead of Aspen? She was terrified of heights, and no one had bothered to grab a ladder. So here I was, clinging to Boone for dear life, trying to hook this damn bat into place.

I exhaled, patience thinning. "My left or your left?"

"Mine!" she yelled back.

Boone shifted obligingly, his steady hands keeping me balanced, and I stretched one last time, finally managing to loop the fishing line over the hook on the barn beam. By some miracle, I got it on the first try.

With a deep grunt, Boone bent slightly, giving me the cue to jump down. I slid off his shoulders, landing lightly on my feet. He straightened, adjusting the ridiculous sheep ears on his head with a lazy grin.

Aspen, in her pink puffy dress, looked like she'd stepped right out of a storybook—the perfect Bo Peep. Boone, ever the devoted sheep, played along with his usual easygoing charm.

He lifted a hand for a high-five. "Great work up there," he teased.

I smirked, slapping my hand against his. "I need a freaking drink after that."

Aspen looped an arm around Boone's waist as she joined us. "The drink table's set up over there. We have punch and other things. Go grab one before the party starts."

Boone pressed a kiss to the top of Aspen's head, his affection so obvious it made my heart squeeze. She glowed, her happiness radiating from the inside out. Seeing her this way made me realize just how much things had changed—how much we'd all grown.

"Alcohol is my preference," I declared, placing my hands on my hips.

Aspen grinned. "There's plenty to choose from. I may have gone a little overboard, so now I'm just hoping enough people actually show up to drink it all."

As if on cue, the first few guests started filtering in through the wide barn doors. The space had completely transformed. Not only were my bats finally hanging where they belonged, but the entire barn was draped in the eerie glow of red string lights. Skeletons perched on hay bales, oversized spiders clung to the walls, and the scent of hay mixed with the crisp autumn air.

Boone wandered to the corner, plugging his phone into the speaker. Within seconds, the deep thrum of bass pulsed through the space, the opening notes of a familiar country song setting the mood.

That was my cue to pour myself a drink and get the party started.

Red Solo cup in hand, I surveyed my options, tapping my chin, one hip popped out as I considered the lineup of drinks. The table was a sea of red, black, and purple, each container labeled with some ominous concoction. Witch's Brew or Zombie Juice? What a hard decision.

"If it helps," a deep voice murmured against my ear, sending a delicious shiver down my spine, "I made the Zombie Juice. Biased or not, it's fucking amazing."

I startled, turning sharply only to find myself nearly chest-to-chest with Mac. He stood close, too close. His scent—whiskey, smoke, and something inherently him—wrapped around me like a lasso. My gaze dipped, my fingers tightening around my cup as I took in every detail of his costume.

Starting at his feet, he wore worn brown cowboy boots, broken in and beat up telling a story. Purple slacks stretched over his long legs, topped with a matching suit coat that clung to his lanky frame just right. But it was his face that stopped me in my tracks.

White paint covered his skin, a wide unsettling grin painted across his mouth, and behind his green-dyed hair that curled around his ears, a cigarette was tucked for safekeeping.

The Joker.

And damn if that didn't do something to me.

A villain had never looked so tempting.

Heat pooled low in my belly, and I bit the inside of my cheek to keep from reacting

I stepped back slightly, arching a brow as I caught him scanning me just as thoroughly. His gaze dragged over every inch of my costume—the tight fabric, the curves I wasn't shy about flaunting, and, of course, the dangerous neckline that left just enough to the imagination.

"Zombie Juice it is," I purred, a smirk tugging at my lips. For good measure, I winked before spinning around to fill my cup to the brim.

When I turned back, I met his gaze head-on, bringing the cup to my lips and taking a long, slow sip, letting the liquid burn down my throat. His eyes darkened, amusement flickering through them.

He wasn't lying, this drink was damn good.

"I like your costume," I mused, wiping the corner of my mouth with the back of my hand, careful not to ruin my lipstick.

Mac grinned, slow and wicked, before spreading his arms wide and giving me a slow turn. "Figured it fit my personality."

I raked my gaze over him again, then tilted my head. "I've always liked a little chaos."

He stepped a fraction closer, just enough that my pulse kicked up. "That so?"

I took another sip, letting the taste of the drink mix with the heat between us. "Guess you'll just have to find out."

Mac let out a gravelly laugh, a rich and deep timbre. His voice was sultry, like every word he said carried the extra weight of seduction.

"Is that a promise?" Mac asked, tilting his head slightly like a cat sizing up its prey.

A teasing smile curved my lips. "One I fully intend to keep."

His gaze flickered with something dark, something promising, before he took a step back, nodding. "I'll hold you to that, Penny."

I shrugged, lifting my cup to my lips, letting the weight of his words settle between us.

But Mac wasn't done.

"By the way," he added, pointing at me with the tip of his beer bottle, his voice smooth as sin, "you look good dressed as a *pussy* cat."

And then he *purred*.

A deep, throaty laugh burst from my lips, my head tipping back as the sound filled the space between us. Mac's smirk deepened, his eyes lingering on me for just a second longer before he turned and walked away, leaving me standing there, biting my lip.

CHAPTER 2

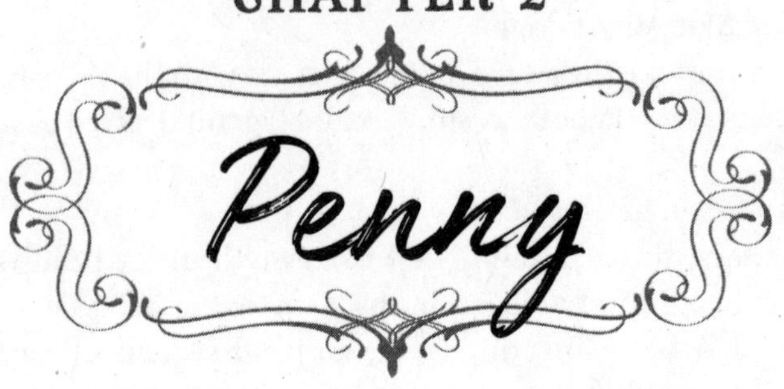

OCTOBER. SEVEN MONTHS AGO.

My friends were by the fire pit, deep in conversation about God-knew-what. It never failed. Whenever we all got together, the *wildest* stories came out.

Take tonight, for instance. I'd just learned *way* too many details about the time Logan walked in on Aspen and Boone getting hot and heavy in the farm stand. Honestly? Good for her. But poor Logan... What I'd give to have been a fly on that wall.

I was filling my cup when I felt a brush on my arm. Expecting to see someone behind me, I spun around, but no one was there.

Brows drawn, I scanned the crowd. Boone and Rhodes were leaning against the wall, beers in hand. Aspen, Theo, and Logan were still by the fire, their laughter carrying across the cool night.

Weird.

I shrugged it off and turned back, only to feel a hand grab me.

Before I could react, I was yanked backward. My drink sloshed over the rim, splashing my wrist as my heels scrambled for traction.

"Jesus!" I gasped, stumbling behind the barn wall. A hand clamped over my mouth, cutting off my yelp.

My pulse slammed in my ears. My eyes widened, frantically adjusting to the dark room. I was ready to fight. No one was going to take me without some kicking and screaming. That was until a flash of neon-green hair caught the dim light.

Heat curled low in my belly.

"Shhh. Keep it down, woman," Mac whispered against my ear, his deep timbre sending a shiver down my spine.

He tugged me farther from the party, weaving us into the shadows, away from the glow of string lights and the hum of conversation. When we were finally hidden, he let go of my mouth.

"What the *hell* was that?" I hissed, running a finger along my bottom lip, checking it in the moonlight to see if my lipstick had smudged.

Mac stepped closer, his presence invading my space like he had every right to be there.

I instinctively backed up, my ankle hitting the first step of the stairs that led up to the loft.

His lips curled into a slow, devilish grin.

A silent dare.

A game.

I stepped up.

He followed.

Step.

Closer.

Step.

Closer.

My heart was loud in my ears until we were finally secluded in the loft, shrouded in the heavy scent of hay, dust, and earth.

The air between us thickened.

And my pulse? *Raced.*

Mac stood a few feet away, the hay chute door cracked open just enough to let in a sliver of moonlight, casting a faint glow across his face. That damn smirk of his hadn't wavered, and despite myself, I found my lips curving into one of my own.

I made one tentative step forward, but he didn't move.

We were stuck in this push and pull, a slow-burning game of tension while our friends partied below, completely unaware.

"I needed to get you away," Mac finally said, pulling the cigarette from behind his ear and fishing a lighter from his pocket.

I stayed rooted in place, so he made the next move, walking past me to a bale of hay before sinking onto it with ease.

Click. Click.

The flame flickered, catching the tip of his cigarette. He inhaled deeply, the end glowing red-hot, before exhaling a slow stream of smoke into the air.

On anyone else, smoking wasn't my type. But Mac? He made it look irresistible.

Deciding to join, I plopped down on the hay beside him, sending a few stray pieces tumbling to the floor.

"And why is that?" I asked, tilting my head as his gaze roamed over me, starting at my heels, trailing up my body, lingering on the cat ears perched on my head. The slow perusal sent heat licking up my spine, my skin prickling in the best way possible.

"Selfish reasons," he admitted, smirking as he took another drag, the smoke curling from his lips like a secret I desperately wanted to know.

I arched a brow. "You do know an open flame around dry hay probably isn't the smartest idea, right?"

Mac shrugged and pulled a makeshift ashtray from his inside pocket—an empty beer can with the top cut off. "It'll be fine." He flicked the cigarette, embers cascading into the bottom with a soft *hiss.*

The hum of music from below felt distant up here, dulled by the quiet tension stretching between us. More space for conversation. More room for whatever the hell he meant by *selfish reasons.*

"Are you going to elaborate on those reasons," I asked, shifting to face him fully, resting an arm on the back of the hay bale, "or leave a woman guessing?"

Mac chuckled, his gaze darkening as he adjusted his position, closing the space between us.

We were already too close, and yet my body hummed for him to be closer.

"Maybe," he murmured, holding the cigarette between his fingers as he reached toward me, his thumb brushing my cheek. The flame hovered dangerously close, yet I didn't move. Didn't even flinch.

"I saw an opportunity to spend some more time with you. One-on-one." His voice dropped lower, rougher. "Without prying eyes."

My pulse fluttered. "And what exactly are your plans for this one-on-one time?" I asked, inching closer, just enough to test him.

His hand fell away, but his gaze never left mine. I tracked the flicker of something dark and unreadable in his eyes before my attention dipped for a second to his mouth. As if sensing it, his tongue darted out, dragging across his bottom lip.

I swallowed hard.

Mac took another slow drag, then dropped the cigarette into the can, watching as it sizzled out, tendrils of smoke curling into the air.

Then, without warning, his hands found my waist.

One firm squeeze—then he grabbed hold and yanked me onto his lap.

A startled breath left my lips, but my body moved instinctively, legs landing on either side of him.

I rose slightly, knees digging into the hay bale as I glared down, hands planted firmly on his shoulders. His grip stayed locked on my waist, keeping me exactly where he wanted me.

"Something like this," he whispered, one hand sliding up to tangle in my hair, pulling me in just enough to bring my face closer to his.

We lingered there, breaths mingling, heat crackling between us. I let my eyes slip shut, feeling his fingers tighten against my skin like he was barely holding himself back.

I was *so* close—close enough that my body ached for it and

heat pooled deep in my stomach.

"I wouldn't be opposed," I murmured, my hands trailing up, cupping his jaw as I leaned the slightest bit closer.

"I've been staring at you all fucking night," he said with a tone so low and masculine it caused the hair on the back of my neck to stand up. "So damn beautiful."

My breath hitched exhale against my lips. My mind was short-circuiting. We were so near danger, so near falling over the cliff into each other.

His hand left my hair and trailed slowly and softly down my sides, following the curve of my waist.

"Especially in that tight outfit, teasing me." He glanced away, and his eyes caught on my breasts. "Showing everyone exactly what is underneath."

Mac glanced up, a wicked grin curling his lips. Heat burst under my skin, every nerve buzzing with raw, unfiltered need.

His thumb brushed over my breast, teasing the aching peak of my nipple through the thin fabric, and I moaned without shame, the sound slipping free like it had a mind of its own.

"Imagine my surprise," he murmured, voice low and full of grit, "when I found out you pierced them." His gaze darkened. "Can't get that image out of my head."

Neither could I.

God, I wanted him to wrap his lips around me, to run his tongue along the bar, to toy with the metal until I shattered from the teasing alone. I was desperate for it, desperate for him.

I couldn't take the tension a second longer. I surged forward, crashing my mouth onto his in a kiss that exploded like fire and brimstone.

His lips crushed mine—firm and demanding. Mac's tongue swept in like he had something to prove, and maybe he did. A low groan rumbled in his chest, and I pressed closer, drinking him in.

Smoke and whiskey. That's what Mac tasted like. Dangerous. Addictive.

A shiver rolled through me, my body unraveling at the seams.

I let go of every last thread of restraint and gave in to the moment, to him.

His hands roamed greedily, gliding over every inch of me like he needed to memorize my shape. Even through the spandex of my costume—which was officially the world's worst cockblock—I burned for him. What the hell had I been thinking, wearing something so tight?

Mac's villain costume, on the other hand? A total fantasy I hadn't known I craved until now. The green-tinged hair. The smudged paint. The delicious chaos.

I rocked against him, feeling the hard press of his cock through his pants. Heat coiled low in my belly as our mouths met again, hot and frantic, like we were trying to make up for lost time.

Why had we spent so much time circling each other instead of *this*? I didn't have the answer, but now that I'd had a taste of Mac Ridley, there was no going back.

I was desperate and horny, craving this like a drug I'd been starved of for far too long. And Mac? He was the cure.

He gripped my ass, kneading through the fabric, groaning at the feel of me. Then, without warning, he stood, hauling me into his arms. My legs wrapped around his waist instinctively as he carried me across the loft.

My back hit the wall with a thud, my breath catching, but Mac held me steady, his body pressing into mine, anchoring me to him.

The sound of the party below was distant, a heavy pulse of bass vibrating through the barn, but up here, in our own little world, the only thing I could hear was the sharp inhale of Mac's breath and the pounding of my heart.

I was trapped between him and the wall, caged in by heat, by tension, by the undeniable pull that had been simmering between us.

And God help me—I never wanted to escape.

Mac fumbled with the zipper at the top of my costume, fingers trembling as I kissed him again and again, devouring every sound he made. When he finally yanked it down, the rush of cool air on my back made me shiver.

I pulled away enough to shove the tight fabric down my arms, but with Mac pinning me to the wall, it was a losing battle.

"A little fucking help," I muttered against his mouth.

He smirked, then set me down abruptly.

His hands were *everywhere*. Yanking, stripping, peeling my costume away with an urgency that made my knees weak.

Just like that, I was bare.

Moonlight streamed through the loft's open door, casting silver shadows across my skin.

Mac's gaze dragged down my body, dark and hungry, his jaw twitching as his cock strained against his dress pants. He reached down, palming himself as his eyes drank me in.

I kicked off my boots, stepping fully out of the discarded suit, leaving nothing but my cat ears perched on top of my head.

Mac's tongue swept along his bottom lip before running over his canine, his smirk downright sinful. "Even better than I imagined," he rasped, voice thick with heat. "You are a fucking *masterpiece*."

I stepped toward him, sliding my hands beneath his jacket, pushing it from his shoulders, letting it drop to the hay-covered floor.

The dress shirt underneath stretched across his broad chest, clinging in all the right places, practically begging me to strip it from his body.

So, I did.

Grabbing each side, I yanked hard.

Buttons popped, scattering across the wooden floor as I tore it open, exposing tattooed skin.

Mac let out a low, rough chuckle, eyes flashing with something dangerous.

"Oh, you're gonna pay for that, Trouble."

The nickname rolled off his tongue, sensual yet commanding. My blood turned molten, heat surging through my veins, my skin prickling with a desperate need for whatever came next.

"Hmm?" I feigned innocence as I tossed his shirt to the floor.

I'd seen Mac shirtless before, but now? Now that I could touch him, *trace* him? I was practically drooling at the thought.

Tattoos covered his smooth, fair skin, each one more captivating than the last. My gaze traced the design on his chest—two hands, fingers nearly touching. Lower, along his ribs, inked words ran the length of his torso, but I couldn't quite make them out. Then, my favorite—two roses, one on each side of the deep V leading down to his—

I snapped my eyes back up, a wicked grin curling my lips.

Mac smirked, knowing exactly where my mind had gone.

The dress pants hung low on his hips, teasing, tempting. I reached out, dragging my fingers over his toned abs, up across his firm chest, then over his broad shoulders, savoring every inch of him.

"What's my punishment?" I murmured, voice dripping with challenge. "How bad have I been?"

I slid my hands into his mop of dark brown hair tinged with green, tugging the strands just enough to earn a sharp inhale from him.

Mac's grip snapped to my lower back, pulling me flush against him.

Bare skin to bare skin.

My nipples brushed against his chest, the friction sending a sharp jolt of pleasure straight down my spine.

His breath fanned against my lips, taunting me.

"First, I'm going to bend that pretty ass over my knee," he replied, his lips hovering close to mine as he spoke. "Then, spank you so fucking hard you'll be screaming for me to stop."

With me firmly in his grasp, Mac dragged me toward the hay bale and sat down as I stood before him.

Slowly, he leaned back, stretching as he lounged. He watched me through hooded eyes, then tapped his thigh in a silent command.

He wanted me in place.

But I didn't move.

I needed to drag this out, to play the game we'd been perfecting for months.

"*Penny*," he growled, his voice edged with warning. His jaw clenched, his eyes darkening with impatience.

Still, I stood my ground, biting back a smirk.

Mac exhaled a slow, controlled breath, shaking his head like I was testing the last thread of his restraint. With stealth and precision, he reached out and grabbed the backs of my thighs before yanking me forward.

I gasped, catching myself on his shoulders before he shifted me into place, flat across his lap, stomach down.

Right where he wanted me.

"I won't ask again," he said, voice a low growl.

He brushed a hand over my bare ass, fingers circling, teasing. Goosebumps formed in his wake.

I huffed, trying to keep my defiant edge, but when I felt that same finger move suddenly between my legs, I lost all sense of power I had.

Mac ran his middle finger through my core, starting at my clit and working his way to my entrance before shoving in once and pulling out completely.

"You're soaked," Mac groaned, repeating the motion, his fingers teasing, testing. "Care to tell me why?"

I swallowed hard, my breath hitching. My mind was chaos, but somehow, I still managed to blurt out a wise-ass remark.

"If I have to explain that, maybe you need a little more experience."

Mac let out a dark, amused chuckle, then without warning—*crack*.

His palm landed hard against my ass, a sharp sting blooming across my skin. I gasped, my body jolting from the impact.

"Did they not teach you that in sex ed? When a female is—"

Crack.

"Not the answer you wanted?" I was testing his patience, and my God, I was drenched.

"Tell me, Pen," he said, rubbing my burning skin. "Is it me that gets you this wet? Because this—you over my knee, soaked and squirming—is what I think about when I stroke my cock."

A whimper left my mouth at his filthy words. I'd always pictured Mac as the silent-but-deadly type. Instead, he was the kind to talk you through it, praise you, and make you crave more.

"Get up," he said. "Be a good girl and stand. Be a bad one..." He trailed off, his voice a promise.

So desperately, I want to be a bad girl, disobey, just to have him punish me more. But my body was raging with arousal, my pulse hammering in my ears. I needed him to fuck me, rough and *hard.*

"Yes, sir," I murmured, standing to my full height.

Mac lounged, pants undone, his cock thick and straining beneath the waistband. He looked wrecked—makeup smudged and hair wild.

"Gimme a spin," he instructed, lazily twirling two fingers in the air.

Slowly, I followed his command, feeling his gaze rake over me, scorching every inch of my exposed skin.

When I turned back to face him, I smirked. "Now what?"

His lips curled, dark amusement flickering in his eyes. "So eager to follow orders now?"

Mac stood, moving toward me with slow, catlike grace—*predatory.*

I nodded, teeth sinking into my bottom lip, anticipation crackling between us.

When he was close enough, I lifted my chin, my breath hitching at his proximity.

Mac's fingers found my jaw, tilting my face up as he held my chin between his thumb and forefinger.

I was his for the taking.

He placed a kiss on my lips and pulled away, mumbling,

"bend over and let me see that pretty pussy, Pen."

"I don't get to see all of you?" I asked, running a hand from his chest down his abs and between the two roses that pointed directly to his cock. "What do you think goes through my mind when I touch myself?"

A growl fell from Mac's lips, and he spun me quickly, slamming me against the bale. With one hand, he held me down, bent at the waist, ass pointing toward him. With the other hand, he pulled out his cock, running it along my entrance, covering himself with me.

"This won't be the last time you're naked for me. We've spent too much time fucking around."

The tip of him ran along me again, teasing my entrance. Pushing back, I silently begged for it.

"I'm on birth control," I huffed, desperately wanting to feel his skin on mine.

"And I'm clean," he replied, rubbing a hand over my backside.

"Then what are you waiting for?"

Without further warning, Mac's cock disappeared inside of me. I didn't know what to expect but when he buried himself to the hilt, I felt him so deep inside me.

I stretched to take all of him, my body adjusting to his size as he fucked me. A moan left my lips, my head tilting back in pleasure. Every thrust, every move of his hips hit the exact spot I needed.

"Oh fuck," I moaned, my voice high-pitched and whiney. I rocked against the hay, Mac's hands still applying pressure between my shoulder blades. "Harder."

Mac obliged, his hips smacking against my ass. Euphoria built at my spine as he changed his angle, thrusting up against the sensitive spot.

Over the bass of the music downstairs, I heard Mac growl, and his hand left my back to fall to my hip. Both hips now in his grasp, he pulled me against him in quick, desperate thrusts.

"Just like that," he coaxed. "You're so fucking tight." The timbre of his voice—his praise—set me on fire. I felt like at any moment I was going to combust and float away into the night.

"You're so good," I panted before I was yanked upward, my back pressed against Mac's front. His hot breath brushed against my skin as he buried his face into my neck.

Mac's teeth latched on, nibbling and sucking as he fucked me from behind. My hand flew up, cupping his face to hold him as close as possible.

He was marking me, placing his claim, which sent me over the edge.

I came, my climax hitting its peak, and my jaw went slack as I let out a satisfied scream.

Mac clapped a hand over my mouth, muffling the noise. "Shhh," he barked, still fucking me through it. "As much as I love how loud you are, you have to stay quiet."

"Mac," I moaned against his hand.

He pulled out, groaning as he came, hot and messy on my back. I collapsed against the hay I'd just been bent over.

Panting, I was trying to get the air my lungs so desperately needed.

There was a soft tap on my shoulder, but I couldn't bring myself to turn around. My heart rate was still high; the pounding echoed in my ears. I needed a moment.

Mac stood next to me, that familiar, cocky grin tugging at his lips.

"How about I help you back into this thing?" he asked, my suit dangling from his grasp.

I exhaled a laugh, still breathless, still buzzing. "Please."

Once we were at least somewhat put together, we snuck back downstairs, slipping into the crowd like nothing had happened. A quick exchange of winks, a lingering glance, and then I was gone, disappearing into the night with my heart pounding against my ribs.

I replayed every moment on an endless loop. The way his hands felt on my skin, the way he tasted, the way my name had sounded on his lips.

When the sun peeked through the blinds the next morning, my first thought was *Mac.*

Because that night wasn't enough.

I wasn't sure it ever would be.

So, when are we doing that again?????

Mac

How did you know I was thinking the same thing?

I usually have that impact on people 

Mac

I'll come over right now if you want me to, no questions asked.

This is going to be dangerous...

Mac

You're my kind of trouble (;

CHAPTER 3

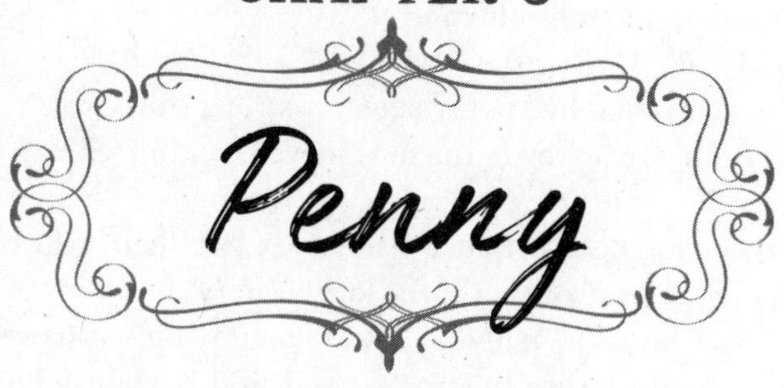

MAY. PRESENT DAY.

"You *son of a bitch*," I muttered, furiously clicking my mouse. "It's the *fucking* twenty-first century—you'd think computers would have learned not to freeze mid-spreadsheet by now."

Letting out a frustrated groan, I dropped my head into my hands. Work was kicking my ass today.

I was knee-deep in budgeting, spreadsheets, and financial reports because, of course, it was *that* time of year. Not only was I the only librarian at Faircloud Public Library, but I had also somehow taken on the role of budget manager, activities coordinator, and school liaison. Apparently, my job wasn't chaotic enough. Clearly, I enjoyed self-inflicted pain. I had a migraine so intense that my eye had started twitching.

I needed a break before I completely lost my ever-loving mind.

Glancing to my left, my eyes landed on a bright pink Post-it note stuck to my desk, a glaring reminder of the never-ending list of tasks I needed to finish by the end of the week.

I was the Post-it note queen. Those little squares of chaos were everywhere: on my walls, my desktop monitor, even covering my refrigerator at home. If I didn't jot something down immediately, it was gone, lost to the void forever.

Call it adulting with ADHD.

Concentration had never been my strong suit. Growing up, I hopped from one hobby to the next, never sticking with anything for long.

Except for books. Books had *never* lost their grip on me. Hence, here I was, working at the local library.

I loved my job—truly, I did. Helping people discover new worlds, lose themselves in stories, and find passion within the pages of a book was what I lived for. Research, creativity, building connections through community events, it all fueled me.

Yet, I'd been stuck in a funk lately.

Where I once found joy in organizing groups and engaging with patrons, I now felt the constant pull to retreat to my office, to hide behind my desk instead of putting myself out there.

With a sigh, I closed the tab I'd been working on and opened a new Word document. I had to plan the rest of the month's reading schedule and, more importantly, find someone to be the group reader.

That was the real struggle.

In a town as small as Faircloud, finding new and exciting people to read to the kids was getting harder.

So far, our biggest hit was Boone. Aspen had somehow convinced her sunshine-in-a-cowboy-hat boyfriend to spend a few Sunday mornings reading to the kids. Let's just say... watching him in that hat, mustache, and deep drawl, captivating a room full of toddlers?

Yeah. I might've been just a tiny bit jealous of Aspen—because, *damn*.

Considering all that, I couldn't ask Boone for more of his time. He'd already done enough.

I could always do it myself, but I already ran the weekday groups, and people would definitely get sick of my voice. Plus, with summer coming, it was time to take a serious look at the budget, which meant one thing: fundraising.

Last year, the Cassidys were kind enough to let me utilize their booth to help raise money. Though it was a hit, I didn't want to be a nag and ask them again this year. That meant I had to get creative.

The mental load of the day had drained me completely, and the Word doc staring back at me felt like too much.

At this point, productivity was a lost cause, and I decided it was time to call it quits and head home.

Besides, I had plans to go out with my friends tonight.

In the last year, our group grew in size. Not to mention, grown closer, too.

Four months ago, Theo had her baby—Frankie, the cutest damn little girl I'd ever seen. She would bring her into the library sometimes, and every time I saw that stroller roll through the door, I couldn't help but squeal.

Frankie was a mini Theo, with dark features and hazel eyes, but her personality? That was *all* Rhodes. It was uncanny, really, considering he wasn't biologically her father. But that man loved that little girl with his entire chest. Watching them together made something tight squeeze inside me.

Then there was Boone's little sister, Ellie, finally back home after nearly a year of traveling the country. Naturally, she'd slipped right into our circle like she always belonged. A lot had changed while she was gone, though, and catching her up had taken time.

So much happened the last year between babies, self-discovery, and new love I couldn't possibly imagine what else life had in store for us.

Shoving my laptop into my tote bag, I grabbed my water bottle and made my way to the door. I needed time to get ready, to mentally prepare for the stress-inducing event I'd have to face tonight.

Seeing *Mac.*

A heavy sigh escaped me at the thought.

It was unfortunate, really, that things between us hadn't worked out. Not for lack of trying on my part, but because that man was a piece of work.

I couldn't even look at him without my stomach flipping like a damn pancake and my anxiety spiking to nearly uncontrollable levels.

But if I wanted to go out with my friends, I had to suck it up because when we went to The Tequila Cowboy, Mac would always be there. I guess I could count my lucky stars that when I saw him, alcohol was always available.

Not a single one of our friends had any idea how much it cost me to show up every time because what Mac and I *had*? It was a secret that ended before it could ever turn into anything more than a friends-with-benefits situation.

Being near him made my heart race uncontrollably, my skin prickle with frustration, with anger. With everything I wished I didn't still feel.

I waved as I said my goodbyes to Crystal at the circulation desk, who returned it with a warm smile. Pushing through the front doors, I stepped into the May air, my skirt billowing around me as I walked down the quiet street.

I lived just a few blocks away, in a small apartment above the local flower shop.

Sandy, the shop's owner, had been running the place since her early twenties. It was her baby, the legacy she and her husband had built together. But after Hank passed away a few years ago, the shop—and the apartment above it—became hers alone.

Sandy was a godsend, the very definition of a Southern grandma. White hair teased into the perfect poof, a spunky spirit, and a slender frame that somehow still carried the strength of a woman who had spent her life tending to flowers and people alike.

Over the years, she'd come to think of me as the granddaughter she never had, and truthfully, I felt strongly about her, too.

Lifting my face to the sky, I let the last remnants of sunlight warm my skin as I made my way home. The streets of Faircloud bustled with familiar faces, and I greeted each one with a smile. In a town this small, you knew everyone. Pleasantries were exchanged in passing, conversations quick but genuine.

When I reached the flower shop's entrance, I pushed open the door and leaned inside.

"Good evening, Sandy!" I called out, gripping the doorframe to hold my weight from falling inside. "Hi, my sweet Penelope!" she chimed, waving at me from behind the counter.

She wore my favorite apron—sage green with a white checkered print, the fabric soft and worn from years of love.

"Do you need anything before I head upstairs?" I asked.

Sandy wiped her hands on her apron, thinking for a moment. "I think I'm good today. Tomorrow may be a different story," she replied with a grin.

"You know where to find me," I answered, chipper as ever.

"Why don't you come down after you get settled? I have some leftover pizza that I made at home. I hate to know you always eat alone."

I sighed. Every night, she tried to convince me to join her for dinner. As much as I appreciated it and sometimes gave in, I did have someplace to be.

"I can't tonight," I said, giving her a sweet smile. "Rain check?"

"Of course, dear."

I blew her a kiss before disappearing up the stairs to my apartment.

The second I stepped inside, I exhaled a deep sigh of relief.

Kicking off my shoes, dropping my bags by the door—I was home.

My safe haven of colors and comfort. The one place where I could let go of the day and just *be*. Here, I didn't have to be anything but myself—chaotic, carefree, light.

Crossing the room, I connected my phone to the kitchen speaker and hit play. Music filled the apartment, wrapping around me like a familiar embrace, loud enough to follow me from room to room.

First task, dinner.

I needed to eat something before heading out tonight. With a couple of hours to spare, I opened the fridge and stared at the contents, debating my options before finally pulling out a salad kit and some fresh fruit to toss in.

After eating, I'd shower and then get ready to meet everyone. I needed to give myself one hell of a pep talk in the mirror.

Swaying my hips to the beat, I dumped the lettuce into the bowl and added fruit, croutons, and some strawberry vinaigrette before carrying it to my dining room table and sitting crisscross apple sauce. The music filled the space, but I sat in my own head, shoveling fork full after fork full of lettuce into my mouth.

CHAPTER 4

PRESENT DAY.

I inhaled deeply, letting the smoke fill my lungs before exhaling around the cigarette dangling from my lips. Another night behind this bar—the same bar I'd grown up in, the same one I couldn't seem to leave.

Working here was in my blood, woven so deep into my DNA that I never saw myself anywhere else. Slinging bottles, pouring drinks, and watching the same faces roll in and out was all I knew.

My father owned this place until the day he died.

I'd like to say he poured his blood, sweat, and tears into keeping it afloat, but that would be a damn lie. The only thing that man ever put effort into was playing pool and getting too fucking drunk to function.

By ten years old, I was pouring draft beers and charming my way into tip money, stuffing every last bill and coin into an old coffee can beneath my bed. Hard work had never been a choice for me—it was a necessity.

"Put that shit out," Lizzie, my sister, barked as she walked by, rolling her eyes. She made it to the window where our neon *Open* sign hung, officially signaling the start of another night of business.

"Mind your damn business," I shot back, taking another slow drag.

"My bar. My rules."

I scoffed, turning my attention away from her and toward the bottles lining the back wall.

Lizzie was a barracuda, ruthless and set in her ways which made us butt heads more often than not.

She was tall and petite, the spitting image of our mother, right down to the sleek brown bob that barely grazed her shoulders—the same color as mine, though I'd never admit we had anything in common because she and I were *nothing* alike.

Our parents never married, and when I was eight and Lizzie was twelve, they finally decided they were better off far away from each other. Mom took Lizzie. And me? I drew the short end of the stick, staying behind with Dad in the cramped one-bedroom apartment above the bar.

While Lizzie had a decent life—sports, friends, college—I was left to fend for myself, playing the fucking adult before I was even old enough to ride a bike without training wheels.

"You are insufferable," I muttered, shaking my head. "Go bark your orders at someone who gives a shit." Waving her off, I focused back on my final count of liquor bottles, scribbling down numbers before the first pour of the night.

The scrape of a stool dragging across the hardwood echoed, mixing with the low twang of country music filtering through the speakers.

I turned, clipboard in hand, slapping it onto the bar top just as Lizzie reached for me.

In one swift motion, she plucked the cigarette from my lips and dropped it into a cup of half-melted ice beside me.

"I said, *put it out*."

My jaw ticked, but I kept my expression carefully blank, both hands flattening against the bar as I leaned in slightly.

"You owe me forty cents for that."

"Will you ever learn?" Lizzie asked, leaning back, tilting her head in that slow, feline way that always made her seem like she was sizing me up. "Just give it up and get over yourself."

She crossed her arms over her chest, all exasperation and superiority.

I rolled my neck from side to side, working through the tension that always formed whenever she decided to spend a night micromanaging *my* bar.

Except it wasn't mine on paper.

There was no way in hell I was ever going to *get over it.* Our father leaving her the bar on his deathbed would never sit right with me. I'd poured years of my life into this place, built the clientele, kept the damn lights on.

This was supposed to be mine.

Yet, in his final moments, my father gave me one last *fuck you* before taking his last breath.

Years ago, after he got sick and Lizzie decided to come back into the picture, I made the mistake of running. I left Faircloud, convinced I'd find something better, a fresh start. Vegas had seemed like the answer—women, an insane bar scene, distractions in every form.

A few months and one big mistake later, I found myself right back here, resuming my position as manager, bartender, and overall CE-fucking-O of The Tequila Cowboy.

Except, in the end, it didn't matter.

Dad never let me forget that I left. He reminded me every damn chance he got. Even now, in *death*, he was still playing his games.

Reaching into my back pocket, I pulled out a small white cardboard box and lighter. Slipping a cigarette between my lips, I ducked my head slightly and lit up, inhaling deeply.

Lizzie scoffed. "See, this is exactly why Dad gave me the bar. You're so damn childish, and that shit will kill you."

I glanced up at her, exhaling a slow stream of smoke into the air.

That same permanent look of disapproval sat on her face, a mirror of our mother. Mom had never been happy, always carried herself like she was waiting for life to disappoint her.

I smirked, unbothered.

"What can I say?" I took another long drag, my voice lazy, taunting. "*C'est la vie.*"

The bell above the door chimed, signaling someone had walked in. Glancing up, I realized it was two *someones*—Aspen and Boone, making their way toward the bar.

Lizzie never stuck around to socialize with my friends. True to form, she stood and disappeared into the back office without so much as a glance in their direction.

Shaking my head, I bent down and grabbed two glasses to make their usual drink of choice. Aspen, a tequila sunrise. Boone, Jack and Coke.

By the time Aspen slid onto the barstool, placing her small purse on the counter, and Boone settled into the seat beside her, their drinks were already in front of them. I took another slow drag from my cigarette before using the half-melted ice in my cup as an ashtray.

"Everything's on the house tonight," I announced, reaching for a shot glass and filling it to the brim with tequila before knocking it back in one go.

If Lizzie wanted to call me childish, I was more than happy to act the part.

Boone scoffed, lifting his drink. "You sure that's a good idea?"

I shrugged. "What do I care?"

"When Lizzie's on your ass for the millionth time, you will."

I let out a dry laugh, leaning against the back of the bar, arms crossing over my chest as I propped one foot over the other.

"Hell will freeze over before I give a shit what she thinks."

And that was the truth. I'd grown up unaffected by her opinions, and I sure as hell wasn't about to start now.

Boone shook his head, giving me a pointed look over the rim of his glass.

"What?" I asked, eyeing him skeptically.

Aspen straightened, leaning forward over the bar, eyes narrowing like she was trying to figure me out.

"Mac..." she drawled, studying my face.

"Yes?"

Her gaze sharpened, then suddenly her expression lit up with amusement.

"Is that a *mustache*?" she gasped, sitting back with a laugh, tipping her head as she grinned behind her glass.

I smirked and strolled toward her before leaning across the bar on my elbow, closing the distance between us.

"It is," I replied with a wink.

Then, tilting my head toward Boone, I added, "I know you have a thing for a mustache. Do we tell him?"

Aspen giggled, shaking her head, playing along.

I extended my hand to her, flashing a cocky grin. "Let's run away, baby."

That smirk? It had gotten me what I wanted more times than I could count.

Boone, unimpressed, cleared his throat and took another sip of his drink. "You're lucky I know you're joking," he muttered. "Otherwise, I'd kick your scrawny ass."

"Whoa there, *cowboy*," I said, stepping back with my hands in the air in mock surrender.

Before Boone could respond, the door swung open again. This time, Theo and Rhodes walked in.

Rhodes held the door open for his woman, and Theo entered with a bright smile, her hair styled in pigtails.

Rhodes removed his hat and raked a hand through his hair before setting it back on his head.

"I didn't know they were coming too," I muttered, tilting my head toward the couple.

Aspen turned toward them, waving. "Rhodes's mom is watching the baby tonight so they could come out."

Theo picked up her pace, leaving Rhodes a few steps behind,

and pulled Aspen into a hug before sliding onto the stool beside her.

Theo and Aspen were also Faircloud natives; we all went to school together. Growing up, we never crossed paths, but ever since Boone started taking a liking to Aspen nearly a year ago, we all became one big happy family.

"What can I get you two?" I asked, tapping the ash off my cigarette before placing it between my lips.

Rhodes clapped Boone on the shoulder in greeting before turning to me. "I'll take a Coors."

"I'll have the same," Theo chimed in, tossing her pigtails over a shoulder.

"Mac's feeling generous tonight," Boone added with a smirk. "Everything's on the house."

Rhodes shot me a suspicious look, brows knitting together. I shrugged, popping the caps off two Coors bottles against the edge of the bar before sliding them over. "It's one of those nights."

Theo laughed, eyes knowing. "Lizzie piss you off again?"

I nodded, my lips pressing into a thin line.

Rhodes smirked as he took a sip. "Penny will be glad to hear everything is on the house."

Her name hit me like a gut punch.

Instantly, my stomach twisted, the air shifting and tightening around me.

Being in the same room as her was hard enough. Pretending everything was fine? Even fucking harder, and unfortunately, I had to pretend way too often.

I'd chosen to ignore her the best I could the last couple of months, but I couldn't take it anymore.

I desperately wanted her to hear me out. To listen to what I had to say. I knew I'd fucked up—I'd admitted my wrong—but she was a woman scorned, and I was in the doghouse.

I wasn't giving up; I just had to find a way to alter my approach, yet every time I tried to corner her, to get a moment alone, she'd find an excuse to run.

Most times, she wouldn't even acknowledge my existence, looking right past me like I didn't fucking exist.

I schooled my expression, doing my best not to let the mere mention of her show on my face. Instead, I busied myself with cutting lemons for garnish, letting my friends fall into easy conversation while I focused on forgetting.

Penny and I had something good. It was fun, effortless—something we both benefited from. The secrecy of everything made it more intoxicating, adding to the pull, the tension, the depth of whatever the hell we were.

But I fucked it up.

Not much of a surprise.

The door swung open again, and this time, a few locals straggled inside. They headed straight for a table on the far side of the room.

Dudley was supposed to be working the bar with me tonight, but the bastard was late—no shock there.

I silently counted my blessings, hoping he'd actually show up so I could slip away, pull Penny aside, and end this shit once and for all. I couldn't keep going like this. I couldn't keep feeling sick at the sound of her name.

With our friends dating, there was no avoiding her.

Tonight, I was fired up. The interaction with my sister was fuel added to the raging fire inside me.

Stepping away from the bar, I ducked into the storage room to grab extra supplies. But when I returned, the group had grown.

Logan and Ellie now stood behind the others, slipping into the fold like they'd always belonged.

Lately, Logan had been coming around more than usual, and Ellie, Boone's little sister, was finally home after nearly a year.

After a brutal breakup, she'd packed her bags and left Faircloud behind, choosing to spend some time alone and rediscover herself.

And honestly? I couldn't blame her one damn bit.

Sometimes, running again sounded like the best possible answer, but I tried that once. This time, it wouldn't fix the problems, because my biggest one would be walking through the door any minute.

TIME TICKED BY, and I held true to my promise. Every drink I poured for my friends was on the house.

Luckily for me, Dudley *finally* showed up, which meant I could focus on them while also managing the rowdy crowd that had packed into the bar.

Music blared over the speakers, the bass thrummed through the floorboards, and the neon lights cast their usual warm glow over the space. The place was packed, double-stacked around the bar, people shoulder to shoulder, making it damn near impossible to keep up.

For a small-town bar, this was busy, and judging by the unfamiliar faces, these weren't just locals.

"You!" I called, pointing at a guy standing toward the back of the mass of people.

He was tall, wearing a cowboy hat, his lips moving as he placed an order. I was great at reading lips; you had to be in a job like this.

Round of shots.

He held up five fingers, mouthing the word *tequila*.

Nodding, I reached out, and he passed his card over the heads of the people between us. "Open or closed?" He gave me the universal sign for the latter.

Wiping my hands on the towel slung over my shoulder, I turned toward the register before finishing the transaction. When I spun back around and glanced up, she was there.

Penny.

Standing at the door, staring directly at me.

The crowd had somehow parted, leaving a perfect line of sight between us, like the universe was taunting me. Testing me.

My throat tightened, and I swallowed hard, forcing myself to focus on the customers before me, but it was useless.

There was no way in hell I would be able to concentrate when my thoughts kept drifting back to her, when my eyes kept scanning the room, searching for another glimpse.

My obsession—the sheer pull she had over me—was becoming impossible to resist.

And maybe that was the real problem.

The more she ignored me, the worse it got.

I had to talk to her.

But first, I needed to get this crowd under control.

Exhaling sharply, I shut my eyes for half a second, steeling myself before pointing to the next customer.

Once the crowd was under control, I would make my move. Until then, I had to power through the racing thoughts and the itch to talk to Penny and focus on work.

Something told me that was going to be really fucking difficult.

CHAPTER 5

"Shit!"

The sharp crack of shattering glass echoed through the bar, loud enough to make a few heads turn.

Third one tonight.

I clenched my jaw, my hands tightening into fists as I stared at the mess at my feet. I was completely useless—every ounce of focus, every goddamn skill I had, had gone right out the front door the second *she* walked in.

And just my luck, Penny looked fucking *stunning*.

Drop-dead gorgeous.

Not that it was a surprise. Penny always looked beautiful.

The way she carried herself, effortless and confident.

The way her laughter rang out over the music, warm and untamed.

The way her damn smile lit up the entire room, brighter than any neon sign could ever dream of being.

She was a walking beam of pure, blinding sunshine. That's what I liked most about her. It was the reason why I was such a goddamn mess, I couldn't get any of it out of my head.

I scrubbed my hands through my hair, exhaling sharply as I tipped my head back toward the ceiling.

I needed a break. Five minutes to pull myself together before I embarrassed myself any further.

With the crowd finally settled, I grabbed a cigarette from my back pocket and stalked toward the back door, shoving it open so hard it cracked against the brick wall before slamming shut behind me.

Fresh air and a smoke. That always helped.

I wedged the cigarette between my lips, flicked my lighter, and took a long, deep inhale. The burn filled my lungs, sharp and grounding. For a second, I let myself believe it might actually do the trick.

Then—

The door banged open again, but I didn't turn around because I swear to God, if that's Lizzie...

"Dude, what the hell is your problem?"

Not Lizzie. Dudley.

Of fucking course.

I turned just enough to see him standing there, arms spread wide like he was ready to throw down. His blond hair was a tangled mess, brown eyes narrowed in irritation.

Where I had tattoos, he had piercings—his lip, his eyebrow, a stud in his nostril. And, as always, he was decked out in all black, the look completed by a cowboy hat.

My blood simmered. I didn't want to deal with him. Didn't want to deal with anyone.

Why the hell couldn't people just leave me the fuck alone?

Why did I always have to explain myself like some schoolboy? First, my sister and now Dudley.

The frustration churned so deep that I didn't even think before I snapped.

"Worry about yourself and get back to work," I barked, my skin prickling, vision blurring at the edges.

I took a step forward. So did he.

Toe to toe.

Both of us stubborn as hell, neither backing down.

Dudley exhaled slowly, jaw twitching before he took a step away, not in the mood for a testosterone-fueled pissing match. I was glad for it because, with how I was feeling right now, I didn't see myself choosing the high ground. I'd say something I'd regret.

Pointing a finger at me, he sighed. "When you're done dropping shit and screwing up drinks, get your ass back inside. Otherwise, I'm taking your tip money, too."

With a shake of his head, he disappeared back inside, leaving me alone with nothing but my cigarette, my frustration, and the mess in my head.

Clearly, he had more to say but chose otherwise.

Dudley was one of my good friends. He and I have been working this bar together nearly every night for years, and to see him pissed at me wasn't a feeling I enjoyed.

Sure, I liked to stir the pot and shake shit up, but I didn't enjoy it when people I cared about were angry at me.

I had to get back to work, service needed to go on as normal.

There wasn't time to finish my cigarette. I snuffed it out on the side of the building and tossed it into the can I kept by the back door.

Rolling my shoulders, I made my way back inside, walking down the narrow hallway from the alley and into the bar. My cowboy boots clacked against the sticky, tiled floor, the familiar sound bringing me back as I reentered the chaos.

By the time I slid back into position behind the bar, Dudley was already in the swing of things. Lucky for me, the crowd seemed satisfied enough that he had it handled.

I used the free moment to stock the bar, but my attention wasn't really on the liquor bottles.

My eyes roamed the dimly lit space, searching, hoping, for a glimpse of Penny, praying she hadn't left already. Considering the rest of the group was still here, it was unlikely she'd be the first to go.

Standing on the balls of my feet, I scanned the bar, the music loud enough to drown out the chatter, the pulse of bass thrumming through the walls.

I found her.

Chestnut hair swaying to the beat.

Penny was on the dance floor, moving with Aspen and Ellie, their hands linked as they spun and laughed, completely lost in the music.

My breath hitched.

I couldn't look away.

The way she moved—hips rolling, body fluid, completely carefree—she was so unapologetically *her.*

I was fucking mesmerized.

A sharp pang of something unfamiliar tightened in my chest. Anxiety then took over, a feeling that was new and very unwelcome, yet it came regardless of how hard I tried to bat it away.

I quickly cleared my throat, forcing my gaze anywhere but her, but it was too late.

Penny spun at just the right moment, catching me watching her before I could fully turn my attention.

For a fleeting second, something unreadable crossed her face—surprise, hesitation, maybe even regret. But even quicker, she masked it, schooling her expression into something cold, detached.

Then, she looked away completely.

Fuck if that didn't sting.

Jaw tight, I busied myself, swapping out the liquor spouts and tossing the empty bottles into the trash, each movement sharper, more forceful than necessary.

I couldn't keep doing this.

This uneasy, gut-churning feeling. This constant, gnawing urge to make things right.

I was living in my own personal hell, watching the woman I'd fallen for pretend I didn't exist.

Ignoring me. Taunting me, whether she realized it or not.

I'd had my eyes on Penny Hudson, and it pissed me off that it wasn't going nearly how I had planned.

Glancing to my left, I saw Dudley on the opposite side of the bar, shamelessly flirting with a brown-haired girl I didn't recognize.

My eyes roamed once more for Lizzie. I hadn't seen my sister all night. Thank God for that. Dealing with her and Penny in the same room? That would've been a hell I wasn't prepared for.

One stressor was more than enough.

Spinning back toward the front of the bar, I froze.

Penny was leaning over the counter, frantically waving toward the end where Dudley stood, trying to get his attention.

My throat tightened, a knot forming so big I could barely breathe. The reaction was instant, visceral—but not the kind I wanted.

My skin prickled. My chest warmed. My heartbeat pounded in my ears.

Forcing a calm front, I took a slow step toward her. Penny still refused to look at me, determined to act like I wasn't standing right fucking here.

This was my chance. It was fate that I spun around when I did.

She chose the wrong spot. The space she crammed into was the only stretch of bar free of sitting patrons, leaving her face to face with me. The perfect opportunity.

"Penny," I said, wiping my hands on the towel slung over my shoulder. The fabric was stark white against my all-black outfit—black T-shirt, tattoos on full display, dark jeans to match.

She ignored me, so I stepped closer.

When I did, her perfume hit me—*vanilla*.

Just like that, I was back there—back to the nights we'd spent tangled together. The way she'd sighed when I nuzzled into her neck, when I kissed along the soft, sensitive skin she loved to be touched.

"Pen, come on," I urged again, reaching out, my fingers brushing against her arm.

She yanked away like my touch had burned her, a scowl forming on her lips as she glared at me. If she had a drink in her hand, there was no doubt in my mind she would've tossed it right in my face.

I pulled back, my patience snapping.

This was fucking insane.

She was pissed—fine. But ignoring me like a child? Pretending I didn't exist?

That was bullshit.

What happened—what the problem was—had *nothing* to do with her.

It was about me, about choices I made years ago. A situation I thought had worked itself out, one I never imagined would come back to haunt me.

But life saw an opportunity when I had something good—something real. And, like clockwork, it shit all over it.

Penny brought her fingers to her mouth and whistled, still trying to get Dudley's attention.

He spun, but I pointed a finger at him, my jaw set.

Dudley got the message. *Stay the fuck out of it.*

With Penny still leaning over the bar, I hooked my hands under her arms and hauled her over the damn counter.

She screamed, legs flailing, nearly knocking over the neatly stacked glasses on the shelf behind me.

"Let me go, you animal!" she shrieked, fists beating against my chest.

I ignored her protests, shifting her effortlessly over my shoulder as I strode toward the back.

Eyes were everywhere, watching, heads turning.

Even over the pounding music, we were causing a scene. I couldn't bring myself to care. I was blinded by rage, blinded by the way she once made me feel, and I clung to that.

All the emotions I felt in the last few hours were surging to the surface. Anger. Disappointment. Longing. Embarrassment. There were so many I'd been harboring the last couple of months, and I'd hit my tipping point.

The moment I got her into the stockroom, I kicked the door shut behind us and let her down. She huffed in frustration, immediately scrambling back against the shelves as if the extra inches between us would make a difference.

"What the hell was that?" she demanded, throwing her hands in the air. Her face was a perfect picture of exasperation, her eyes blazing with annoyance.

I'd pulled her away from her night, from the fun she was having, and I was probably the last person she wanted to be stuck in a room with.

"If you'd just listen to me—" I started, crossing my arms over my chest.

"Mac, there's nothing to hear," she shot back, voice sharp and unwavering. "You lied to me. You kept a big fucking secret."

"I didn't lie!" The words came out too loud, my voice cracking with desperation.

I forced my eyes shut, dragging in a breath to steady myself. I knew she had every right to be furious. I should've told her sooner. I should've come clean. But I never once lied.

"Come on, Trouble," I sighed.

She popped her hip and angled her head, her expression calling me out on my bullshit.

"Don't you dare call me that. You lost the right."

"There was nothing to lie about," I muttered.

She exhaled sharply, shaking her head. "I can't do this right now." Penny made a move to push past me, but I caught her arm.

"When, then?" I demanded, my grip gentle but firm. "You name the time and place, and I'll be there."

She sighed, rolling her eyes, but there was something else lurking beneath the surface—something that made my stomach drop. Sadness? Regret?

"I don't know," she admitted, her voice quieter now.

I softened instantly, my frustration crumbling under the weight of what I felt for her. "I'm begging you, Penny. Please..." My voice was rough with emotion. Under the dim stockroom light, she tucked her hair behind both ears—a nervous tell I'd come to memorize.

"I'll let you know when I'm ready," she finally said. Then she turned, disappearing out the stockroom door before I could stop her.

I groaned, raking my hands through my hair.

That was the first time I'd been alone with her in over a month. I wasn't letting it end this way. I wasn't going to let her slip through my fingers that easily.

I needed to know what she wanted from me, what she *needed* me to do.

The moon? I'd rope it.

On my knees? I'd beg.

A confession of every feeling I'd ever had for her? I would, without batting an eye.

I wasn't going to stop until she heard me out because those months together in secret were the best damn months of my life.

The flicker in her gaze, the softness that took over her voice just a moment ago, let me know she still felt something, too.

CHAPTER 6

DECEMBER. FIVE MONTHS AGO.

Answer my FaceTime!!

Mac
I'm about to get in the shower...

And?

Mac
As much as I love the thought of you and my shower. You'll have to take me to dinner first, Trouble (; I can't keep giving myself away so easily

I opened my camera, snapping a naked photo of me in the mirror and hit send.

What about now?

Mac

You're naughty... how am I supposed to say no when you look like that?

I leaned back in my chair, my phone propped up on FaceTime with Theo and Aspen. We were in the middle of a battle—me trying my hardest to convince Theo to let us throw her a baby shower, and her stubbornly resisting.

Despite her protests, this was her *first* baby, and she was going to need everything she could get.

I had plans: raffles at the library to gather supplies, inviting people from around town to pitch in, making sure Theo felt as loved as she deserved because she *did* deserve it.

Seeing her smile like this, like she was right now? A real, genuine smile? It had been too damn long.

Theo found something in Rhodes—something solid, something safe. He understood her in a way no one else did. They were two people who thrived in each other's simplicity.

It was kind of beautiful...

Aspen was at the farm stand, the glow of string lights behind her as she flitted around, the hem of her dress catching the air. Theo sat cross-legged on her bed, folding some of the cutest little onesies I'd ever seen.

Baby fever was a bitch.

I had to keep reminding myself that whenever I needed a little dose, I'd just have to steal Frankie.

"I really don't want anything big and elaborate," Theo said, placing a onesie down and giving us her full attention. "The gender reveal was plenty, and while I loved it, it completely wiped me out."

She had a point. Aspen and I would handle everything, but once the dust settled, Theo would be the one left drained. And that wasn't fair.

With a sigh, I leaned back further in my chair, holding my phone up toward the ceiling.

"Fine, fine, I get it. Nothing big, but I still—"

A sound caught my attention. I sat up, and there was Mac, standing in the doorway of my office.

I shot him a pointed look, widening my eyes and waving him over with a sharp nod—*shut the door, stay quiet.*

Mac grinned, the corner of his mouth tilting up, infuriating me in the best way possible. With both hands behind his back, he obeyed and stepped closer.

My mind was pulled between the conversation going on and curiosity about what Mac was holding behind his back. With a smirk like that, I knew there was *something.*

Stopping next to me, he finally showed his hand, and my breath hitched.

A bouquet of red roses. The color vibrant, the leaves full of life and perfectly green.

I schooled my face, ignoring the way my heart stupidly flipped in my chest.

Keeping my expression neutral, I turned my focus back to the phone screen, making sure Mac stayed out of view.

I wanted to smile. Wanted to tell him how beautiful they were. But I couldn't. Not right now.

Mac laughed silently, shaking his head before setting the bouquet across my keyboard. Then, as if he belonged there, he perched himself on the edge of my desk.

My gaze flicked to him, just for a second.

Big mistake. He looked so damn good.

That perfect mess of hair I loved, the soft Henley hanging loose on his frame, the top buttons undone just enough to reveal a sliver of his chest tattoo.

The way his sleeves were rolled up was like he was about to get down to business.

Not to mention, his hands flexed with each deliberate move, the tattoos on the backs moving in just a way that made anticipation pool in my belly.

Mac reached out, seemingly to touch me, but I kicked my leg

to shoo him away. The bastard pulled back, making me kick the side of my desk instead.

"Who was that?" Aspen asked.

My skin prickled, shit.

I cleared my throat before responding. "No one." I shrugged. "Anyway, I still want to do something for you, Theo. You deserve it."

I needed to redirect the conversation and take the heat off me before either of them caught on.

What Mac and I were doing—this little game, this secret—was fun. It was hot. For now, it was just *ours*.

There was something thrilling in the hiding, in the tension that crackled between us when no one was looking. And Mac? He loved it just as much as I did.

Theo hesitated like she was considering caving, but instead, she sighed, shaking her head.

"I appreciate it, but really, I'm okay." A small smile touched her lips as she folded another onesie. "Maybe we could just have a small get-together? No gifts. Just the three of us and maybe the guys hanging out."

Aspen's face lit up. "I could bake some goodies!"

I trusted Aspen with anything baked. She made a pretty good blueberry muffin. I couldn't bring anything like that, but I knew there was one thing I was good at.

"I'll bring the fun," I added, grinning.

Theo giggled. "Rhodes might be up for cooking something."

Ugh. A man who cooks? *Be still, my heart.*

A sudden thud against my desk chair snapped my attention back.

Mac.

Still perched there. Still waiting.

I glanced at him out of the corner of my eye. He pointed at himself, mouthing something I couldn't quite catch.

I didn't dare acknowledge him—if I did, Theo and Aspen would know.

So instead, out of view, I reached down and pinched his leg.

A silent warning.

A reminder that I knew he was still there.

Judging by the slow, wicked grin that spread across his face, Mac loved every second of it. The idea that no one knew he was sitting so close to me, that once again, it was our little secret.

My body betrayed me, reacting in ways I had zero capacity to handle right now. Heat pooled low in my stomach, my pulse kicking up as Mac's hand slid onto my thigh.

Asshole.

"Speaking of Rhodes," Aspen said, a sly smile creeping onto her lips, "how are things going?"

"Ooh, ooh, did he like the pictures?" I asked, desperate to focus on anything other than the man beside me, whose hand was teasing my inner thigh. The same man who was very much enjoying my torment.

Theo burst into laughter. "Yes, he did. He keeps it in his truck, actually. So... I guess you could say things are going great."

Mac's fingers stilled like he was waiting for me to look at him. Instead, I kicked his leg *again*, a silent warning for him to back off.

The urge to end this conversation and deal with Mac head-on was *so* strong, but I forced myself to stay present.

"Hot!" I sighed dramatically, dragging my focus back to the call. "That is every girl's dream."

Mac stood from my desk, moving enough to catch my attention before casually making his way to the opposite side.

One by one, he started clearing off my desk.

What the hell is he doing?

Every item—my planner, my pens, even my phone stand—moved elsewhere, making space for something else.

"You're happy," Aspen said softly, resting both hands on the counter as she peered through the phone.

"I am," Theo admitted, her smile soft, content. "Rhodes has been so supportive, so kind. Being with him is... easy. I've always liked being alone, but being with him is better. He makes me feel understood, heard. He gives me a kind of comfort I haven't felt in a long time."

I should've been invested in the conversation. I wanted to be. But my focus? It was fully hijacked.

Out of the corner of his eye, Mac glanced at me as that irresistible smirk spread across his face.

He was taunting me.

"I have to go," Theo mumbled suddenly, cutting out before Aspen and I could respond.

I blinked, snapping back to reality as Aspen shrugged. "Well, that was—"

"Ugh, me too," I blurted, already hitting end before she could question it.

Mac let out a low, satisfied snort because he knew he won. I was intrigued and desperate to know what the hell was happening.

Locking my phone screen, I set it down and finally turned my full attention to him.

"What are you doing here?" I asked, glancing at the bouquet of roses he'd brought me.

Roses. I loved roses.

He knew they were my favorite. I always kept a pitcher full of them on my counter, never letting it go empty.

"Well," Mac said, strolling toward me as I sat in my desk chair. "I had some time before the bar opened and thought I'd come see what you were up to."

"Working," I replied dryly.

Mac stopped in front of me, leaning down, his hands bracing on the armrests of my chair. His face was dangerously close now, eyes locked on mine.

My breath hitched, but I held my ground, staring right back at him.

I shifted under his gaze, my pulse betraying me as I tucked my hair behind both ears—*damn it.*

"You nervous, Trouble?"

He caught me, just like he always did.

Being nervous around Mac was part of the course, though I never let it show beyond that tick. But he knew. He always knew and he used it to his advantage every damn time.

His hand came up, fingertips skimming my cheek in a touch so soft, so damn tender, it stole my breath.

A shiver rolled down my spine. My body warmed under the simple touch, betraying me completely, but I kept the rest of myself calm and collected.

I met his gaze with a smirk. "Why would I be nervous around *you*?"

Mac scoffed, his fingers falling away as he straightened to his full height. He ran his tongue along the inside of his cheek, exhaling like I was *exhausting* him.

"You love to play these games..." His voice was rough, edged with something dangerous.

"Hmm?" I tilted my head, feigning innocence, bringing my manicured hand up to inspect my nails. "Whatever do you mean?"

His eyes darkened.

In one swift motion, Mac picked me up, lifting me right out of the desk chair.

I gasped, clinging to his shoulders as a giggle slipped past my lips.

With purpose, he carried me toward the exact spot he'd meticulously cleared off while I was on the phone.

A man on a mission.

I had a feeling I knew exactly what he had in mind.

"You pretend to be unaffected, but I know it's a lie," Mac murmured against my neck, his warm breath tickling the sensitive skin.

A shiver ran down my spine.

"I know your body, Pen. I see how you respond to me. The way your skin blushes... right... here." The tip of his finger danced across the swell of my chest, goosebumps forming in its wake.

My hand slid to the back of his head, fingers tangling in his hair, holding him close.

His lips found the spot he knew drove me crazy, kissing and nibbling with slow, torturous precision. Two months into whatever this was, and he already knew my body better than I had in twenty-six years.

"I'm not affected by you," I whispered, a small smile tugging at my lips even though he couldn't see it. "You can keep thinking I am, whatever makes you sleep at night."

His mouth curved against my skin, his hands gripping my waist.

"Tsk, tsk..." He ran his tongue along the shell of my ear before pressing a lingering kiss to my jaw. "We both know you just can't control it."

He was right.

My body reacted the second I saw him in a room. My pulse spiked, anticipation coiling tight, my every thought consumed with getting him alone.

But it wasn't just this—wasn't just the heat and the tension.

Mac made me laugh, too. He was playful, sharp-witted, the perfect match for my own chaotic energy.

That's what made this dangerous.

My palm pressed against his chest, pushing him back slightly. His gaze snapped up, locking onto mine, heat flashing in his dark eyes.

I licked my lips, and his smile turned downright wicked.

In one smooth motion, I hopped down from my desk, my body pressing flush against his. I had to stop this before it went too far, not here.

"You wanna see just how much I *can* control it?" I teased, my voice low, taunting.

Mac's jaw ticked as he glanced down, right to the strain in his jeans.

"If I'm being honest?" His voice was rough, edged with need. "No."

I laughed—a real, head-tilting-back kind of laugh.

Brushing my fingers over his length, I watched in delight as his breath hitched, a quiet, involuntary whimper escaping him.

Before either of us could push this further, I stepped out of his orbit entirely, because if I didn't, I'd prove him right and lose all of my control.

"As hot as it would be to have you take me on my desk," I mused, flashing him a smirk, "this is a place full of children. And I love my job."

Distance. I needed distance.

Because Mac?

He had the kind of pull that made a woman forget everything—morals, rules, ethics—until all she wanted to do was obey his every damn command.

CHAPTER 7

PRESENT DAY.

I needed a distraction. After last night, my blood felt like it was at a permanent rolling boil.

The night had been fine, fantastic even, until Mac pulled that caveman stunt, yanking me over the damn bar and dragging me into the storage closet.

Who the hell did he think he was?

I made it perfectly clear that I needed space. That whatever we had was over because my trust was worn thin.

Grabbing the next book from my cart, I checked the label, funneled through the shelf, and slammed it into the empty space with more force than necessary.

The battle in my head raged on, my face scrunched in frustration. If anyone were watching me, they'd probably think I was insane as I argued with the voices inside my head.

I was beyond frustrated with how things had ended between us. *Six months.* That's how long it had been. Six months of stolen glances, of laughter, of whispered conversations in the dark. Six months of tangled sheets and tangled emotions.

And then, one morning, it all blew up.

Everything we did, every unspoken promise, burned to the ground.

I ran, not looking back, and put as much distance between us as I possibly could, given the circumstances.

My heart *hurt*.

I was wounded and stubborn enough to let the pain keep me from turning around, from letting him in again.

For a brief moment in that closet, I had considered hearing him out—letting him explain why he hadn't told me. Maybe I would have understood if it had only been a month or two. But six whole months spent together? He'd chosen to keep a secret that big, knowing damn well the entire time.

"Stupid bastard," I muttered under my breath, turning on my heel, gripping the book in my hand a little too tightly.

As I spun, I nearly collided with something small yet solid. I jolted back just in time to see a little girl standing before me, wide-eyed and curious.

Winnie.

Her mom was a frequent visitor to the library, and at seven years old, Winnie was already reading far beyond her age. I knew that because she always came to me for help with the "big words" she couldn't quite figure out. Normally, she curled up in one of the bean bag chairs with her favorite short chapter books, completely lost in the pages.

But today, she was standing in front of me, head tilted to the side, blonde curls bouncing around her face, and a bright pink bow perched on top.

"What's a bastard?" she asked, her voice as innocent as could be.

Shit.

I cleared my throat, willing my face to look composed even though panic was flaring inside me. Dropping into a squat, my dress pooling around my knees, I placed a gentle hand on her arm.

"I said, Buster," I corrected smoothly, smiling like I wasn't a filthy liar. "The other one is a bad word, and we don't say those kinds of words here."

Winnie's little brows pinched together in confusion. "But Mommy says that to Daddy all the time."

A laugh bubbled up before I could stop it. Oh, this poor kid.

I ruffled my hand over her curls, then stood and held out my hand for her to take.

"Well, why don't we go find Mommy and see if she'd like to tell you what that means?" I suggested.

Winnie slipped her small hand into mine, but instead of moving, she gazed up at me with those big brown eyes, blinking sweetly.

"Can we skip Miss Penny?" she asked.

Instantly, my heart swelled, an ache settling deep.

"Of course, sweetie. Did she tell you where she would be?" I asked, scanning the library in search of those familiar blonde curls somewhere near the adult section.

Winnie let out a dramatic sigh, her tiny shoulders rising and falling as she paused, clearly searching for the right word. I glanced down as she pursed her lips in determination.

"The e-e—aerobics," she finally said, her voice laced with confidence despite her stumble.

My heart warmed at her effort, but I didn't correct her. Instead, I grinned and gave her hand a gentle squeeze.

Lucky for her, I knew what she meant. We took off skipping as I guided her toward the erotica section in hopes of finding Mom.

THE SUN WAS setting, casting a golden glow over the quiet streets. The air was the perfect balance of warm and cool, and a gentle breeze brushed against my skin as I made my way home.

Tonight was mine—reserved for catching up on my favorite shows, drinking wine until my head felt light, and dancing around my apartment like no one was watching because no one *was* watching.

It was later than usual. I'd stayed behind at the library, finishing up the book cart I'd claimed earlier in the day. A school field trip had interrupted me that afternoon, pulling me into an impromptu lesson on how to properly use a search engine, which was desperately needed for their end-of-the-year final papers.

With summer fast approaching and school nearly out, my job was about to shift into high gear. During the school year, the library hummed quietly, busiest in the evenings when students filled the space for clubs, homework help, or just a quiet place to exist. But summer? Summer brought a different kind of energy. Days packed with eager kids and restless adults, bringing in a constant flow of visitors. I liked to fill it with programs, keeping the young minds engaged while giving the regulars their much-needed escape.

Letting out a slow breath, I tried to shake the day off. I refused to carry work home with me—especially not the stress, or the lingering frustration over *Mac*. Just thinking about him made irritation stir low in my gut, threatening to ruin my night before it had even begun.

No. Not here. My home was my sanctuary, my peace. And I refused to let anything—or anyone—disrupt that.

The steady tap of my loafers echoed against the concrete as I dug through my bag for my keys. My fingers brushed against the cool metal just as I looked inside Sandy's flower shop.

The lights were still on.

Curiosity piqued, I hesitated in front of the picture window. It was too late for Sandy to still be here. The sun nearly dipped below the horizon, and that went against her number one rule: *always be home before dark.*

Frowning, I stepped into the small vestibule and then pushed open the front door of Petal Pushers.

The chime above rang softly, the scent of fresh-cut flowers curling around me like an embrace.

But Sandy was nowhere to be found.

"Sandy?" I called out, leaving my bag by the door.

Silence.

My pulse ticked up as I moved deeper into the shop, my eyes flicking toward the back room.

Something felt... off.

Keeping my head on a swivel, I took a cautious step forward and then another until I knew the front of the store was empty.

Pushing through the swinging doors into her prep area, I found her sitting on the floor, back against the stainless-steel table leg, like she'd accepted her fate.

"Oh my gosh!" I huffed, rushing toward her.

Sandy's head snapped up, and she gave me a small, sheepish smile. "Oh, thank goodness," she sighed, reaching for my extended hand as I pulled her to her feet.

She dusted her hands off on the front of her apron, brushing away whatever debris had stuck to her from the floor.

"I dropped a vase," she admitted, gesturing to the mess around us. "Bent down to pick up the bigger chunks of glass, lost my balance, and well, here we are."

She turned her hands over, revealing tiny scrapes—evidence of her attempt to catch herself.

My stomach dropped. "Are you hurt? Do you need me to take you to the emergency clinic?" I grabbed her biceps, scanning her from head to toe for anything else she wasn't telling me.

Sandy laughed—actually *laughed*—then grabbed my cheeks, tilting my head up so I had no choice but to look at her. The concern must've been written all over my face. My heart was still thudding in my ears. I was full of adrenaline, bracing for the worst.

"No, sweetie, I'm okay." Her smile softened, and my shoulders sagged in relief. "I'm just glad your nosiness got the best of you and made you check on me."

I rolled my eyes, finally exhaling a deep breath. "You *scared* me!" My voice rose as I planted my hands on my hips. "Next time, use a broom and dustpan."

Sandy chuckled and patted my arm, guiding me toward the little table and chair she usually perched at while assembling her bouquets.

"Take a seat. Let me get you a drink."

I huffed. "*I* should be getting *you* the drink and making *you* sit down."

"I've been sitting for..." She glanced at her watch. "Forty-five minutes."

Before I could argue, she disappeared for a moment, then returned with iced tea and a plate of cookies.

I accepted the tea with a grumble. "How many times have I told you, begged you, to keep your phone in your apron?" I scowled, biting into a cookie and washing it down with a sip.

Sandy waved me off, already turning toward the other side of the narrow space, acting as if she hadn't just spent nearly an hour stranded on the floor.

"Stubborn woman," I muttered, shaking my head.

With a dustpan and broom finally in hand—the choice she should've made from the start—Sandy began sweeping up the shattered glass.

"Did you need my help with Mother's Day weekend again this year?" I asked, steering the conversation in a new direction.

For the last few years, I've dedicated my weekends to helping Sandy fulfill the holiday orders. Usually, there was a huge influx, and without anyone else working the shop, Sandy could hardly keep up.

"Yes," she replied, squatting to grab the dustpan.

My breath hitched.

"Penelope," Sandy scolded.

I rolled my eyes. "What days were you thinking? You know I'm free the whole weekend."

It wasn't like I had Mother's Day plans. My relationship with my parents was nonexistent, which made it an easy choice to spend my time helping Sandy however she needed.

"I could use that creative eye of yours to help me put together some arrangements. *And* I might need help loading up a pretty big order for the community center."

Sandy straightened, pivoting toward the trash can before dumping the last of the glass inside.

Mother's Day was still two weekends away, so I made a mental note to jot it down in my calendar once I finally got upstairs.

"Well, you put me to work, and we'll get it done," I assured her.

Finally, Sandy sank into the chair across from me, grabbing a cookie and biting into it before lazily pointing it in my direction.

"I was thinking," she mused between chews, "maybe you could ask that Ridley boy to help us load those orders and drop them off. I haven't seen him around here in a while."

A knot the size of a damn tennis ball formed in my throat, and I tried to clear it away. When that didn't work, I took a long sip of tea and shook my head.

"I don't think so," I said firmly. "He and I don't talk like that anymore."

Sandy sighed, giving me a look that hovered between sympathy and pity. Coming from anyone else, I might have spoken up, but I let it slide.

"That's a shame," she said, shaking her head. "He was a nice boy... and pretty easy on the eyes." She winked.

I couldn't help but laugh, nodding in agreement. As infuriating as he was, he was nice to look at. A blessing and a curse.

When I used to sneak Mac into my apartment, there was no getting past Sandy. She was the only person who knew we'd been spending time together, and luckily for us, she wasn't much of a gossip.

He'd stop in and check on her, make sure she was doing all right, and then buy me roses. He never forgot, never let the pitcher go empty.

I couldn't help but smile, thinking about those moments with him.

I got to see the sweet side he kept hidden away from the world. I'd learned a lot about Mac, about the man he is.

No.

I didn't like that my anger was softening toward him. He didn't deserve it. He played me and made me look like a fool.

My feelings were warranted, and I wasn't giving up that easily.

I sighed and took another sip before giving Sandy my attention and moving on to a safer topic.

Because my mind—my heart—couldn't take it.

"I can ask another brawny, easy-on-the-eyes guy," I said.

There was one other guy in Faircloud I knew who probably wouldn't be doing anything that weekend. His parents, too, weren't very present in his life.

"Oh yeah?" Sandy asked, wiggling her eyebrows. "And who is that?"

"Logan Walker, Boone's friend."

Logan was sweet, even though we didn't see him much. He spent most of his time working or by himself.

"That would be lovely," Sandy replied.

By the time I'd finished my third cookie and drained the last of my tea, I decided to call it a night. I hugged Sandy, reminding her again to keep her phone in her apron.

In true stubborn old-lady fashion, she ignored me completely and sent me on my way with the rest of the baked goods... and the entire pitcher of tea.

CHAPTER 8

PRESENT DAY.

Angus flopped against my chair, sending it rolling back before he let out a deep, bone-weary sigh and sprawled across the floor like he owned the place.

With a faint smirk, I reached down, scratching behind his floppy ear. All one hundred and twenty pounds of him made it impossible to move my chair back, so I stayed put, working on my computer from an awkward distance.

Technically, today was my day off from bartending. The administrative work, though? That never stopped.

If I wasn't pouring drinks, I was back here making sure we had enough money to keep the doors open.

I'd done this dance with Dad for years—acting as the accountant, janitor, and wearing every other hat possible. He was usually too drunk to notice or tell me how to run the place, so I had full control. Lizzie, on the other hand, thought she always knew best, when in reality, she didn't know a damn thing.

I hadn't seen her since she got on my case about smoking in the bar, and not seeing her didn't bother me one bit.

Reaching down, I pulled a cigarette from the box, lit it up, and took a slow drag—just out of sheer fucking spite.

My head was a tangled mess.

It had been a few nights since my run-in with Penny, and for whatever reason, it was still messing me up.

Maybe it was the way her face softened, that flicker in her eyes—the smallest hesitation that told me, *maybe*, things weren't completely broken.

Or at least, that's what I wanted to believe.

Maybe I was reading into things. Hell, I probably was. But it wasn't like I had anyone to talk to about it, and truth be told? I didn't need the bullshit of anyone else's opinions messing with my head.

If a small chance was all I had to hold onto, I'd have a death grip on it.

Chance meant there was hope.

A loud thud echoed from the main room. We weren't open yet, which meant only one thing—Lizzie was here.

I had a plan: finish up this last task, go upstairs, and avoid her entirely. Going upstairs was my only relief because leaving wasn't an option, considering I lived above the bar.

Even on the rare occasion I had a day off, I was never really gone. The constant thrum of old country music shook my floorboards, forcing me to either crank my TV up to an unreasonable volume or come downstairs and end up working anyway.

My fingers tightened around the pen in my hand. I took a long drag off my cigarette, holding it between my teeth before exhaling toward the ceiling, watching the smoke curl and disappear.

Lizzie's figure flew past the open office door in a blur of blue, moving back and forth like a hurricane. Out of the corner of my eye, I watched her throw shit around, slam doors, even listen to her mumble shit under her breath.

I rolled my eyes and spun my chair to face her theatrics.

Clearly, she wanted my attention. Dramatic entrances and mumbled words were her preferred methods of communication instead of just saying what the hell was wrong.

I tucked the pen behind my ear then leaned back, hands clasped across my chest.

Cigarette still dangling from my lips, I called out lazily, "Did you have something to say, or is this your audition for a soap opera?"

That did it. Lizzie went off like a Roman candle, spinning on her heel and storming into the office, smoke practically pouring from her ears.

Her face was red, jaw clenched tight, and when she jabbed a finger in my direction, I braced for impact.

"You don't know when to shut up, do you?" she snapped. "You can never just leave me be, let me have my peace without some wise-ass comment."

I stayed perfectly relaxed, reclining back in my chair with a slow shrug. I knew I was being a dick, still didn't care.

"Why shut up when toying with you is just too damn fun?" I smirked, tilting my head, watching her fume.

Lizzie and I had never gotten along. Not as kids, *definitely* not as adults. Hell, I hadn't seen her for over a decade before she waltzed in here, tossed our father's will onto the bar, and upended my entire life.

She was the one who started this.

She was the one who barged in on her high horse, never once giving a damn about how I felt or what I had to say.

This place was *mine*.

And she took it.

Without this bar, I had nothing.

Lizzie let out a frustrated groan and stomped her foot, looking all of five years old. "It's not just me you can't keep your shit together around. So don't act like this is just for fun and games." She threw up her hands. "You're pissed because of how things went down. You think I *wanna* be here?"

That sent my blood pressure through the damn roof.

I shot to my feet, matching her energy.

Angus huffed from his spot on the floor, then, like the world's most unbothered soul, got up and padded out to the bar. Even my own damn dog was over our shit.

Since her arrival, we hadn't had a moment of calm between us. The fights were more and more frequent with every day that passed, especially since we were spending so much time around each other.

"If you don't want to be here, then fucking leave," I bit out. "Give me the damn bar and go back to your perfect little life far away from here."

Lizzie rolled her eyes so hard I thought they'd get stuck. Hand on her hip, she let out a dry, humorless laugh. "I can't give you the bar, dumbass. Think long and hard about why."

My stomach dropped. My smirk vanished. My eyes narrowed.

How the hell did she know about that?

"Me running away has nothing to do with my ability to handle this bar!" I shouted, throwing my hands out.

Leaving Faircloud had been a one-time mistake, a ghost from my past that I thought I'd buried. But lately? That ghost had been clawing its way back, haunting me in ways I never saw coming.

"Look," Lizzie said, arms crossed, expression set in stone. She was ready to stand her ground. "Nothing is changing. You can throw all the grown-man tantrums you want, but it won't fix what's already happened. So grow up and suck it up."

I let out a humorless laugh. "Says the one who just stomped her damn foot like a little girl."

She scoffed. "You can be mad at me all you want. But you *can't* be taking it out on everyone else around here—like Dudley, for example. He isn't your emotional punching bag."

My jaw ticked. "I don't treat him like my punching bag."

Lizzie arched a brow. "Right. So the testosterone showdown in the back alley was, what? A love confession?"

I clenched my fists, the memory of why that fight happened slamming into me like a freight train. It wasn't my sister, it wasn't the damn bar—it was *Penny.* Seeing her on that dance floor, watching her move like she hadn't spent a single night losing sleep over me, had sent me straight into a tailspin.

Lizzie exhaled sharply. "All I'm saying is, get your shit together. No more dropped glasses. No more storming out in a rage. No more fighting the employees—"

"Oh, come on," I cut in, scowling. "You act like it's a habit."

"Don't *make* it a habit." Her voice softened slightly, but her eyes stayed sharp. "Learn to rein it in. Not everyone needs front-row seats to your personal crisis."

The last frayed thread holding me back from demanding Penny talk to me, *really* talk to me, finally snapped. I was unraveling, and there was no stopping it now. The last damn thing I needed was my sister, of all people, trying to put me in check.

With a sharp exhale, I grabbed my keys and wallet from where I'd tossed them on the desk and stormed past Lizzie. The force of my exit sent a gust of air whipping past her, shifting her hair from her face.

"And no more free drinks for your friends, asshole!" she shouted after me, but the slam of the front door nearly swallowed her words whole.

I didn't care.

I wasn't waiting any longer for Penny to come to me. Who the hell knew how long that would take? I was done sitting on my hands, drowning in regret. I was standing up and fighting for this.

Penny was never just a fling, no matter how many times we swore that's all it would be—just a casual, no-strings thing. The more time I spent with her, the deeper I sank. She wasn't just a habit; she was the air I breathed. I'd be damned if I let her slip away without a fight.

Falling for Penny Hudson had been inevitable.

She was the best trouble I'd ever been in.

I'd do whatever it took to make her see, make her *feel,* how sorry I was.

I was a determined son of a bitch, and she was about to find out what lengths I'd go to get what I wanted.

CHAPTER 9

JANUARY. FOUR MONTHS AGO.

Why the hell was I checking my hair?

I stood in front of the tiny mirror in my bathroom, running a hand through the unruly mess on top of my head. My reflection stared back, brows pinched in confusion as I tilted my head left, then right. With a huff, I wet my fingers and smoothed down the stubborn flyaways—not too much, just enough to look somewhat put together.

Not that Penny cared.

She liked me a little rough around the edges, liked when I was unkempt and untamed. But I cared. I wanted to impress her. Somehow, against all odds, I was completely and utterly smitten. A word that had never once existed in my vocabulary until Penny Hudson crashed into my life like a beautifully reckless storm.

Trouble.

Smirking to myself, I checked my teeth in the mirror next, swishing some mouthwash for good measure before flicking off the light and stepping back into my apartment.

I had a pep in my step since October—since the night I finally snapped, pulled Penny into me, and let my desire for her take the lead. I'd always been the type to go after what I wanted, never one to hesitate, never one to care too much about how people saw me. Their expectations didn't mean a damn thing.

But lately?

I cared about *her* expectations. I cared about what Penny thought and how she felt. Enough that I was making sure I looked decent just to show up at her door.

That was the thing about Penny.

She was trouble—the kind that settled deep under your skin, the kind that made a man obsessed without him even realizing it. That woman had a pull like no other. She walked into a room, and people noticed. She didn't ask for attention; she commanded it. And somehow, against every odd, I was the lucky bastard who got to have those deep brown eyes locked on me.

Damn, if that didn't make me the richest man in the world.

Stepping into my cowboy boots, I tugged my jeans over the tops and adjusted the Henley that clung to my frame. With my keys, wallet, and phone in hand, I strode out the door.

Jogging down the steps to the main bar, I wove through the crowd that had already gathered. Tonight was my night off, and I planned on taking full advantage of it.

Dudley was behind the bar, working alongside Jolie, their movements fluid as they kept up with the steady stream of orders. I threw up a lazy salute in Dudley's direction, and he returned it without missing a beat, already pouring a drink for the next customer.

The night sky was thick with clouds, swallowing up the stars and leaving the town cast in an eerie half-darkness. Rain threatened on the horizon, the kind that could roll in fast and leave you drenched before you had a chance to curse at it. Penny didn't live far—just a few blocks—but I wasn't about to risk getting soaked walking home later.

Rounding the corner, I picked up my pace, making my way to my truck. The old beater sat under the dim glow of a flickering streetlight, its rusted fenders and dented body a familiar sight.

When I yanked open the door, it let out the same ear-piercing squeak it always did.

Sliding behind the wheel, I turned the key in the ignition. The engine grumbled to life before throwing it into drive. The town was quiet, the streets nearly empty with the occasional light glowing in the distance.

Within minutes, I was parked a few doors down from Petal Pusher, the flower shop Penny lived above.

Parking a little away from the shop was imperative so people wouldn't put together that Penny and I were seeing each other.

Neither of us wanted that.

The rain started to fall, fat droplets splattering against the windshield.

Ducking into the vestibule, I shook the dampness from my hair and glanced toward the warmly lit shop. Before heading up to Penny's door, I poked my head inside.

"Sandy!" I called out, ruffling a hand through my wet hair before tucking a strand behind my ear, and making my way inside.

From behind the counter, Sandy held up a finger, silently telling me to wait while she finished counting the register. I smirked and rocked back on my heels, slipping my hands into my front pockets as I took in the shop.

The exposed brick walls, the bursts of color from the carefully arranged displays, the lingering scent of fresh blooms—it was cozy, a stark contrast to the storm creeping in outside.

The sharp slam of the register drawer snapped my attention back.

"You on your way up to see our girl?" Sandy asked, leaning forward on the butcher block counter with a knowing grin.

I nodded. "Yes, ma'am."

With a tap on the counter, she turned, rummaging behind her for something. When she faced me again, she held out a single red rose.

I stopped in often, always grabbing flowers for Penny. Sandy knew the drill.

Reaching into my back pocket, I pulled out my wallet, peeling off a few bills. “Keep the change,” I said, offering her a smile as I extended my hand for the rose.

Sandy just shook her head. “It was an extra. You just take it up to her, okay?”

Not wanting to tell the woman no because I knew I’d never get away with it, I took the flower. “You need anything before I head up?”

She shook her head and waved me off. With simple goodbyes, I departed, exiting through the front door.

When I got to Penny’s door, I looked down at the doormat, which read, “Come On In I’m Still Not Ready,” and chuckled. Raising my fist, I knocked against her door, waiting for the familiar sound of her voice.

“It’s open!” Penny called, her voice muffled but warm.

I turned the knob and pushed the door open, immediately hit with the mouthwatering scent of garlic.

“You really should lock this,” I said, kicking off my wet boots and leaving them by the entrance before stepping further inside.

Penny never locked her door. Her ability to trust was endearing and also incredibly frightening.

The walls of her apartment were a vibrant mismatch of color, covered in gold-framed paintings of all shapes and sizes. Nothing matched, but everything radiated with personality—just like her.

Soft music hummed from the kitchen, a melody weaving through the air, pulling me in.

I found her at the counter, rolling out pizza dough, her hips swaying lazily to the beat. A small smile tugged at my lips. She had no idea how effortlessly beautiful she was—how damn intoxicating the sight of her could be.

She wore the cutest apron, dotted with tiny pink flowers, her hair piled into a messy top knot. A few stray curls had escaped, framing her face. I had the sudden urge to reach out, to tuck them behind her ear just for an excuse to touch her.

“Meh,” she said, not bothering to look up as she pressed her fingers into the dough. "I could take whoever decided to come through that door. Joke's on them, I have a taser."

She finally glanced up, flashing me a lopsided grin—the kind that sent a spark straight through my chest.

I chuckled, stepping closer. "You and a taser sound like a dangerous combination."

Before she could fire back, I leaned in, brushing a kiss against her cheek, letting my lips linger just long enough to feel the heat rise beneath her skin.

Penny giggled, leaning into my kiss, soft and warm against me. When I finally pulled away, I leaned my hip against the counter as I watched her.

"I have something for you," I said, my voice quieter than I intended.

Her eyes snapped up to mine, curiosity flickering in their depths. She paused mid-knead, flour-dusted fingers stilled against the dough, giving me her full attention.

I pulled out the rose from behind my back.

Her lips parted slightly, eyes widening as they flickered from the flower to my face. Slowly, as if savoring the moment, she reached out, her delicate fingers brushing against mine as she took the stem. That simple touch sent a spark straight through me, heat pooling beneath my skin.

"Mac," she sighed, her voice wrapping around my name like silk.

Bringing the rose to her nose, she inhaled deeply, a smile blooming across her face.

I simply stood there, watching her, completely and utterly mesmerized because that's all I could do. The way she twirled the flower between her fingers, the way she savored something so small—it made my chest tighten, and something profound inside me shifted.

A feeling I'd never had before. A sensation I wasn't sure how to name, but one I knew, without a doubt, belonged to her.

Without thinking, I gave in to the temptation and reached

out, tucking a stray wisp of hair behind her ear. My fingers grazed gently against her ear as I did.

"What can I do to help?" I asked, my voice a little rougher than before.

Penny scoffed, turning away, but not before I caught the smile playing on her lips. She moved with a sway that was impossible to ignore, her fitted leggings hugging her curves, her cropped sweater teasing just the smallest sliver of skin.

I was done for.

"I already kneaded the dough for both pizzas," she said, placing the rose into the pitcher on the table. "You can add the sauce."

Snapping myself out of whatever daze she'd put me in, I pushed off the counter, moving toward the drawer. I grabbed a spoon, popped the lid off the jar sitting nearby, and tried to focus.

Tried.

Because Penny Hudson made it real damn hard to concentrate on anything other than her.

Like we'd fallen into some unspoken rhythm, Penny came up behind me, wrapping her arms around my waist and resting her cheek against my back.

The warmth of her, the way she fit so easily against me, settled me.

"How was your day?" I asked, taking a dollop of sauce and spreading it in the center of the dough.

"Pretty calm," she murmured, giving me one last squeeze before slipping away, leaving the heat of her touch lingering. "Boone came by today and read *The Cat in the Hat* to a group of kids."

Behind me, the fridge door opened and closed, and then Penny was beside me again, her shoulder brushing mine as I worked the sauce over the dough.

I huffed out a laugh. "Are you shitting me?" That man was too damn much for his own good.

"Nope. All the moms stayed for once, too." I slid the first

pizza toward her, a knowing smile playing on her lips. "I can't blame them. A man in a cowboy hat *and* a mustache?"

My hand stilled, fingers tightening around the spoon. My eyes cut to hers, narrowing slightly. I knew she was teasing, but something in my gut twisted at the thought of her thinking of anyone else besides me.

Penny let out a soft laugh, clearly enjoying herself, and sprinkled cheese onto the pizza before reaching for the next one.

"Not to mention," she added, sliding the first pizza into the oven. I turned, my back pressing against the counter, grabbing a towel to wipe my hands. "Reading to little kids?"

She was testing me.

Taunting me.

Penny loved knowing when she had me right where she wanted me—wrapped around her damn finger.

I let out a slow, measured breath, my gaze raking over her as she came back toward me. She was waiting for me to take the bait, but I held my ground, saying nothing. Instead, I watched, arms crossed, as she layered cheese over the last pizza, then placed the pepperoni just how I liked it before sliding that one into the oven as well.

Satisfied, she turned, wiping her hands on the towel I hadn't even realized she'd taken from me. Strong eye contact. A teasing grin.

"You know," I drawled, stepping closer, placing my hands on her hips, and pulling her flush against me, "I can come read, too. If you ever need someone."

Penny tilted her head, her arms looping lazily around my neck.

"You can read? Maybe you'll have to come visit me at work to sign up for a library card," she teased.

Damn woman.

"Ha-ha," I said, locking eyes with her deep brown ones. That sparkle—playful, full of mischief—never dulled. "You'd be surprised. There's a lot I can do that you don't know about."

Penny arched a brow, amusement flickering across her face. “Is that so?”

Grinning, I reached behind me, grabbed her phone from the counter, and turned up the volume, letting the soft strum of music fill the air. The melody wrapped around us, thick and warm.

Moving from her grip, I put enough distance between us to hold out my hand. She eyed it skeptically, hesitation flickering in her expression, but after a beat, she placed hers in mine.

I loved the way curiosity played across her features—the way her brows pulled together just slightly, her lips twitching like she was trying to figure me out.

Still holding her gaze, I tugged her away from the kitchen and into the open space of her living room. With a quick flick of my wrist, I spun her in a slow, graceful circle, then pulled her flush against me.

Our bodies pressed together, and I swayed us to the music.

In the middle of her apartment, under the soft glow of lamplight, we danced—our own little world wrapped up in the sound of an old country love song.

I led us into an easy two-step, guiding her left before shifting our bodies in sync. With each turn, each playful sway, I let my touch linger, fingers trailing down her arms, her back. The heat between us simmered—familiar and intoxicating.

Then, with a teasing grin, I spun her out again, only to bring her right back in, catching her against my chest.

“Okay, look at you go,” she said breathlessly, her laughter bright as she looked up at me. “Who knew Mac Ridley had moves?”

I chuckled, keeping my grip steady. “This is the extent of my dancing.”

Slow swaying, a two-step, and a few simple twirls were all I needed to know to impress anyone. Anything past this became very questionable.

Penny smirked. “Oh, I don’t know... I think you’ve got a little more in you.”

She dipped back playfully, trusting me to hold her, and when

I did, she laughed before righting herself, her arms looping around my neck.

The song slowed, and with it, so did we.

Penny rested her head against my chest, and I let my chin brush the top of her hair, breathing her in. Our sock-covered feet glided effortlessly across the wooden floor, moving in perfect sync, like we'd been dancing together our whole lives.

And with every step, every twirl, I felt myself sinking deeper into her.

She glanced up, that familiar longing glimmering in her eyes, and just like that—I softened.

Completely.

Hopelessly.

And I knew right then... I was a goner for this woman.

CHAPTER 10

PRESENT DAY.

Spin. Shuffle. Hip sway.

The beat pulsed through my speaker, and I moved with it, completely lost in my own little world. The vacuum became my dance partner, the living room my stage, and I belted out every lyric like I was performing for a sold-out crowd.

Chores didn't have to be miserable—not if you found ways to make them fun.

Laundry? I sang like I was headlining the Grand Ole Opry.

Dishes? I played in the suds, shaping bubbles into beards, blowing them into the air just to watch them pop.

Finding joy in the little things—that was the secret to making the hard days feel less suffocating. Those tiny, ridiculous moments? They were the ones I looked forward to, the ones that reminded me life didn't always have to be so heavy.

That's why my home was more than just a place to sleep. It was my safe haven. My castle. A space where only a select few were granted entry—only those I trusted, only those who truly mattered.

No matter how exhausting or chaotic the outside world got,

I always had this.

The walls painted in colors that made me feel alive. The air thick with the soothing scents of vanilla and spice. Every piece, every detail, carefully chosen to be more than just decor. It was comfort. It was a sanctuary.

It was mine.

I dipped the vacuum low in a dramatic swoop, then spun—only to freeze when a shadow moved in my periphery.

My heart lurched into my throat, and every alarm bell rang.

I let out a loud shriek, stumbling backward as the vacuum crashed to the floor with a loud clatter. My pulse pounded against my ribs, my breath coming in sharp gasps as the surge of adrenaline rocketed through me.

"What the fuck!" I clutched my chest, feeling the wild hammering of my heart beneath my palm. "Are you crazy!"

With a shaky hand, I smacked the vacuum's power button, cutting off its low rumble.

Mac stood in front of me, his chest rising and falling like he'd just sprinted a marathon. His expression was unreadable—except for the way his lips parted slightly, like he was struggling to catch his breath.

He stood completely still and silent, staring at me like he wasn't the one who'd nearly given me a heart attack.

I narrowed my eyes and repeated myself. "What. The. Fuck."

A surge of anger flooded in at the reminder he'd walked into my apartment unannounced and sure as hell unwelcomed.

Mac reached behind himself and—*click*—slid the deadbolt into place.

My stomach dropped as my eyes went wide. The anger morphed into a low tingle of fear and apprehension. Instinctively, I took a few steps back, putting space between us. "Mac?" My voice was edged with caution.

He started pacing, his boots scuffing against the floor as his hands raked through his hair. He gripped the strands, tugging roughly before locking his fingers behind his neck.

"Mac..." I tried again, softer this time.

His head snapped up, dark eyes locking onto mine.

"I need you to talk to me." His voice was raw, thick with something desperate.

I stilled, my breath catching.

Not this. Not *again*.

Had he already forgotten the other night? I told him—*on my terms. On my time.*

Barging in here like this, demanding answers, backing me into a corner. He was ignoring everything I'd said.

He couldn't be that stupid.

"I have nothing to say right now," I replied, my voice clipped and controlled.

Walking into the kitchen, I grabbed a towel and started wiping down the counters with unnecessary force, like scrubbing hard enough could erase him from my life.

Maybe if I ignored him, he'd get the hint.

Nope.

Heavy footsteps followed. The heat of his presence curled around me as he stopped behind me. Close enough that I could feel the weight of his presence pressing into my back.

"Pen..." he exhaled, his voice low, almost pleading.

I closed my eyes, tilting my head up toward the ceiling as frustration coiled in my chest. Then, with a sharp breath, I threw the towel down, the sound of damp fabric smacking against the countertop breaking the silence between us.

I'd spent energy and time trying to erase him as best I could. Trying to shove every memory, every whispered promise, every stolen glance into some locked-away part of my heart.

Mac didn't realize *that* morning, my heart had been ripped straight from my chest by a woman I'd never even met. Then, he was the one to step on it.

I stood there, listening to her words, knowing I was never meant to hear them—*that* was the moment everything shattered.

Trust wasn't something you played with. My emotions

weren't a game.

Yet, Mac Ridley had handled them like they were. Not with care. Not like they mattered.

Maybe he hadn't *lied*.

But he had hidden something, a secret so big it made every kiss, every touch, every whispered what-are-we feel like a cruel joke.

The only thing that kept me from breaking completely?

We hadn't planned a future together.

Not yet.

But that hadn't stopped *me* from dreaming about it on my own.

Finally, I spun around, my chest heaving, my skin burning with anger.

"Get. Out." I pointed toward the door, my voice sharp enough to cut through the tension. "I don't want you here. I don't want to hear you out. I don't care."

Mac didn't flinch.

Instead, he shrugged off his jacket, acting like I'd just invited him to stay awhile. He draped it over the stool beside him, crossed his arms over his broad chest, and leveled me with a look that made my blood simmer.

"I'm not leaving until you listen to me."

I let out a scoff, followed by an exasperated groan. My gaze locked onto his, onto those deep, familiar eyes I'd stared into so many times. I could describe them to a painter, guiding their brushstrokes until they captured them perfectly in a masterpiece that belonged nowhere but on a wall.

Brown as the bark of an old oak tree.

Warm as the first golden rays of spring after a brutal winter.

Soft, yet sharp enough to bring even the strongest to their knees.

And damn it, I hated that I still noticed.

"I guess we're going to be here all night then," I muttered.

"Fine by me." He leaned against the counter, one ankle

crossing over the other, looking like he had all the time in the world. "There's nowhere else I'd rather be."

I tilted my head side to side, rolling out the tension coiling in my neck, but it didn't help. Not when *he* was standing there. Not when his presence made my skin prickle and my stomach churn.

Ignoring him, I moved down the hallway to my bedroom, resuming my night like I didn't have a six-foot-something shadow trailing behind me. The music still played—traitorous love songs mocking me with every lyric.

Mac was right there, hovering like a damn gnat that refused to be swatted away.

"If you're not going to stop for a minute and hear me out, I'll just talk at you instead," he said.

"Oh, *thank God*," I mumbled, dripping in sarcasm.

His jaw ticked. "If I had known she was going to show up, I would've told you."

I barked out a hollow laugh, bending down to lift the laundry basket. "Oh wow, that makes me feel so much better!"

Mac groaned, dragging a hand through his hair. "That came out wrong. What I *meant* is, if I knew she was going to show back up, if I thought she was still tied to my life in *any* way, I would have warned you."

I shoved past him, my shoulder brushing against his chest as I made my way to the little hall closet where my washer and dryer were tucked away.

"I was stupid for not saying something," he admitted, his voice following me. "But I genuinely thought it was done. That it was handled years ago."

I stayed silent, methodically tossing in clothes, focusing on the task instead of the ache creeping into my chest.

Of course, if he'd known, he would have told me. But that wasn't the point.

The point was that he hadn't told me when it mattered, when it counted.

I poured in detergent, added fabric softener, then shut the

lid harder than necessary. Without a word, I walked away, my feet tapping against the wooden floors as I moved toward my hobby basket in the living room. If I was going to be bothered, I might as well make use of the time.

Settling at the dining table, I pulled out my crochet hook and yarn.

Mac followed. Of course, he did.

He dragged a chair out and sat across from me, silent, watching.

The minutes stretched, his stare pressing into me, but I refused to meet it. Instead, I focused on the rhythm of my hands, on the simple, mindless motion of creating something out of nothing.

Crochet over. Into the loop. Pull through—probably a bit too hard.

Repeat.

I swallowed, the weight of something unspoken pressing into my ribs.

"Your pitcher is empty," he said finally.

"Yup."

That ceramic pitcher I'd always kept filled with fresh roses sat empty on my table.

The day it all went down, I swore I'd never put another rose in it again.

"I made a mistake. I'm sorry." Mac's voice was raw, edged with a sincerity that made my chest tighten. "I can't even begin to tell you how much I know I fucked up because the words don't exist." He leaned forward, resting his elbows on the table, his fingers threading together like he was holding himself together. "I know I can't take back what I did. I can't go back in time and make it all go away."

My jaw clenched. My heart wavered. Damn it.

"You and I..." He exhaled slowly, shaking his head. "We had something special. *You're* special. I was a lucky bastard that you even gave me the time of day."

"If that's true," I whispered, voice barely audible over the hum of the room, "why didn't you come find me? Why didn't you say something sooner? It's been two months, Mac."

I finally looked up, letting him see the hurt still carved into me, the wound he'd left behind. The crochet hook slipped from my hand, landing on the table with a soft clatter.

Mac's throat bobbed as he swallowed. "I panicked." His voice cracked. I saw it—regret, tangled with something heavier. "I've never had something like this before. Never felt so desperate to make something work." He dragged a hand down his face. "I hid. I was scared. I was unsure how to handle emotions. I knew you were upset, but I didn't know what to say, so I avoided it." His eyes met mine, pleading. "I'm not saying it was right. I know it wasn't. I just—I handled it wrong."

"And now?"

His chest rose and fell in a slow, measured breath. "I've spent a lot of time thinking. Preparing. Reevaluating every step I took." He let out a humorless laugh, leaning back in his chair. "I've done so much fucking thinking."

I picked up my crochet project, my fingers wrapping around the yarn like it could tether me to something steady. "I hope you learned your fucking lesson."

Mac groaned, tilting his head back, staring at the ceiling like it held the answers he couldn't find in me.

He wasn't going to walk in here, say a few sweet words, admit he'd screwed up, and expect me to just get over it. It would take so much more than that because I knew what one omission of the truth after another did.

I lived it.

I watched my parents' relationship crack under the weight of lies and half-truths until there was nothing left but hurt and regret.

I swore I'd never find myself in that same situation.

"I'm so fucking sorry, Trou—" Mac started, but his words faded into nothing.

I clenched my jaw, staring at my stitches. “You have no idea the mental shit I’ve been through since.”

His voice dropped lower. “If it’s been anything like mine... yeah, I do.”

I finally looked up, my gaze locking onto his. “Why tonight? Why show up now with this big protest?”

Mac’s eyes traced the movements of my hands as I twisted the yarn, looping it through the hook. His voice was quieter this time, but steady.

“Because I can’t block it out any longer.” He exhaled sharply. “You consume me. Every thought. Every second. Awake or asleep.”

The air between us grew heavier, thick with the weight of everything unspoken.

I didn’t know what to say. How to think.

The anger still simmered beneath my skin. But something else knocked at the door, too.

CHAPTER 11

MARCH. TWO MONTHS AGO.

Our lips brushed, soft and teasing, before Mac's hand slid up to cradle my face. His touch was fire against my skin, a slow, smoldering burn that sent a shiver down my spine. I deepened the kiss, my tongue tracing his in a slow dance, savoring the way he tasted—like warmth and smoke and something unmistakably *him.*

The early morning sun peeked through the curtains, casting golden light over us, turning the moment hazy, dreamlike.

I loved when he touched me. It was electrifying, earth-defying—something I'd never experienced before. Mac had unlocked a part of me that belonged solely to him.

These past few months had been more than I ever anticipated. Hot hookups. Fun. Low stakes. No strings attached. Existing in the now, tangled up in him.

Yet, there was a lingering feeling of permanence. I didn't want to hide this forever. The urge to shout and tell everyone, especially my best friends, how happy Mac made me was relentless.

Breaking away from the kiss, I grinned at him, my fingers grazing the warm, taut muscles of his abdomen. I trailed my touch lower... and lower...

Mac chuckled, his voice dripping with amusement and warning. "Whoa there, Trouble," he murmured, eyes darkening with heat. "If I'm gonna be the one getting breakfast, you gotta let me go."

I pouted, slipping my fingers into the waistband of his boxers, toying with the elastic.

His breath hitched.

"As much as I love your hand wrapped around my cock..." His voice rasped, low and rough. "If we start again, I'm not leaving this bed. And neither are you."

I bit my lip, my fingers dipping lower, teasing over the velvety tip. He was already hard—his protest was futile. I laughed, low and wicked.

"One more round, then breakfast?" I countered, stroking along his length, pushing him toward the inevitable.

Mac let out a quiet curse, his restraint fraying. He crushed his mouth against mine, his grip tightening around my neck just enough to make my breath catch, sending a dizzy, heated rush straight through me.

His teeth grazed my lower lip, tugging playfully before he pulled back just far enough to whisper, "Mmm. I love the way you taste." His voice was thick, hungry. "Maybe you're all I need for breakfast."

Before I could tease him back, he rolled me onto my back, the blankets slipping away to expose my bare skin to the cool air. He straddled me, one hand pinning my wrists above my head.

I gasped, arching into him. "I wouldn't be opposed," I murmured, moaning as his lips trailed down my throat.

Then, just as quickly as he'd taken control, he pulled away, hovering above me. His hair was a disheveled mess from the night before, his eyes dark with something that sent heat curling low in my stomach.

"First," he said, voice thick with reluctance, "I need a cigarette and real breakfast." He kissed me once more, lingering just long enough to make me whimper in protest. Then he climbed off the bed, his muscles flexing as he stretched. "Plus," he added with a smirk, "the longer I make you wait, the more needy you'll be when I get back."

"You tease," I hissed, sitting up and stretching, my arms overhead, breasts bare to the morning air as I stood from the bed.

Mac chuckled as he stepped into his jeans, tugging them up over his hips with a little hop. They sat low, revealing the sharp cut of his V and the tattoos I'd come to love.

My gaze traced over his ink, my fingers following suit as I stepped closer, running my hands over the two roses etched onto his lower stomach—the ones I'd claimed as my favorites.

Roses would never mean the same thing to me again.

Mac inhaled sharply, his resolve flickering. "I can't help it," he murmured, pressing a kiss to the top of my head.

"If you don't hurry back," I warned, a smirk curling at my lips, "I might have to take care of the ache *you* caused myself."

His eyes darkened.

I pulled away just enough to grab his discarded flannel from the floor, slipping it over my shoulders and buttoning it up. It fell mid-thigh, covering exactly what it needed to.

The sweatshirt he'd been about to pull over his head stalled in his hands. His jaw tensed, his fingers clenching the fabric. His stare raked over me, heat crackling in the space between us.

"Fuck," he muttered under his breath.

If there was one thing Mac Ridley loved, it was placing his claim.

"I'll be quick," he said, tapping his jean pockets to make sure he had everything before he practically ran to his front door, slipped his boots on without caring how his jeans bunched up, and blew me a kiss before slamming the door.

A laugh bubbled from my lips, light and easy. While Mac was gone, I'd make coffee and get things ready for when he came back with breakfast. He was just running to the diner a few doors down from the bar—it wouldn't take long. So, I acted fast, shuffling to the counter and pulling out the coffee grounds.

I measured them into the machine, and my thoughts drifted back to last night, which inevitably led me down the rabbit hole of *us*.

No strings attached. That was the deal. But lately... it didn't feel so simple.

I liked being with Mac. I liked the late-night drives to the overlook, the stolen moments in his truck, the way his laughter filled the quiet spaces between us. More and more, we spent our nights together. Sometimes at his place, sometimes sneaking around to mine. It wasn't just about the sex—it was the ease of it, the comfort.

If I was being honest with myself, I'd started thinking about the *what ifs*.

What if we stopped keeping this to ourselves?

What if we stopped pretending it was just casual?

What if I told him I wanted more?

The idea sent a nervous flutter through my stomach, equal parts excitement and fear. Because if we stripped away the secrecy, if we took the thrill of the unknown and replaced it with reality... would the magic of it disappear?

Shaking my head, I pushed the thoughts away. In typical *me* fashion, I grabbed my phone, turned on my go-to playlist, and let the music fill the apartment at a low hum as I got back to my task.

A few moments passed, and then—

A soft knock.

Smiling, I skipped toward the door, ready to fling it open, expecting to see Mac standing there with his hands full of food.

"That was fa—"

Except it *wasn't* Mac.

The smile dropped from my lips, my body going still as I took in the stranger before me.

Tall.

Blonde.

Bright blue eyes.

The exact opposite of me.

A strange, unfamiliar unease coiled in my stomach.

"Is Mac Ridley home?" she asked, her voice smooth, practiced.

My stomach dropped. Her gaze flicked down, taking in my bare legs, the flannel I wore—Mac's flannel—that barely covered my breasts.

Who the hell is she?

I forced my expression to stay neutral, though my fingers curled into the fabric at my sides. "Who's asking?" My voice was even, but my heart was pounding.

The woman cleared her throat, tightening her grip on the yellow folder in her hands.

"I'm Mimi. I know Mac from a few years ago." A pause. "Is he home?"

She tried to peer around me, her curiosity apparent, but when she didn't see him, her sharp blue eyes returned to mine.

I swallowed hard, my mind spinning. *Why was she here? How did she know Mac?*

"No," I answered, my voice clipped. "He's grabbing breakfast. He should be back soon."

Mimi shook her head and extended the folder toward me.

"Can you give this to him?" she asked. "Tell him to take care of it as soon as possible. It's urgent."

Urgent.

The word sent a fresh wave of nerves through me.

My hands were unsteady as I reached for it, my fingers brushing the thick envelope. *Why am I shaking?*

"Uh, yeah. Sure." I nodded stiffly.

She gave me the smallest, barely-there smile before turning on her heel and disappearing down the steps.

I stayed there, frozen, the door still cracked open as I watched her go.

Then, slowly, I shut it.

My breath came shallow, my pulse hammering against my ribs. I didn't know what made me do it—jealousy? Curiosity?—but my fingers slid beneath the flap, peeling it open before I could stop myself.

A thick stack of papers sat inside. I pulled them halfway out, my eyes scanning the first page.

And that's when I felt it.

The sharp, sinking heat of realization.

My skin went cold. My vision blurred.

The bold, block letters at the top of the page read:

DECREE OF DIVORCE.

And beneath it, two names.

MIMI MARTIN.

MAC RIDLEY.

The world tilted.

I stumbled back, my shoulder hitting the door as my grip on the papers tightened. My pulse roared in my ears, drowning out every other sound.

Mac. *Married.*

The truth slammed into me like a freight train, knocking the air from my lungs.

She was his *wife.*

CHAPTER 12

PRESENT DAY.

I stared into Penny's eyes, searching for something—anything—but the sparkle that had once lived there was gone.

Her features were flat, distant, like she was reliving that moment all over again, feeling every ounce of betrayal, every shred of heartbreak.

That morning, when I'd come back... she was already gone.

She'd left in a hurry, so fast that the ghost of her still lingered. Her shampoo was still sitting in my bathroom, her clothes tucked neatly in my top drawer. As if she'd vanished, as if this world we'd built in the shadows had never really existed at all.

I hadn't had the courage to get rid of any of it, either.

I'd walked in, arms full of food, a stupidly big smile on my face, expecting to see my girl bare-legged, wrapped in my clothes while she waited for me to come back. Instead, I was met with an empty apartment.

Then, I saw it.

The yellow envelope, ripped open on my dining room table.

The second my eyes scanned the words, realization crashed into me, all-consuming and suffocating. Even now, months later,

I felt that same searing panic—the kind that clawed through my chest and made it hard to breathe.

Before Penny, I didn't care about much. I was easygoing, letting life roll off my back, never letting anything stick to me. But after that morning? I barely recognized myself. I'd been drowning in guilt and regret since.

I'd spent the time avoiding everything, thinking she would come around and all would fall back into what it was. I was stupid to think a woman like her would ever settle.

Coming here tonight was my last shot. My final attempt before I let us slip through my fingers for good.

I should've chased after her the second I saw those papers. Should've barged in, told her everything, made it crystal clear. But I didn't.

I played the coward.

I convinced myself she would come back to me. Then... time passed, and it felt too late.

Days. Weeks. It never got better, in fact, the more I watched her from a distance, the worse it felt.

Sitting at Penny's table for hours now, I watched as she did everything in her power to ignore me. I asked her about work. I apologized too many times to count.

I wasn't leaving until we worked something out.

Still, we sat.

At some point, Penny got up and grabbed a snack, didn't ask if I wanted anything, which I didn't expect her to. The clock crept past midnight, and she flipped through the pages of her book, snacking as if I weren't sitting right there, waiting—*pleading*—for some kind of opening.

I stared at her, watching every little movement, every blink, every flick of her fingers against the pages.

Then, to my surprise, she spoke first.

Closing her book, she wiped her hands on her pants and leveled me with a look.

"Why did you get married?"

The question hit like a sucker punch. My breath stalled, my mind reeled. But I caught myself, masking my reaction.

She was curious.

That was a good sign.

I swallowed hard, my voice steady but low. "When my dad got sick, I left. Moved to Vegas for a while." I hesitated, running a hand down my jaw. "I needed a break from... everything. Mostly the pressure I knew I'd be under. I don't know if it was the right choice, but—"

"What pressure?" Penny asked.

I exhaled, dragging my fingers through my hair. "With his diagnosis, I assumed the bar would be mine when he died. I'd already been running most of it, but it was still his. Still his responsibility. But with him gone, it would all be mine."

I ran from the weight of knowing that. I knew that if shit went south, it would be me left to deal with the debris. I was immature, and instead of growing up, I decided to bolt.

Penny nodded, her expression unreadable.

"So, how did Mimi happen?"

I leaned back, rubbing a hand over my face. "I worked at a bar on the Strip. It was loud, busy, nothing like Faircloud. It was easy—not a single thought about home. Mimi worked there, too. She also ran from something in her hometown. We spent most of our shifts together, talking about our experiences. We got close, became friends."

Penny's eyes were locked onto mine.

I took a breath and forced myself to continue.

"One night, we got too drunk, and in true dumbass fashion, we thought it'd be funny to run off and get married by Elvis. We'd seen so many couples come in and do it that we figured, why not?" I shook my head, letting out a humorless laugh. "Sober me could've answered that question. But insanely drunk, younger me? Not a damn chance. It was a joke. A stupid, reckless joke."

The truth was, I hadn't even realized it was real at the time. I thought it was just some Vegas bit, something fake for the tourists.

I had no clue a fake Elvis actually had the legal power to marry someone.

Dumb.

I was *so* damn dumb.

Penny didn't flinch. Didn't react. Just studied me.

"Why did she show up that day?"

"She wanted to *actually* get married. Went to file the paperwork, and turns out, she already was." I dragged a hand down my face, feeling the exhaustion deep in my bones. "I swear, I didn't even know it was legally binding until she showed up."

Silence stretched between us.

Penny sat still, her hands pressed together in her lap, her lips barely parted.

I ran a hand through my hair, the weight of it all settling on my chest.

When I came home, I lived for years without knowing what had really happened in Vegas. Dad got better—sort of—and stubbornly hung on, living much longer than the doctors predicted. That damn old bastard never gave up.

He didn't know I'd gotten married. He never knew the mess I'd created for myself, the mess that ended up costing me so much. Even in the end, he still left the bar to my sister.

"I can't give you the bar, dumbass," Lizzie had said earlier, and it finally made sense. She knew. It wasn't just because I ran.

How she knew was a mystery I couldn't solve, but I understood now.

Penny was silent, her gaze unfocused, drifting just past me. I couldn't look away from her. I could see the tension in her shoulders, the way her chest rose and fell with every breath, as if she were holding herself together by sheer force of will.

Her eyes flickered to mine, and my heart slammed in my chest.

"Did you love her?"

That four-word question was a punch to my gut, nearly knocking me off my chair.

Love?

Fuck no.

My face fell to a soft, vulnerable expression. "No. Nothing even close to that ever happened between us. I didn't even know what it felt like to love someone before. Now I—"

She held up a hand and looked away from me, her throat bobbing as she swallowed.

"I'm so fucking sorry, Pen." My voice cracked, the words getting caught in the tightness of my throat. "If I ever thought it would hurt you... I wouldn't have done it. I swear, I wouldn't have—"

I stopped, the weight of my mistakes crashing over me. I placed my hands on my face, the exhaustion of it all sinking deep into my bones. I had fucked this up. I had hurt her—*ruined* us—and I didn't know if I could ever forgive myself, even if she found a way to forgive me.

I couldn't even look at her anymore. I was a coward who had stayed silent for too long.

"I know..." she said softly, her voice carrying the weight of everything she was feeling. "I know you feel bad, guilty, but that doesn't change how hurt I am."

I nodded, because honestly, it was all I could do.

"You broke my trust, Mac. Do you have any idea what it was like for me to open that door, wearing nothing but your shirt and a *thong* to see another woman standing there?" She tilted her head, her eyes searching mine, daring me to understand. "Put yourself in my position."

"I—I can't imagine." The words felt hollow, inadequate against how she was feeling, but they were the only honest response I had.

"And then... to find out she was your *wife*?" Penny's voice cracked, the last word drenched in venom.

Fuck.

My chest tightened, a sharp, unforgiving pressure that made it hard to breathe. The weight pressed down like a boulder, threatening to crush me from the inside out.

"You never once came to talk to me." Her voice trembled slightly, but she held firm, unyielding. "You sent me a text a whole damn day later, like nothing happened." She sucked in a sharp breath, her arms tightening around herself. "It made me feel... disposable. Like everything we shared for those months, everything I thought we were meant nothing."

"That's the farthest thing from the truth," I rasped, my voice hoarse with desperation.

She studied me, her expression unreadable. Those chestnut eyes locked on mine with an intensity that told me she had already made up her mind.

"I know I was a coward," I admitted, the words tasting bitter in my mouth. "I was stupid to pretend like everything was fine, that I didn't know what was going on. But I didn't know what to do. You left, and—"

Penny's hands slammed down on the table.

The glass near her rattled, liquid sloshing dangerously close to the rim.

I stilled, watching as she reached out and tapped the surface again, punctuating each word with a sharp, deliberate strike.

"I left because the thought of having to confront you, having to see your stupid face fucking destroyed me."

The pain in her voice shredded through me, leaving nothing but raw, exposed nerves in its wake.

Without thinking, I reached for her, my fingers brushing against hers before settling gently over them. The contact sent a jolt through my system, dragging me back to the nights we'd spent tangled in each other, her skin beneath mine, her laughter filling this very apartment.

"Then tell me," I whispered, leaning closer, needing her to feel the sincerity in every syllable. "Tell me what I have to do to make you believe me. Believe that everything we had *meant* something to me. Believe how fucking sorry I am."

My hands trembled as I fully clasped hers, desperate for any connection, any small piece of her that I could still hold onto.

The past month had drained me, like my energy had been leeched by something else.

"I'll do anything," I vowed, my voice thick with emotion. "I'll prove it. Just please, Penny. Give me a second chance."

For a moment, she didn't move. Didn't breathe.

Then, ever so slightly, her posture softened.

She leaned in, closing the space between us, her breath warm against my skin.

I could smell her—vanilla and spice, the scent that had been imprinted in my memory. It was ironic how she smelled like vanilla, because she was anything but.

Her eyes glistened, whether from exhaustion or the weight of everything between us, I couldn't tell.

Every muscle in my body ached to reach out, to cup her face and wipe away the tears that threatened to spill.

Instead, I closed my eyes for a fleeting second, breathing her in, savoring the nearness, the sliver of hope that still lingered in the air.

I wanted this. *Her.*

I was shit at using words, but I needed to find the right ones now.

"Tell me..." My voice barely broke the space between us. My eyes searched hers, pleading, willing her to let me in.

Something flickered across her face—a shadow of something softer, something real—before she sat back, crossing her arms over her chest.

I recoiled slightly, left grasping at the empty space.

"I'll give you one chance," she said, holding up a single finger.

"That's all I need," I replied confidently. I'd done enough thinking and ruminating to know that I was capable of proving myself.

With a sharp sniffle, Penny nodded, wiping her nose with the sleeve of her crew neck. Then there was a hint of a smile, like she was thinking of the perfect plot, the perfect punishment.

The smile wasn't sweet or forgiving; it was devious.

"You better learn to grovel, bitch."

Beneath the bite, I felt it—a crack in the armor. A small opening, a chance she hadn't slammed the door shut completely.

She was hurt. Scorned.

But she wasn't walking away.

A slow, determined smirk tugged at my lips as I leaned in, resting my forearms on the table.

"I'd move fucking mountains," I swore, my voice dropping low, rough with conviction. "Walk barefoot across hot coals. Brand my skin with your initials, Penny." My fingers curled into fists. "You have no idea how goddamn determined I am."

A spark flickered behind her eyes, something unreadable, something that felt an awful lot like intrigue.

The fire inside me ignited, adrenaline pumping hot through my veins.

Game on.

CHAPTER 13

"Grovel," I muttered to myself, rolling the word around on my tongue like it was foreign. Well, because it was.

Tapping a pencil against the edge of my small dining room table, I stared at the blank sheet of paper in front of me. My phone lay open beside it, the search engine filled with articles, forums, and desperate advice from men who had clearly screwed up just as badly as I had.

The more I scrolled, the more I realized one thing—I'd never done this before. Not once in my life. I didn't even know where to begin.

I could think of a million small, subtle gestures, but none of them would do.

Penny deserved more than easy. She deserved something real. Something that made it crystal fucking clear that I wasn't just sorry—I was hers, if she'd still have me.

After she'd thrown down that challenge, she all but shoved me out the door, making it clear I'd overstayed my welcome. And yeah, maybe I'd pushed her, worn her down, forced her hand into giving me the slightest crack of hope. But I wasn't ashamed of it.

I was a man who knew exactly what he wanted.

And I wanted Penny Hudson—desperately.

Sitting in my apartment, drink in hand, I let the possibilities race through my mind. All the ways I could show her. Prove to her.

Win her back because one thing was certain.

I'd make groveling my bitch. I'd do *whatever* it took.

Losing her for good? That wasn't an option.

And my end goal? To take whatever we had and mend it into something more. Something real.

No more sneaking around, no more stolen moments behind closed doors. I wanted her in the daylight, out in the open, where everyone could see that this was more than just a passing fling.

I was about to kick this groveling shit into high gear.

I'd flirt, I'd charm, I'd win her over because Penny was going to be mine again, for good.

But first, I needed a plan. A damn good one.

I sat at my dining table, pen poised over a blank sheet of paper, ready to map out my strategy. Stage one—small, thoughtful gestures to break through the walls she'd built around herself. I couldn't come on too strong, couldn't lay my entire hand on the table just yet.

Patience was key.

Instant gratification wasn't an option this time.

Next to me, Angus sat with a heavy sigh, watching me with those big, soulful eyes. His pink tongue lolled out, while I was here, drowning in my own indecision.

"What do you think?" I asked, waiting like he'd actually answer.

When he didn't, I dropped my pen onto the table and reached out, rubbing behind his ears. He tilted his head into my touch, groaning like he didn't give a shit what I was going through; all he wanted was for me to keep giving him the attention.

"What can I do?" I mused, thinking out loud.

My mind was blank.

Not just blank—completely useless, like that damn cartoon monkey clashing cymbals together inside my head.

I needed inspiration. Guidance. *Something.*

With a sigh, I bent down and kissed Angus on the snout. He licked my chin in return, tail thumping against the floor like he approved of whatever scheme I was about to cook up.

Laughing, I gave him one strong pat before standing up and grabbing my pen again. I started pacing, tapping the end of it against my chin.

"Think, Mac. Think."

Flowers? Too cliché—but let's be real, I'd probably end up buying a hell of a lot of them anyway.

Chocolate? No, Penny wasn't into sweets. She liked fruit. Apples, mostly.

Maybe I could bake her something?

Jesus, no. I was a terrible cook.

The last thing I wanted was to poison the woman I was trying to win back. That would just create more problems for me, and I couldn't afford another setback.

I let out another sigh, stopping at the table to stare down at my paper.

I needed something personal. Something that would remind her why we worked.

In those months we'd spent, we'd learned so much about each other, this should be fucking easy.

My boots scuffed against the floor as my thoughts churned, resuming my pacing once more.

Movement helped me think. Sitting still drove me crazy—it always had.

That was why bartending suited me so well. The constant motion, the rush of orders, the feeling that my hands were never idle. My brain thrived in chaos.

Penny was the same way. One of the many things we had in common, one of the things that made us click from the start.

Since we both thrived on experience, maybe I should take her somewhere new, something she would never forget.

I rifled through my memories, mentally flipping through the folder labeled *All Things Penny.* Conversations we'd had, little things she'd mentioned, places she'd always wanted to go.

And yet, the second I reached for something solid, the drawer in my mind jammed shut.

"For fuck's sake," I groaned, tossing my pen onto the table with a sharp clatter.

I hated admitting when I was out of my depth, but I couldn't do this on my own. I needed help, which meant swallowing my damn pride and going to the one person who knew Penny better than anyone.

Determined, I grabbed my jacket off the back of the couch and shrugged it on. My fingers tapped against my pockets, checking for the essentials—phone, wallet, keys.

Then, without another thought to talk myself out of the decision, I stormed out the door.

THE TIRES CRUNCHED over the gravel driveway leading up to the cabins on Cassidy Ranch. The Texas sun blazed overhead, not a single cloud in sight to offer even a hint of relief from the growing heat.

Pastures stretched endlessly around me, speckled with grazing horses and cattle, their slow movements contrasting the quickened beat of my pulse.

Growing up around guys like Boone and the others, you'd think I would've ended up just like them—spending my days working cattle, sweating under the open sky, putting in hard hours in any and every condition. But I'd never had much interest in that life. The bar was easy. Convenient. At first, it was a steady gig that didn't ask much of me beyond pouring drinks, making conversation, and keeping the lights on. Now, I've come to love it and couldn't see myself anywhere else.

Still, there were days—especially when my dad was still alive—when I'd wondered if I should've done something different. If maybe I had it in me to follow in his footsteps.

I shook off the thought as quickly as it came. I knew I wasn't cut out for that life.

I pulled my truck to a stop in front of the better-kept cabin on the property. Flowers overflowed from ceramic pots on the porch, the swing draped with throw pillows and a knitted blanket that fluttered slightly in the warm breeze.

Taking a final drag of my cigarette, I let the smoke linger for a second before exhaling, then crushed the ember out in the ashtray in my cupholder.

Here goes nothing.

Time to do something else I wasn't used to doing—asking for help.

Shoving my hands deep into my front pockets, I made my way up the steps, but before I could knock, the door swung open.

Aspen stood there, arms crossed, eyebrows pulled tight as she studied me with a mix of confusion and suspicion. One hip popped out as she assessed me, waiting for an explanation.

I never showed up at her place, especially without warning, so her curiosity was warranted.

"Hi," I exhaled. "I know I'm here unannounced, but I need your help. And I promise to tell you everything, on one condition."

Aspen scoffed, and she playfully shook her head. "Why would I agree to something before knowing what it is?"

"Because it has to do with your best friend," I said, voice steady but low. "And righting my wrongs."

Her expression shifted in an instant, skepticism giving way to something else.

She hesitated only for a moment before stepping aside, but I didn't move just yet. I needed her to agree before I stepped inside.

"Promise me you won't tell anyone," I said, voice barely above a whisper. My eyes flicked toward the neighboring house. If Boone finds out I'm here, he'll eat this up like it's his last damn meal.

I pointed at her, my tone firm. "Not even Boone."

Aspen's brows shot up, and she let out a low whistle. "This must be serious."

My skin prickled with heat, embarrassment creeping up my neck like a slow burn. I swallowed hard, then admitted, "I fucked up."

Aspen's lips parted slightly, but whatever she was about to say, she must've thought better of it. Instead, she gave me a quick nod, then gestured sharply with her hands.

"Okay, *fine*—but get inside before Boone sees you. Then I have to tell him."

I didn't need to be told twice.

I slipped past her, the door clicking shut behind me.

"I have to say, I'm surprised you came to see me," Aspen added, her voice dripping with curiosity as she trailed behind me.

I barely made it to her open living room before spinning on my heel, hands planted on my hips. She was in the kitchen, head buried in the fridge, rummaging through its contents.

"Yeah," I scoffed. "Me too."

Aspen didn't react, just kept digging through shelves like she'd find treasure between the ketchup and leftover takeout.

"Want something to drink? Water? Beer?" she asked, finally glancing over her shoulder.

"Beer, please."

She spun around, the hem of her dress catching the momentum, as she reached for a bottle opener. With practiced ease, she popped the cap off a cold one and stepped toward me, her fingers wrapped around the sweating glass.

"Should we sit?" She shot a glance at the dining table, but I shook my head.

"Well," she huffed dramatically, lowering herself into a chair anyway, "I am. I've been on my feet all damn day, and they're killing me."

Her ponytail was slightly messy, loose strands slipping from the elastic to frame the curve of her jaw. She looked comfortable, confident—meanwhile, I felt like my ribs were in a vice grip.

I stayed where I was, jaw locked, words getting stuck somewhere in my throat. Aspen tilted her head, her sharp gaze locked onto me, studying me like I was a puzzle she wasn't sure she wanted to solve.

Where the hell did I even start?

Did I lay it all out there? Spill every last regrettable detail? If I said it out loud, it meant other people would know what a mess I'd made, and I wasn't sure I was ready for that level of exposure.

I needed Aspen's help, but I didn't need to hand her my entire disaster on a silver platter. I could leave some things out.

Halloween. That was a safe enough place to begin. I'd tread carefully.

"Penny and I have been hooking up since the Halloween party at the barn," I said, my voice carefully even. "That night, we snuck off while you all were downstairs."

Aspen's lips parted—then, suddenly, she burst out laughing.

"I knew it." Her eyes glowed with mischief, her tone smug. "You two mysteriously vanished, and no one could find you. Oh my God." She sat forward, gripping the armrests. "So, let me get this straight—you and Penny have been sneaking around behind everyone's backs for seven months?"

"Well, *were*," I corrected. "Past tense. That's why I'm here." I exhaled sharply, rubbing a hand over my jaw. "Like I said, I fucked up. Penny and I haven't really spoken in like two months. Up until last night."

Aspen's expression shifted, curiosity melting into confusion. She shifted in her chair, smoothing out her dress as she crossed her legs.

"Nothing ever seemed off when we were all together?" she asked, reaching for her water.

I let out a slow breath and wandered toward the kitchen, gripping my beer like it was the only thing keeping me steady. I didn't want to sit, but I needed something solid under me.

So, I did what any self-respecting man in crisis would do—I leaned against the counter and crossed one ankle over the other to brace myself for the rest of this conversation.

"It doesn't matter," I said, waving a dismissive hand. I took a long pull from my beer, letting the burn of regret settle in my chest. "I need your help getting her back."

Aspen blinked at me, unimpressed. "I feel like I'm missing a *lot* of information to be able to help you."

Groaning, I set down the beer and then dragged both hands down my face, like I could scrub away the sheer stupidity of this situation. God, I needed a cigarette to cope with this shit.

I shouldn't have come here. I should've sat with my own failure a little longer, figured out how to grovel on my own.

But no, here I was.

"I'm not going into detail," I said, my tone a little too sharp, but I didn't care. "But I hid something pretty... big from her. Penny and I had a conversation last night, and it ended with her telling me to—and I quote—'*grovel, bitch*.'" I even threw in air quotes for dramatic effect.

Aspen snorted. "That definitely sounds like something she'd say."

I nodded grimly. "So, here I am. How the hell do I grovel? What do I need to do?"

Aspen inhaled deeply, letting out a long, drawn-out sigh like she was already exhausted for me. "Okay, since you won't tell me what you did, can you at least rate it on a scale from one to ten? How bad are we talking?"

My jaw tensed. I rolled my neck, trying to shake off the weight pressing down on me.

"9.5."

Aspen let out a low whistle, leaning back in her chair. "Damn. Yeah, you did mess up."

"No shit," I grumbled, pushing off the counter. Frustration simmered under my skin as I stalked toward the dining table, yanking out a chair and dropping into it with all the grace of a guy who'd just realized he was completely screwed. I slammed my beer onto the table for extra emphasis.

Aspen, meanwhile, looked thrilled.

"Is that why she had Theo and I come with her that one day? With the glitter?" Aspen's grin was front and fucking center. There was no hiding how amused she was.

"Yup."

She let out a laugh, nodding in understanding.

"It's gonna be fine," she assured me, sitting up straighter. She reached into a woven basket on the table, pulled out a notepad and pen, and pressed the tip against the paper. "We'll come up with a plan. I'll help you by using what she loves, stuff that'll actually work to win her back."

I'd expected Aspen to talk me through this, maybe drop some half-baked advice and send me on my way. What I hadn't expected was her grabbing a goddamn notebook like this was a full-blown strategy session.

I narrowed my eyes. "Like what?"

Aspen didn't answer right away. She was too busy biting her lip in concentration, scribbling things down like some kind of evil genius plotting world domination.

I leaned in slightly, trying to get a look at whatever the hell she was writing. When that didn't work, I sat up straighter, my eyes bouncing between her face and the words on the page.

Whatever was coming next, I wasn't sure if I would be relieved or terrified.

"Groveling is going to require you to take everything you've ever done in the past to win a girl over and throw it in the trash," Aspen said, pausing her furious note-taking to look me dead in the eye.

I frowned. "What the hell does that even mean?"

"It means flowers, charming pickup lines, and pure sex appeal won't help you here."

I sucked in a deep breath, leaning back slightly. Well, shit. I relied on my good looks *a lot*.

"Because," she continued, her expression unyielding, "she already knows how you look. She knows you're capable of doing the small things." Aspen hesitated. "She *does* know that, right?"

"Yes," I muttered, my mind drifting back to all the little things I'd done—dinners, dancing, thoughtful gifts. Things she probably set on fire and then threw into the garbage disposal for good measure.

Aspen nodded, satisfied. "Good. Because now it's all about action. Prepare to make yourself feel like a fool."

I grimaced. That sounded awful, but my feelings didn't really matter.

I'd dress up as a damn clown if Aspen thought it would work.

"I don't even know where to start," I admitted, my gaze dropping to the table. I picked at the beer label, giving my hands something to do.

"Well," she said, grinning like she was actually enjoying this, "you're in luck."

I lifted a skeptical brow. "Yeah? How's that?"

"Penny *loves* romance novels," Aspen said, her smile widening like she was about to deliver the most obvious solution in the history of solutions. "You've got an entire genre of advice at your fingertips."

Of course. Why hadn't I thought of that?

A slow, disbelieving smile crept onto my face. "Aspen, you're a genius."

She did a dramatic half-bow from her chair, like she was accepting an award she definitely deserved. "Thank you, thank you."

"I should rent some of her favorites from the library," I said, half to myself.

"Bingo." Aspen pointed at me. Then she tore the paper she'd been writing on and slid it across the table. "I took liberties and made a list of books to start with."

I grabbed the note and scanned the list. A few titles, a couple of authors I'd never heard of, but I was making a mental note to hit the library first thing tomorrow.

"I say we meet once a week," Aspen announced, reaching down into a massive tote bag and pulling out a planner. She flipped through the pages, pen poised like this was a real job.

"Weekly?" I asked, skeptically.

Aspen's gaze snapped up to mine. "Are you serious about

getting back on her good side or not?"

I was. Absolutely.

"Then once a week it is." She didn't even wait for my agreement. "I can come by the bar in the mornings when Ellie's working the stand."

"Wait," I cut in. "Ellie's working there again?"

Aspen groaned. "Yeah. Just until she finds something else. But this isn't about Ellie right now. Focus."

Rolling my eyes, I leaned back in the chair.

"How about Thursday morning?" Aspen asked after pondering over her schedule for a beat.

Considering I lived at the bar, she could show up whenever the hell she wanted. I didn't need to check my calendar.

"Sounds good to me," I said.

She extended a hand over the table, all business. "It's going to be a pleasure working with you, Mac."

Scoffing, I reached out, shaking her hand firmly. "You too, Miss Westgrove."

CHAPTER 14

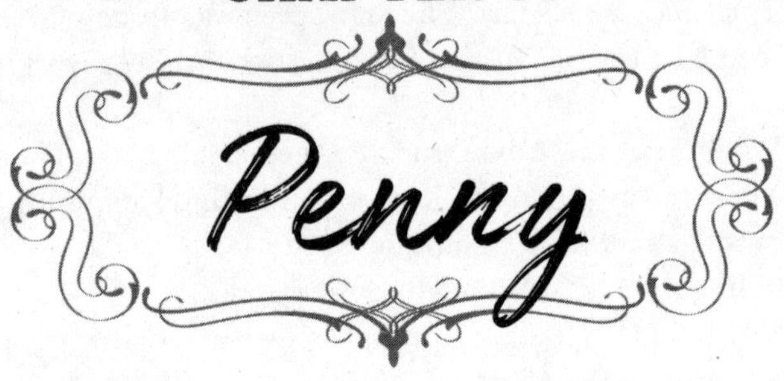

Unknown Number

I can't stop thinking about you

Thanks... but who is this?

Unknown Number

Mac...

Ah, yes. I deleted your number 

Unknown Number

Fairrr does this mean you'll add it back?

Oh no way it's a privilege to be saved in my phone.

Unknown Number

One day, you'll save my number again... mark my words.

We'll see about that

One of our employees called out sick this morning, which meant one thing—I was on front desk duty.

Not that I minded. It shook up my routine, gave me time to tackle tasks I didn't get to often, and, best of all, put me in the perfect position to mingle.

Working the circ desk was where I got my start. My very first job was right here, checking books in and out, helping patrons find their way, and shelving returns when things were slow. The library wasn't just a job to me; it was a calling. A place where stories lived, where knowledge was free, and where anyone could walk in and leave a little richer than when they arrived.

Sure, libraries housed books, but that was just the beginning. We had computers, programs, resources—but beyond the physical, we were a community. Faircloud's library wasn't just a building; it was a safe space.

Hell, it had been my safe space, too. Even on my worst days, even when I was drowning in stress, the library was the kind of stress that distracted me from the deeper, heavier things pressing down on me. The things I didn't want to think about.

And today? I needed that distraction. More than ever.

It had been two days since Mac barged into my apartment and basically put us on lockdown. Like a soldier on a mission, he planted himself in my space and held his ground.

I had to give him credit—sitting at my table, barely speaking, just existing in my orbit for hours. That was dedication. It was a sliver of proof that maybe he really did regret what happened.

If I were being honest with myself, I knew Mac was sorry. My whole attitude after that night had shifted into something else entirely. Something more about proving a point than genuinely believing he didn't care.

I was still hurt. That wasn't going to change overnight. But it didn't mean I couldn't see how hard he was willing to try.

Before then, I was sure I'd never let him back in. His lack of effort had been abysmal, and I knew my worth. I wasn't some girl who would sit around waiting for a man to figure out I was worth the work.

But clearly, Mac had gotten sick of waiting for me to come back around.

He wasn't used to having to chase—he was always the one being chased. Women practically threw themselves at him, mesmerized by that cocky smirk and those unfairly good looks. One flash of that dimpled grin and poof—panties vanished like a damn magic trick.

That was where Mac and I had always been alike. We were both the ones people wanted.

Our relationship had been a game for us—push, pull, tease, retreat—until one of us would run out of energy to keep playing and either left or wanted something serious.

Unfortunately, we hadn't gotten to that point.

But now? Oh, Mac was in for it.

I wasn't about to make this easy on him.

Did I forgive him? Not entirely.

Was I going to drag this out, have a little fun while he worked to win me back?

Oh, hell yeah.

I smiled to myself as I crouched down, reaching for the books stacked at the bottom of the rolling cart. My fingers brushed over the worn spines, my mind still lingering on Mac. I was eager—maybe too eager—to see what he'd come up with next.

Then, a throat cleared behind me.

The sound wasn't just a polite little cough. No, it was the kind that demanded attention.

I shot up quickly, books clutched to my chest, my dress billowing around my legs as I spun to greet whoever was waiting.

"Hi! How can I help—"

My words died in my throat.

Mac.

The same Mac who had been haunting my thoughts, standing right in front of the desk like he belonged there.

He was dressed in all black—a fitted tee to show off those tattooed arms, each one a patchwork of mismatched ink that I knew far too well.

My gaze dipped, memories rushing back of tracing those very designs with my fingertips, lying beside him in the dark, whispering about each of their meanings.

Spoiler alert: none of them meant a damn thing. Just random choices, impulsive decisions, and things he thought looked cool at the time.

I inhaled sharply. *Get a grip, Penny.*

"You," I finished my sentence, forcing a bright, pleasant smile as I shifted my weight, popping a hip and tilting my head for effect.

Mac responded with that damn grin, the one that made my knees threaten to give out. And now, with the addition of the mustache he'd grown?

I was in trouble.

Deep, *deep* trouble.

Somewhere in the back of my mind, I was still trying to play it cool, trying not to let my thoughts spiral into places they had no business going.

"Well, hello there, Penelope," he said smoothly, setting a stack of books on the counter.

Penelope.

At the start of our relationship, Mac and I had been flipping through an old yearbook, laughing over bad haircuts and cringeworthy memories.

He saw my full name underneath a shockingly good middle school picture and had decided, right then and there, that he *loved* it.

Since then, I was either Pen, Penelope, or—on his most charming days—*Trouble.*

That one was my favorite.

"I'm checking out some books," Mac said casually, drumming

his fingers on the top of the pile.

I tilted my head, scanning the titles.

Then I froze.

There sat a rather large stack of romance.

Not just any romance books—*my* favorites. Everything from *The Notebook* to the newer releases that were on my need-to-reread list.

I lifted my gaze, skepticism all over my face.

"What exactly are you doing with these?"

"It's fine literature," he replied, widening his stance and crossing his arms like he was taking up as much space as he could. Not that he had to because his presence was already all-consuming enough.

"Yes, I know that," I shot back. "But why are you suddenly so eager to expose yourself to such *fine literature*?"

Mac bit down on his bottom lip—his tell. A sign that he was scheming something.

Then, he leaned down, resting his elbows on the counter, putting him just below my eye level. His gaze lifted, dark and hooded, as his voice dropped into a low, gravelly register.

"Now, what would be the fun in telling you all my secrets?" he murmured. "Don't you like a little mystery?"

I scoffed, shaking my head—but I couldn't stop the smirk that curved my lips.

This was him. The Mac I knew. The unapologetic flirt who had never met a challenge he couldn't charm his way out of.

So, being me, I leaned down, too, closing the space between us.

Our lips hovered close.

The warmth of his breath brushed against my skin, a slow exhale that sent heat skimming down my spine.

Mac's hand lay flat on the desk, his fingers twitching slightly.

I let mine drift forward, tracing the tattooed ink on the back of his hand with just the tip of my finger. Deliberate. Slow.

His breath hitched.

"I get my ideas from romance novels, too," I whispered, my voice sweet and laced with something wicked. "That's where I learned the thing with my tongue you liked oh so much... the one that had you begging me to do it again."

I batted my lashes once. Then, before he could respond, I stood to my full height, stepping back just enough to regain the upper hand.

Mac straightened too, shaking his head slightly, his mouth ticking up at the corner.

"Well," he replied, nodding toward the books. "Let's hope you'll allow yourself to benefit from all this research."

Mac reached into his back pocket and took out his wallet. His fingers shifted through its contents and pulled out a white, plastic card, which he laid down on the top of his stack.

My gaze was locked on it and the picture in the top corner. I took that photo of him when he came to visit me at work. Somehow, I convinced him to get a library card, though he never used it... until now.

Clearing my throat with a nonchalant nod, I acted as unbothered as I possibly could and started scanning each book.

But I felt his eyes on me, which made keeping my composure that much harder.

His stare was unwavering. Intense.

By the time I ripped the receipt from the machine, my skin was warm and prickling like a live wire.

"Here," I said, sticking the slip inside the top book. "Return date is on the receipt. You're free to go."

Mac took the books into his arms, lingering just a second too long before flashing me a slow, knowing grin.

"You look devastating today, Penelope."

"Thanks," I said as my voice cracked a little on the last syllable. I could kick myself for letting his effects show even in the smallest ways.

With a wink and one last shameless glance down my frame, he spun on his heel and strolled out the door.

I watched him through the glass, my pulse still unsteady as he strode toward his truck, tossing the books into the passenger seat before rounding the front and slipping behind the wheel.

The second he was gone, I let out the breath I'd been holding—then bit my lip to keep from smiling.

Because, damn it, things were already feeling charged and we were just getting started.

CHAPTER 15

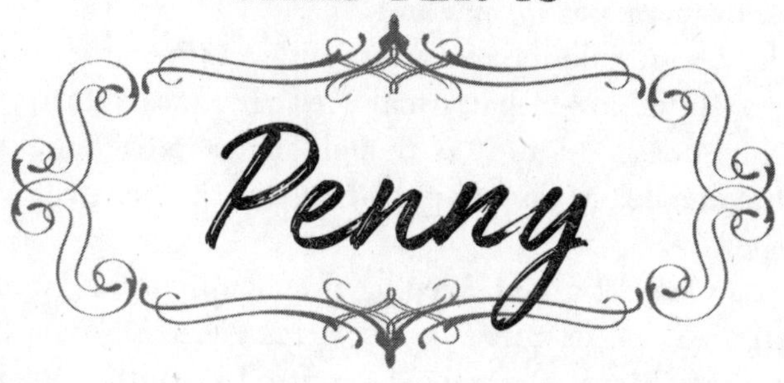

"Sandy!" I called, the bell above the front door of Petal Pusher jingling as it shut behind me. A large, grease-stained pizza box balanced in my hands—the unmistakable scent of extra pepperoni filling the air, mine and Sandy's favorite, no question.

I made my way through the flower shop, weaving between bouquets of pastel lilies and bright sunflowers, past the chalkboard sign that read *Today's Mood: Petal to the Metal*, and straight into the back room.

Sandy stood at the wash station, sleeves rolled up, elbow-deep in soapy water as she rinsed out a cluster of glass vases. The soft clink of one tapping against another echoed lightly in the room.

"It's about time," she said, flipping the last vase upside down on the drying rack before wiping her hands on the front of her floral apron. "I was starting to think my Penelope stood me up. You know my rule."

I let out a little laugh as I set the pizza box on the small table we always used. "I know, I know," I said, huffing as I brushed some flower scraps from the table. "Home before dark."

Sandy gave a knowing smile and nodded, untying her apron. "Let me lock the door. Plates are in the cabinet, same as always," she added, pointing in that direction with a flick of her wrist like I hadn't eaten dinner here at least a hundred times.

This little tradition of ours had become a rhythm. Neither of us had anyone waiting at home, so we found comfort in sharing these simple moments together. A makeshift family stitched together by pizza, gossip, and love.

The swinging doors creaked as Sandy returned from the front, her steps a little slower than usual. Her hand moved instinctively to her hip, pressing into it as though she were trying to soothe something tender. My brows pulled together as I set plates in our usual spots.

“You okay?” I asked, keeping my tone light but laced with concern. I turned to fully face her, arms folded across my chest as I watched the way she walked—controlled, a little too careful. She straightened up when she saw me watching, a practiced smile sliding across her face.

But her eyes told a different story.

“Sandy...” I said, the single word heavy with meaning as I followed her toward the office.

“I’m fine,” she replied quickly, shrugging out of her apron and tossing it over the back of her desk chair. “I just twisted my hip a little funny, that’s all.”

I didn’t believe her for a second.

Sandy was the kind of woman who would climb a ladder with a sprained ankle just to hang eucalyptus garlands across her storefront. She didn’t let people in easily—not really. When she did admit to needing help, it was usually more about keeping me from fussing than about her actually asking.

Still, I didn’t push. Not yet.

I made a quiet promise to myself that I’d totally be asking about this later.

“Come on, Penelope,” Sandy said as she brushed past me and out of her office. A gust of rose-scented perfume lingered in her wake, trailing through the air. I stood still for a second, watching her try her damnedest to hide the limp in her stride.

I sighed and followed after her, catching up just in time to beat her to the table. I pulled out her chair and offered my arm in a silent assist.

"Will you *please*," she said with a light laugh, brushing me off. "I'm okay."

"Okay, okay," I said, backing off with my hands in the air in mock surrender. "I just worry about you, that's all."

"And I appreciate that," she replied with a pointed look, "but I don't need you to coddle me."

I opened the pizza box and grabbed two slices, handing her one before sitting down across from her. "I'm going to anyway," I said with a wink, biting into my slice.

Sandy shook her head, trying to smother her smile as she took a bite of her own.

She could pretend to be annoyed, but we both knew better.

Sandy had been a constant in my life since I moved into the tiny apartment above Petal Pusher after high school. At this point, she was less of a landlord and more of a grandmother—sharp-tongued, quick-witted, and the most fiercely independent woman I knew. But that didn't mean she got to limp around like her hip wasn't screaming for rest without me stepping in.

She could push me away all she wanted, but I wasn't going anywhere. I checked in, I hovered, I annoyed the hell out of her—and I'd keep doing it. Because once someone was in my circle, I loved them hard.

Maybe too hard sometimes.

I made them my priority, often at the cost of myself. I was working on that—slowly, painfully learning that I mattered too. That taking care of myself didn't mean abandoning the people I loved. So for now, I took a deep breath, refocused on the pepperoni in front of me and the way Sandy folded her napkin like she was setting a place at a five-star restaurant.

"Have you heard from your mother?" she asked suddenly, dabbing her mouth with that perfectly creased napkin before placing it neatly back on the table.

With the holiday approaching, I guess I didn't need to be so thrown off by her curiosity.

I let out a short, bitter scoff and leaned back in my chair, crossing my legs beneath the hem of my dress.

"Nope," I said, tossing my hair over my shoulder. "Don't plan to, either."

Sandy didn't reply, just nodded with that soft understanding that came from someone who knew the situation.

I usually saw my mother once a year—*if* she felt like coming back to Faircloud.

The day I turned eighteen, I was handed my freedom like a set of hand-me-down keys and a goodbye. My mom sold her house, packed her things, and disappeared from my life like she'd been waiting for the exact moment I was no longer her legal responsibility.

It wasn't that my childhood was tragic—it was just... bare. Minimal. I had food, a roof, and clothes, but no one tucked me in. No one showed up for parent-teacher conferences or clapped from the bleachers. I spent most of my time raising myself.

That's probably why I'd latched onto Aspen and her family so fiercely. They'd given me something I never had—a sense of being wanted. Being chosen.

I didn't carry resentment toward my mom. I'd made peace with the absence, the silence, the indifference. But I'd be lying if I said it didn't leave marks.

I think that's why I poured so much of myself into others. Because deep down, there was a little girl in me who never thought she mattered in the first place. The same little girl that had no one cheering in her corner.

So, I learned to clap for myself.

I became my own cheerleader.

And somehow, in the quiet glow of a flower shop back room, with pizza on mismatched plates and a woman who pretended not to limp, I continued to learn I was worth something more.

Sandy had been there for me, and I was always going to be there for her.

For the rest of our dinner, Sandy and I laughed and gossiped like we always did—an easy rhythm between us, filled with warmth and routine. She filled me in on the latest Faircloud drama, from Mrs. Winchester throwing a fit at the new candy shop owner over a parking spot to something juicier—news about the new chef in town.

Apparently, some big-deal city chef had packed up his knives and moved to Faircloud of all places. Rumor was, he bought The Coffee Cup—the same little café where Aspen used to work before moving to Cassidy Ranch. Ironically, a few doors down from Petal Pusher.

The people of Faircloud were already stirring about it, naturally. Some were concerned he'd attract the "wrong crowd," whatever that meant. I, for one, didn't see the problem. Honestly, Faircloud could use a little shaking up. Some fresh energy. And, selfishly, maybe even a dish that didn't involve pepperoni and a cardboard box.

A girl can only eat so many slices of pizza before the spark fades.

Sandy, on the other hand, was practically buzzing with opinions. She leaned back in her chair, clutching her mug of chamomile tea like it was gospel.

"Can you believe it?" she huffed. "He wants to turn it into some fancy steakhouse. *A steakhouse*, Penelope. Is that what we need?"

I smiled as I picked up her plate and headed for the sink. "Don't be so close-minded. It could be good for everyone."

She waved a dismissive hand at me. "No, Penelope. It isn't."

"What about southern hospitality?" I teased. "Aren't we supposed to be welcoming?"

She took a long, dramatic sip from her mug. "Bless his heart," she muttered with every ounce of southern sarcasm she had.

I laughed, the sound echoing softly in the quiet shop as I rinsed our dishes.

When everything was clean and put away, I stayed with Sandy while she locked up, making sure she got to her car safely.

Then I headed upstairs to my apartment, the warm smell of

flowers still lingering in my hair and clothes. But as I reached the top step, something unusual caught my eye—a small something on the floor near my door.

I stepped closer.

A bouquet.

The red petals were unmistakable. I bent down slowly and picked it up, the scent sweet and familiar, the stems cool and dewy in my hands. A note was tucked between them, the paper rough under my fingertips. I flipped it over, heart already skipping ahead of me.

Penelope,

I'll never let your pitcher go empty. It's my promise to you.

Forever,

Mac.

I stared at the note, my heart thrumming as my breath caught somewhere between my chest and throat. He must've come straight from the library. And if these were from Sandy's shop, which of course they were, she hadn't said a word.

"That woman," I whispered with a smile, shaking my head.

The grin that spread across my face was instant, unstoppable. My cheeks flushed, heart fluttering like I was seventeen again, and I held the bouquet close to my chest.

I walked through the door, the quiet of home wrapping around me like a soft blanket. And the very first thing I did?

I filled the pitcher.

For the first time in months, I watched the water rise to the brim and gently lowered the roses inside. They fit perfectly.

Then I dug through my purse until I found my phone and snapped a picture of the flowers right there on my little kitchen table.

I got the flowers. They're beautiful 😉

Unknown Number

Glad they didn't wilt. They look good

OMG how long were they up here?

Unknown Number

Dropped them off before work, right after the library. Sandy said they'd be fine. That woman is never wrong 😉

Suck-up 🙄

I laughed to myself as I walked toward the kitchen. I turned on the speaker and connected my phone, locking the screen and setting it face down on the counter.

Reaching into my fridge, I filled my wine glass with wine until it kissed the rim. Then, I leaned back against the counter and glanced across the room.

The pitcher caught my eye once again.

It looked foreign, being full—like a part of me I'd forgotten had come back to life.

Roses had always been my favorite. But after Mac... they carried more weight. More meaning. They were tattooed on him, inked on his skin in a place I had been close enough to kiss. Close enough to memorize.

I closed my eyes and took a long sip of wine, letting the memories rush over me like a tide.

Happiness.

Comfort.

Thrill.

He brought out a side of me I always enjoyed. And I knew, deep down, I did the same for him.

But no matter how much I wanted to lean in, to let the past go and fall again with abandon, I couldn't. Not yet.

The hurt was still there, curled in the corners of my heart, waiting. And if I gave in too easily, if I folded now because of a few flirtatious words and a bouquet of my favorite flowers... what message would that send?

No. He needed to earn it.

Because this time, I wasn't giving myself away so freely.

CHAPTER 16

Thursday morning had arrived, which meant one thing: my penciled-in appointment with Aspen at the bar.

I'd been doing my homework—literally. The stack of romance novels Penny had helped me check out from the library sat in a neat pile upstairs on my little dining table, their spines already worn from how often I flipped through them. I had to admit, they weren't half bad. Actually... they were kind of addictive.

Some of them were funny as hell, and even though I wouldn't say it out loud, I'd caught myself lying in bed last night, laughing like a damn fool. I never thought I'd relate to a guy in a romance novel, working to win back the girl, but here we were.

Aspen had insisted I use little sticky tabs to mark the parts that stood out—lines I liked, things I could maybe steal and adapt for my own version to use on Penny.

I went overboard, of course. There were tabs everywhere. Bright neon slivers stuck out like confetti from every edge of the pages. Dialogue that made me smirk. Scenes that sparked ideas.

I hadn't expected *so* much sex. These sweet little covers with pastel colors and sun-dappled fields? They were hiding a lot of heat.

It made me wonder—if these were Penny's favorites, did that mean she'd fantasized about all this? About being wanted like that?

My chest tightened, pulse picking up. The thought of her reading those pages, biting her lip, cheeks flushed—it was enough to scramble my focus.

The book was still open on the bar top, one arm propped beneath me as I hunched forward to keep reading while I waited for Aspen. I brought the cigarette I held in my fingers to my mouth, taking a long drag and then exhaling. My eyes scanned the paragraph again, but I wasn't really processing the words anymore.

Before I could make it past the next page, the front door opened with a familiar chime. Aspen strolled in like she owned the place. Her blond hair was clipped up in a messy twist, and she wore a cap-sleeved dress with worn-in sneakers that somehow made her look effortlessly put together.

I straightened to my full height, closed the book, and placed both hands on the bar.

"I see you're already getting to work," she teased, sliding onto a stool and tossing her tote onto the seat next to her.

"Already finished two," I said, holding up the book I'd just been reading like a trophy. "This is number three."

Aspen let out a low whistle. "And?"

I tilted my head, rolling it side to side in a noncommittal shrug. "First of all, I wasn't expecting that much sex," I said with a laugh. "But hey, I'm not complaining."

The bell above the door chimed again, and before I even glanced up, instinct took over. I grabbed the book and tucked it under the bar like it was contraband. The last thing I needed was anyone catching me reading *that* and trying to figure out why.

When I did look up, adjusting myself like I hadn't just been hiding something, I saw Theo walking toward us.

My brows pulled together in confusion. I turned to Aspen, expecting her to glance behind her to see who it was—but she didn't. She was already looking at me, that pained, guilty smile written all over her face.

"You knew she was coming," I whispered, my voice low and

tense.

Aspen didn't deny it. "I had to tell her, Mac. She's my best friend."

I groaned. "You gossip."

"I had my fingers crossed!" she said, trying to sound innocent.

Theo slid onto the stool beside Aspen, propping her chin up with her hand and sighing dramatically. "Oh, Mac... you're in some *serious* trouble, I hear."

I dropped my head forward, groaning again as my shoulders sagged.

"I'm aware," I muttered. "Not that I had any control over you hearing about it."

Theo rolled her eyes.

"But yeah." Sighing, I leaned against the back of the bar. "I'm in deep. Now I'm just trying to climb my way out of the hole. Please tell me you came with advice and not just to enjoy the show."

Theo grinned, unapologetic. "I'm fully up to speed on the plan."

Perfect.

"The books," she added with a nod. "That's genius. If there's one way to get back into Penny's heart, it's through her love of literature."

I rubbed the back of my neck. "Yeah, well... being creative is the problem."

Following instructions? No issue. Showing up and doing the work? Fine. But coming up with something heartfelt and original, something that actually stood a chance of reaching her? That's where I froze.

"That's why we're here," Aspen said with a grin.

I let out a humorless laugh, more exasperated than amused. "Great. Because if there's something better than one opinion, it's two," I said, my tone laced with sarcasm

Aspen and Theo exchanged a look.

Immediately suspicious, my eyes bounced between them. "What did you do?"

Like I summoned them with my words, the door chimed *again.*

In walked Boone, his worn cowboy hat sitting perfectly on his head like always, followed by Rhodes, who had a baby strapped to his chest.

I snapped my gaze to Aspen. "You're kidding me."

"I tell Boone everything," she said defensively, lifting her hands.

"And I don't hide anything from Rhodes," Theo added smoothly. "Maybe you should try it sometime."

I scowled, pushing away from the bar and standing up straight, frustration crawling over my skin.

Boone was the first to approach, sliding behind Aspen and leaning down to kiss the top of her head. Rhodes joined Theo's side, wrapping his arm around her shoulder as Frankie let out a happy coo.

Was this some kind of intervention? All my friends gathered here, watching me like I was a lost cause.

My hands dragged down my face as I groaned again, this time wishing I could rub them all out of existence. But when I looked up, they were still there. Still watching. Still waiting.

They all wore the same expression: gentle sympathy. And somehow, that was worse than judgment.

"You really didn't have to come," I muttered to Boone and Rhodes.

"We wanted to," Boone said, his voice steady and calm. "Aspen told us what happened. We're here to help."

Yeah, well I wish she hadn't.

But there was no going back, so whatever was done was final, and I might as well use it to my advantage.

"So," Rhodes said, leaning on the bar, a smirk tugging at his lips. "You gonna start, or should we?"

I blinked. "Start what?"

"If we are going to help you, we need to know what happened," Theo said.

So, this *was* an intervention. They were cornering me, forcing the truth and wanting me to admit my problem out loud.

At this point, there was no avoiding it, no beating around the bush, because I had four pairs of eyes staring at me from four people who wouldn't take no for an answer.

With a mutter of expletives and a roll of my eyes, I spoke.

"I was married. Years ago. She showed up at my apartment, and Penny answered the door while I wasn't home."

Those four sets of eyes bore into me even harder, widening slightly.

Blink.

Blink.

The silence was creeping up my spine, coiling in my gut as the nerves set in. I needed someone to say something.

"You were *married*, Mac. Married. And you didn't think to mention it? Not even to us?" Rhodes finally broke the silence.

I hadn't. I'd told no one—not a single soul—about Vegas. There wasn't a reason to because it was nothing. A blur of neon lights, too much whiskey, and a choice I regretted as soon as the liquor dried and the truth came out. If I'd known it would come back years later to bite me in the ass and become a hot topic for my entire friend group, I might've handled things differently.

Like I told Penny, if I could go back and rewrite that chapter, I would in a heartbeat.

"It was nothing," I muttered, my voice low and tight. "She was nobody, a coworker. A stupid, drunken mistake I clearly *really* regret now."

Right about now, embarrassment felt like a second skin. The one thing I wanted to keep buried, locked away and forgotten, had become front-page news among my closest people... and apparently, even my sister, judging by what she'd implied the other night.

How the hell did it get this far?

If Mimi had just called me instead of showing up out of nowhere...

The papers were signed, and I delivered them back to her. Everything was settled, on its way to being okay.

"I just can't believe you were dumb enough to actually go through with it," Theo said with a laugh, the kind that was half disbelief, half amusement.

I shot her a look. "Whiskey will do that to you," I said flatly. "Most of my dumbass decisions involve alcohol."

I'd always loved the party scene—the noise, the music, the laughter echoing through crowded spaces. It was my comfort zone. People cutting loose, losing their filters, letting the night take over... yeah, that was a part of me I never really tried to change.

Then came Penny.

She fit right into that world without ever needing to prove anything. She could sit at a bar with a cocktail in hand and talk circles around anyone. Or she could hit the dance floor like she owned it. I'd spent too many nights pretending I was focused on working, when really, I was watching her. Admiring how effortlessly she moved through the very culture that shaped me.

"So," Boone said, arms crossed. "What's your game plan?"

That question punched the air right out of my lungs.

Game plan? I didn't have one. I was so early into this whole thing that formulating a plan still felt so far off.

The silence that followed was deafening. My friends stared at me like they were waiting for some brilliant, heartfelt strategy, but I had nothing. Just two romance novels down, a cluttered head, and a heart that couldn't stop chasing a girl who, right now, was really testing it.

Boone gave a slow nod, like he already knew. He pulled out the stool with Aspen's tote bag, set it aside, and took a seat.

"Well," he said, settling in, "we're gonna be here a while."

My friends and I huddled together in that dimly lit bar like we were planning the heist of the century—except what I wanted to steal back was a heart I'd already broken.

We'd scribbled on napkins, scratched out bad ideas, circled the good ones, and laughed harder than we had in weeks.

The apprehension I felt when I first saw them all come in here had vanished and been replaced with comfort. As badly as I hadn't wanted more people to know, maybe it turned out to be a good thing.

My hand ached from gripping the pen too tight, and my knuckles were smudged with ink. But damn, my heart... my heart felt full for the first time in a long time.

Somewhere between Theo's teasing, Boone's practical suggestions, Rhodes's side commentary, and Aspen's relentless optimism, I found it—that flicker of.

As I looked around the bar top at the chaos of our ideas and the unwavering support in my friends' eyes, I felt something I hadn't expected. A fragile, reckless kind of feeling that maybe, just maybe, things in my life would work out for the better.

The last thing I needed?

Penny Hudson—messy, stubborn, brilliant, beautiful Penelope—to be mine.

Not just for tonight.

Not just in memory.

But for good.

Forever.

CHAPTER 17

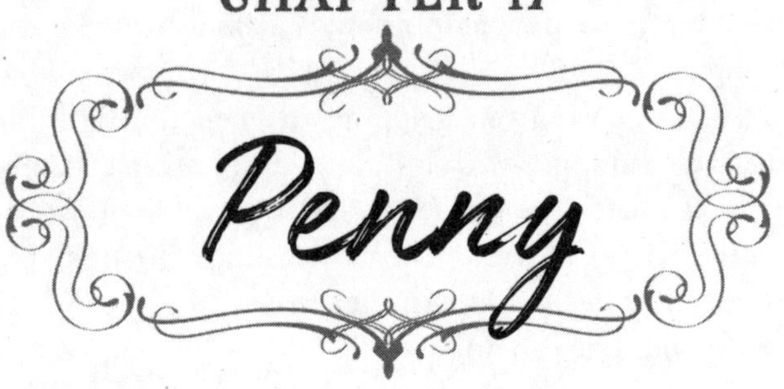

"What do you mean you can't make it?" I groaned, wedging my phone between my ear and shoulder as I dragged a lumpy, well-loved bean bag across the library's carpet floor toward the youth section. The thing skipped with every tug, like it was just as overworked as I was.

It was barely ten in the morning—only an hour into our day—and I already felt like I'd run a marathon. My dress stuck to my back from the hustle, and my to-do list kept growing like it had a personal vendetta against me.

Boone was supposed to be my reader for a second-grade field trip, but currently, he was on the other end of the line, claiming he'd "fallen ill." Total bullshit if you asked me. His cough sounded about as fake as a toddler apologizing after drawing on the books with a marker. Trust me, I knew exactly what that sounded like.

As if that weren't enough, I had a group of elderly crafters arriving soon to set up for their weekend craft show in one of the rec rooms. I'd promised to help them with tables, chairs, and making sure the hot glue guns didn't burn down the building.

Oh, and because I apparently hate myself, I also volunteered to man the circulation desk while Crystal—our new hire—took her daughter to the dentist.

One body. Three tasks. No clones in sight.

If someone asked me what superpower I wanted at the

moment, I wouldn't have hesitated—*the power to be in multiple places at once.* Or maybe to stop time. Either one would do.

I stopped halfway across the lobby, letting the bean bag fall from my hand with a dramatic *thud.* My chest rose and fell with an exaggerated sigh as I looked up to the ceiling, silently praying for strength, patience, or maybe divine intervention.

"I'm really sorry, Pen," Boone said through the speaker, followed by another pitiful excuse for a cough.

I pinched the bridge of my nose, closing my eyes. "It's okay," I muttered, half to him, half to myself. "I'll figure it out. I always do."

We said our goodbyes—him adding one final, theatrical cough—and I slipped my phone into the side pocket of my floral dress.

I *did* always figure it out. When life threw impossible decisions and chaotic days my way, I somehow managed to walk out of them victorious. Flustered, sure. Maybe a little sweaty. But victorious nonetheless.

Still, this morning? This was pushing it.

My mind was spinning, a dizzying carousel of logistics and timelines. There was no room for panic, so I shoved it down and turned on my inner machine.

No more dragging. I heaved the bean bag into my arms and power-walked toward the story circle like I was competing in the library Olympics.

I dropped it in place with another dull *whump* and glanced at my watch. Twenty minutes until the kids started pouring in.

Plenty of time for a breakdown. But instead, I grabbed the hair tie from around my wrist and whipped my mop of chestnut-brown hair into a bun. A few rebellious strands framed my face, but I let them stay. They softened the exhausted edge in my reflection when I caught it in the window.

With a deep breath and a fresh—if totally fake—smile, I made a beeline for the circulation desk. This was the kind of smile you wear not because you feel it, but because people need to see it.

That's what being dependable looked like—showing up, smiling, and pretending everything was fine even when your brain was screaming otherwise.

I'd never been a girl with a lot of strong opinions—at least not about the everyday stuff. What to eat? Didn't matter. What to do on a date? I was happy just being with someone I cared about.

But ask me whether aliens had been to Earth? Buckle up because I had thoughts.

I was easy, go with the flow, but right now, I felt like I was being pulled so tight I was going to snap.

I reached the circulation desk and pulled up the hold list. First task: check if any of the returned books matched holds, and if so, make the calls. Usually, this was quick... unless I got stuck on the line with one of our chatty locals.

In those cases? I'd pretend someone just walked in, toss in a polite excuse, and hang up before getting roped into a thirty-minute debate over who made the best peach cobbler in town.

I spun around, arms full of returned books freshly collected from the bin, barely managing to keep them balanced in my grasp. Just as I turned back toward the desk, a figure appeared out of nowhere.

"Geez," I gasped, clutching the books tighter as my heart jumped in my chest. I let out a shaky breath. "You scared me."

Mac was popping up out of nowhere way too often lately.

He stood with that infuriatingly perfect grin tugging at the corner of his mouth. His hair was tousled like he'd just rolled out of bed, and those impossibly dreamy eyes locked onto mine like he had all the time in the world.

"I didn't mean to," he said smoothly. "I was going to say something, but you turned around too fast."

I placed the stack of books on the counter a little harder than necessary and shifted my weight, cocking a hip with an exasperated sigh. My expression must have said it all—I didn't have time for his games today.

"Look," I said, my tone sharp. "Unless you're here to help

me set up for the craft show, run the circ desk, or read to a pack of hyper second graders, this is really not the time for you to be bothering me."

My voice came out tight, clipped. Harsher than I'd intended, but I was hanging by a thread. My nerves were shot, my to-do list was growing by the minute, and my brain had officially reached maximum capacity.

Lately, it felt like I lived at the edge of a breakdown. Since... well, since *everything* between Mac and me, I hadn't felt quite right. Like I was a coil wound too tightly, holding in more than I could manage.

"You're in luck," he said, sliding his hands casually into his jeans pockets, every inch of him relaxed while I was anything but. His eyes stayed fixed on mine, stubborn and steady. "I'm here for option three."

I blinked, unsure if I'd heard him right. "What?"

He shifted his weight like this was no big deal. "I'm taking Boone's spot."

I stared at him, eyebrows shooting up so high they probably disappeared into my hairline. My jaw dropped—and then I laughed. It bubbled out before I could stop it, a mix of disbelief and the tiniest bit of unhinged amusement.

Mac Ridley? Reading to second graders?

I tried to picture it. Boone had flair—he used voices, exaggerated expressions, and dramatic pauses that had the kids hanging on every word. He turned story time into a whole performance. Mac... well, Mac had never struck me as the *flair* type.

He had big cowboy boots to fill, and I wasn't entirely sure he knew what he'd signed up for.

Before I could say as much, he held up a hand like he knew exactly what was coming.

"Before you hit me with some smartass comment, let me remind you we've already established I can read. Remember when I checked out those books last week?"

I folded my arms, watching him with wary amusement.

He grinned wider. "And really, how hard could it be?"

MAC SAT IN the wooden-backed chair, the book propped open on his lap like it belonged there, like he belonged there.

I didn't bother asking another question, didn't hit him with a wise-ass comment or a reminder that this wasn't some performance to wing—it didn't matter. He showed up. That was enough. So I pointed him toward the reading corner and let him take over. If Mac Ridley believed he could handle a room full of second graders, who was I to tell a grown man no?

He got himself settled, long legs stretched out, cowboy boots on. His posture relaxed in a way only someone like him could pull off without looking lazy. As the kids arrived—backpacks bouncing, voices chirping—I guided them toward the man in the chair.

"Go sit with Mr. Ridley," I said with a small smile. "He's got a few books about dragons picked just for you."

And then I left him to it. I didn't have the time—or honestly, the energy—to babysit a bartender playing story time hero. There were tables to move, decorations to hang, and a group of silver-haired crafters bossing me around like drill sergeants. I didn't mind; in fact, their take-no-prisoners attitude gave me something to focus on.

But now? Now I needed a breather. Five minutes of peace and a drink of water before I went back into the crafting trenches.

Maybe I wanted to check in on Mac, too.

I sipped from my bottle as I quietly stood in the back of the kids' section, keeping to the edge of the room. What I saw made my breath hitch in a way I didn't expect.

Mac was into it.

His voice shifted from soft and growly to squeaky and shrill as he brought the dragon characters to life. His expressions were animated, eyes wide, brows rising, mouth twisting into exaggerated shapes with every turn of the page. The kids? They were enraptured. Completely locked in on him, giggling and gasping at every twist in the story.

And me?

I was locked in, too.

Something warm cracked through my chest, just enough to make me suck in a slow breath. The wall I'd carefully built between Mac and my heart had a fracture now—a thin, glittering line of something...

We'd never gotten serious enough to talk about the future. Kids, family, that kind of thing—it was all just too far away then. But now, standing there watching him like this, the urge stirred in me. A tiny ache, sweet and slow, crept up my spine. A vision I hadn't asked for slipped into my mind.

Little feet pounding through our house. Laughter echoing off the walls. Mac making those same ridiculous faces, telling bedtime stories to children with his eyes full of love and mischief. *Our* children.

My head tilted to the side, like some cliché out of a rom-com—the moment the female lead realizes, *Oh no, I'm falling for him.* Time didn't quite stop, but it slowed just enough for my heart to thud a little harder.

Then Mac grinned.

Those dimples. That damn smile. All white teeth and charm and something magnetic that pulled me in without asking.

Nope.

I blinked, snapping myself out of it. I spun on my heels so fast I nearly lost my footing.

I needed to get back to work. Whatever that moment was, it was too much. Too dangerous. Too real. Too soon.

Taking one last sip of water, I headed back toward the rec room. I'd taken this little moment to cool down... and somehow ended up feeling anything but.

CHAPTER 18

I was fucking exhausted.

Who knew reading to second graders could feel like putting on a damn five-act show? My throat was raw, my face ached from over-exaggerating every single expression, and I was pretty sure I pulled something in my jaw trying to mimic a baby dragon's squeal.

When Boone pitched the idea of me filling in for him, he didn't exactly undersell it. He laid out all the rules—no monotone reading, no sitting there like a statue, and definitely no skimming the pages. These kids wanted a performance. And I... well, theatrics weren't really in my skill set.

Sure, I was charming. Women liked me. But that brand of wit didn't always translate to kids hopped up on imagination.

Boone wasn't sick. We'd planned this since Thursday morning after everyone ambushed me at the bar. Their ambush meant well. They saw something in Penny and me and wanted to help get that something back.

Hell, I saw it, too.

The more everyone around us believed it, the more I started to trust those gut punches I'd been feeling since I started paying attention. Really paying attention to Penny.

With the kids satisfied and their little minds off in dragon worlds, I figured it was time to find *Miss Hudson* so she could escort them to their next adventure.

Boots hitting soft carpet, I wandered toward the rec room—I'd only found it because Penny had muttered something about it earlier while half-talking to herself. She did that sometimes when she was frazzled, and I'd be lying if I said I didn't find it endearing as hell.

My eyes scanned the room.

Gray hair everywhere. A sea of cardigans and sensible shoes. But then I saw her.

Penny stood tall, arms crossed under her chest, that familiar mop of rich brown hair piled messily on her head. Her dress hugged her in all the right places, cinching at the waist, draping low across her chest. My gaze dipped without permission, catching just the edge of that neckline which was just enough for me to recall a detail no one else in this town would ever know.

The silver bars piercing both of her pale pink nipples.

A memory so vivid it slammed into me, capable of knocking me on my ass if I let it: my tongue tracing the cool metal, the way her back arched, the way she moaned my name like it was a prayer and a curse all at once.

Fuck.

Not the time. *Definitely* not the place.

Clearing my throat, I stepped from carpet to vinyl, the sound of my boots sharper now as I crossed the room toward her. She was laughing with a group of older women—probably organizing some craft show uprising—and when I got close, the entire group quieted like I wandered into some sacred coven I wasn't supposed to know about.

"Ladies," I greeted with a tight nod, eyes already on Penny. "Sorry to break up the gossip circle, but I've gotta steal her. The second graders are calling, and apparently, Miss Hudson is the only one who can answer."

Penny smirked and muttered something that made the women laugh before they scattered like sparrows. None of them gave a damn about me—and that wasn't new. Most older women didn't like me... unless they were looking for a good time.

Maybe it was the tattoos.

Once we were alone, I bumped her shoulder lightly. Penny glanced up at me with those warm brown eyes, and something inside me pulled tight.

"I didn't do half bad," I said, throwing her a grin.

"Hmm, is that so?" she replied, amusement playing on her lips.

"Don't act like you didn't sneak in to watch."

She stopped walking. I took a few more steps before realizing, then turned to face her.

"I was making sure the kids were okay," she said, arching a brow. "You don't know the first thing about children. For all I knew, you passed out cigarettes and taught them how to light them."

I barked a laugh, planting my hands on my hips. "The teacher was literally five feet away. You think I'd corrupt her, too?"

I gave her a once-over—subtle, but not enough to go unnoticed. I watched the way her chest rose and fell, saw the blush coloring her skin, fading just below the neckline of her dress.

When my gaze met hers again, she was throwing daggers.

"Stop looking at me like you're gonna eat me," she rasped, voice lower than before. Not angry. Not warning. No—there was a softness in her tone that said she didn't hate it.

"I can't help it, Penelope," I murmured, stepping just a breath closer. "You have that effect on me."

She made a sound—barely a whimper—and shook her head, smiling despite herself.

Her fingers reached for my arm, warm and light. "Thank you, Mac. It means a lot that you came today. You really saved my ass."

The teasing fell away, and something steadier settled between us.

Being flirty with Penny came naturally. It always had. But if I really wanted her—if I wanted more—then I had to show her the side of me I'd been quietly building. The part I'd uncovered reading romance novels I wouldn't admit to borrowing, or after long conversations with Rhodes that forced me to feel shit instead of pushing it away.

"Anything you need," I said, voice low, steady. "I'll be there. You call, I'm yours."

Penny's eyes searched mine. "They did seem to like you."

I smirked. "What can I say? I have that effect on people."

She giggled—sweet, soft—and took a step back.

"Well, I better wrangle the little monsters and get them to their next event. The ladies are probably wondering where I am, too. If you see anyone at the front desk, can you let them know I'll be right there?"

"Of course. I'll see you around, Penelope."

She waved, fingers fluttering, and turned toward the youth section while I headed for the exit.

As I passed the front desk, an older man stood waiting, so I made good on my promise and let him know Penny would be back soon.

Then the warm Texas air hit me like a wave.

I slipped a cigarette from my back pocket, lit it against the breeze, and leaned back into the sun. That had been one hell of a morning, and I'd do it again in a heartbeat.

As I walked to the truck, I remembered how I'd caught a glimpse of her watching me, that faint, knowing smile tugging at her lips. Yeah. I was getting through to her. Slowly but surely, I was showing her the man I wanted to be—for her.

That was validation I was doing something right, and I'd latch onto that small sliver of hope 'til the end.

Climbing into the driver's seat, I glanced down and spotted a stubborn speck of pink glitter on the floorboard.

I laughed softly to myself.

Glitter had been in here for months. No matter how many times I vacuumed, it never went away, so I stopped trying and left it there.

A reminder. A memory.

I realized just how special Penny truly was, because glittering my truck? Yeah, that was exactly the kind of wild thing *I* would do.

The thing about a woman like her?

You don't just let her walk away.

You fight for her.

You stay.

And you figure out how to love her the way she deserves—no matter what it takes.

CHAPTER 19

DECEMBER. FIVE MONTHS AGO.

Come on in when you get here, the doors open

Penny

Is your sister there?? Do I need to mentally prepare?

Nah, she hasn't been here yet today.

Make sure to lock the door behind you.

I can't have anyone walking in with what I'm about to do to you, Trouble.

Penny

Oh? And what is that?

You'll just have to wait and see...

I tapped the tip of my pen against the desk, eyes glued to the latest expense report. The bar was doing well—thank God.

We weren't raking in anything crazy, but we were solid. Profitable. Enough to keep the lights on and tuck a little something extra into our pockets.

Tourist season had wrapped about a month ago, and Faircloud had seen an impressive surge this year. The town's proximity to the city meant we caught the overflow—people looking for a taste of *real* Texas. Small towns, open skies, cattle, ranches... and cowboys...

The bell above the front door chimed, and I didn't need to look up to know who it was.

A slow smile tugged at my lips before I could stop it. But I kept my gaze locked on the screen, trying to summon my most nonchalant expression.

Penny.

For the last month and a half—ever since that Halloween party—Penny and I had been unable to keep our hands off each other.

We'd agreed not to tell anyone—not our friends, not our coworkers. We knew exactly what would happen if we did: a chorus of *"Finally!"* and *"Told you so."* Besides, keeping it quiet made it easier. If things fizzled out, we could walk away clean. No drama. No explanations.

But deep down? I didn't see it fizzling.

Penny had a way of matching me, stride for stride. She stirred something wild in me, something I usually kept locked away.

I wasn't the type to romanticize sex. I enjoyed it, respected it—whether it was for one night or more. But with Penny? It was different. There was a need—a feral, consuming need—that hit me the moment she walked into a room like, I'd go insane if I didn't touch her.

The soft scent of vanilla and spice drifted through the air, and I finally glanced up.

She was leaning against the doorframe, a smirk on her lips and mischief in her eyes.

"Well, hello there, Penelope."

"Hello," she purred, giving me a slow wave with her fingers.

"I'll be done in just a second," I said, my voice low. "Then you're all mine."

She laughed, that warm, wicked sound that always lit me up from the inside. Pushing off the frame, she sauntered toward the desk and hopped up onto the edge with casual ease, bracing herself with her hands behind her.

"I don't have all day," she warned. "This is my lunch break. The library gives me thirty minutes, but I blocked myself off for an hour. If anyone asks, I was doing professional development from twelve-thirty to one."

I turned my chair to face her fully, leaning back as my gaze swept slowly down her body.

That dress.

It clung to her in all the right places, just tight enough to tempt, just loose enough to imagine slipping it out of my way. The hem brushed below her knees, a whisper of fabric I could already see bunched around her hips. The neckline cut straight across her breasts, simple, elegant—and criminally distracting.

I nodded to myself, tongue sweeping across my bottom lip without thought.

"Hungry?" Penny asked, tilting her head with a feline sort of grace.

I sat up straighter and rolled the chair closer to her, the wheels sliding across the hardwood floor. My hands found the insides of her knees, and with a gentle but insistent pressure, I nudged them apart.

She opened for me, slow and deliberate, the trust in her movement making my pulse thrum louder in my ears.

I moved between her legs, eyes locked on hers as I dragged

my fingers up the soft, heated skin of her inner thigh. Her breath hitched as the hem of her dress rode up under my touch, inch by inch, until that delicate pink lace was exposed.

I murmured, voice low and rough, "I'm fucking starved."

My gaze shifted from between her thighs back up to her face. She was already watching me, eyes dark with heat, lips parted just enough to send a fresh wave of need coursing through me.

A soft smile curved her mouth as she reached out and tangled her fingers in the hair at the back of my neck. With a slow, purposeful tug, she tilted my face up, holding me there so she could look down at me like I belonged to her.

God, maybe I did.

I planted my hands on her knees again, gripping tight. My forearms flexed as I urged her thighs wider, baring more of that mouthwatering view. The fabric of her dress gathered high on her hips, and I swore I could feel the heat radiating off her.

She was absolutely breathtaking.

I leaned in, close enough to feel the warmth of her skin, to inhale—sweet, heady, and mine. My hand slid forward, fingers trailing a line straight down her center.

She was soaked.

Soaked for *me*.

The pads of my fingers barely grazed her through the lace, and a soft, helpless whimper escaped her throat. The sound hit me like a lightning strike.

I didn't just want to touch her.

I wanted to devour her.

Penny's breath hitched again, her fingers tightening in my hair as I brushed my mouth against the inside of her thigh. She trembled under my lips, an involuntary shiver that made my cock ache behind the zipper of my jeans.

I kissed my way higher, taking my time even though every part of me burned to tear that lace aside and feast.

But she deserved the build-up. She deserved to be worshiped.

My hands slid under the backs of her thighs, lifting her just enough so I could hook my fingers into her panties and drag them down. She responded like a good girl, lifting her hips for me. I pulled the lace down her legs, kissing her knees as I did, and then tossed them aside without a second glance.

She was spread wide for me now, dripping with need.

"Jesus, Penny," I murmured, my voice rough with want. "You're perfect."

I leaned in and ran my tongue through her in a slow, deliberate stroke, groaning as her taste hit my tongue. She was everything I craved and everything I shouldn't want this much.

Her thighs tensed around me, and she let out a strangled sound—half moan, half plea. Her hands clutched at my hair again, but not to push me away. No, she was guiding me, pulling me in deeper.

I gave her what she wanted, what *we* wanted.

I circled her clit with my tongue, then sucked it between my lips, earning a gasp and a sharp jerk of her hips. She rolled against my mouth, already needy, already right on the edge. I could feel it in every tremble, every choked sound that spilled from her lips.

"You taste like heaven," I growled, earning me a moan. "I could spend all fucking day right here."

I pushed a finger inside her, slow and deep. In response, her head fell back with a sharp cry. Her walls clenched around me, so tight and wet, that my whole body tensed with restraint. I added another finger, curling just right as I kept my mouth on her clit, licking, sucking, driving her higher.

"Don't stop," she whispered, her voice raw, breathless. "Please, don't stop."

She rocked against my face, one hand still tangled in my hair, the other fisting the edge of the desk behind her. She was close—I could feel it, *taste* it. Every moan grew louder, more urgent, her thighs trembling around my shoulders.

Then she shattered.

Her body arched, legs clamping tight around my head as her orgasm ripped through her. She cried out, loud and unfiltered, and I didn't stop—just slowed enough to ride the waves with her, licking her through every pulse, every aftershock.

When she finally sagged back against the desk, chest rising and falling, flushed and breathless, I looked up at her.

Hair a mess. Lips parted. Eyes glassy with pleasure.

"Lunch break," I said with a grin, wiping my mouth with the back of my hand, "might need to be extended."

She laughed—soft and spent—and reached for me, pulling me up by the front of my shirt.

"Your turn," she whispered, eyes smoldering. "Close the door."

My chest tightened at the look in her eyes. They were dark, hungry, and full of promise. Still catching her breath, flushed and glowing, Penny pulled me in like gravity.

I reached back and nudged the office door shut with a firm kick. The soft click of the latch felt final, like sealing ourselves off from the world.

By the time I turned back around, she was already sliding off the desk.

Her dress fell back down her thighs, only half-covering her, but she didn't bother fixing it. Instead, she stepped into me, her hands already tugging at the hem of my shirt, lifting it over my head with impatient fingers.

"You're wearing too much," she murmured, lips brushing my chest as she spoke.

"Fix it, then," I growled, grabbing her waist and pressing her back against the desk.

She made quick work of my belt, unbuttoning and unzipping me while I groaned against her neck, trailing kisses from her collarbone to that perfect spot just behind her ear. My jeans hit the floor, and my boxers followed, my cock springing free. I was hard, aching, ready for her.

Penny's eyes dropped, and her lips parted slightly as she looked at me. "God, you're—"

I didn't let her finish. I lifted her onto the desk again, pushing her thighs apart as I lined myself up against her slick heat.

She fumbled for the purse sitting next to her on my desk and pulled out a condom. Bringing it to her mouth, she ripped it open with her teeth as her eyes stayed locked on mine.

My heart raced, skin prickling with intense desire. This woman made me weak in so many ways.

"No teasing this time," she whispered, breath hitching.

I met her eyes, my voice low and ragged. "Not a fucking chance."

She pulled the condom from the foil and rolled it down my length. The movements were deliberate as she brushed her fingers along the shaft.

My body surged like a live wire. I had to burry myself deep in her now or I would lose all fucking composure.

"I thought you said no teasing?" I quipped.

"No teasing *me*, I didn't mean I couldn't tease you," she replied with a devilish grin.

"You brat," I growled before I buried my shaft until I was completely lost inside of her.

Her nails dug into my shoulders, her head tipping back as I filled her, stretching her open. I claimed every inch. She was so tight, so wet, the heat of her wrapped around me like a goddamn vice.

"Fuck, Penny," I groaned, pressing my forehead to hers. "You feel—*fuck*—you feel incredible."

She clung to me as her hips rolled, already matching my rhythm. I drove into her harder, gripping her hips, the desk creaking beneath us. Every thrust had her gasping my name, every grind of her hips drew me closer to the edge.

Our mouths found each other hot, messy, hungry. She kissed like she fucked: desperate, no holding back. I bit her bottom lip, and she moaned into my mouth, her legs wrapping tighter around my waist.

"Right there," she gasped. "Don't stop—don't you dare stop."

"Not. Stopping," I growled, each word punctuated with

another deep thrust.

She was so close. I could feel her building again, her body trembling against mine.

I reached between us, my thumb finding her clit, rubbing tight circles while I kept thrusting deep and hard. Her whole body tensed, and then she came again.

Her walls clenched around me, and it took everything I had to hold back for just a few more strokes—until the tension snapped and I came with a low groan, spilling into her as her name tore from my lips.

We stayed like that for a moment, still tangled, bodies shaking, hearts racing.

Then she leaned in, forehead against mine, smiling.

"Think I can call the rest of the day *professional development* too?" she asked, breathless.

I laughed, still inside her, not ready to let go.

"Pen," I said, brushing a kiss to her lips, "at this rate, I'll write you a whole damn curriculum."

CHAPTER 20

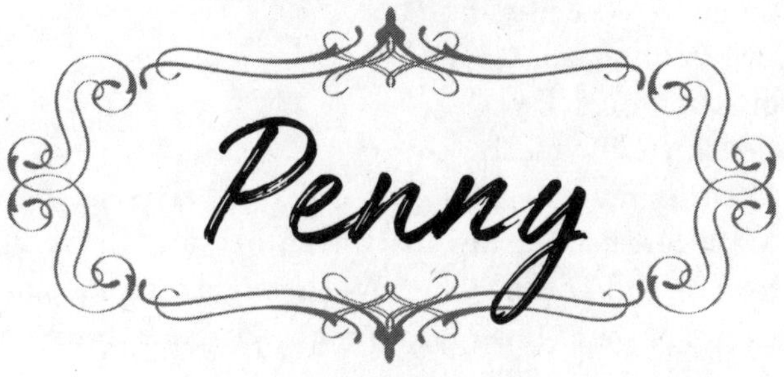

PRESENT DAY.

Aspen

The Tequila Cowboy tonight?

You think I'd say no?

Do you even know who I am?

Theo

I'm gonna skip out. Rhodes and I are hooked on this show and have to watch to see how it ends

Ellie

I'm in! I'll come by after closing the stand! 😘

I bolted straight home after work, practically peeling off my modest dress and diving into my closet. Ellie and Aspen were already waiting at the bar for our long-overdue girls' night out, even though we were missing Theo.

Cowboy boots on? Check.

Low-cut top? Hell yes.

Mini skirt? Obviously.

Clutching my cow-print purse like a statement, I strutted down Main Street from my apartment, one foot in front of the other, toward The Tequila Cowboy. The night air kissed my skin, and the hum of small-town Friday night wrapped around me like a promise.

A low, nagging guilt tugged at the edges of my excitement. None of them knew about Mac. Not the sweet beginnings, not the explosive fallout. Not the long silences or the way he was now, trying to claw his way out of the doghouse. And with everything that happened the last week, I didn't know how well I'd be able to hold it together.

It wasn't like me to not tell my friends what was going on in the world of Penny. I was always the oversharer—the first to admit my intrusive thoughts, the one who never hesitated to say the quiet parts out loud. But this? What happened with Mac? It was still too raw. The pain too real. The words too tangled to unravel just yet.

Maybe once the dust settled, I'd open up. Maybe when or *if* things got repaired, I'd explain it all to them. But not tonight.

Tonight, I'd dance until my feet ached and my head spun. I'd laugh too loud, toss my hair just right, and pretend like nothing in the world was weighing on me.

Music would be my armor.

I smiled, lips curling at the edges as the stars shimmered above me.

I'd give Mac a run for his money. Let him watch from the bar while I flirted just enough to keep him guessing. Just enough to remind him what he stood to lose.

And no one would question a thing—because the best way to keep a secret... is to put on a show.

Deep down, I knew it wasn't a complete show. There was a genuine need for this man that still simmered underneath. The more he came around, the more I'd been easing up.

The bass could be heard from the sidewalk outside. I gripped the cool metal handle, and I flung the bar door open. Instantly, I was swallowed by a wave of chatter, the low hum of conversation mixing with moody neon lights that painted everything in hues of red and violet.

I scanned the room quickly, my eyes landing on two familiar heads of blond hair, backs turned to me. A smile tugged at my lips.

Skipping over, I landed behind them, slinging an arm around each of their shoulders and leaning in between.

"Can I buy you two pretty ladies a drink?" I purred in my best imitation of a guy trying way too hard.

Their heads snapped toward me, recognition lighting their faces just before the laughter came. Ellie grinned and pulled her purse off the stool she'd been saving.

"I'd never say no to that," she said with a wink.

"Thank God!" Aspen added. "We've been dying for a drink. We waited for you, but now I'm thirsty."

"I know, I know," I said, throwing my hands up dramatically. "I'm here now! What's it gonna be?"

"Tequila!" they chorused like it was rehearsed.

I raised a hand in the air, lifting slightly on my stool as I tried to catch Jolie's attention behind the bar.

She was working with *him* tonight.

Mac was on the other side, towel slung casually from the back pocket of his jeans, leaning on his forearms as he talked to a couple of locals. His body language screamed effortless ease.

My gaze trailed over him, soaking in the way his arms flexed with just the slightest movement, how the soft mess of his hair curled at the nape of his neck.

Tendrils of smoke curled around him—of course, he had a cigarette clenched between his lips.

My chest tightened, a heat creeping up my neck. Just looking at him was like flipping a switch I swore I'd turned off.

Jolie finally looked up and spotted me, her full lips curling into a soft smile, and she nodded, which made her curls bounce. She was effortlessly stunning—rich brown skin, striking green eyes, curves that made every girl just a little jealous. With three bottles in one hand, she tapped Mac on the shoulder to get his attention.

He turned toward her, cigarette still hanging by a thread from his lips. Jolie pointed our way, and then his eyes landed on me.

His smirk was subtle—just a twitch on one side of his mouth—but it shot straight to my core. He reached up, tucked a strand of hair behind his ear, and started walking toward us, hips moving with that easy, unbothered saunter that was my personal brand of kryptonite.

I bit my bottom lip before I could stop myself.

There was a full-on war going on inside me—heart screaming *caution*, body ready to toss every damn rule out the window. If he asked me to go upstairs right now, I couldn't promise I'd say no.

Hell, I wasn't sure I'd even try to deny it.

"What can I get ya?"

Mac's voice rumbled low as he leaned forward, both hands braced on the edge of the bar. His gaze moved from Aspen, to Ellie, and finally—hot and heavy—landed on me.

"Three shots of tequila and three sunrises," I said, breaking the stare as I rummaged through my purse, trying to fish out my wallet.

Mac knocked twice on the wood in acknowledgment, then straightened to his full height.

With the easy grace that always got to me, he grabbed three shot glasses and three short tumblers. The bottle gleamed under the bar lights as he tipped it, the pour spout gliding like second nature. His forearms flexed with every movement, tattoos shifting with muscle as he moved glass to glass, pouring with perfect precision—no measuring, no hesitation. Just muscle memory and charm.

He returned with the drinks a moment later, setting them down in front of us like an offering. I found my card, sliding it toward him, but he only shook his head and flashed that cocky grin.

"Don't worry about it," he said, plucking the cigarette from his lips to ash it. "I got it covered."

Then the bastard winked.

"You can't," Aspen cut in, tilting her head with a laugh. "Lizzie's gonna have your head on a stick, parading it up and down Main Street."

Mac sighed dramatically, folding his tattooed arms across his chest, the sleeves of his black T-shirt bunching around his biceps. "Come on. You know me by now."

Aspen threw her hands up in mock surrender. "I'm just saying it's a bold move."

"Is giving away drinks something you do often?" Ellie asked, sipping slowly from her glass, all cool curiosity while enjoying that free drink.

He shrugged, nonchalant. "Lately, yeah."

It was typical Mac—pushing buttons just to see if they'd push back. Especially when it came to his sister. Since Lizzie's return to Faircloud, it had been one battle after another. I hadn't known Mac before she came back, but I'd heard enough to understand they didn't exactly play nice.

He'd confided in me that it still stung, the way their dad left the bar to Lizzie after he passed. All the years Mac had invested into the place—his time, sweat, and frustration—felt like they hadn't meant a damn thing. I'd gently encouraged him to talk to her, to say what he was really feeling, but he always brushed it off with a wave of his hand and that same old line: *"It'll work itself out."*

Sounded familiar...

He used to talk about his dad late at night, in between sips of his whiskey and my wine. The stories weren't good ones. And while I didn't know the man well, the few times I had seen him, he wasn't hard to remember. Scruffy beard, long hair in a thick braid, and never once sober.

I didn't have much ground to stand on when it came to family advice. I'd let go of that fantasy a long time ago. These days, I built my own kind of family. People I chose. People who stayed.

Still, sometimes, I missed my mom. Watching Aspen, Theo, even Ellie with their moms—it hit me in quiet moments, a soft ache I rarely let linger. My own mother hadn't been around in over a year. Usually, she'd breeze through town in the summer just long enough to say she still hadn't given up on me completely.

Mac and I had that in common, too—our family ties were dressed in different clothes, but the fabric felt the same.

"Pen?"

A hand on my shoulder pulled me out of my thoughts. I blinked up at Aspen, who was now standing beside me.

"I said we're going to the dance floor," she said with a teasing smile. "You coming?"

I glanced around. Mac was already back at the far end of the bar, pouring drinks and talking to someone I didn't recognize.

"Ugh, yes," I said, grabbing my shot glass. Without a second thought, I tipped it back, the tequila burning smooth and sharp down my throat.

We moved to the dance floor, music vibrating through the floorboards, laughter curling around us like smoke. But I couldn't help it—I glanced over my shoulder.

And there he was.

Mac was pouring a drink, but his eyes? They were on *me*.

I smiled, flipping my hair over my shoulder with purpose, and threw him a wink before turning away again.

Every step I took after was deliberate. My hips swayed just a little more than usual, teasing and hypnotic—because I knew *he* was watching.

And I wanted him to feel it. Every. Damn. Step.

This was my payback.

I could've thrown a drink in Mac Ridley's face, God knows I'd fantasized about it more than once. Or spat the sharp words I'd whispered to myself during sleepless nights, curled up and aching from the weight of wanting someone who had given up so quickly.

But no.

That wasn't how you got to Mac.

Not really.

If I wanted to rattle him, truly rattle him, I had to hit where it hurt.

And Mac? He was a jealous creature.

And me? That was my weakness. My favorite non-sexual kink was a man who couldn't hide it when he wanted me.

So tonight, I was going to make damn sure he remembered exactly what he pushed away.

The bar was alive with music, bodies moving under low lights, the scent of liquor and sweat and temptation thick in the air. Tequila burned in my chest and the beat in my bones as I moved to the edge of the dance floor.

I didn't even have to look to know where he was. I felt him watching me from behind the bar like he always did. That unreadable expression, that tight jaw, those sharp, whiskey-colored eyes that followed my every move.

Good.

Let him watch.

My hips found the rhythm easily, swaying to the slow, sultry beat. I let my body move with the music, fluid and effortless.

I turned away from him, keeping my back to the bar, letting him see the curve of my spine, the way my skirt hugged me tight. I slid my fingers into my hair, tousling it as I tilted my head back and pretended to laugh at something no one said, just for show.

Just for him.

Someone behind me brushed a little too close, but I didn't step away. I let it happen. Let the illusion bloom. I arched slightly, shifting my weight like I might press into someone. Like I was open to the idea. Like I wasn't thinking of *him*.

But I was.

Every single move I made was for him.

I knew what he looked like when he was about to break—when his knuckles went white on the edge of the bar, when his eyes narrowed and that little muscle in his jaw ticked because someone else had the nerve to look at me the way he did.

So I kept dancing. Just long enough to make him burn. Just long enough to stir that possessive part of him I knew too well.

And when I finally looked over my shoulder, when our eyes locked through the low light and thick air, I smiled.

Slow. Knowing. Dangerous.

Checkmate.

CHAPTER 21

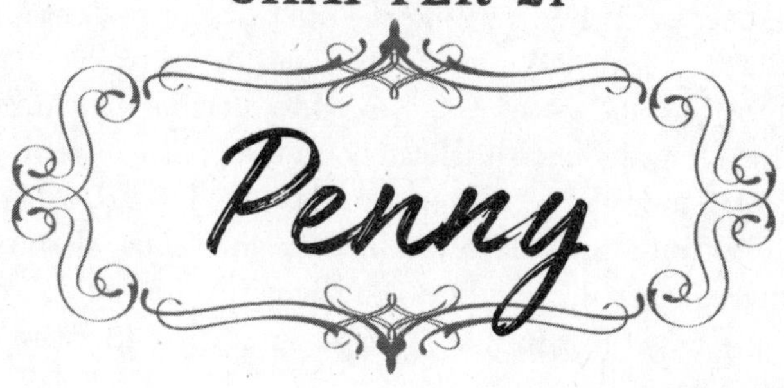

"You're dangerous," Mac said, his voice low and rough as he leaned across the bar. His face hovered just inches from mine, close enough that I could feel the heat radiating off his skin.

I'd slipped away from the dance floor a little while ago, leaving Ellie and Aspen to carry on without me. I could've stayed, continued the torture. Instead, I found myself gravitating back to the bar, back to *him.*

The crowd had thinned, the noise dulled into the background. It was just quiet enough that Mac could give me his full, undivided attention—and God, did I drink it in.

I liked the way he looked at me like I was a mystery he wanted to get lost in. Every time he laughed, every time his hand brushed close to mine, it was like lighting a match to something already smoldering.

Before everything fell apart, before the heartbreak and the silence, we lived in this tension. A charged kind of dance, a will-they-won't-they that stretched on for months.

Me—showing up to the bar dressed to turn heads, but only ever wanting to catch *his* eye.

Him—leaning across the counter, eyes trailing down my body, never making a move.

Not until the Halloween party.

Not until everything changed.

Mac had always been magnetic. With him, it never felt like a choice. We were two ends of a live wire, sparking when we got too close. I'd never felt anything like it—not before, not since.

"But you love it," I murmured, letting my voice dip into something low and sweet. I sat straighter, resting my chin in my palm, my elbow balanced delicately on the polished wood of the bar. For good measure, I fluttered my lashes. Slowly. Deliberately.

He let out a soft, almost pained laugh. "Those damn eyes," he muttered, gaze flicking between them, like he couldn't decide which one to get lost in first. "They could bring any man to his knees, Penelope."

My name from his lips did something to me.

"Oh?" I arched a brow, letting my lips curl. "You? On your knees for *me*?"

The image hit me hard.

Mac, on the floor, eyes dark and reverent, staring up at me like I was the center of his universe. My fingers in his messy hair, the tips of my fingers dragging across his shoulder, circling him while he waited. Watched. *Worshipped.*

A shiver rolled down my spine, goosebumps rising beneath the thin fabric of my top.

My pulse thundered in my ears.

"Come back to me," Mac whispered, his voice like smoke, and when I blinked, I realized he was even closer now. Just a breath away.

Too close.

I closed my eyes, just for a second. A heartbeat. A breath. I needed to break the spell before I drowned in it.

Before I forgot every reason we weren't supposed to do this, not yet.

His words landed with more weight than they should have—soft and simple, but layered.

Come back to me.

Not just to the moment, but to him. To his bed, his hands, his heartbeat next to mine.

I exhaled slowly, dragging myself back from the edge of that thought. My gaze drifted to his face, familiar in every way that still made my chest ache. I studied him like I had so many times before. The subtle dusting of hair above his upper lip was new and maddeningly attractive. The faint freckles dusted across the bridge of his nose, the ones I used to trace with my fingertips, still made my stomach flip.

"Sorry," I said, forcing a casual tone as I leaned back on my stool, putting some distance between us. It was the only way to quiet the fire that had been lit low in my belly. "I got a little distracted. I was picturing you... worshipping me."

He didn't flinch. Instead, Mac stood up straighter, arms folding over his chest, sleeves bunching against his tattooed arms. He tilted his head, eyes narrowing like he was dissecting every word.

"Is that what you need from me?" he asked, voice cool but laced with something darker. "Would that help fix this? Because I saw you out there on that dance floor. You were putting on a show for me, and you know it."

I let out a low chuckle, dragging my tongue across the edge of my canine before smirking. "I just needed to remind you what you're missing. That's all."

"Oh, Pen," Mac said, almost like a breath. "You don't need to remind me. I know exactly what I lost."

That line and *that* look—the one where his eyes darkened, his lips turned up into a smirk—hit me low and hot. It wasn't just what he said. It was the way his eyes dropped, lingering shamelessly over my chest, letting the memory of me soak in like he was starving for it. It was the way he looked at me, like he wanted to devour me and remember what it felt like to be full.

This was the Mac I remembered—the flirty, cocky charmer with a laugh like sin and a smirk that could undo me in seconds. That was the version that pulled me in, but it wasn't the one that made me stay.

That's what I was waiting to see now. How far was he willing to go—not just to flirt, but to fight?

"I'm not letting you off that easy," I said, folding my arms across my chest in a move that matched his own.

His smirk deepened. "Then why don't you stay past closing tonight?" he asked, casually pulling a cigarette from his back pocket. "Keep me company while I clean up."

I paused.

Was this a setup? Some carefully orchestrated plan to reel me in, only to pull me straight back into his bed? Because if that's what he thought... he had another thing coming.

I studied him sideways, arms still folded, guarded. Measuring.

He laughed, warm and unbothered. "Relax, Pen," he said. "I'm not gonna try anything. I just want a little more time with you. That's it. Then I'll walk you home."

The offer sat between us, tempting.

I had the day off tomorrow. Time wasn't the issue. Willpower was.

I wanted to believe that this wasn't a trap. That he just wanted to be near me again.

If I ever wanted things to find their way back to something real, trust was the first step, even if it wasn't yet fully deserved.

"Okay," I said at last, letting my posture soften. Mac's smile bloomed instantly—wide and boyish, like he'd won something big.

I lifted one hand, stopping him with a raised brow. "One condition."

"Hit me," he said, eyes dancing.

"You have to make me that popcorn."

His grin turned into a full-on laugh. "Penelope, I'll make you ten bags of popcorn if it means you'll hang out with me a little longer."

I waited for him to shake on it. If I was going to risk staying late with him, I was damn sure getting a snack out of it.

The popcorn—seasoned with whatever black magic he worked in the kitchen—was addictive. The number of bags I'd inhaled when we were... us? Borderline shameful.

Mac's hand landed in mine, his warm skin heated up every one of my nerves. He squeezed gently before leaning down and bringing the back of my hand to his lips, placing a kiss, his eyes still locked on mine.

The butterflies in my stomach betrayed me, fluttering and swirling as they tickled.

"Mac!" Dudley's voice called across the bar.

He pulled back and took a few.

Mac glanced over his shoulder reluctantly. Dudley waved him over with a gesture that clearly said *I need help now.*

Mac looked back at me, eyes warm. "Go on, have some fun," he said. "Looks like duty calls."

"After my drink," I said, lifting the glass to my lips.

He gave me a knowing smirk before turning to walk away, leaving a trail of cigarette smoke and temptation behind.

But I didn't move from that stool.

I had no intention of dancing.

Not when I could spend the rest of the night watching *him.*

CHAPTER 22

"I'll be okay," I said softly, pulling Aspen into a hug goodbye. She and Ellie were calling it a night—one shot of tequila proving to be one too many.

Boone stood nearby, waiting to play chauffeur. His signature smirk firmly in place as he leaned against the edge of the bar, watching Aspen cling to me like she might never let go. Her arms were locked around me with a grip so tight it nearly cut off my circulation. Ellie, tucked under her brother's arm, was practically asleep on her feet, her eyes fluttering shut.

"Are you sure you want to stay here with *him*?" Aspen asked, her voice low and pointed as she peered around my shoulder to shoot Mac a sharp glare.

Mac stood a few feet away with his arms crossed, eyebrows furrowed.

I laughed, stepping back from her suffocating hug and placing my hands on her arms, grounding her. "Yes," I said, drawing the word out slowly, my head tilting with confusion. "Why wouldn't I?"

Aspen's eyes widened. She swallowed hard, blinking like I'd just caught her in a lie. "No reason," she rushed out, waving her hand dismissively. "Nope. None at all."

Something about the way she said it knotted suspicion low in my stomach, but before I could press, she slipped from my grasp like water through fingers.

"I'll see you later," she said. "Text me when you get home. I probably won't answer, but do it anyway." She giggled, flicking her gaze toward Boone with that smile that only he seemed to inspire.

One more tight hug, and then she was gone with Boone trailing behind, his arm lazily slung around Ellie as they made their way to the exit.

"You better behave!" I called after them, cupping my hands around my mouth to project over the soft hum of music still playing through the speakers.

"No promises!" Boone hollered back, tossing a wink over his shoulder before the door swung shut behind him with a final, echoing *thud.*

The bar was quiet now. The last of our friends had cleared out, leaving only Mac and me, the silence between us thick with possibility.

Mac moved then, rounding the bar with slow, easy steps. He tossed me a sideways glance, cigarette dangling between his fingers, the ember glowing faintly. His smirk curved just slightly as he twisted the lock on the door and turned the deadbolt.

I let out a long breath and made my way back to the barstool, dropping onto it with a soft sigh and resting my head against the cool surface of the bar top. I was exhausted, my body aching for bed, but I wasn't ready to leave.

"If you wanna go home," Mac said, his voice quieter now, stripped of bravado, "I can walk you before I clean up."

I lifted my head and looked at him. His eyes met mine without flinching, like he really meant it. Like he'd walk me all the way back right now if I simply asked. Yet, there was a crackle in the air, one that told me even though he'd do it for me, he wished I wouldn't say yes.

I shook my head.

"I'm okay," I whispered. "I want to stay."

Mac's shoulders dropped ever so slightly, the faintest sign of relief softening his features. He brought the cigarette to his lips, took a slow drag, and exhaled with a satisfied grin.

"Good," he said, voice low, like the idea of me staying meant more than he would admit.

I smirked, leaning back on the barstool, crossing my arms in a lazy sort of challenge. "So... what's step one of closing up shop?"

"Well," Mac said, flicking ash into the tray, "I usually deal with the money first."

"Can I help with something?"

He paused. Then, with a shrug, he gestured with a tilt of his head—*yeah, sure, why not.*

He crooked a finger, beckoning me around the bar, and turned on his heel like he already knew I'd follow. And I did. Like a moth to the flame, or a kid chasing after candy. The pull toward him was almost embarrassing in its intensity.

"I can have you wipe down the bar top," Mac said, glancing over his shoulder as he walked backward down the hallway that led to the supply closet. "That okay?"

I nodded, trailing him into the narrow corridor where the air smelled faintly of lemons and dust. A red bucket sat on the floor beside a water spout. Mac crouched, filling it with warm water, then poured in a splash of cleaner. I leaned against the doorframe and watched him, arms folded across my chest, quietly soaking him in.

He stood to his full height and turned toward me, holding out the bucket. As I reached for it, our hands brushed—barely, just skin grazing skin—but it lit something in me like a match catching fire.

The breath stilled in my lungs.

Instinctively, my head snapped up, and I caught him looking at me. The hallway light was dim, but it was enough. Enough to see the way his expression shifted, just slightly. Enough to make my pulse trip over itself.

For a heartbeat, I saw the Mac I'd fallen for—unfiltered, present, maybe even a little bit regretful.

There was a painful, longing kind of ache. The kind that

whispered *if only.*

If only things hadn't changed.

If only the secret hadn't shattered the illusion.

If only we could go back to the before.

I wanted to fall into him. I wanted to press my face against his chest and inhale that scent of cigarettes, citrus, and the faintest hint of cologne he probably didn't even know lingered on him. I wanted to let him be that safe place again.

Instead, I swallowed hard and turned, walking away before I gave in. I needed air. I needed distance. I needed *control.*

I marched back to the bar, setting the bucket down with more force than necessary. Water sloshed over the rim, droplets scattering across the surface. I stared down at them like they held the answers, but all they did was blur everything more.

What the hell was I doing?

Was this worth it?

Was forcing Mac to earn his way back into my life really going to give me the clarity I was chasing?

Or was I just clinging to a game I didn't know how to end?

I groaned under my breath and plunged my hand into the warm bucket, pulling out a yellow rag. I wrung it out, even though my hands shook, even though my eyes were starting to sting.

I started at the far end of the bar—away from him, away from the ache, away from that damn office in the back.

The same office where we—

"For fuck's sake," I muttered, scrubbing a little harder than necessary.

I wiped in wide circles, stretching my arm as far as it would go to the side of the bar. My fingertips just barely grazed the edge, but it wasn't enough. I rocked up onto my tiptoes, determined to get every inch, my body curving over the wood.

Then I felt it—that heavy, magnetic presence behind me.

A warm chest pressed into my back, solid and familiar, sending a jolt through my spine. My breath hitched as a tattooed hand settled over mine, guiding my movements to the spot I couldn't quite reach.

My heart kicked into overdrive, pounding in my ears so loud it drowned out everything else. The heat of him, the way his body curved to mine—it was too much and not enough all at once.

"You looked like you were struggling," Mac murmured, his voice brushing along the shell of my ear, low and rough and entirely too intimate.

We leaned forward together, over the bar top, his front molded to my back in a way that made every inch of me hum. I swallowed hard, desperate for composure, for air, for space.

"I was," I admitted softly as we straightened. My body still tingled from the contact, the fit of him against me too perfect, like we were puzzle pieces that had once been whole.

I turned then, slowly, until I was facing him head-on. Mac watched me with that boyish expression—dimples showing, eyes like warm whiskey, lips too full for their own good. There was something soft in his gaze, something reverent which disarmed all my armor.

His hand lifted, thumb brushing along my cheek. My skin burned in its wake.

My body turned to lead, rooted in place by the weight of memory, desire, and every unsaid word between us.

But, I ducked beneath his arm, grabbing the bucket with a deep exhale. My pulse was still racing as I retreated to the opposite end of the bar.

Mac hadn't moved. He stayed where I left him, posture slightly slumped, his focus lingering on the door like he was trying to talk himself out of something.

"I think you're forgetting something," I called, glancing over my shoulder at him.

At the sound of my voice, he snapped out of it. His eyes found mine again.

Mac tilted his head, thought for a beat, then lifted a finger in realization.

"Ahhh," he exhaled, grinning. "You don't forget about the

popcorn."

I smiled, shaking my head. "That's one thing I don't mess around with."

"Oh, I know, Penelope." He laughed, warm and nostalgic. "Whenever you were having a rough day, I made sure I was fully stocked."

A laugh slipped from my lips before I could stop it, soft and unguarded. I loved that he remembered.

"That," he added with a smirk, "and a good orgasm always helped."

A wide grin pulled at my lips as I stood. "Two of my favorite things," I said.

Mac left, leaving to make one of my favorite things come true because the second was completely off the table.

I let out a breath I didn't realize I'd been holding and turned back to the bar. My rag moved in slow strokes this time, my thoughts trying and failing to focus solely on the task at hand.

"ALL RIGHT!" I shouted, bouncing on the balls of my feet. "Open wide!"

Mac stood a few feet away, knees bent slightly, mouth wide open. I grinned, holding up a piece of popcorn between my fingers before tossing it in his direction.

The piece arced just a little to the left, and Mac shifted, moving with it like he'd been training for this moment his whole life. It landed square in his mouth.

He stood up straight with a victorious cheer, both hands raised like he'd just won gold.

I squealed, laughing as I jumped up and down. "That was so good! Even though my throw was absolutely awful."

"You're lucky I'm agile," he said, chuckling as he reached into his bowl for another piece. "Okay, Penelope. The trick is to follow it with your eyes. Don't look away. Stay under it."

I gave him a determined nod, planting my feet wide and bracing like I was about to catch a winning touchdown.

"On the count of three," he said, his gaze locked with mine. "One... two... three."

He tossed it, and I tracked it through the air, shuffling a little to the right. I opened my mouth just in time, and the popcorn landed perfectly on my tongue.

I gasped, stunned for half a second, before snapping my eyes to his. "Finally!"

Mac clapped like I'd just nailed the shot of the century. "I knew you had it in you."

I rolled my eyes and tapped my phone where it sat on the table beside me, the lock screen lighting up. Time had flown. Mac and I had cleaned the bar over an hour ago, but somehow we'd fallen into this silly, mindless game just like old times.

"Oh geez," I muttered. "It's late. I should get home. I need my beauty rest."

Mac grinned, leaning his hip against the bar. "Can't imagine you could get any more beautiful."

I smiled, cheeks warming. "Charmer."

"I'll walk you."

Normally, I would've insisted he didn't need to, but this time I didn't, maybe because the idea of walking home alone sounded... heavy. Lonely. And maybe because part of me just wasn't ready to let go of tonight yet.

I reached for my popcorn bowl, but Mac stopped me with a gentle touch to my wrist.

"Leave it," he said, already stepping beside me. "I'll take care of it when I get back."

"You sure?" I asked, my hand hovering.

"Yeah." He gave me a small smile. "Come on, Trouble. Let's get you home."

The nickname hit like a sucker punch.

I froze. My heart dropped to my feet. The air shifted—charged and bittersweet. Mac must've felt it too, because he stilled, like he hadn't meant for it to slip out.

It was a name that once meant so much.

"I'm sorr—"

"Don't," I cut in gently. "Don't worry about it."

Silence stretched between us, but we moved together toward the front door without another word.

Mac locked up behind us, the sound of the deadbolt loud in the quiet night. I couldn't take the weight of it, so I cleared my throat.

"I had fun tonight," I said, trying to sound casual. Like my heart wasn't still thudding from one word—*Trouble*.

He turned toward me, tucking his hands into his pockets. "Me too."

The stars were out, twinkling like a thousand secrets overhead. The air was cool for May, a soft breeze sweeping across the pavement. I wrapped my arms around myself as we walked in sync toward my apartment.

"You can come over whenever you want," Mac said quietly.

I looked up at him, uncertain. That felt like a door creaking open. Was I ready to walk through it?

"Is this your subtle way of trying to get in my pants, Mac Ridley?" I teased, raising a brow and flashing him a flirtatious smile.

He matched it, shaking his head. "No," he said. "Even though I wouldn't exactly be against that... I like spending time with you outside of sex."

I looked away, down at the sidewalk, tucking a loose strand of hair behind my ear. A shiver rolled up my spine, stealing into my bones.

Without a word, Mac slid his arm around my shoulders and pulled me in close. His warmth spread through me, anchoring me to something that felt so achingly familiar.

"I like spending time with you, too," I said, my voice softer than his, like the words might crack if I said them too loud.

Mac's arm tightened around me just a little as we continued

down the quiet sidewalk. "We could always work on your popcorn-catching skills," he teased.

I tilted my head toward him, letting it rest lightly against his shoulder. Just a little. Just enough to feel him there. "It did take me an embarrassing number of tries to catch that last one."

"At least fifteen," he said, all smug.

I groaned. "Okay, okay. We don't have to assign an actual number."

He chuckled, and I felt the sound more than heard it—the low rumble vibrating through his chest and into me. It made me smile.

When we reached my apartment building, I reluctantly stepped away from his warmth. The night air hit me immediately, cool and sharp in comparison. But the chill was short-lived when I saw the look in his eyes—that playful, daring glint that made my pulse skip and my cheeks flare up.

He took a small step forward, closing the space between us, and I knew it. He was going to kiss me.

My heart squeezed, emotions tangling inside me. I wasn't sure if I was ready for that. Not yet.

Mac must've sensed it—something in my eyes or the way I shifted—and he stopped. Leaning back just enough, he gave me space without making it awkward. I felt both disappointment and relief rush through me at once.

"Good night, Penelope," he said, his voice low, warm. His hands tucked back into the front pockets of his jeans like he needed to keep them there to stop himself from reaching for me again.

"Good night," I whispered.

He nodded toward the door. "Go on. I'm not leaving until I see you safely inside."

Rolling my eyes, I tried to hide the smile pulling at my lips. "Yes, Daddy," I quipped, shooting him a teasing glance as I turned on my heel.

Behind me, I swore I heard a low groan, but I didn't stop to gloat. The front door clicked open, and I stepped into the quiet vestibule. The lights of Petal Pusher were dark, the streetlamps casting a soft golden glow over everything inside.

When I reached the top of the stairs, I turned and looked through the glass. Mac was still there, hands in his pockets, watching.

I lifted my hand in a wave, and he returned it with a small smile.

Then, finally, we turned and went our separate ways.

For tonight.

CHAPTER 23

Last night with Penny hadn't left my mind. I walked her home, almost kissed her, and then spent the rest of the night tossing and turning like a man caught between two timelines—the past we shared and the future we might still have.

There'd been something in the air between us, a flicker of what we used to be. That effortless rhythm. The unspoken pull. It gave me hope—dangerous, addictive hope.

But I knew I wasn't out of the doghouse.

There were still things I needed to do, things I wanted to prove. I had plans tucked up my sleeve, and patience tucked somewhere deeper.

When she agreed to stay after closing, I nearly cracked. Every part of me wanted to show her how happy that made me. But I held it in, kept my cool, and played it safe. Still, something had shifted. I felt it in the way she moved around me, in the way her eyes lingered a little longer than before. The spark was back.

God, I wanted to kiss her. So badly.

But I hadn't earned that right, not yet.

A sudden knock on my apartment door jolted me out of my thoughts. I blinked, glanced at the book I'd been trying to read while finishing my lunch. It sat on the table, still open, pages fluttering from the breeze drifting in through the cracked window.

Brushing the crumbs from my fingers against my jeans, I

crossed to the door. No one ever really showed up unannounced, especially not in the middle of the day. Cautiously, I turned the knob and cracked it open.

Boone stood in the narrow hallway, arms crossed, no cowboy hat in sight—just his usual white tee and worn jeans.

"Oh, hey, man." I opened the door wider, stepping aside. "What're you doing here?"

Boone didn't usually make daytime appearances. He spent most of his days out on the ranch, and when he did stop by, it was late during the bar scene.

He gave me a shrug and stepped in. "Thought I'd check in." A sly smile tugged at the corner of his mouth. "Plus, now that I'm the boss, I can do what I want."

I snorted as I shut the door behind him. "Fair enough."

Boone pulled out a chair from the small kitchen table and dropped into it like he owned the place. I followed and flopped into the seat across from him, my legs stretching out under the table.

"So how's it going? The whole taking over the ranch thing?" I asked.

He ran a hand through his hair and exhaled. "Good. I'm liking it. It's a lot, but it feels right."

Boone had officially taken the reins from his dad, giving his parents the freedom to finally enjoy some rest. His mom stepped away from teaching, and they'd been off doing the retirement dream thing—this weekend, it was a road trip in their new RV to some lakeside campground a few states over, right on time for Mother's Day.

A brief ache stirred in my chest, sharp and familiar, but it faded as quickly as it came. It always did.

"I'm glad it's working out," I said, meaning it.

Boone leaned back, lacing his hands behind his head. "Yeah, yeah. But I'm not here to talk about me. I'm here to talk about last night." His smirk deepened. "What happened with Penny?"

I laughed, shaking my head. "Not much."

Boone rolled his eyes like I was giving him nothing, which, in all fairness, I kind of was. "Seriously? She stayed behind. I thought for sure I'd be driving all three of them home, playing chauffeur."

"I don't know," I admitted. "I asked her to stay on a whim, and she said yes."

It wasn't some grand plan. It was instinct. A last-second choice I wasn't sure she'd go for, but she had. Those stolen hours with her, just the two of us, had been everything. Quiet. Easy. Familiar.

"It's gotta make you feel good, yeah?" Boone asked as his head tilted just enough to read me.

A slow smile tugged at the corner of my mouth, and I shrugged, trying not to let too much show. "I guess it did."

"What's next on your list of ways to win her back?" Boone asked.

I let out a heavy breath. I was always looking, searching for some spark of inspiration. And today, finally, it struck.

"I'm planning to make a few drinks at the bar," I said, watching his reaction. "Name them after her. Subtle stuff, things only she'd pick up on. Kind of like a secret code."

Boone arched a brow, curious now.

"I wanna pull ingredients from memories we've made, her favorite liquors, the flavors she'd always gravitate toward. Then give them names only she'd understand. It's not some big public declaration, but it's personal. It shows her I remember."

It felt like the perfect in-between with just enough to say, *I still see you,* without screaming it to the whole damn town.

If I thought she'd be okay with it, I'd climb on top of the bar and shout to the world how gone I am for her. But that might be... premature.

Boone gave a small nod, pressing his lips into a line like he approved, though something in his eyes flickered with caution.

Still, the question buzzed in my brain like static. Would this be enough? Would she see what I was trying to do?

If I let doubt keep steering the ship, I'd never move forward. I had to trust my gut and keep going.

"Penny's not the kind to hold a grudge," Boone said after a beat. "If you put in the effort, I can't see her not giving you another shot."

"Oh, I am putting in the effort," I said with a huff of a laugh, and he smiled.

"I know you are." There was a pause before he added, "Still can't believe you were married."

I rolled my eyes and leaned back, hands behind my head, spine cracking with the stretch. "This whole marriage thing? Needs to be behind me already. I'm so fucking tired of it being the center of every goddamn conversation."

"Can you blame us?" Boone leaned in, resting his elbows on the table. "I find out my best friend's been secretly married? And the woman you're trying to get back with finds out, too?"

Groaning, I grabbed the white cigarette box, fished one out, and lit it. Inhaling deep.

"I get why it's being talked about. Doesn't mean it's not frustrating as hell."

Another thought had been gnawing at me for days—one I hadn't said out loud yet.

"It's not just Penny," I said slowly. "I think that drunk mistake is why my sister's being an ass about the bar, too."

Saying it out loud released something. I'd been carrying that weight since the night her and I fought. Which also happened to be the last night we'd really spoken, actually. Since then, I'd done what I do best—avoid.

Boone's brows shot up. He turned his head like he was trying to make sure he heard me right. "Go on."

"We were arguing, again, and she said she *couldn't* give me the bar. Not that she didn't want to, but like something was stopping her."

I'd been running it through my head since. But the only thing that made sense? She knew. She knew about the marriage. After Dad died and the bar became hers, she somehow knew and kept it in her name.

"No shit..." Boone murmured. "But how would she even find that out?"

I took a hard drag from the cigarette and tapped ash into the tray. "No fucking clue."

"It never made sense why she stayed in Faircloud," he added, voice low. "She always looks miserable behind that bar."

A quiet laugh slipped from my throat. "That's her default expression."

"Have you talked to her about it?"

"Nah." I exhaled a cloud of smoke. "A civil conversation? That's never gonna happen. She's impossible."

Boone hummed like he wasn't convinced.

I squinted at him. "What?"

He threw his hands up like I was accusing him of something. "Nothing, man."

Bullshit. I could see the gears turning behind his eyes.

"Spill it."

"I just think... maybe you both make having a civil conversation impossible."

My head tilted. I didn't love the way that landed.

"I'm just saying," Boone continued, cautious, "every time I've seen you two talk, it's like watching two firecrackers light each other up."

I didn't argue. I couldn't because deep down, I knew he was right. No matter what the topic was—bar business or personal—we always ended up at each other's throats.

I crushed the cigarette in the tray and didn't say a word.

"Did you know," Boone said, changing gears fast—thank God, "Logan's going to Petal Pusher tomorrow to help Penny?"

I straightened, leaning on my elbows. "Logan?"

That was my job. *My* thing.

When Penny needed help with Sandy, I was the one she called—whether it was cleaning vases or making deliveries during peak seasons.

A flicker of jealousy burned through my chest. She'd asked

someone else.

"And you're telling me this... why?"

Boone glanced down at his phone, thumbs idle. "Just do what you want with that information."

"Wait—"

"I should get going," he said, rubbing his palms on his jeans. "Can't leave everyone alone too long, even with Rhodes holding down the fort."

Logan's going to help Penny...

I sat with that thought a second longer before something clicked. I looked up at Boone, a slow smirk spreading across my face.

He was already watching me, grinning like he knew I'd finally caught up.

"Thanks for stopping by," I said, standing to see him out. "Even if you did interrupt my lunch."

"And the romance book you've got sitting on the table?" he teased, nodding toward the pink paperback, cartoon couple mid-kiss on the cover.

"They're not half bad," I said, shrugging. "You should try one sometime. The stuff you learn..." I gave a low whistle. "It's a goldmine."

"My girlfriend writes them," Boone said with a cocky grin. "Trust me. I know exactly what's in those pages."

I laughed. "Fair point."

We said our goodbyes, and once the door clicked shut behind him, I reached for my phone, opened my messages, and pulled up Logan's number.

Time to send a text and make myself busy this weekend.

CHAPTER 24

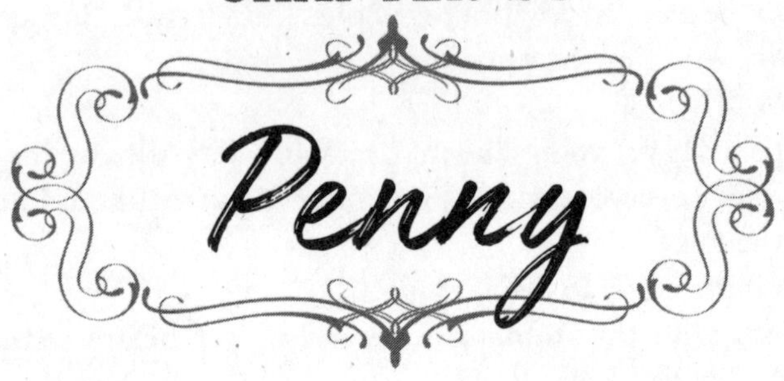

"Penelope!"

My name floated up the staircase, sharp and familiar, just as everything in my arms began to slip. I huffed, trying to hold on to the wobbling stack of books and the trio of bags tangled around my shoulders. My lunchbox dug into my side, my purse strap slid down my arm, and the oversized work tote—my trusty, overstuffed companion—threatened to drag me off balance.

The books were heavier than I expected, so right now, I regret taking them off the library's hands. We'd gotten new editions of a few well-loved titles, and the worn-out copies weren't being checked out anymore. Normally, they'd be carted off to the recycling center, their pages pulped and forgotten. But that never sat right with me.

There was a Little Free Library on the edge of Faircloud Community Park. It wasn't much, just a weathered wooden box with a glass front and a squeaky hinge. I figured it was the perfect spot for someone else to discover these old stories and give them a second life.

Still, by the time I made it to my front door, I was pretty sure my shoulder was going to give out.

Grunting, I twisted my head as far as I could. Down at the bottom of the stairs stood Sandy, hands on her hips, expression unreadable but determined.

Of course.

I hadn't stopped into the shop after work, mostly because I was on the verge of toppling over, but clearly, she had something on her mind.

"Give me one second, Sandy!" I called, fumbling with the doorknob. "Let me just put this stuff down before I collapse!"

With a final burst of effort—and maybe a prayer—I managed to push open the door and stumble inside. The books nearly tumbled from my arms, but I caught them just in time and deposited them onto the dining table with a loud *thunk*, followed by a sigh as I let my bags slide to the floor in a heap.

Light footsteps pattered up the stairs, and within seconds, Sandy appeared in my doorway. Her signature puff of silver hair bounced with each step. She wore her floral apron tied in a perfect bow at her waist, a pair of faded blue capri pants, and her well-worn white sneakers that somehow always looked spotless.

Hands on my hips, I turned to her, still catching my breath.

"To what do I owe the pleasure?" I asked, huffing out a breath with exaggerated flair.

"Well, don't you look lovely today!" she sang, her eyes twinkling as they swept over me.

I glanced down at my dress—Aztec-inspired patterns in bold reds and sun-kissed oranges, with cap sleeves that fluttered as I moved. It was one of my favorite pieces, especially paired with my brown mule heels. I smoothed a hand down the fabric instinctively, a shy smile tugging at my lips.

"Thank you," I murmured, giving a little twirl that sent the hem swirling around my knees. "But I'm guessing you didn't chase me up here just to compliment my outfit."

Sandy laughed, stepping deeper into the apartment. "That Logan boy is still coming tomorrow to help with deliveries, right?"

I nodded, pulling out a dining chair and sinking into it gratefully. "As far as I know."

Sandy pursed her lips thoughtfully. "Well, the crochet club ladies just sent over a last-minute request. They want to hand out free flowers to moms at the park tomorrow." She paused. "Sweet, right?"

"It's a lovely idea," I said, smiling warmly.

"It is," she agreed, but there was hesitation in her voice. "Thing is... between the regular orders, the walk-ins, and now this one, I don't think you and I can handle it all ourselves."

She glanced down at her sneakers, then up at me through her lashes, sheepish and hopeful.

"You need another set of hands?" I offered gently.

Her whole face lit up. "Oh, sweetheart, that would be wonderful. I didn't want to burden you, but I was starting to feel a little overwhelmed."

"You could've just asked," I chuckled softly.

She waved a hand as if to say *where's the fun in that?* And gave a dramatic shrug.

Fortunately for her, I already had someone in mind. Someone who loved flowers almost as much as I did—and who just so happened to be free this weekend.

As I opened my mouth to tell her, Sandy tilted her head slightly, eyes drifting past me. She squinted toward the dining table, then nodded approvingly.

"Well, aren't those just the loveliest things?" she cooed, a mischievous sparkle in her eyes.

I turned to see what she was talking about—and froze.

The ceramic pitcher on the table now held a bouquet of fresh, vibrant roses. When I'd left for work that morning, the arrangement had looked tired, its leaves drooping, the petals starting to brown. But now? They looked brand new. Dew-kissed. Like they'd just been plucked from a garden an hour ago.

I spun back toward the doorway—but Sandy was already gone and the door was now shut.

Her retreating footsteps echoed softly down the stairs, followed moments later by the cheerful chime of the shop door below.

"This woman," I muttered with a shake of my head, making

my way toward the pitcher.

There was only one person who knew how to get into my apartment. One person who knew I rarely remembered to lock the door.

As I walked back to the table, I paused in front of the pitcher. The roses were flawless. Fresh, soft petals curled open just enough, their red edges deepening toward the center. My lips curved into a smile, and something light and fluttery stirred in my chest.

A dozen roses. Always the same amount. Always the same flower.

They were from Mac. I didn't even have to question it.

Bending down, I rifled through my purse until I found my phone. His number wasn't saved, but I knew exactly which one was his. Without a second thought, I hit the FaceTime icon.

It only rang twice before the familiar *ding* echoed, and his face filled the screen.

"What's up, Penelope?" he asked casually. His phone was propped up somewhere on the bar. Behind him, the soft glow of the bottle wall cast light over the space.

"You know," I said, making my way toward the kitchen, "it's technically a crime to break into someone's apartment, even if you're just leaving flowers."

"Is it really breaking in," he replied, smirking, "if she leaves the door unlocked?"

I laughed, the sound bubbling up before I could stop it. "Touché. You got me there."

I set the phone on the counter, still grinning, and opened the fridge. A cold wave rushed out and stopped me in my tracks.

It was full.

Apples. Iced tea. Pre-made salad kits. Even a few of my favorite chocolate bars, tucked neatly on the top shelf. None of this had been here this morning.

I turned slowly, narrowing my eyes at the screen.

Mac was leaning against the bar now, his arms braced on either side of the camera. Relaxed. Watching me.

"Did you do this too?" I asked, cocking my hip and pointing toward the fridge with a raised brow.

"Maybe," he said, that maddening grin tugging at one side of his mouth. "Does it make it more of a crime if I opened your fridge after breaking in?"

I rolled my eyes but couldn't fight the warmth spreading through me. Turning back to the fridge, something else caught my attention—a white to-go container, carefully placed on the center shelf.

The logo gave it away instantly.

It was the only Italian place in town. Also, coincidentally, the only decent pizza, too.

"Mac..." I said slowly, pulling the container out and setting it on the counter. I angled the camera so he could see more than just my face now.

"If this is what I think it is..."

"There's only one way to find out," he said, his voice full of that low, teasing drawl.

I popped the lid.

Chicken Parmesan.

Golden-fried chicken, blanketed in marinara, smothered in cheese, and laid gently over a bed of angel hair pasta—my favorite. My cheeks lifted into a grin as a quiet *oh my God* slipped from my lips.

"How'd I do?" he asked, clearly pleased with himself as he watched me practically drool over the container in front of me.

"You did *very* well," I said, already reaching for a plate.

As I dished the food and slid it into the microwave, he leaned in a little closer to the screen.

"So I guess you can't really be mad about the whole breaking-and-entering thing, right?"

I shook my head, glancing over my shoulder with a smirk. "If this is what you do when you break in, I'll leave the door wide open."

"At least I didn't throw glitter all over your stuff," he said with a wink.

I narrowed my eyes. "I never confirmed or denied that it was me who did that."

"Innocent until proven guilty," he replied with a slow nod. Mac tilted his head just slightly, that dimple showing up again. "Still... I do wonder who else would draw a giant *P* on my dashboard."

"Could've been Patrick," I said with a shrug, biting back a grin.

Mac arched a brow. "I don't know a Patrick."

"Maybe it was an upside-down lowercase *d*," I teased. "Ooo, *Dudley!*" I pointed at the camera, eyes wide with mock realization.

He rolled his eyes and shook his head. Reaching into his back pocket, he pulled out a cigarette and lit it with one fluid flick of his lighter. The flame illuminated his features for a heartbeat—strong jaw, focused eyes—before he exhaled a slow stream of smoke into the air. He leaned forward to grab an ashtray, placing it beside him with practiced ease.

"Something tells me no," he said, voice low and amused. "But it was still funny. Even if the guilty party refuses to come forward."

To Mac's credit, he'd taken it like a champ. Not that I would've cared if it pissed him off.

He started texting after that. Showing up more. Then there was *that* night at The Tequila Cowboy—when he pulled me over the bar like he couldn't wait another second to get me alone to start the conversation.

I blinked, pulling myself out of the memory fog and looked up at the screen. "Thank you," I said softly.

Mac nodded, taking another drag of his cigarette. "No problem, Pen. Wasn't a big deal."

The microwave dinged, pulling me from the moment. I walked over, retrieved my food, and grabbed my phone before settling into my usual spot at the table. I propped Mac up against the napkin holder, and with an eager sigh, twirled a forkful of pasta and took a bite.

A satisfied groan escaped me. "This is so good," I mumbled through a mouthful, covering my mouth with my hand. "They *never* mess this up."

Mac chuckled, watching me like it was the best show in town. "Glad I get to see you enjoy it."

I grinned and held a loaded fork toward the screen. "Want a bite?"

"You tease," he muttered, lips twitching with amusement.

I wiggled the fork like bait. "You know you want it."

Before he could respond, his attention flicked away from the screen. I could hear new voices and music growing louder in the background.

"Josie!" Mac called out, his voice carrying above the hum of chatter. "Can you take care of Mr. Skully, please?"

He grabbed the phone again and brought it close, lowering his voice to talk to his other bartender. "I'm on the phone. I'll be out in a bit."

I couldn't hear her reply, but I could tell the bar was picking up. The familiar buzz of people, clinking glasses, and soft country music filled the space between us.

"You can go if you need to," I said, swirling the pasta around my plate. "I just wanted to say thank you."

"No way." His voice was firm. "I've got your attention. I don't wanna lose it."

"My attention means more than the tips you're missing out on?" I teased. "You must really be sorry."

Mac moved down a dim hallway, the grainy lighting blurring out his face. He pushed open a door and stepped outside, taking a seat on the back steps. Crickets chirped in the background, the lit cigarette dangled from his lip.

"Tips don't mean shit if I can't spend them on you."

I swallowed hard, trying to play it cool, but my heart stuttered. That simple confession short-circuited something inside me.

I didn't know how he did it. He could tear down every defense I had with one quiet truth. The standard I was trying to set was being challenged, pushed until I gave in.

Mac was doing it on purpose, but whether he knew it or not, his sweet confessions and acts of service were taking my walls down faster than I'd imagined.

It wasn't just about sex. We hadn't even been together like that in almost two months. Still, he had this undeniable effect on me like he'd unlocked something buried—something soft and vulnerable and aching to be seen.

Mac didn't just get under my skin; he was seared into my mind.

"Any plans for the night?" Mac asked, his voice easy, casual.

I shook my head, twirling my fork as I took another bite. "Nah. Might do some crocheting later."

He leaned back slightly, lifting the cigarette to his lips before exhaling a soft cloud of smoke into the night air. "What about this weekend?"

I swallowed and reached for my water bottle. "Helping Sandy tomorrow. Mother's Day prep, you know how it is. She came up here earlier, dropping not-so-subtle hints that she's gonna need extra hands besides me, so... I'll be tied up all day."

Mac nodded, thoughtful. "Who're you thinking to ask?"

The question sat in the space between us for a beat. Was he hoping I'd say him?

"Logan's coming over to help with deliveries," I said, trying to read his expression, "and I was thinking Ellie might be my second."

Ellie's parents were away for the weekend, so I was hoping she'd be free. Boone was off with Aspen, which ruled both of them out.

And honestly? I liked Ellie. We didn't hang out alone often, but when we did, it was always a good time. She was spunky, a little sassy, and had the biggest heart. The kind of girl who'd give the shirt off her back and make you laugh while doing it. Plus, she had a thing for flowers—she knew her way around a bouquet better than most.

"Sounds like the dream team," Mac said, a small smile tugging at the corner of his mouth.

"That reminds me—" I dabbed my lips with a napkin and pushed back my chair. "I should call her before it gets too late."

Mac ground his cigarette into the pavement with the toe of his boot. "Right, you probably should."

I hesitated, then looked at him—really looked. His hair was a little messy, his eyes soft but searching.

"Thank you again, Mac," I said, my voice quieter, more tender than before.

He didn't say anything right away. Just gave me a slow, thoughtful smile like he was savoring whatever this moment was.

"You're welcome, Penny."

He said my name—low, gentle, like a promise that would stick with me long after I ended the call. I waved at him, and he waved back as his eyes lingered on the screen.

I let out a heavy sigh and dropped my head back against the chair.

What a mess.

A mess of emotions. A mess of wanting to get in my car and drive to him right now. Of craving more time, more of *him*. But I knew myself. I knew the second I let him off the hook, the second I made this too easy, it would chip away at what I was trying to prove.

He needed to come to *me*. He needed to show me that I was worth the effort after he'd shown me the opposite.

Because no matter how badly I wanted to roll over like some damn golden retriever begging for affection...

Mac Ridley still had some groveling to do.

CHAPTER 25

Boone said you were helping out at Petal Pusher tomorrow???

Logan

yeah man why what's up?

Mind if I join you?

Logan

sure thing, that would be great. I'll swing by and grab you in the morning.

I tugged on my cowboy boots, the worn leather fitting like a glove, and double-checked that my wallet and phone were tucked securely in my pockets. With a quick glance around my apartment, I shut the door and jogged down the steps into the main part of the bar.

The place was quiet, just the soft hum of the coolers and the faint scent of spilled beer clinging to the air. I swung behind the bar and grabbed my pack of cigarettes, stuffing them into my back pocket.

Logan was due any minute. We were heading down to Petal Pusher. The best part was that Penny didn't know I was tagging along to help. Not that I expected a big welcome. Hell, I didn't know if she would be angry or pissed off, but only time would tell. Still, it felt good, doing something for her. Something she didn't see coming.

"Where the hell do you think you're going?" a voice snapped from behind me.

My sister stepped out from the back office, all tight lips and crossed arms, a permanent scowl etched across her face. Her sharp bob swayed with the motion, eyes raking over me like she was trying to read something that wasn't even there.

"Out," I said flatly. No warmth. No charm. Hoping she would take the hint and leave me alone.

She propped a hand on her hip, clearly settling in for a fight. "You're supposed to work the bar in a few hours. You will be back in time... right?"

I rounded the bar until I stood face-to-face with her, arms folded, my patience already wearing thin. I gave her the same once-over she gave me—cold, assessing. Then took a slow breath to keep my mouth in check.

"Have I ever missed a shift?" I asked, my tone sharp but controlled.

"Who knows what stupid shit you'll pull," she shot back.

I barked out a dry laugh as I shook my head. "That's rich to assume my character, especially coming from someone who didn't show her face in over a decade."

I turned on my heel and stalked toward the door, not giving her a chance to respond. "Not that I owe you a damn explanation, but Josie's covering my shift tonight. Don't wait up... *Mommy dearest.*"

The silence behind me cracked like a whip, no room for a final jab. Pushing through the door, I stepped onto the sidewalk, letting the cool morning air slap some sense back into me.

Logan wasn't there yet, but I didn't care. I'd rather wait outside in the street than stand another second in that room with her.

One of these days, I'd have to actually talk to Lizzie. But now that I had even the slightest inkling she might know about the marriage—that she was here because of it—it lit a fuse under my already simmering frustration.

Why wouldn't she just say something?

The resentment I felt wasn't just about the bar.

It went deeper.

She'd left me behind. Took off with our mother while I stayed. While I *struggled,* and I was supposed to just welcome her back like it was no big deal?

I was jealous. There, I said it even if it wasn't out loud.

Lizzie got a life. A different one. One where she didn't have to scrape and fight and grind her way through every damn day. And maybe I ended up building something I was proud of, something I wouldn't trade, but that didn't mean the resentment didn't burn just beneath the surface.

That, despite no help from her or our mother, I'd made a life for myself that didn't follow in our dad's shitty footsteps either.

She should be lucky I wasn't some worthless drunk making my problems everyone else's.

I pulled the carton of cigarettes from my back pocket and tapped it rhythmically against my palm, the soft thump grounding me more than I cared to admit. Flipping the lid open, I slid a cigarette between my lips and patted down my pockets, searching for my lighter.

Shit.

I must've left it behind the bar when Lizzie came storming out. Groaning under my breath, I tilted my head back, let the sunlight warm my face for a second, and pulled the unlit cigarette from my mouth, returning it to the pack.

So much for that.

I leaned against the rough brick wall, the heat from it soaking through the back of my shirt. Crossing one ankle over the other, I watched as locals milled about across the street, the breeze tugging softly.

It was a perfect day, sun-drenched with just enough wind to keep the heat from settling in. Even with the weather working overtime, my mind lingered on Lizzie. A part of me half-expected her to barrel out the front door and finish what she started. But the minutes passed and all I got was the sound of slow-moving traffic and the occasional chirp of a bird overhead.

I stayed where I was—smokeless and stubborn—refusing to go back inside.

Thank God, Logan pulled up a few minutes later. My emotions practically radiating off me, I climbed into the passenger seat, the familiar creak of his old truck welcoming me like an old friend.

"Here, man," Logan said, reaching for the console and popping out the lighter. His truck was so damn old it still had the original cigarette lighter. I took it with a small grin, fingers curling around the warm metal.

"What gave it away?" I muttered, lifting an eyebrow.

Logan shrugged with a smirk. "The fact that you weren't smoking when I pulled up. Plus, you had that look like you were ready to punch a stop sign or something."

I chuckled low in my chest and shook my head. "Sounds about right."

I pressed the lighter to the tip of my cigarette and inhaled deeply, letting the fire catch. One, two, three puffs—then the soft red glow was alive. The first drag felt like a necessary evil, familiar and grounding.

"I'm that predictable?" I asked, exhaling slowly out the open window.

"When it comes to you and nicotine?" Logan laughed. "You might as well be a walking Marlboro ad."

I've been smoking since I was fifteen, even back then, the world felt heavier than it should've, and a cigarette felt like the only thing that made sense. It wasn't just a habit anymore. It was part of me.

Maybe one day I'd quit, but I didn't see that happening anytime soon.

Logan shifted into drive and eased away from the curb. "Your text didn't give much away," he said, eyes flicking toward the road.

"You haven't heard?" I asked, resting my elbow on the edge of the window, smoke curling from my fingers into the breeze.

"Oh, I've heard," he replied with a pointed glance.

"Let me guess... Aspen?"

Logan snorted. "Rhodes who heard it from Theo."

"Of course," I muttered, rolling my eyes.

"So, you're going to help Penny. But why not just... show up on your own?"

I stared at the street ahead, lips twitching into a half-smile. "She doesn't know I'm coming."

Logan looked at me sideways. "And now I'm being roped into one of your grand schemes."

"I guess you could say that," I said with a shrug. "It's a soft entrance."

He shook his head with a small laugh, but didn't press.

When we pulled up in front of Petal Pusher, Logan shifted into park and killed the engine.

I took one last drag from my cigarette before snuffing it out in the truck's ashtray, the final ember flaring before it died, then I exited the vehicle.

"If she's pissed," Logan said, rounding the front of the truck to meet me. "I'm pinning this all on you."

He tapped his fingers against my chest and turned toward the shop door with a grin, but I caught the quick flicker of nerves in his eyes.

"Fair enough," I murmured, my gaze already drifting to the soft glow of the shop window.

THE COOL AIR of the flower shop hit my skin the moment Logan and I stepped through the door.

Inside, the space was already buzzing with early-morning customers, all of them searching for the perfect last-minute bouquet for a mom or a special woman in their life. I glanced at my phone. Eight o'clock sharp. The day was only just beginning, but Petal Pusher was alive with color, scent, and soft conversation.

Behind the counter stood Ellie, ringing up purchases with her usual bright smile. The resemblance to her mother, Mrs. Cassidy, was borderline eerie—same sharp cheekbones, same infectious energy. Her blond hair contrasted the rich brown she used to wear, softening her features in a way that made her seem more kiddish than she already was.

I'd always seen Ellie as a little sister, just like I'd seen Logan as a little brother. Both were a few years younger than the rest of us.

She looked up as Logan and I neared, her face lighting up with recognition. With a quick wave, she acknowledged us before returning her full attention to the elderly Mrs. Winchester at the register, handling her with the kindness and patience Ellie had always been known for.

Logan gave her a quick wave back, his long stride taking him ahead of me.

To my left, a kid stood still in front of one of the tall coolers, anxiety seeping from his pores. He couldn't have been older than seventeen, and the way he tapped his chin, surveyed the flowers while rubbing his hands over his face told me this wasn't just about picking something nice for his mom. This was something else.

A girlfriend, maybe?

I watched as he reached out for a bouquet of soft pink flowers, hesitated, then drew his hand back like he might make the wrong move and ruin it all.

I stepped up beside him, keeping my voice low. "Hey, man. You can never go wrong with red roses."

He looked over at me, startled at first, then grateful as I grabbed a bouquet of classic red roses—the same ones I always bought for Penny—and offered them to him.

"Really?" he asked, hope creeping into his voice as he took the flowers from my hand.

I nodded. "Really. Let me guess, these for your girlfriend or her mom?"

His mouth twitched into a shy smile. "Both."

I grinned and reached for a fresh bouquet of tulips. "Roses for the girlfriend. Tulips for her mom. Can't miss."

He took both bouquets carefully, like he'd just been handed a roadmap to survival, and tucked them under one arm. Then, surprisingly, he held out his hand.

"Thanks for your help."

I shook his hand, impressed by the simple gesture and the genuine look in his eyes. There was something sweet about a kid trying so hard to get it right.

Hell, I was a grown ass man *still* trying to get it right.

Without another word, he spun on his heels and jogged off toward the counter, hope restored and flowers in hand.

I shook my head with a quiet smile and made my way toward the counter where Logan now stood shoulder to shoulder with Ellie. The two of them were chatting easily with a customer, completely in sync. That was my cue to slip away and see if I could be more useful in the back.

My boots echoed softly against the hardwood floor as I rounded the counter and pushed through the black swinging doors into the prep area.

The air back here was thick with the scent of fresh-cut flowers—roses, eucalyptus, and something sweet I couldn't place. Penny and Sandy stood at a stainless-steel table, hands busy snipping stems and arranging blooms. Buckets of flowers lined the floor, waiting their turn to be part of someone's special bouquet.

Penny's back was to me, her shoulder blades moving as she worked quickly, efficiently.

"Thank goodness," Sandy said as she glanced up, flashing me a sly smile and a wink. "Reinforcements have arrived."

"Ugh," Penny groaned, letting her arms drop to her sides in exaggerated relief. She tilted her head back and stared at the ceiling. "Logan, I need you to—"

She turned and froze.

For a beat, her expression flickered from expectation to surprise. Her eyes widened, just slightly, and her lips parted like she might speak but forgot what she was going to say.

"Not Logan," I said smoothly, trying not to grin too hard. "The better-looking, taller, and obviously funnier one. Reporting for duty."

Penny cocked her head, giving me the kind of once-over that warmed places only she could. Then she rolled her eyes and turned back to her flowers.

"Funnier?" she said with a smirk. "That's a stretch."

"Oh, come on," I replied, walking toward them. "I'm hilarious."

She raised a brow. "Then tell me a joke."

Just like that, my mind went blank. Completely blank. All I could think of were the worst knock-knock jokes imaginable and none of them would help my case.

"See? Not funny," she said, grinning in triumph.

"Definitely good-looking, though," Sandy added with a mischievous grin, not missing a beat.

Penny and I both turned to her. Penny was startled, while I was thankful. Sandy just giggled like she'd dropped a bomb and walked away unscathed.

"As much as I'd enjoy a battle of wits, we're on a schedule," Penny said, stepping close and giving me a playful shove to redirect me. Her hand landed lightly against my chest, and I didn't miss the way her fingers lingered for a second longer than necessary.

I turned, and she pressed her palm to my back, nudging me

forward.

"I can walk, you know," I teased. "Or is this just an excuse to touch me?"

She scoffed under her breath but didn't deny it.

Reaching around me, Penny pushed open the back door, and the sunlight spilled in like a warm welcome. The golden rays kissed my skin, chasing away the cooler air from inside the shop.

She bent to secure the doorstop, holding it open as we stepped outside. The delivery van sat just beyond the threshold, waiting.

And for a moment, I couldn't decide what was more distracting—the heat of the sun, or the woman beside me. It was a no-brainer because Penny always pulled my attention.

"I'm going to need you to start loading those flowers," Penny said, pointing to two cardboard boxes just inside the hallway. "The top box needs to be dropped at the community hall. The one on the bottom goes to the crochet club." She turned to a nearby stack of white florist boxes, each big enough to hold a single bouquet. "These are all deliveries. You and Logan need to start with the boxes on the bottom and work your way up."

I stood there, taking in every word like it was gospel. The last thing I was going to do was screw this up, especially not with Penny watching.

"Got it?" she asked, planting her hands on her hips. The look she gave me was no-nonsense, but I saw the warmth beneath it.

She was wearing a pale floral apron tied snugly at her waist, a loose tank top with a deep neckline, and jeans that fit like they were made just for her. Her hair was tossed up in a messy bun—my favorite look on her, hands down. Soft pieces had fallen loose, framing her heart-shaped face and making her look infuriatingly beautiful.

A loud snap of her fingers pulled me out of it.

"Earth to Mac," she said, waving a hand in front of my face.

I grinned, unashamed. "These go to the community and crochet ladies," I said, pointing to the first boxes. "These"—I gestured to the white delivery boxes—"need to be delivered, starting with the top."

Penny's eyes narrowed, fists clenching slightly at her sides, her mouth parting in disbelief. Before she could scold me, I reached out and gently wrapped my hands around her biceps.

"I'm kidding," I said softly, my thumb brushing her skin. A shiver ran beneath my touch. "I got it, I promise."

Her body relaxed, and she let out a long breath, her lips curving into a half-smile.

"Thanks for coming today," she said, her voice quieter now, her eyes locked on mine. "I didn't ask because... I mean, it's not that I didn't think you'd show, I just..."

"I get it," I said gently, my hands still resting on her arms. "But just know, if you ever need me, I'll be there. Always."

Penny looked away for a second, tucking a loose strand of hair behind her ear. When her gaze returned to mine, something unspoken passed between us.

"Noted," she said softly.

I stepped just a little closer. "Since we probably won't get much time together today," I said, slowly letting my hands fall back to my sides, "I wanted to ask if you'd come by the bar tomorrow night."

She studied me, eyes searching my face like she was trying to find a catch I hadn't voiced. I could practically hear the internal debate.

"Sure," she finally said. "What time?"

"Whenever you can," I replied, trying to keep it casual, even though my chest had just filled with relief.

She bit her bottom lip, then crossed her arms, rubbing one lightly with her hand. "I'll stop by after work."

There was a pause between us.

"Well, I've got orders to deliver. Stop distracting me, or I'm telling Sandy."

She gasped, smacking my arm lightly in mock offense. Acting on instinct, I leaned in and pressed a soft kiss to her cheek.

The second my lips met her skin, warmth spread through

my chest. I felt the moment for what it was—small, innocent, but meaningful. I pulled away slowly, studying her face for a reaction.

To my surprise, she didn't flinch or pull back. She didn't tell me she wasn't ready. Instead, she smiled.

"I'll go get Logan, that is, if I can manage to pull him away from Ellie," she said with a shake of her head.

She turned and walked back through the door, disappearing into the hallway.

I stood there for a moment, heart thudding like a drumline in my chest. I'd kissed her. Just her cheek, sure, but still.

I missed that connection. I missed touching her, being close, sharing even the tiniest moment that when I thought about them now felt like so much more. We were getting there—slowly but surely. I could feel it in my bones.

CHAPTER 26

"Yes, you got it, Mrs. Conrad! I'll stop by tomorrow after work," Logan called out, walking backward toward the van with that charming grin he wore like armor.

I stayed where I was, propped in the passenger seat with my boot resting against the dashboard, a cigarette hanging between my fingers.

Bringing it to my lips, I took a long drag and exhaled slowly out the open window, watching the smoke curl into the warm spring air.

"You don't need my number, I promise I'll be there!" Logan added, voice pitched just enough to carry back to the small crowd of older women who'd been surrounding him like a pack of coyotes in cardigans.

I couldn't help the laugh that slipped out, my lips quirking into a grin. Logan was being completely overrun by a group of flirtatious grandmas, all batting their lashes and pretending they didn't know exactly what they were doing.

Could I have saved him? Sure.

Was I enjoying this a little too much? Absolutely.

Finally, with one last wave and a desperate smile, Logan turned on his heel, yanked open the van door, and climbed inside. His expression dropped the second he sat down.

"I'm never coming back here," he muttered, slumping against

the driver's seat with the dramatic exhaustion of someone who just barely escaped with his dignity intact.

This had been stop number two on our flower delivery route. The ladies from the crochet club now had their flowers to pass out around town, which left the door-to-door deliveries still ahead of us.

"Did I hear you lining up a hot date with Mrs. Conrad?" I asked, taking another pull from my cigarette. "Didn't peg you as the widow type."

Logan gave me a sideways glare, shifting the van into drive. "She needs help lifting 'heavy things,'" he said, air quotes and all. "Apparently, my muscles will do the trick."

I snorted, my head falling back as I laughed.

Logan was pretty ripped. He might've been the youngest and shortest in our crew, but his physique gave Rhodes and Boone a real run for their money. His arms were the size of damn tree trunks—hard not to notice when he was constantly in T-shirts a size too small.

I glanced down at my own leaner frame and gave a one-shouldered shrug.

"Guess that's why she didn't ask me," I muttered.

"That, and you barely got out of the van to say two words to them."

"Yeah, well, it's not exactly a secret that most of the older ladies in this town aren't my biggest fans."

I'd never been the golden boy type—not like Logan. I'd started smoking young, worked in a bar before I was old enough to legally drink, and never made much effort to hide the rougher edges of who I was.

Tattoos covered most of my arms, stretched across my chest, even snuck up the sides of my hands. I wasn't what they wanted their daughters—or granddaughters—bringing home. And my dad being the town drunk hadn't helped matters. His reputation clung to me like smoke, no matter how hard I tried to shake it.

Not that I really did.

"I wonder why," Logan said dryly, pulling onto Main Street toward our next delivery.

"Wise ass," I grumbled.

He chuckled, clearing his throat, and gave me a quick glance. "So, how are things with Penny? She didn't seem pissed about you tagging along today."

"I think... good," I said finally, flicking ash out the window. "She doesn't act like she wants to murder me anymore. So that's progress."

Logan didn't say anything, but the knowing smile that tugged at his lips said enough.

"I'm actually enjoying all this groveling," I said, surprising even myself. I wasn't the kind of guy who chased, but chasing Penny? That had been... kind of incredible.

"Oh?" Logan's voice carried too much amusement for my liking. "The hunted becomes the hunter?"

I rolled my eyes and let out a sarcastic laugh. "Very funny." Then, softer, more honest: "I like making her happy. I know I screwed up, and I'd do just about anything to fix it. Seeing her the way she was before—distant, cold, avoiding—it sucked." I shook my head, trying to clear the memory.

"I get it," Logan said, glancing over at me before turning back to the road. "Her happiness matters more to you than your pride."

It did. I'd beg, I'd crawl, I'd do whatever it took. Knowing I'd been the reason behind that flicker of sadness in her eyes... it gutted me like someone had driven a blade straight through my chest.

I glanced at Logan and caught it—a flicker of something passing across his face. His jaw clenched. One hand tightened on the steering wheel, his knuckles going pale.

"You got something you want to add?" I asked, narrowing my eyes.

He looked at me, startled—like I'd caught him mid-thought—and cleared his throat. "Nah. Nothing."

"Come on, man. You know all my shit. Least you could do is

give me a crumb of yours. Help a guy's bruised ego out."

Logan hesitated, his brows furrowing as he mulled something over. Then he exhaled through his nose and said, "I'm in love with Ellie."

I blinked. Then scoffed. "I said, tell me something I don't know. That doesn't count."

"What?" Logan looked genuinely taken aback as he pulled up to the only traffic light in Faircloud. He turned to face me, confusion creasing his features.

I shrugged. "Pretty sure everyone already knows. You've been in love with Ellie since the dawn of time, right?"

Logan had been trailing after Ellie Cassidy since the moment he became a permanent fixture at Cassidy Ranch. His mom traveled constantly for barrel racing, which meant he spent more time with our crew than he did at home. And wherever Ellie went, Logan followed.

She needed help? He was there. She smiled? He lit up.

And when she left town for almost a year? So did he—at least emotionally. He distanced himself, vanished for random trips, barely showed face. At first, I thought he'd grown tired of us. But the more I thought about it, the more the puzzle pieces clicked into place.

"You know?" Logan's voice went tight. "Does Boone?"

"Don't know," I said. "We've never talked about it. But if I picked up on it, I'd bet others have too."

The light turned green, and I pointed ahead. "Eyes on the road, Romeo."

Logan shifted into gear, driving us down Main Street and onto one of the quieter back roads that led out of town.

"So what if Boone does find out?" I asked. "What's the big deal?"

Logan scoffed. "You mean besides the fact I'm in love with my best friend's little sister?"

"You're practically his brother," I said. "Boone's not an idiot. And if he hasn't noticed by now, that's on him. Besides, it's not like you've hidden it well. You've had heart-eyes for that girl since you were a freaking kid."

"I don't know..." he murmured, and I could see the war inside him. He opened his mouth like he wanted to say more, then clamped it shut again.

"Come on," I coaxed. "I'm feeling soft today. Say what you gotta say now or forever hold your peace."

He huffed a laugh and rubbed the back of his neck. "I think I've always loved her. I just never knew how she felt about me. And then she dated Buck, so I backed off. Figured that was my sign to let it go. But now..." His voice trailed off into the quiet hum of the van.

"You want to know if there's still a chance," I finished for him.

Logan nodded slowly, his voice barely more than a whisper. "Yeah."

If I'd learned anything lately, it was to speak up before you lose what matters.

This thing with Penny had changed me. More than any fight I'd been in, more than any mistake I'd made, more than all the years I spent trying to outrun the inevitable.

I had the urge to say all that to Logan. To crack my chest open and spill everything out onto the floor between us. But instead, I nodded and said, "Go for it. Deal with Boone later."

Logan didn't respond, and silence settled in the van as we turned down a quiet street. When we pulled up to the first house on the delivery list, I climbed out and rounded the back to grab the bouquet. I figured I'd take this one. Let Logan sit in his thoughts for a minute.

Mine were already spiraling anyway.

I started walking toward the porch, the flowers cradled in one arm, and let myself drift.

If I were being honest, I wasn't entirely sure I'd ever really been loved. Not in the way people talked about in songs or movies. I didn't grow up knowing what that looked like.

But the way I felt around Penny—the way my chest tightened

when she laughed, or how her presence lit my nerves on fire like a live wire—that felt like a damn good place to start.

I knew I loved her. That much had been clear the day she left that little pink glitter bomb in retaliation for everything that happened.

In that moment, every emotion hit me like a freight train; everything crashed down at once.

Anger.

Sadness.

Guilt.

Fear.

There was sadness for her, for me, even. Guilt for the way I'd handled everything in the beginning. Regret for not doing things sooner. Happiness, because I reflected on the moments when things were so damn good.

Penny made me *feel*.

CHAPTER 27

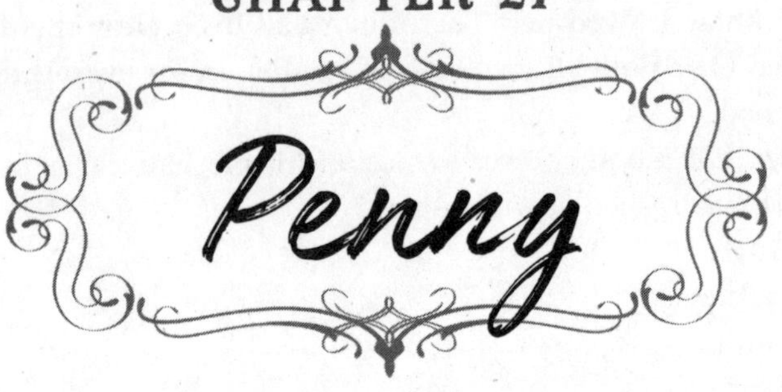

Thank you for coming today I'm glad everything worked out 😮‍💨

Mac

Who is this?

Seriously???? You should be careful, you're still on my shit list.

Mac

Well, then good thing I have a few more things up my sleeve.

Mac

Can you at least tell me, is it working?

Now, what would be in the fun in that?

Mac

Since you said the word fun, I'm assuming it is working 😉

Let's just say, you're on the right track

CHAPTER 28

I slammed my laptop shut and tossed it into my oversized tote, eager to get a move on. Tonight, I was stopping by the bar after work, and I didn't want to waste a second.

Mac showing up yesterday, completely unprompted, to help at Petal Pusher had lit a burning flame inside me. I couldn't stop thinking about it or about him.

He hadn't just shown up—he *performed*. Every delivery was spot on, dropped off with care and perfectly on time. When he and Logan returned to the shop, Mac didn't check out or disappear.

Instead, he rolled up his sleeves and stayed until close.

He swept floors, helped customers choose arrangements, smiled at strangers, and charmed even the grumpiest regulars.

I hadn't even asked him to help. I'd called Logan and Ellie. Not Mac.

And yet, he stayed later than anyone else.

When the store started to look like itself again, Mac convinced Sandy to head home before dark, remembering her rule without needing to be reminded. When everyone was gone, he still stayed with me.

We closed up shop together, moving through the motions in comfortable silence and playful teasing. He was patient, gentle, respectful. The kind of man who made sure everything was done right—not for praise, but because it mattered to me.

The night was spent laughing, talking, wrapped up in that familiar thread of banter that had always been ours.

Finally, when the lights were off and the doors locked, he still stayed until I was safely inside my apartment.

It was getting harder to hold onto my no-shits-given attitude—harder still to keep Mac guessing. Because the truth was, it *was* working. Every gesture, every look, every shift was pulling me in all over again, and I wasn't sure what that said about me.

Maybe I was weak.

Maybe I was pathetic for letting the gravity of him affect me so soon.

But the part that got me the most? It didn't feel forced. His attempts, his charm, his presence weren't manufactured or manipulative. It was like we'd fallen back into a rhythm that had always been there, waiting. Effortless. Familiar. And soaked in that spark we used to call *us*.

The teasing banter. The way we orbited around each other like planets tugged by an invisible thread. It all felt natural again. Dangerous, but natural.

Yet, six months wasn't nearly enough time to fully get to know someone like Mac Ridley. We'd only scratched the surface of each other. Deep inside, there was this part of me—dormant, now awakened—that wanted to know more. Craved it.

That's how I knew my defenses were crumbling.

It wasn't just about attraction anymore, though that still burned hot and wild between us. No, I wanted more. I wanted the pieces of Mac he didn't give easily. The layers he kept tucked behind those sharp eyes and that crooked smile.

My tote bag bounced lightly against my hip as I adjusted the strap on my shoulder and kept moving forward, heart thudding in my chest with each step.

I wore a thin-strapped sundress, one that brushed just below my knees with soft, flowing fabric that caught the breeze. My hair was curled in loose beachy waves down my back, my sandals clicking softly against the concrete.

But this wasn't just a dress.

This dress had history.

A smile played at the corners of my mouth as my hand ran absently down the front of the fabric. This was my statement. My answer to all the teasing, the tension, the way he'd been testing my limits.

I wanted him to see this dress and remember. Remember the way I'd worn it for him—here, in his bar. More specifically, the day in his back office, ruining me with nothing but his hands, his mouth, and his...

The smile deepened into something darker, something electric, and I bit my lip as the memory took hold.

My body flushed with heat, my thoughts unraveling into want. My skin buzzed with the idea of him and all the ways he used to touch me, *worship* me.

God, I missed it.

The way Mac had always made me feel like the only woman in the world, like my body was a gift he never got tired of unwrapping.

And right now?

I wanted to feel that again. I wanted *him*.

Country music spilled into my ears the second I stepped through the door, wrapping around me like a familiar hug. Locals perched at the bar, low voices rumbling in conversation, and a few couples swayed lazily on the dance floor. Midweek meant things were slow.

My gaze swept to the right, then the left, and landed on him.

Mac was behind the bar, and as if he'd felt me before he saw me, his head snapped up the moment I stepped in. His lips curved into a slow smile, and he gave me a small nod, one that said *come here*...like I wouldn't. Like I hadn't already been halfway across the room after catching a glimpse of him.

I made my way over, my shoes clicking softly on the hardwood floor. When I reached the bar, I leaned slightly over the surface. Mac mirrored me, pushing up on his hands and leaning forward. His forearms flexed under his weight, veins prominent beneath the swirling black ink of his tattoos.

God help me.

"Go ahead and bring your stuff to the office," he said, voice low and casual. "It'll be safe in there. No need to carry it around all night."

"Carry it?" I arched a brow. "I planned on plopping myself on a stool and letting you feed me drinks until close."

Mac's smile deepened, the dusting of hair above his lip curling with it. "Still, put it back there anyway. I'd hate for anything to happen to it."

I rolled my eyes playfully. "Sure thing, Dad."

He smirked. "I liked it better when you called me Daddy."

"I bet you did," I shot back, walking away before he could see the heat that climbed up my neck, swaying my hips a little extra for emphasis.

The hallway was dim, quiet. The moment I stepped into the back office, memories came rushing at me like a flood.

I placed my bag gently on the floor and stepped toward the desk, letting my fingers trail across the smooth, dark wood. I could still feel Mac's hands on me—still hear the rasp of his voice, still taste the urgency in the air. So many afternoons we'd stolen in here. So many secrets whispered into skin.

"Hey, Penny," a voice said behind me.

I turned quickly and found Dudley leaning in the doorway. He smiled, the silver ring in his lip catching the light.

"Hi, Dudley." I folded my arms and took a few steps closer.

"Nice to see you back around."

I smiled softly. "It's nice to be back." And for once, I meant it.

Dudley nodded and disappeared down the hallway, and I followed not long after, heart thudding a little harder than I wanted to admit.

Mac was on me in seconds, a cigarette tucked between his lips and a mischievous glint in his eye. He was holding something behind his back.

"What's that?" I asked, pointing to him with narrowed eyes.

He pulled out a laminated menu, the edges catching the neon glow above the bar. With exaggerated ceremony, he slid it across the counter to me.

My gaze dropped.

Love on the Rocks, the header read.

And then my eyes kept moving:

Penny's Potion

Vanilla and Spice

Comeback Kiss

The Apology Shot

Blushing Rose

Let's Not Be Over

My heart stuttered.

Color bloomed high on my cheeks, hot and all-consuming. I blinked up at him. Mac's gaze was steady, like he was trying to read me.

Good luck, because at that moment, my brain had gone blank.

"Does everyone get this?" I asked, lifting the menu.

He nodded. "They're tonight's specials."

This man had made a menu—an actual, laminated, public menu—with my *name* on it?

A menu with cocktail names that read like a romance novel?

My heart squeezed tight in my chest, and a slow smile crept across my lips. I shook my head in disbelief, setting the menu down gently. My fingers traced the edge absentmindedly as I pressed my lips together in thought.

This wasn't just a cute stunt. This was Mac standing in the middle of his bar, in front of everyone, offering a quiet confession that he'd messed up.

I glanced up at him, resting my chin in my hand. "So... what's in *Penny's Potion*?"

Mac leaned in slightly, one arm braced on the bar. "Your favorites. Tequila, orange juice, and grenadine."

I raised a brow. "So basically a tequila sunrise... with a romantic rebrand?"

He smirked, already reaching for a glass beneath the bar. "Only the best for my muse."

That made me laugh. I tilted my head, watching him work—how his hands moved with easy confidence, flexed with practiced motion as he scooped ice and poured the tequila. There was something hypnotic about it. Or maybe it was just *him*.

"I guess it's only right I try one of everything," I said, voice light. "Starting with my potion."

Mac nodded, not taking his eyes off the drink. "Bold move. Starting with the showstopper."

He finished the pour and added the grenadine last, letting the syrup swirl like a sunset through the glass. Then, as always, he fished two cherries from the bars container and dropped them gently on top because he knew I liked an extra. He slid the drink across the bar toward me, a little grin tugging at his lips.

"I have to admit, coming up with the names wasn't easy."

"Oh yeah?" I lifted the glass, letting the cold bite against my palm. "Well, they're pretty damn creative."

He grinned. "Glad you think so. Dudley said *The Apology Shot* was a little bland.

I sipped, letting the citrus hit my tongue. Sweet. Bright. Exactly what I needed.

"Maybe," I said, setting the glass down, "but it's also honest. Which, let's be real, isn't exactly your default setting."

"Ouch," he said with a mock wince. "Low blow, Penelope."

I leaned forward, a smile teasing my lips. "Truth hurts, Ridley."

He studied me for a second, then exhaled slowly. "It does. But you know what hurts more?"

"What?"

"The thought of you walking out without giving me a chance to show I've changed."

My stomach flipped. His voice had softened, just a little, but it was enough to slip through my defenses.

Still, I kept my expression playful. "That line part of your cocktail pitch too?"

He grinned, wide and boyish. "Nope. That one's straight from the heart." Mac tapped his chest, right where his heart was.

Hearing Mac say anything *from the heart* stirred something deep in my chest—an emotion I wasn't sure I was ready to feel.

Clearing my throat, I took another sip of my drink and set the glass down gently on the bar.

"Oh, shit," I muttered with a groan.

Mac's brows furrowed in concern. "What's wrong?"

"I meant to grab my book from my bag," I said, a sheepish grin tugging at my lips. "Figured I could read a little while I, you know... subtly watched you work."

He blinked. "You're going to read in the middle of a bar?"

"Why not?" I replied, instantly on the defense as I leaned back and crossed my arms over my chest.

Mac raised both hands in mock surrender. "Hey, I'm not judging. Just asking. Is it in your bag?"

I nodded. Without another word, he stepped out from behind the bar and disappeared down the hallway toward his office. I shifted in my seat, trying to peek past Dudley's broad shoulders to catch a glimpse of Mac.

Moments later, he returned, holding something in the air. As he got closer, I saw it was my book.

"This one?" he asked, a teasing glint in his eye.

"Yes!" I grinned and stretched my hand out toward him.

But he pulled up short, tucking the book under his arm as he leaned in across the bar. His face hovered close to mine, and instinctively, I leaned in too. The space between us shrank until only a breath separated our mouths.

His warm exhale brushed against my upper lip. My tongue darted out to wet my bottom lip, and his eyes tracked the movement like a man starving.

"Hand it over, Mac," I said, my voice low.

"I want something first," he murmured, gaze dropping to my mouth.

"You're not getting a kiss," I warned, even as my heart pounded in my chest. God, I wanted to kiss him. I wanted to taste the heat of his mouth, the familiar hint of tobacco and adrenaline that always lingered on his lips.

"Not even on the cheek?" he asked, tilting his head just enough to make it a dare.

I narrowed my eyes at him and reached out, grabbing his chin firmly and turning his face away.

"Don't try that stupid trick where you turn your head at the last second," I said, narrowing my eyes playfully.

He chuckled under his breath, the sound low and amused.

Then I leaned in and pressed a slow kiss to his cheek. His skin was warm, the faintest trace of sweat on his jawline. I lingered a heartbeat longer than necessary, inhaling him, letting myself feel it.

"Perfect," he murmured, turning his head back to me. Our eyes locked, and the air between us went still. My stomach somersaulted as I stared into that familiar gaze—intense, hungry, soft around the edges, only for me.

I was dangerously close to grabbing the collar of his shirt and kissing him until the world disappeared.

But I didn't.

I pulled back, lips curving into a smile that didn't quite mask the desire crackling beneath the surface. "Good," I said, settling back onto my stool. "Because that's all you're gonna get."

CHAPTER 29

"Boo!" Penny yelled, slapping her hand against the bar top with a playful scowl. "You were totally hovering!"

"Was not, little lady!" Harry shot back with a bark of laughter, fanning out a handful of cards like a magician. "You just weren't quick enough."

"*Me* not quick enough?" Penny raised a brow as she picked up her drink. "Please. I've got more agility in one toe than you do in your whole body, Harry. Let's be honest here."

She brought the straw to her lips and took a long sip of what was now her sixth drink of the night. When she said she was going to try one of everything, she wasn't bluffing. She was draining the last of the *Let's Not Be Over*—a whiskey sour that had clearly added some extra sass to her already fiery charm.

Harry let out a deep, belly-shaking laugh as he slapped his cards onto the bar top in defeat.

Dudley leaned toward me and murmured, "Who knew a card game could get this competitive?"

I smirked, keeping my eyes on the scene unfolding in front of me. "It's Penny we're talking about."

Dudley nodded knowingly and moved off to the other end of the bar to start closing out tabs.

"I hate to break up this championship round," I said, stepping closer to where Penny and Harry were locked in a dramatic stare-down. "But we're closing soon, and Harry, I need you to settle your tab."

Harry huffed, stalling for dramatic effect before finally relenting. He pulled out his wallet with a sigh, muttering something under his breath about "youthful reflexes" as Penny grinned, victorious.

About two hours earlier, she'd run into my office and returned with a deck of cards. Since then, she and Harry had been in a heated battle of slapjack, drawing in the attention of a few locals and even Dudley, who cheered from the sidelines. It was the kind of spontaneous joy only Penny could bring into a room.

As Harry stood from his stool, he leaned over and pressed a quick, gentlemanly kiss to Penny's cheek.

"This was fun," he said, his grin warm. "Should we do it again?"

Penny extended her hand, meeting him with a firm shake. "You've got yourself a deal."

After closing the tab, I returned and grabbed a bar towel from my back pocket, wiping down the damp rings the glasses left behind.

"Can I do anything to help?" Penny asked, her voice softer now, but still laced with that bubbly energy.

I glanced around. The bar had emptied, save for a few lingering regulars making their way out. Dudley was almost done settling up the last checks. The music softened to background static, and the steady buzz of conversation had finally quieted.

"You can lock the door," I said with a smile. "Not much left to do at this point."

With a sparkle in her eye, Penny hopped down from her stool and dashed to the door. She held it open for the last few guests, sending them off with bright goodbyes and that signature Penny warmth that made people feel like they mattered.

Dudley appeared beside me, dragging his own towel along the bar. "Why don't I handle clean-up?" he offered. "You should walk her home... or at least take her upstairs."

I raised a brow. "She's not that bad."

"I didn't mean she was," Dudley said, glancing in her direction with a knowing smirk. "I meant you should spend the time with her."

I paused, watching her laugh with the last straggler on their way out. Her hair bounced over her shoulders, those beachy waves swaying as she turned back inside. The soft flush on her cheeks, the sparkle in her eyes, the way she moved like the whole world was still full of magic...

Maybe taking her upstairs—if she was willing—wasn't such a bad idea after all. Like Dudley said, we could spend time together. Real time. Quiet time. Just... us.

I nodded, tossed the towel on the counter, and clapped Dudley on the shoulder.

"Lock up behind yourself after you're done."

Dudley gave a lazy salute and turned, gathering the last few glasses and heading for the back.

Penny came skipping up to the bar, light on her feet and glowing from the whiskey and whatever thrill she'd gotten from absolutely demolishing Harry at slapjack. She stopped short, her gaze playful, curious.

"Now what?"

I leaned my elbows on the bar, keeping my voice easy.

"Want to head upstairs... or should I walk you home?"

I asked like it didn't matter. Like I'd be fine either way. But it wasn't true. I wanted her to choose upstairs because walking her home meant goodbye. It meant distance. If I got her upstairs, even just for a while, it would mean time.

Her smile wavered. Not gone—but flickering like a candle in the wind. I could see the conflict in her eyes, the way they danced like she was flipping through every version of what this night could become.

I didn't say anything else. Didn't push.

Then, finally, she breathed out, almost like surrender, and said the words that lit me up like a goddamn Christmas tree.

"Let's go upstairs."

I tried not to react too quickly, but relief and desire surged through me as I rounded the bar. She met me at the end, her eyes a little softer now, a little more open.

"You want to grab your stuff now or later?" I asked.

"Later," she said with a smile that made my chest tighten.

I held out my hand, not sure if she'd take it, but I hoped she would.

Her gaze flicked from my hand to my face, searching for something. I didn't move. Instead, I waited.

Then, with an almost imperceptible breath, she slipped her hand into mine.

For the first time in months, I felt her—slim, warm, familiar. I curled my hand around hers, cradling it, anchoring us both, and led her toward the narrow staircase that spiraled up to my apartment.

Each step felt loud in the silence, and with every beat of my heart pounding in my ears, I reminded myself to stay calm.

This was the first time Penny had been back in my space since *that* morning.

The morning everything shattered.

Still holding her hand, I opened the apartment door, trying to keep it casual even as my pulse throbbed at the base of my throat.

My apartment looked almost the same as when she left—too much the same. Her shampoo was still in the shower. I was pretty sure one of her hair ties was still wrapped around the lamp switch by the bed. And her sweatshirt? That was tucked in the top drawer of my dresser.

Maybe I should've cleaned it all up. Maybe it would've been less complicated.

But none of this was part of any plan.

The second we stepped inside, I felt the shift in her body. Her hand tensed beneath mine, a little flicker of hesitation in her fingertips.

I turned us around and shut the door, placing my back

against it to give her space to breathe. Penny stood in the middle of the living room, illuminated by a slant of moonlight pouring in through the window.

The soft glow wrapped around her like silver ribbon, tracing the outline of her dress, catching in the waves of her hair. She looked like something out of a dream.

No—my dream.

Angus's loud and heavy footsteps came casually walking toward us. Penny let a soft smile form on her lips as she crouched down and coaxed him to come closer. His tail wagged fast, and excitement bubbled as he picked up speed and trotted over to her.

I stood back and watched them interact. He'd missed her.

Many mornings were spent while the three of us lay in bed, often Angus between. With his size, he had no business being in my bed, but I found it hard to deny a face like that.

"What are you feeding him?" Penny asked, looking at me with a smirk. "He looks like he's gained like ten pounds since I last saw him."

"I'll have you know, the vet thinks his weight is perfect. Angus panicked a little when I told him we'd have to cut back on his nightly ice cream, but that ended up being a false alarm."

Penny gasped, and I winked, taking a step closer and patting Angus on the head. "Come on, buddy." I moved toward the bed to slide the door to my bedroom closed to keep him away.

If I let him, he'd soak up every ounce of Penny, and right now I wanted the time to myself.

Angus huffed and followed with a groan, and once he was settled, I slid the door closed.

Like she was seeing my apartment again for the first time, Penny's eyes scanned the room slowly. She took in the little dining room table we'd spent nights laughing at, the scuffed floorboards she'd walk across barefoot, the bed we'd been wrapped in time and time again. The blanket was the same. I hadn't washed it. I couldn't.

"You didn't change anything," she said softly.

"No." I paused, watching the rise and fall of her chest. "Didn't want to."

She looked back at me then, her gaze catching mine like a hook. There was something in her eyes that broke me open a little—recognition, sadness, warmth... maybe even longing.

"It's weird," she whispered, "how familiar this all still feels."

Stepping forward, I closed the space between us, one slow footstep in front of the other.

I reached for her hand again, this time bringing it to my chest so she could feel the way my heart pounded. Her fingers curled slightly over the fabric of my shirt.

"I miss this," I said, voice low. "I miss *you*."

Her eyes shimmered, but she blinked quickly, turning her face slightly as if afraid of being too seen.

"I didn't mean to," she said. "Miss you. Miss us. But I do. Every damn day."

That undid me.

To know she missed me, to hear those words fall from her lips, was everything I needed.

The playful energy that was downstairs hadn't followed us up here. It was like being in this space again, together, alone, had spun everything into a tangled web of feelings and truths.

I raised my hand to her jaw, brushing my knuckles across her cheek. Her skin was warm, soft, familiar in a way that made my chest ache.

The shift in the air brought a sense of comfort.

"I'll take it."

Her laugh was breathless, a little broken, like she was fighting off the same weight I was.

Then she tilted her head, leaning into my palm.

"Are you feeling okay?" I asked, needing to know she was sober enough to make this choice. I felt the shift in our energy, felt the pull like we were tethered by a string that kept getting shorter.

Penny had quite a few drinks, I could tell she was fine, but I needed to make sure.

She smiled softly like she appreciated the fact that I checked in, because I cared about her. I wanted to ensure we were doing this the right way.

"Yes. I want this. I want...you."

That's all it took to break the restraint I'd been holding on to out of respect for her, but I couldn't any longer.

I leaned in and took a split second before I pressed my lips against hers. Slow, deep, reverent. The kind of kiss you give someone when you're scared—but hope like hell she wanted it, too.

Penny melted against me, her hands finding the back of my neck, pulling me closer. I wrapped my arms around her waist and lifted her slightly, just enough for her to rise on her toes.

The tenderness turned to hunger in a matter of seconds. Once you've tasted something you thought you'd lost forever, it's impossible not to want more.

Her fingers slid beneath the collar of my shirt, nails grazing skin. My breath hitched as I guided her backward toward the dining room table, kissing her like she was the only thing that had ever mattered.

Because she was.

We broke apart just long enough for her to whisper, "I don't want to think tonight."

I looked her in the eye. "Then don't. Just feel."

"I-I don't know if I'm ready," she whispered, her eyes flickering between mine—uncertain, vulnerable, *beautiful.*

I exhaled slowly, leaning in until my forehead touched hers as I caressed her cheek. "I'm here for *you*, Pen. Whatever you want... whatever you need. Always."

There wasn't a part of me that wanted to pressure her. I'd already broken her trust once. And if I'd learned anything, it was that real intimacy was so much more than physical. It was emotional. It was trust rebuilt. It was being willing to wait.

Before Penelope Hudson, I didn't understand that. But now, I was a man who would wait forever if it meant earning her heart again.

Her hands slid to my sides, grounding me in the moment. I pulled back, and in her gaze, I saw resolve beginning to settle beside hesitation. She stepped back slowly, tugging me with her, until the backs of her knees hit the chair at the table.

She sat.

And I dropped to my knees before her.

There was no performance in it, just reverence. My place was at her feet, worshiping her in all the ways I hadn't when I was too blind to see what I had.

Penny sat tall, her posture proud, as her hands came up to cradle my face. I looked up at her, lost in the warmth of her touch and the intensity behind her eyes.

The room was quiet, thick with anticipation, with something deep and sparking hanging in the air between us.

I slid my hands slowly up her thighs, feeling the rise of her dress as I went. Inch by inch, fabric gave way to soft skin, to heat, to a glimpse of delicate lace where her legs met. My fingers twitched with restraint, every muscle in my body tense with the desire to touch, to claim, to bend her over the table and lose myself in her.

But I didn't move. Not until she did.

I dragged my hands back down, a teasing trail of warmth over her skin, and met her stare again. Her lips parted as her eyes fluttered closed, breath catching from the gentle stroke of my fingertips.

Finally, she leaned down and kissed me as she held my face in her hands. Slow. Lingering. Like we had all the time in the world.

Her mouth molded to mine in lazy, sultry kisses that made the world fade away. I gripped her thigh tighter, anchoring myself in her as my heart threatened to burst from my chest.

Then she pulled back, lips brushing mine as she whispered, "Do you know what I want?"

I swallowed, shaking my head slightly.

"Release." Her voice was like a secret, a confession, a demand wrapped in velvet.

A sound, almost a whimper, escaped me. "Whatever you

want, Pen. I'm yours."

I reached for her again, but she caught my wrist and gently pushed my hand away. Then she leaned back in the chair, a sly smile curving her lips.

"No," she murmured.

My brow lifted in surprise, but I stayed still, watching as she slowly, tantalizingly, slid the thin straps of her dress off her shoulders.

My breath caught in my throat.

She tugged the neckline down, baring her perfect breasts, silver piercings glinting in the moonlight, my greatest temptation. My mouth watered. Every primal instinct in me screamed to taste her, to run my tongue over those perfect peaks until she begged for mercy.

"I'm going to pleasure myself," she said, rising from the chair and letting her dress fall to the floor. She stood tall, radiant, stepping out of the fabric and kicking her shoes aside.

Then, with one slow, deliberate motion, she slipped her panties down and off.

My mouth dried. My cock strained painfully against my jeans.

"And you're going to watch."

Her bare pussy hovered inches from my mouth, the scent of her driving me wild.

"I'll be a good boy," I promised hoarsely. "I'll keep my hands to myself."

She reached out, placing one finger beneath my chin, and tilted my gaze back up to hers.

"I knew I'd like seeing you on your knees for me," she said, her voice low and teasing, "but I didn't know I'd love it this much."

With a groan, I reached down and palmed the rigid line of my cock through my jeans. I was rock fucking hard, my whole body straining with need as Penny stood before me—bare, bold, and about to make one of my most wicked fantasies come true.

As much as I wanted to be the one to pull every moan from

her throat, I was more than willing to sit back and watch her unravel herself.

"Submission might just be my new kink," I growled.

Penny smirked and stepped back, sinking into the chair with deliberate grace. My breath hitched, turning into ragged pants as her hands roamed upward, starting at her breasts and exploring every inch of her body like it was the first time she'd ever touched herself. Every slow glide of her fingers was mesmerizing.

Her head tipped back, lips parting in a soft gasp as she brushed her fingertips over her flushed skin. My mind filled with every memory of those curves under my hands—how her nipples would harden when I teased them, how she'd whimper when I sucked a little too hard, how her back would arch when I found just the right rhythm.

Then her fingers drifted lower, slipping between her legs.

And fuck me, I almost lost it.

She started slow, rubbing gentle circles into her thigh, edging toward the place I was desperate to be. Her lip caught between her teeth, eyes fluttering closed as she began to stroke herself.

"Fuck, Pen," I moaned, grabbing myself again and adjusting against the painful pressure in my jeans. I wasn't going to last. Watching her touch herself like this? It was the most erotic thing I'd seen.

She moaned softly, adding another finger as she picked up speed. Her free hand found her breast again, rolling the soft peak between her fingers. My mind flashed with images of my tongue tracing that same path, of my hands spreading her open and tasting her until she begged for more.

"Faster," I groaned, hips shifting helplessly. "You like it faster. You always have."

She let out a breathy sound, pushing her fingers deeper. "Yes..."

She worked herself with practiced rhythm, two fingers dipping down, gathering her slickness, then circling her clit again. Her legs were spread wide, and the view was heaven and hell all at once.

"You are so fucking beautiful," I whispered hoarsely. "I can't take my eyes off you."

My palm rubbed against my length, stroking it with the friction of the fabric, adding a deeper sensation.

"Mac..." Her voice broke on my name, thick with need. "God, it's so good..."

My name on her lips, said like a prayer, was the final push. I came, groaning low as release rushed through me, hot and uncontrollable, spilling into my jeans with the kind of intensity that made my body tremble.

When I finally opened my eyes, hers were on me as she bit her bottom lip, and her eyes gleamed with victory

"You like watching?" she asked.

"I love watching," I said honestly, still breathless. "But now?"

I stood, towering over her as she sat sprawled in the chair, glowing and fucking wild. I reached out and slid my thumb along her cheek, then down to trace her jaw. "Now I want my turn."

Without waiting for permission, I dropped to my knees again—but this time, not to worship from afar.

This time, I was going to taste her, and I wasn't stopping until she screamed my name again.

Penny didn't protest when I latched my mouth onto her center. Her thighs parted like an invitation, and I dove in, my tongue flicking out to taste her, savoring every drop of her arousal like it was the only thing I'd ever crave again.

She moaned, head falling back with a sharp gasp as her fingers tangled in my hair. She gripped hard, pulling me closer, practically shoving my face into her like she couldn't get enough. I never wanted her to.

Growling low in my throat, I shook my head side to side, devouring her like a man who hadn't eaten in months. I licked, sucked, gave her clit every ounce of attention it deserved before dipping lower and pushing my tongue into her tight, wet heat.

"Yes—yes," she cried, her legs starting to tremble.

I didn't stop. I couldn't.

I pushed her right past that first wave of release, straight through the eye of the storm and off the edge into something deeper, wilder. Her body tried to retreat, instinctively twitching away from the intensity, but I wasn't letting her go.

I pressed a firm hand to her lower stomach, anchoring her in place as I finished her off. And when she finally came—loud and unfiltered—I licked her clean, drinking down every last drop of her pleasure.

Penny screamed, her voice cracking, then whimpered and moaned as her entire body went boneless.

"You..." she managed between breaths, voice airy and spent.

"I know," I murmured, sitting back and wiping my mouth with the back of my hand. "You said I couldn't touch. I promised I'd be a good boy... but no one makes you come like I do, Pen."

She let out a breathless laugh.

"That is true."

I reached down to grab her dress from the floor, then stood and offered her my hand. She slipped hers into mine without hesitation, and I helped her to her feet, steadying her when her knees wobbled.

Lowering to one knee, I held the dress open for her. She placed a hand on my shoulder for balance, and carefully, I guided the fabric back over her legs, then up her body. Once she was covered, I stood and adjusted the straps over her shoulders, pressing a soft kiss to her skin as I did.

"Why don't you stay a little longer?" I asked, my voice low, warm. "We can talk, throw on a movie... whatever you want. I just want you here. With me."

Her arms circled my neck, and she rested her head against my chest, quiet for a moment before answering.

"If I say no," she whispered, "it'll look like I'm not giving you a fair shot at winning me back."

My lips curved against her temple.

"So, because I'm a woman of equal opportunity," she added with a playful smirk, "I'll stay a little longer."

I chuckled, voice rough with affection. "No other reason?"

"Nope," she said, popping the p with a grin.
But her eyes said everything her words didn't.
She wanted to stay for more than just equal opportunity.

CHAPTER 30

I'm running a few minutes behind! I'm coming, I promise 😭

Is Ellie there yet?

Aspen

Nope!!!

Theo

Don't worry, we added a time buffer just for you (;

Aspen

Think you can get here in an hour?

Did you two add a whole hour extra for me?

Theo

...

Aspen

Do you blame us?

Nope. Have I told you guys I love you lately?

* Penny changed the group chat name to F.R.I.E.N.D.S But Feral *

Rummaging through my top drawer, I frantically searched for my favorite bathing suit. I was already running late—despite the generous buffer my friends had built in, knowing full well I'd need it.

"Where the hell is it?" I huffed, tossing items over my shoulder one by one. Underwear, bras, and socks flew across the room, decorating the floor like chaotic confetti.

Everyone had the day off and was meeting at Cassidy Ranch to celebrate Ellie's birthday. Aspen had come up with the idea—a laid-back, picnic-style party at the swimming hole with our closest friends. Ellie didn't know about it, which made me showing up on time even more important.

Finally, with one last dig, my fingers brushed against familiar stretchy fabric. I yanked it free from the drawer with a triumphant grin.

"Yes!" I shouted, pumping the hot pink bathing suit in the air like a victory flag. The vibrant color felt like a sign telling me I was about to get back on track.

Stripping out of my pajamas, I slid into the cheeky bottoms and tied the triangle top. On my way to the closet, I caught a glimpse of myself in the mirror and stopped in my tracks.

For a beat, I just stared, taking in my body, the curve of my waist, the way the suit hugged my hips. A smirk curled across my lips.

Mac was going to die. I looked *good*.

I let out a laugh, spinning slightly to check out my ass and giving a nod of approval.

The other night with Mac... well, it'd taken a turn I should've expected the moment I agreed to go upstairs with him. Sure, I'd had a few drinks, but I knew what I was doing. I was fully present, fully in control.

At first, my plan had been simple: tease him, torment him, let him watch while I took the pleasure part into my own hands. But when he broke the rules and stepped in to finish what I'd started, it was like a switch flipped. I'd forgotten how good he was—how good *we* were—and I couldn't bring myself to stop it.

He'd been right... No one did it like he did. Not even myself.

You're supposed to know your own body better than anyone. And yet, somehow, Mac had learned every part of mine like it was a language only he could speak.

There wasn't a single ounce of regret. Not for giving in. Not for wanting more.

In fact, the only thing I felt now was the urge to do it all over again. I felt recharged, like the battery in me died and now I was back, baby, back to full strength.

From across the room, my phone started ringing, which was the last thing I needed. I reached into my closet, snatched the biggest T-shirt I could find, and sprinted toward the sound, half-blind as I wrestled to get my head through the neck hole.

On the final ring, I hit accept and put it on speaker.

"Hello?" I said, slightly breathless, still struggling to get the shirt on right.

"Penny! Just the person I was hoping to reach," my boss, Gerry, said cheerfully.

I internally groaned and tilted my head back in frustration. It was my day off, and he knew that.

"You called me. Who else did you think was going to answer?" I replied, a little sharper than intended. Gerry was a good boss, just one who occasionally forgot about boundaries. I'd learned to take the good with the annoying.

He let out a deep, hearty laugh. "I know, I know you're off today."

Then why are you calling me? I screamed silently.

"But the board's looking for an update on this year's fundraiser," he continued. "Last year was a hit, and they're eager to know what's coming next."

Seriously? He was calling me on my day off... to talk business?

"I hate to be that person," I said, grabbing my sandals, gift bag, and purse, tucking my phone between my ear and shoulder, "but is this something that could wait until I'm back in the office?"

"Oh! Of course, of course," Gerry backpedaled quickly. "They've been blowing up my email, and I wanted to give them something to chew on."

With a resigned sigh, I closed my apartment door behind me and hurried down the steps. I glanced into Petal Pusher and spotted Sandy cleaning the front window. I waved, and she returned it with a sunny smile.

I could give him *something*, a placeholder to keep the board off his back. Honestly, I didn't even have a plan yet.

"Fine," I said. "Romance has been flying off the shelves this year. I was thinking of tailoring the event to that crowd. It fits the small-town vibe."

Total bluff. I pulled that straight from thin air. But as I said it, the idea started to take shape. Maybe it wasn't such a bad plan after all.

Fumbling through my purse, I found my sunglasses and slid them on.

Maybe we could host something at the bar... an adults-only night? That sounded like *Librarian Penny* talking. *Off-duty Penny* was climbing into her car, ready to spend the day swimming and drinking with her closest friends.

"Great!" Gerry said. "They'll love that. You young people and staying up to date with the trends, changing the book world one post at a time!"

I laughed, starting my car. One of the rare times social media was actually working in the world's favor.

"I've got to go," I said, clearing my throat. "I'll stop by when I'm back in the office."

After a round of goodbyes, I hung up and pulled out of the alley, heading toward Cassidy Ranch, more than ready to dive in and have a damn good afternoon.

"I'M HERE! I'M here!" I called out, breathless as I jogged through the clearing in the woods that opened up to the swimming hole. Everyone was already there—everyone except the birthday girl. So technically... I made it on time. *Ish.*

Pausing to catch my breath, I bent over, hands on my knees, lungs burning just a little from the sprint.

"If someone had a gun to my head and told me to pick the friend most likely to be late," Theo said, strolling over with a teasing smirk, "I'd pick you every damn time."

I laughed, holding out my gift bag and purse for her to take. "What an honor."

Theo was wearing baggy cutoff shorts that were unbuttoned and a dark blue bikini, her tattoos on full display. Her hair was braided into two playful pigtails, and her smile was pure mischief.

She took my things with ease, then pulled me into a tight, familiar hug. I melted into it, still breathless.

"Please tell me you brought the baby," I said as we walked toward the group gathered off to the side. "I need a hit of that new baby smell."

"Oh my *God*," she laughed, shaking her head. "No baby today. My mom all but begged to keep her for a few nights. She took some time off work and swears there's no better way to spend it than with her granddaughter."

"Well, your mom isn't wrong," I said with a grin.

As we approached the rest of the group, Boone turned toward me. "You know what I'm getting you for *your* birthday, Penny?"

I stopped and placed my hands on my hips, scanning the familiar faces. My gaze caught on *him* immediately—Mac, already looking at me like he knew every thought in my head. That slow, crooked smile of his made heat rise in my chest.

"Let me guess, something time-management related?" I said, leaning down to hug Aspen from behind.

She was sitting on a rock, cheeks puffed as she blew up a bright pink floaty, her eyes wide as she gave me a thumbs-up mid-breath.

"She's fine," Aspen said when she ran out of breath and needed a break, defending me like the angel she was. "We all know to build in the buffer."

I kissed her cheek and murmured, "This is why you're my favorite."

I stood and scanned the area for an open spot. There was only one, which was an old log that had been turned into a makeshift seat. It just so happened to be right next to Mac.

Before heading over, I peeled off my oversized T-shirt to use it to brush away any dirt from the log. The sun filtered through the trees above, dappled light kissing my skin, warm but not harsh.

As I walked past him, Mac lifted a bottle in my direction—offering it wordlessly, the hint of a grin still tugging at his lips.

That smile, that look... it was all there, leaving me even more breathless.

I took the bottle from Mac's hand, letting my fingers brush his on purpose—just lightly, just enough.

Electric.

He felt it too. His jaw ticked, that almost-imperceptible shift in his shoulders, like he was grounding himself against the jolt of it.

"Thanks," I said, my voice softer than before. Almost shy, which wasn't like me. Not usually.

I had to keep myself in check today because our friends still didn't know what was happening.

I don't know why I still hadn't gone to Aspen to help with the mess inside my head. Maybe a part of me felt silly for not cutting things off for good, for giving him the chance to yearn and grovel his way back into my life.

Mac tilted his head, watching me. "Hot pink, huh?" His gaze dipped for the briefest second, enough to make heat crawl up the back of my neck. "The color of angels."

I rolled my eyes, but I smiled anyway. "You sound like you thought hard about that one."

"I didn't." He leaned back on his palms, his thigh brushing against mine as I sat down next to him on the log. "But I *have* been thinking about you nonstop in less than that since the other night."

That earned him a sharp inhale from me, and a heartbeat that stumbled in my chest.

"Mac..."

He didn't say anything right away. Just looked ahead at the water glimmering in the sunlight, the ripple of movement from the light breeze. The sound of chatter fell into the background from our friends next to us.

Then he turned his head toward me, voice low and steady. "If you want to pretend it didn't happen because that's what you need, fine. But I won't."

"I'm not pretending," I said, barely above a whisper. "I just... I don't know what to do with it."

"Then don't do anything," he said, his voice like gravel and velvet all at once.

I swallowed hard, not sure how to relieve the ache that started to press into my chest.

We sat in silence for a minute, yet it was anything but quiet because my mind was swirling.

Every nerve in me was alive, way too aware of his proximity. My fingers curled around the edge of the log just to keep them from doing something stupid.

"You always did know how to get under my skin," I murmured.

Mac leaned closer, his voice a breath against my ear. "That's because you've always let me."

The hairs on the back of my neck stood up, and my whole body went still, except for my heart—my traitorous, unrelenting heart—pounding like a drum against my ribs.

I turned my head, only slightly, and there he was. So close.

Too close.

Not close enough at the same time.

"She's coming!" Aspen hissed, snapping my attention away from Mac.

Rhodes, Theo, Boone, and Aspen stood off to the side, waiting for Ellie. Logan was in charge of distracting her and leading her here. It was his job to make sure the surprise went off without a hitch.

Even though I looked away from Mac, I could still feel the weight of his fixed look on me, like a tether pulling tight between us, and it left a buzz under my skin I couldn't shake.

Voices drifted through the trees, quiet at first, then clearer as footsteps approached. A few moments later, Ellie stepped through the clearing. She stopped short, her long blond hair catching the dappled sunlight as she reached up and tucked a few strands behind her ears.

"Surprise!" we all yelled, the word echoing across the water and into the woods.

Ellie blinked, eyes wide, and then broke into a breathless laugh. Her gaze swept over the setup—the pop-up table full of snacks, the coolers loaded with drinks, the blankets and floaties scattered across the grass—and finally landed on us.

"What the heck?" she asked, putting her hand over her chest.

Aspen was the first to reach her, wrapping her in a hug. "We wanted to throw you a little birthday get-together."

"We figured something small, just the core group," Rhodes added, smiling warmly.

Ellie turned toward Logan. "Did you know about this?"

He shrugged with a grin that betrayed him instantly. "Maybe."

She swatted his arm, laughing. When she turned back, Logan

touched the spot like it still tingled, the grin lingering on his face even when he thought no one was watching.

Everyone began settling in—grabbing drinks, finding seats, tossing jokes across the circle. Ellie, beaming, finally declared, "Okay. Enough chit-chat. I'm getting in the water."

This spot had always been a Cassidy family favorite—full of childhood memories, secret teenage parties, and sun-drenched summer days. The trees created a shaded canopy overhead, the light filtering through in golden specks. The water shimmered beneath it, clear and inviting.

Boone was the first to make a splash, leaping in with a front flip. Mac followed with a running start and some kind of half-twist that sent water crashing over the rocks.

I set my drink carefully on a nearby boulder and backed up a few steps.

With a grin, I took off running, launching myself into the air and mimicking Boone's flip. For a second, I flew, and then the cool water welcomed me in a rush.

I let myself sink, the shock of the temperature calming my overheated skin. I stayed under just a moment longer than necessary, eyes closed, savoring the quiet.

Eventually, I popped up to the surface and swam toward the others. We floated, joked, and basked in the ease of it all. At one point, the group naturally split—girls on one side, guys on the other.

Ellie raised her drink. "Thank you all, seriously. You've been so inviting since I came back. I didn't realize how much I needed this."

I reached out and rubbed her forearm. "You're one of us now. You've got us for life."

"Facts," Aspen chimed in. "We're happy to have you."

"We need a girls' night," Theo said with a mischievous grin.

"Ooh, maybe at Aspen's cabin?" I suggested.

Aspen's face lit up. "Yes! Spa night, wine, music, maybe some deep, emotional soul-bonding."

I laughed. "And secrets. We're spilling all the secrets."

That last part was for me. Maybe a girls' night would be the perfect opportunity to finally say out loud what I hadn't told any of them.

I glanced across the water, finding Mac immediately. Just seeing him sent a rush through me. The memories of what it felt like to be on the verge of something with him—teetering between casual fun and something real—hit me.

We were finding our way back, step by step. But deep down, I knew I needed more than flirtation and stolen moments. I needed reassurance that this time, it was different. That I wouldn't be left picking up the pieces again.

I felt us edging what we once were, but I needed that final mile, that honest conversation, that *proof* before I handed him my heart again.

CHAPTER 31

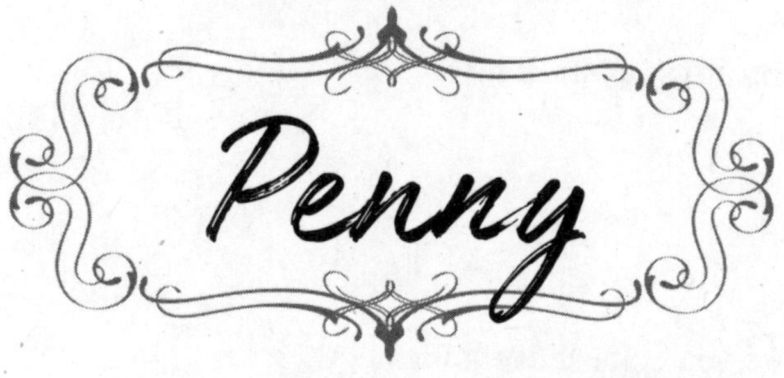

Pick up pick up! I have to show you what I found!

Mac

I'll be free in a second, I'm with the guys

It won't be here in a second!

Mac

Jesus okay, I'm calling now

Mac

Seriously? Are you not going to answer me?

LOOK!

Mac

Is that a turtle... in your apartment?

YUP!

Mac

you are something else

Mac

Are you coming over tonight? Or am I coming to you?

I'll be over in ten minutes!

Mac

My ten or your ten?

HA! SO FUNNY MAC!!!!

Mac

I'm gonna need an answer, Penelope, because we have very different timetables here

My ten...

Mac

FaceTime at lunch?

It's a date (;

How many books are too many?

Mac

I don't think there is a right answer to the question... It feels like a trick.

Mac

How many would make you happy?

A man after my heart...

Did you want to come over for dinner tomorrow night?

Mac

Let me get Jolie to cover my shift and I'm in

Mac

Can I bring anything?

Just yourself (;

CHAPTER 32

A rush of déjà vu swept over me so suddenly it made me pause. I'd been in this exact moment before—or something close to it a few months ago. Same nerves, same anticipation. Same girl.

I dampened my fingertips under the faucet and ran my hands through my hair, smoothing down the loose strands to curl behind my ears.

After a quick spin in front of the mirror, I nodded once to myself, turned off the bathroom light, and stepped into the living room.

Flowers—check. Phone, wallet, keys—check.

For the second time in just over a week, I'd managed to get a shift covered at the bar. That was saying something.

Before all this, I never took time off. I was the guy to *cover*, not the one who needed covering. When Dudley, Jolie—hell, sometimes both at once—called, I was always there.

That had been part of my problem. I didn't know how to give myself a life outside of that building. If I spent time with friends, it was within those four walls, sneaking in laughter between drink orders and last calls. I'd never been good at carving out space for joy, not intentionally. That was a foreign language I never learned to speak.

"You be a good boy," I said, pointing at Angus, who offered a long-suffering sigh before flopping onto his side like the dramatic prince he was.

"Don't give me that attitude," I muttered, grinning. That dog had more sass than most people I knew.

Pulling on my boots, I jogged down the stairs and through the bar—flowers in one hand, cigarette in the other. Outside, I paused at the edge of the sidewalk, slipping the bouquet between my knees as I lit the end of the cigarette. The paper crackled, and I drew in a slow breath, holding the smoke in my lungs for a beat before letting it go.

The weather was warm, the last golden rays of the day slipping behind the mountain ridge. The town was quiet in that almost-sacred, in-between hour when the day is ending but night hasn't quite begun.

I walked in peace, savoring the feel of this—the moment before something good.

Going over to have dinner at her place was Penny's idea. Through nonstop texting, late-night FaceTime calls, over the last few days, I'd earned my spot at her dinner table—in her sanctuary—this time invited.

People passed me on the sidewalk, their eyes flicking briefly to the bouquet in my hand before moving on. No one stopped, no one asked.

Not that I wanted them to. I'd watched people devour every detail of Boone's life, pick apart Ellie's departure like it was a movie they were all entitled to direct. I didn't crave that. I liked being a quiet mystery.

I smiled, taking another slow drag before letting the smoke drift out and up.

When I reached Penny's place, I stomped out my cigarette and tucked the butt into the container near the stairs before pulling open the door.

As I jogged up the steps, a rush of happiness surged through me at the thought of seeing her again, so much so that I skipped the formality of knocking. She had a bad habit of leaving her door unlocked, something I knew probably would never change.

I twisted the knob and stepped inside, instantly greeted by the sound of music floating from a speaker and the sight of Penny in the kitchen, barefoot, dancing slightly as she stirred something on the stove.

Her eyes caught mine the second I walked in.

Her smile hit me—wide, warm, and blooming so big it nearly knocked the air out of my lungs.

"Welcome to House de Penny," she announced with mock grandeur. "The finest restaurant in all of Faircloud."

I grinned and started pulling off my boots near the door. "What's on the menu tonight, Chef?"

"Pasta!" she squealed. "Rhodes's recipe. He was sweet enough to send it over when I asked, even though it's apparently sacred Dunn family stuff."

"Well," I said, stepping into the kitchen and offering her the flowers I brought, "what can I do to earn my stay?"

Penny's smile softened as she took the bouquet from me. She lifted it to her nose and inhaled, closing her eyes as if she were letting the scent sink in.

"They're beautiful," she muttered quietly. Then her expression shifted—mischievous and playful.

Tapping a finger against my chest, Penny replied, "I left the breadstick for you this time. Your turn to suffer."

I chuckled as she moved past me, pulling the limp, sad-looking bouquet from the pitcher on the table and replacing it with the one I brought.

"Watch and learn, Hudson," I teased, rolling up my shirt sleeves with a dramatic flair. I was already halfway to the freezer by the time she jumped up to sit on the kitchen counter, wine glass in hand.

I worked on laying out the frozen breadsticks on a tray while the pasta sauce simmered behind me, the scent filling the kitchen in warm, spicy waves.

"You're staring, Pen," I said, not turning but fully aware of her eyes on me.

"I know," she replied shamelessly, her voice low and sultry. "I wasn't trying to hide it. I like the way your muscles flex when you move."

I smirked, placing the last breadstick on the tray before turning to look at her with a raised brow. "So it's just my biceps you're after, huh?"

"Well," she said, swirling her wine and giving me a look that made my skin flush, "and the tattoos are a strong selling point."

"Noted," I replied, sliding the tray into the oven and setting the timer.

Penny set her wine glass down with a soft clink and hopped down from the counter, her eyes shining beneath the low light of the kitchen. The soft hum of music drifted from the speaker near the window, something acoustic and slow. Her hand lifted slightly, palm open in invitation.

"Dance with me?" she asked, her voice confident and strong.

Abso-fucking-lutely. I always looked for a reason to have her close to me.

I reached for her hand and let her pull me toward the middle of the living room. There wasn't much space between the couch and the coffee table, but that didn't matter when she fit against me so perfectly.

I wrapped my arms around her waist, and she curled hers around my neck, drawing me close like it was instinct. The moment we started to sway, it hit me—muscle memory and emotion colliding in my chest.

"You remember the first time we did this?" I asked, my voice low, lips brushing the shell of her ear.

Penny's head tilted against my shoulder. "Of course I do. You told me this was the extent of your dancing abilities, but then proved that wrong when you danced for Theo, even though I somehow missed it."

God, I didn't want to relive that moment again. A couple of months ago, Rhodes asked us all to cheer up Theo and unfortunately, it involved all of us dancing like idiots to "My

Humps." Penny and Aspen were supposed to be there, but luckily, they were running late. Per usual for Penny.

"I'm so glad you did," I murmured, smiling against her hair. "That was a level of embarrassment I never plan to reach again."

Penny chuckled against my chest, sending a vibration surging through me.

"Remember the other time when you tried to dip me halfway through the second song and nearly dropped me on the floor."

Somehow, dancing in the comfort of this space had become our thing. There were many nights spent practicing our amateur moves to the music coming from this same worn speaker.

"I *did* drop you."

"You did," she agreed, pulling back just enough to look at me, her lips curved in a soft grin. "Then we ended up staying on the floor and didn't get up until morning."

Her smile faltered, just slightly. Not because the moment had slipped away, but because it had shifted into something deeper, weightier. Her hand came to my cheek, her fingers soft and slow as they traced the line of my jaw, like she was memorizing me all over again, piece by piece.

"Can I admit something?" she asked, her voice barely above a whisper.

My heartbeat kicked up, thudding hard in my chest. I didn't answer right away—just met her gaze, where something unguarded shimmered just beneath the surface.

I gave her a small nod, holding the space open for her.

"I think I was falling in love with you then," she said, breath catching on the confession. "I felt... consumed by you. In the best, most terrifying way. But I was scared to admit it because I didn't think you wanted that kind of commitment." Her voice wavered, just enough to crack something in me. "I didn't know what was real, what to believe."

I felt the tension ripple through her body, her hands tightening slightly against me. I pressed my palms gently into her hips, grounding her, silently telling her I was here and that she didn't have to hold herself so tightly.

"I wasn't pretending," I said quietly, my voice low and steady. "Not for a second. And I know I broke something along the way, but I want to fix it. I want to earn that trust back... earn *you* back."

I knew I loved her, but I couldn't say it in this moment. The words wouldn't mean enough, not without action behind them. After everything I'd done, my promises needed to be lived, not spoken.

The silence settled between us again, but it wasn't uncomfortable. It was full—rich with reflection and possibility, like the past and future were both pressing in on this one moment. We swayed gently, locked in that fragile stillness.

Then she exhaled—a long, slow breath against my chest—and her arms curled tighter around me.

"Can I admit something else?" she asked.

"I'm all ears, Pen."

"You still make me feel safe," she said, the words trembling. "There's something about being near you that feels... calm. Like I can breathe again."

My throat tightened. "Then let me keep doing that. Let this be our second chance. No games, no walls. Just us."

A soft buzz came from the kitchen—the timer, probably—but neither of us moved. Her head stayed right where it was, resting on my chest, her breath warm through the fabric of my shirt.

She was thinking, weighing everything in real time. And that alone—her consideration—was more than I deserved. It meant the door hadn't fully closed.

Penny looked up at me with a soft smirk as the timer continued to blare. "If you burn the breadsticks after all that, you're never getting invited over again."

I laughed, brushing my lips to her forehead before letting her go. "You burn one batch of breadsticks and suddenly *I'm* the problem? Bold statement, Trouble."

I grinned as I turned toward the oven.

"Bold is one of my best traits, didn't you know?" she asked.

Penny leaned on the counter, sipping her wine as I pulled the tray from the oven and gave the breadsticks a proud once-over. "Perfect golden brown," I declared. "Feel free to start drafting my redemption arc."

"Redemption arc?" she scoffed. "Let's not get ahead of ourselves."

With everything plated and the sauce steaming, we carried our dishes to the small table tucked beside her window. Penny lit a candle for ambiance, she claimed, but I saw the way her eyes flicked toward me when the soft light hit my face.

"This smells amazing," I said, twirling my fork through the pasta. "You sure you didn't just charm Rhodes into doing all the hard work?"

"I'll have you know I diced those tomatoes myself," she said proudly, then narrowed her eyes. "And when I say 'diced,' I mean chopped at them until they vaguely resembled pieces."

"Sounds like a culinary masterpiece."

She shrugged. "You're easy to impress."

I leaned across the table slightly and whispered, "Only when it comes to you."

Her fork paused halfway to her mouth. Her eyes flicked to mine, caught off guard as a smile curved on her lips.

I took a bite of the pasta, nodding in exaggerated approval. "Okay... yeah. That's dangerously good."

"I'm texting Rhodes later to tell him you cried into your plate at how amazing it was."

"Oh, I will cry," I said with mock seriousness. "But only because I realize I wasted years not letting you cook for me more often."

"Years, huh?" she teased, swirling her own fork. "So dramatic."

"What can I say? You bring it out of me."

She laughed, that soft, melodic laugh I hadn't realized I missed so much. We kept eating, exchanging stories and banter between bites, each moment folding over the next like soft layers in something new, something warm.

By the time we were finished, her cheeks were pink from the

wine and the candlelight, and I was thoroughly full and completely charmed by her.

"So," she said, leaning back in her chair and eyeing me. "Did dinner win me any points?"

I tilted my head. "Depends. Am I staying for dessert?"

Penny raised an eyebrow, the corner of her mouth lifting. "What kind of dessert are we talking about?"

I stood slowly, rounding the table to her side. "Wait, shouldn't *I* be the one trying to win the points?"

She tilted her face up toward mine, eyes dancing. "Smart man."

"Let me start with the dishes, and then we can see if I earn something a little sweeter," I whispered.

"You just might," she murmured.

We moved into the kitchen together, side by side. Everything tonight felt heightened—sharper, warmer, charged. I filled the sink, silent except for the music in the background as the water ran.

Penny handed me the first plate, and our fingers touched—intentionally, neither of us pulling away.

"I have a favor to ask you," Penny said, mischief lighting her eyes. "And saying yes will definitely earn you some of those points. Could even get you out of the doghouse faster."

"Oh?" I glanced at her, amused, as I scrubbed a plate clean. "Do tell."

"Last year, I worked with the Cassidys for the library fundraiser," she explained, stepping closer, her hip brushing mine. "This year, the board is already on my case about what I'm planning. So, I was thinking..."

I grabbed the next plate from her hands but kept my eyes locked on hers. I knew that tone. She was buttering me up.

"You want to use the bar for some kind of fundraiser, don't you?" I asked with a grin.

She winked, her smile teasing. "Exactly."

I playfully rolled my eyes, placing the plate in the drying

rack. Penny could ask me to shut down the bar for a week and I wouldn't bat an eye. Whatever she needed, I'd make it happen. Hell, I'd rebuild the damn place if she asked.

"Sure," I said casually, returning to the sink. "What are you thinking?"

She sighed dramatically and leaned against the counter, her head dropping between her shoulders. "I don't know yet. I haven't really mapped it out. But whatever we do, it needs to happen soon."

"Well, whatever it is, the bar's yours," I told her.

Penny tapped her chin thoughtfully. "Hear me out, we could get the guys involved. And maybe..." She lifted her hands in the air as if defending herself. "A mechanical bull?"

I barked out a laugh, tilting my head back. "You want a mechanical bull inside The Tequila Cowboy?"

She nodded eagerly. "Please?" She moved closer, gripping my biceps with her hands. She gave me that damn pouty face, bouncing slightly on her toes. "Pretty please?"

It wasn't that I was against it—it was just... the bar wasn't exactly that kind of place. We had cover bands and the very occasional line-dancing lesson. But a full-on theatrical bull ride? That was another level.

Still... she was looking at me like that, and it melted me into a puddle, completely at her mercy.

"Fine."

"Yes!" Penny squealed, lifting up on her toes and pressing a quick, triumphant kiss to my lips. "You're the best. Now I really have to get planning."

CHAPTER 33

Penny. Penny. Penny.

She was all I could think about.

I was at the bar, hands working on autopilot as I wiped down a rack of clean glasses, but my mind? It was nowhere near The Tequila Cowboy. I was stuck in the last few days with her—replaying each moment, each look, each stolen touch that had somehow grounded me and set me on fire all at once.

I was entirely, hopelessly gone over Penny Hudson. And that wasn't a revelation, it was a quiet truth I'd carried for the better part of a year.

If there were two things in this life I knew were meant to be mine, it was this bar and Penny. Lately, both had been weighing heavily on my mind, but one was starting to feel possible again... the other, not so much.

I placed a polished glass on the counter, reaching for the next. I had some time to kill before Aspen was coming to the bar for a *check-in* about how things were going with Penny. Her idea, not mine.

The silence of the bar was almost peaceful without Lizzie buzzing in my ear, which gave me time to think. We hadn't spoken much since our last blowout, and I preferred it that way. Since I'd called her out for throwing a tantrum and micromanaging everything I touched, she'd kept her distance. It was easier.

Quieter. Less tense.

Until now.

The familiar chime above the door rang out, a cold draft sneaking in behind it. I didn't even need to look up to know it was her—Lizzie, her pristine look and pinched expression.

Funny how quickly the mood could shift. A moment ago, I was riding the warmth of memories with Penny. Now, the room felt ten degrees colder.

She approached the bar with practiced confidence, her dark bob curled perfectly at her chin, one side tucked neatly behind her ear. The sight of her always pulled something tight in my chest—reminded me too much of our mother. Staring at Lizzie was like staring down my lack of childhood in heels and lipstick.

I kept wiping the glass in my hand, pretending she wasn't there.

"No smoking inside?" she asked, dropping her oversized purse onto a barstool as she slid onto the seat.

It would be much easier if she ignored me as much as I was trying to ignore her. Instead, she always fucking sat down—commanding attention like she was entitled to it.

I rolled my head from side to side, working out the tension her presence had instantly brought with it. With a sigh, I placed both hands on the bar and let my head hang for a second before meeting her eyes.

"No, Lizzie. But now that you mention it, I am craving some menthol."

I didn't move to grab the pack from my back pocket, though. Just stared her down.

"Don't get mad when I ask this," she started, and instantly, I was already mad. Nothing good ever followed that sentence.

"What now?"

"I saw Penny leaving the other morning." She tilted her head slightly, watching me too closely. "Is there something going on between you two?"

I stood straighter, shoulders rolling back. "I'm not sure what to call it, but that's none of your business."

There was no way I was about to open up to her about something so personal, not when we barely managed to share floor space. She didn't get access to that part of me.

"Right," Lizzie muttered. "I didn't see you walk her out. What if she stole something? People shouldn't just be walking through the bar unattended, especially people you aren't sure about."

I stared at her like she'd grown a second head.

"Are you fucking serious?" I asked, disbelief thick in my voice. "Penny Hudson? You really think she'd steal from the bar?"

"I'm just trying to protect the business," she replied, lifting her hands in mock surrender.

Did my sister lose one of her very few fucking marbles?

"No, you're being nosy." I stepped forward, voice lowering. "For your information, I did walk her down, just didn't make it all the way to the door because I was in my boxers and figured the morning crowd didn't need that kind of show."

Lizzie hummed like she didn't believe me, then reached into her tote and pulled out a laminated menu.

She slid it across the bar like she was presenting evidence in a court case.

"And this?" she asked, tone clipped. "You made this without even running it by me."

I barely glanced down at the menu before looking back up. "So what?"

"You just said you didn't know what was going on with her. But you're making personalized menus?"

I picked up the next glass and dried it with more force than necessary, my patience with her and this conversation wearing thin. "Just say what you're really trying to say and get it over with."

Lizzie huffed, then reached into her bag again. This time she tossed down a handful of wrinkled, half-torn flyers.

I threw the towel over my shoulder and picked one up. It was a promotional flyer for the fundraiser Penny had mentioned—cowboy hats, cacti, and bold fonts carefully curated on the page.

Mechanical bull, themed drinks, line dancing, *real* cowboys. Saturday night. Right here.

Despite myself, I grinned. It was over-the-top and dramatic—pure Penny.

"What about it?" I asked.

"Did you tell your *girlfriend* she could use the bar for a fundraiser?" Lizzie's voice had sharpened.

"Yeah," I said. "And? You got a problem supporting the library? Helping kids keep access to books and computers and a safe place to go?"

I leaned in close, voice dropping. "Go ahead. Shut it down. See how well that goes over in this town."

"All I'm asking for is some transparency," Lizzie said, her voice tight. "Is that really too much to ask?"

"Yes," I said flatly. "It is."

Her eyes narrowed. "Whatever resentment you've been carrying around since childhood? Put it aside and grow up. This is business, not personal."

I laughed—a humorless, bitter sound that echoed too sharply in the quiet bar. The sheer audacity of her comment burned like cheap whiskey going down the wrong damn pipe.

"Not personal?" I leaned both palms on the bar and stared her down. "It's pretty damn personal to me. This place has been my life since I was tall enough to see over this counter. And now you come in here, on your high horse, expecting me to nod and jump every time you bark out an order? That's not business, Lizzie. That's arrogance."

I tapped my finger hard against the bar top, each word punctuated with the weight of a lifetime. "I grew up behind this damn wood. You didn't."

She stayed on her stool, arms crossed, lips pressed in a line—unbothered, at least on the surface. But that only fueled the fire roaring inside me.

Maybe it was her accusing Penny of stealing. Maybe it was just years of built-up shit between us. But I wasn't holding back anymore.

"Why is it that every time you walk through that door, you have to push every one of my buttons?" I snapped. "You don't say hello. You don't check in. You just pick something to complain about—something to fix, something I'm apparently screwing up."

"Me?" she shot back, hand on her chest, voice edged with sarcasm. "*I'm* the one pushing buttons? Give me a break, Mac. You do shit just to get a rise out of me."

"Because I'm tired, Lizzie," I said, stepping back and throwing my hands in the air. "Tired of being micromanaged. Tired of the nagging. Since the moment you came back, it's been one thing after another. I've offered more than once to take this place off your hands and let you walk away."

"I didn't ask—"

"Yeah, yeah," I cut her off, waving a hand between us. "You didn't ask for this. Boo-fucking-hoo. But you stayed. You keep coming around. So, what is it? What's keeping you here if you hate it so much?"

She mumbled something under her breath, arms crossed again, eyes shifting away.

"If it was that easy," she said, tone sour.

"Then say what's so hard about it," I pushed. "What? Is it the fact I was married?"

Her head snapped up so fast I knew I'd hit a nerve.

Gotcha.

I held her gaze. "Yeah. I figured you knew."

Reaching into my back pocket, I pulled out the cigarette box I hadn't touched since this conversation started, then grabbed the ashtray from beneath the bar. With a flick of the lighter, I lit one and drew in the smoke, letting it steady me.

"I figured you were just waiting for me to say it out loud," I muttered, exhaling slowly. "You could've just asked. You could've been honest."

She said nothing. Just stared at me with something unreadable in her eyes.

"If that's what's been making this so difficult, me being married, then let me save you the energy." I took another drag and tapped the ash into the tray. "It's over. It's been over. So if that was your reason for holding out, it's gone."

"If you figured I knew," Lizzie snapped, "why not say something sooner and get your precious bar back?"

I took a slow drag of my cigarette, exhaling to the side as her words settled over me.

"Because I didn't really know that was why, not at first," I said. "Not until everything else started to fall apart because of that damn marriage. That's when it clicked. It was the only thing that made sense."

I pointed the burning tip of the cigarette toward her, not in anger, but with emphasis.

"I did the research, Lizzie. I get why you held onto it. You thought she'd be entitled to a piece. But if you'd just picked up the phone and called a lawyer, like I did, you'd know that's not true."

"What do you mean?" she asked, arms folding tighter across her chest.

"In Texas, it would've been mine. Married or not. The bar was always going to be my property. It had nothing to do with her." I ashed the cigarette, then placed it between my lips again. "But instead of talking to me, you just assumed. You came in here with your attitude and condescending tone, acting like you knew everything. Just like Mom."

I blew out a long stream of smoke, feeling the bitter truth loosen from my lungs.

Lizzie's jaw tightened. She tucked her hair behind her ears—both sides now. She was trying to hold onto that composed, self-righteous thing she did, but I could see it cracking.

"Well, there was a reason Dad gave it to me," she said, quieter this time. "Maybe he trusted me more."

I barked a dry laugh, full of venom. "Yeah, more like a final *fuck you* from beyond the grave. That man made it his life's mission to screw with me. Why not do it in death, too? Or maybe he was so far gone, he didn't even realize whose name he wrote down."

Her face flushed with frustration. "How was I supposed to know? I hadn't spoken to the man in years, and then suddenly I get a call saying I'm the proud new owner of his dive bar?"

"You could've asked, Lizzie. You could've picked up the damn phone instead of assuming you knew the whole story. Dad didn't even know I was married. Hell, I barely remembered it myself until Penny—" I stopped, raising both hands in surrender. "Forget it. Doesn't matter now. You know the truth."

I turned away, pretending to busy myself with the glasses again, needing the distance more than I wanted to admit.

The silence that followed was the loudest part of the conversation. Lizzie, for once, had nothing to say. No smug retort. No carefully phrased insult. Just... silence.

I didn't turn around when I said, "Aspen should be here any minute. You can run and hide like you usually do."

The soft rustle of her bag and the shifting of feet on the wood floor told me she'd taken the invitation. When the office door shut in the distance, I let out a breath I hadn't realized I'd been holding.

It felt good. Saying the things I'd swallowed for a while. I'd always masked it with sarcasm, treated our tension like some sibling rivalry, a game of verbal sparring. But that hadn't gotten me anywhere. Not with her. Not with this bar.

I braced my hands on the bar top, let my head hang between my arms, and took another long drag from the cigarette. It helped settle the edge still crackling in my chest.

This conversation was far from over. But for now, I needed a second to breathe.

Of course, the universe had perfect timing.

The front door creaked open and Aspen stepped inside. I didn't look at her right away—didn't need to. I heard her familiar sigh, the scrape of the stool as she slid into the very spot Lizzie had just left.

When I finally turned and looked up, her eyes went wide. Her brows pulled together in something that looked like worry, maybe even pain.

"What the hell happened to you?" she whispered.

CHAPTER 34

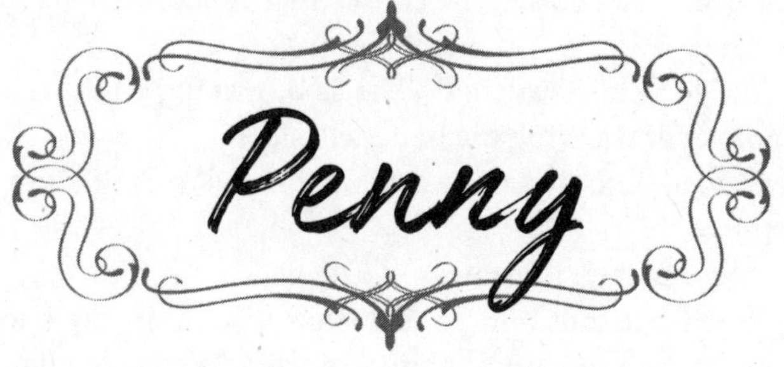

"Sandy," I called, dragging myself into Petal Pusher like a kid on the verge of a tantrum.

I needed to talk to someone—someone who at least had a sliver of understanding about this whole Mac situation. Sandy knew we'd once been a thing. She knew it had been secret. She knew we ended it. What she didn't know were the details. And right now, I regretted not sharing them sooner. Maybe if I had, I wouldn't feel so alone with all this.

I could've called Aspen, but I didn't have the emotional bandwidth to unravel the entire mess. I needed a soft place to land. A quick fix. Someone to help me piece my head back together before I spun out completely.

The same questions kept circling. Was it too soon to feel the way I was feeling about Mac? In every movie, the girl always waited until the final scene to forgive him. But me? I was ready to crash right now—ready to throw myself headfirst into *us* again. But was I really ready? Had I given myself enough time?

Sandy was my best bet.

She stood behind the counter, wrapping a bouquet in brown paper, her hands graceful and practiced, each movement filled with purpose. The way she worked was almost meditative.

"Hello, sweetie," she said, not missing a beat as she secured the bouquet.

I let my tote drop to the floor with a thud and sighed loudly. Loud enough to pull her attention. Her eyebrows pinched as she gave me a slow once-over, the concern settling into her face like a storm cloud.

"You don't look so good," she said, placing a sticker on the brown paper and sliding the bouquet aside.

I flopped onto the counter, folding myself in half like a soggy napkin.

"My brain feels like mush," I groaned.

She reached out and rubbed slow circles on my back, her touch grounding me more than I expected. We sat in a few beats of silence before she gently asked, "And you came to talk about it?"

I nodded, cheek mashed against the counter. The friction made a tiny squeaking noise that would've been funny if I didn't feel so emotionally drained.

"Want to head out back and talk in private? I can close up shop," she offered, removing her hand as I straightened.

"No," I sighed. "Can I help with bouquets instead? Emotions always feel easier when my hands are busy."

Fidgeting, picking, tapping—anything to let my hands distract my heart long enough to form a coherent sentence.

"Come around," Sandy said with a small wave, motioning me beside her.

She had a bucket full of fresh-cut blooms, all sorts of colors and textures spilling over the rim. I scanned the selection, eventually picking a few stems I thought looked pretty together.

Sandy had already laid out brown paper for me. I started trimming stems, arranging them mindlessly as my mouth opened, words tumbling out without much thought.

"I need advice. It's about Mac."

She hummed softly, enough to tell me she was listening but waiting for more.

"You know we were secretly seeing each other for a while," I said, placing down a few Gerbera daisies and fussing over their angle.

"Six months," she replied casually.

I scoffed. Of course she knew. If I ever doubted I'd come to the right place, that was proof enough.

"Yeah. Six. Then something happened and we ended it. But a few weeks ago, he came back, demanding a second chance."

"What happened?" she asked, her voice warm but firm. "If you want my advice, I need the full story."

I picked up a sprig of baby's breath, tucking it into the daisies as I spoke. "He was married. Never told me. I was at his house, in his flannel and my underwear, when a woman showed up and served him divorce papers."

"I beg your pardon?" Sandy turned toward me fully, her hand landing flat on the counter, those bright blue eyes locked onto mine.

"Exactly," I muttered. "So I left because I was pissed."

"And? What else?" she prodded.

I tilted my head, confused. What else?

"If it was just a secret hook-up, two people having fun," she said, "why was him being married in the past such a dealbreaker? What made you run before knowing the full story?"

I stared at her, stunned. I didn't think about it like that.

I turned back to the bouquet, rearranging it even though it didn't need it. The flowers became a stand-in for the chaos I felt in my chest.

"I was hurt," I admitted. "Betrayed. Embarrassed. My head was spinning and I didn't know what to believe."

"Because?" she prompted.

I'd already known but refused to say it to someone else out loud.

"Because I was falling for him," I whispered, throat tight. "And I was scared. I felt stupid for catching feelings for someone I was only supposed to be hooking up with."

I slammed a final flower into place a little too hard. A few petals drifted off like casualties to my anger.

"But that doesn't excuse him," I added quickly. "He didn't

call. He didn't text. And when he finally did, it was like nothing had even happened."

Sandy reached out, her fingers curling gently around my arm.

"No, it doesn't excuse him," she said softly. "But maybe... maybe you weren't just running because of what he did. Maybe, deep down, you were looking for an exit because you didn't know how he felt about you. Maybe sabotaging it felt safer than waiting around to be disappointed."

Her words hit me like a freight train.

My head tilted back slightly, eyes fluttering shut. The rush of reality was nearly too much for me to bear.

Sandy watched me for a long moment, her fingers still resting on my arm, grounding me.

"You know," she said quietly, her eyes softening, "you remind me a lot of myself at your age."

I blinked, surprised. "Me?"

She nodded, pulling her hand away and reaching beneath the counter for another roll of brown paper. "I was twenty-six, working in my aunt's flower shop. Thought I had it all figured out. I met this super cute guy through a supplier. He was charming in that dangerous kind of way. Said all the right things. Made me feel seen in a way I didn't even realize I was craving."

Her smile faded just a little. "We dated in secret for months. Not because we had to, but because I didn't want to ruin the fantasy by letting the real world in."

She glanced at me. "Sound familiar?"

I nodded, heart tight. Too familiar.

"One day, I showed up at his place with cinnamon rolls, his favorite." She gave a small laugh, full of regret and old wounds. "And when he opened the door, he was... holding a toddler."

My mouth dropped open. "Oh my God."

"Turns out, he had a child, which he conveniently forgot to mention. I was humiliated. I left without a word and never looked back. Didn't even give him the chance to explain. It hurt too much."

She paused to lay out more paper, her fingers still calm and steady. "But here's what I learned later. He wasn't a bad man, Penelope. He had his reasons. And I'd gotten so wrapped up in my hurt that I never gave myself the chance to hear the full story. I let pride drive the getaway car."

I stayed quiet, the weight of her words settling into my chest.

"Was he the one that got away?" I asked, almost afraid of the answer.

Sandy smiled, soft and fond. "For me, no, because I met Hank shortly after that, and that man was my whole world. Though I sometimes wonder what would've happened if I'd let my heart be just a little braver."

She turned fully toward me now, her eyes shining with quiet certainty. "What Mac did hurt you. And you have *every* right to be angry, to feel betrayed. But don't confuse your hurt with the whole truth. Ask yourself this, is your pride protecting you, or is it keeping you from something that could be real?"

I looked down at my half-finished bouquet, the petals now trembling in my hands.

"I don't want to get hurt again," I whispered.

Sandy reached for my hand and gave it a gentle squeeze. "No one does. But the best love stories? They're built on choosing to stay even after things fall apart. Not because it's easy but because it's worth it."

Her words hit a place I'd been avoiding for weeks.

I looked down at the bouquet again, watching how the soft cloud of baby's breaths curled around the bold daisies.

"I should also mention," I said, folding one side of the brown paper, then the other, and tucking the bottom beneath to create the perfect wrap, "I've been making him grovel for the last few weeks. Earn my trust back, inch by inch."

Sandy let out a full, delighted laugh—the kind that shook her shoulders and tilted her head back. "Oh, Penelope. Only you would have a man on his knees."

I shot her a playful wink. "Literally"

She grinned. “Oh, my. To be young again.”

We worked in quiet rhythm for a while, the gentle snips of scissors and rustling paper filling the space. I found comfort in the movement, in the way my hands kept busy even when my thoughts refused to sit still. But the question had been building in my chest, pushing harder with every heartbeat.

“Do you think it’s too soon?” I finally asked, pausing with my hand resting on the edge of the counter. “To give in? Should I stick to my word?”

Sandy looked at me, no judgment in her expression—just calm, steady warmth. “Too soon says who? You’re the one setting the standard here, sweetie. No one else. You created those boundaries because you needed them. Because he needed to work to earn his way back to you.”

I nodded slowly, still unsure.

“Do you think he’s done that?” she asked.

There it was—vulnerability, thick in my throat. I didn’t know. I was still living in the shadow of the unknown. But talking to Sandy cracked something open. Her story. Her kindness. It reminded me that love didn’t have to come perfectly packaged to be real.

“You don’t have to decide today,” she said softly. “Take a few days. Sit with everything we talked about. Ask yourself what you want, not just in this moment, but in the long run. You’re smart. Passionate. Beautiful inside and out. You already know the answer, you just have to trust yourself to hear it.”

Her words wrapped around me like a warm breeze. I felt something close to clarity—not certainty, not yet. There was peace, and maybe that was enough for now.

“But if it were me,” Sandy added with a mischievous grin, giving my shoulder a playful bump with hers, “I’d make him sweat it out a little longer. It’s more fun that way.”

I laughed, wrapping my arm around her shoulders and pressing a grateful kiss to her cheek. She smiled into it, leaning against me with the kind of warmth that made you feel instantly safe.

"Thank you, Sandy. For everything."

As we pulled apart, she brushed her hands off on her apron, and her smile stayed soft.

"Oh, I saw that flyer you posted at the grocery store this morning, about the bar," she said casually. "The crochet club would love to come out and support the library fundraiser."

"That would be amazing," I said, my heart lifting a little. "The more the merrier."

"You know who the ladies are hoping shows up, though?" she asked, her tone dipping into something gossipy and gleeful.

I hummed, slapping a sticker onto the paper to seal the bouquet. "Who?"

"That Logan boy. Especially if he gets up on that mechanical bull, shirtless." Sandy giggled like a teenager. "Those muscles on him..."

"Oh my God," I groaned with a laugh, shaking my head. "You're incorrigible."

"If I had my way, though," she said slyly, "I'd like to see that cute bartender hop up on the bull."

My head whipped toward her, eyes wide. "Wait... Mac?"

She burst into laughter and waved her hand. "Oh, no, no. The one with all the piercings."

"Dudley?"

"Yes!" she exclaimed, pointing a finger at me, delight lighting up her entire face. "That one's too handsome for his own good."

I couldn't help it—I laughed so hard my eyes watered.

"Unbelievable," I said, shaking my head, but feeling lighter than I had when I walked in.

CHAPTER 35

The bar was packed. Wall-to-wall bodies, sweat and laughter clinging to the air like cheap perfume. In all my years working here, I'd never seen anything like it. Penny's fundraiser wasn't just a success it was making fucking history.

Leave it to Penny Hudson to pull off an event like this with barely any lead time.

She'd pitched the idea to me a few nights ago, in her kitchen. I'd tried to resist, but she had a way of making no sound like yes. One look from her—those big, stubborn eyes—and I was done for.

She ran it by her boss the next day, and the board jumped at the chance. They wanted it done fast, to take advantage of the tourist spillover from the neighboring cities' rodeo season.

Penny handled every detail. I sat at her dining table one morning, coffee in hand, and watched her work her magic. She demolished every half-formed idea I offered with something sharper, smarter, better. Her brow was furrowed in concentration, tongue tucked between her lips as her fingers flew across the keyboard like lightning. I'd never been so turned on by logistics.

Now, here I was bartending her masterpiece.

I was damn good at my job. I'd slung drinks on the Vegas Strip, but nothing could've prepared me for the crowd crammed into the bar tonight. This small town had never seen action like this.

The mechanical bull was the main event, of course. Against my better judgment, I'd let her rent the damn thing. But I had to admit—it was genius. That, and the themed drink menu we came up with.

Penny even made sure Jolie, Dudley, and I had custom shirts for the night. Mine read *Ride of Your Life*. I'd snipped the sides clean off, exposing every inch of ink down my ribs and the sharp cut of my torso. Paired it with dark bootcut jeans, my well-worn cowboy boots, and a cigarette tucked behind one ear.

Somehow, she even roped in Logan, Boone, and Rhodes to help work the floor. Better yet, she had them walking around *shirtless*, cowboy hats on, passing out shots like they were straight out of a raunchy fantasy.

If one more woman tried to climb Boone like a tree, I wouldn't be surprised if he made a sign that said, *Happily Taken and She's Over There* and pointed it directly at Aspen.

Speaking of, Aspen, Theo, and Ellie were parked at the bar, laughing and drinking while the guys navigated the crowd like cattle through a gate.

Women were slipping dollar bills into the waistbands of their jeans as they passed, putting on a show.

Somehow, in all this madness, all I could think about was Penny.

Tonight, she had her hair down, her own cowboy hat tipped low as she moved through the bar with the kind of casual confidence that could kill a man. Her shirt—if you could even call it that—was cropped high enough to drive me insane, and her boots hit just below the knee, hugging her long, toned legs like a damn dream.

I was fucking putty.

Every step she took, every glance she tossed my way, every teasing wink. It was a slow, torturous game she was playing. And I was her willing victim.

"Some of these women are *savages*," Rhodes muttered, stepping up to the service counter and dropping his tray like it had personally offended him.

The speakers pumped out a steady country beat that pulsed through the old wooden walls, vibrating beneath our boots.

I grabbed the red tip bucket from behind the bar and held it out toward Rhodes with a grin. "Come on, pay up. The library thanks you for your service."

Rhodes sighed, reached into the waistband of his jeans, and pulled out a wad of cash. After dropping every last dollar into the bucket, he removed the cowboy hat he'd borrowed from Boone, swiping at the sweat on his brow before raking a hand through his damp hair, and slapping it back on.

"These ladies from the crochet club keep grabbing my ass," Logan said, sliding in beside Rhodes and looking both exhausted and vaguely traumatized. "I can feel their little hands *pinching* me."

I barked a laugh, and so did Rhodes.

Logan dropped a few more bills into the bucket with a shake of his head. "This better get Penny back on your side."

"Yeah," Rhodes added, smirking. "I still don't know how the three of us got roped into your fuck-up."

I had the best damn friends a man could ask for—something I maybe hadn't always appreciated the way I should have. Watching them strut around this bar, getting harassed by women twice their age while flaunting their ranch-built bodies? Yeah, I was damn lucky.

"I'll buy you all a round for your troubles," I offered, smirking.

"Cheap bastard," Logan muttered, resting his forearms on the bar.

I chuckled, tugged the cigarette from behind my ear, and turned to light it. A few quick drags, and I exhaled into the air, letting the nicotine settle the restless hum beneath my skin.

Boone was the next to join us, squeezing into the service space and leaning a hand on the bar as he scanned the crowd.

"I'm pretty sure Aspen's enjoying this way too much," he said, nodding toward the girls at the far end of the bar.

All three of them—Aspen, Theo, and Ellie—looked right at

us, winked, and blew kisses.

"She is," I said. "I brought them their drinks earlier. Pretty sure I saw a tally sheet in front of them."

If I had to guess, one for every time one of the guys was hit on by someone.

"Where's Penny anyway?" Logan asked, glancing around.

I shrugged.

I hadn't seen her in a while, if I were being honest. She'd been working the room like a pro. She was handing out raffle tickets at the door, checking in on tables, laughing, smiling... making sure everyone felt seen.

But now?

I stood on my toes, scanning the crowd, but between the crush of bodies and the sea of cowboy hats, spotting her was impossible.

"You know what you need to do," Rhodes said, shooting me a look.

I tilted my head. "What?"

"Get on that bull."

"Oh, hell no," I said immediately, taking a sharp inhale off my smoke.

"Rhodes has a point," Boone chimed in, nodding. "You want to make a statement? Prove something? That'll do it."

"Damn right," Rhodes said, slapping a hand against Boone's chest. "Didn't you pull that move with Aspen?"

Boone grinned. "Worked like a charm."

"Let's go!" Dudley's voice cut through the noise behind me. I spun to find him grinning like a devil, motioning for me to move. I flipped him off, and he blew me a kiss in return.

I turned back to my friends. "You guys need more shots?"

They all groaned and nodded in unison.

As much as I didn't want to get up on that bull and make a spectacle of myself, I knew I had to. They were right, it was time to make myself a spectacle in the name of impressing the girl.

I clapped Dudley on both shoulders, leaning in close.

"You two hold down the bar for a minute?"

He didn't miss a beat. "We've been holding it down for the last ten while you were running your mouth. What's a few more?" His tone was serious, but the smirk he wore was anything but.

I grinned, snuffed out my cigarette in the nearest tray, and ducked around the back of the bar. My boots thudded against the worn wooden floor as I pushed through the thick press of bodies, making my way toward the bull in the far corner.

She was already there.

Penny.

Laughing with a group of girls, her smile wide and wild, her cheeks flushed from whiskey and heat. She tossed her hair over her shoulder like she knew damn well how magnetic she was.

Part of me wanted to make a scene. The jealous, reckless part, the part that still felt the sting of not having her the way I used to. I wanted every guy in the bar to know she wasn't theirs to look at like that. She was mine, whether she admitted it yet or not.

I stalked over to the guy manning the controls and said, "I'm up next."

He gave me a slow nod, then motioned toward the bull.

Stretching my neck side to side, I stepped onto the platform just as a buzzer split through the air, signaling the next rider. The crowd shifted, turning toward the mat like they knew something good was coming. I swung my leg over the cold, fake hide of the bull and settled into position. One hand gripped the rope. The other stayed loose, raised in the air.

Then I heard it.

Her laugh.

Somehow it cut through the music, through the crowd noise, slicing right into my chest. I didn't look at her yet, I needed all my focus to be on me and this bull.

The operator flipped the switch, and the bull lurched beneath me. I clenched my jaw, shifting my weight.

I looked up and immediately found her in the crowd, a big mistake.

Penny stood near the edge, arms folded under her chest, head tilted, mouth parted like she was caught between amusement and something else. Something hotter. Her eyes locked with mine, and there it was.

Possession. Challenge. Hunger.

I brought my attention back. My hips rolled with the bull's rhythm, every movement calculated, controlled. It shifted beneath me, jerking into a hard spin, the world blurring for a beat before snapping straight again. I stayed grounded, locked in.

Facing the crowd again, I winked at Penny and sent her a dimpled smirk before I let go.

Both hands shot into the air, fingers spread wide, a show of confidence that wasn't entirely fake. It was strength, yeah, but it was also pure adrenaline. I clenched with my core, kept myself anchored with nothing but muscle and the burning need to impress her.

The bull kicked harder, more unpredictable now, testing my balance. I moved with it, riding each surge like it was second nature. Every twist of my torso, every snap of my hips, was a silent message. Every flex of my body was aimed at *her.*

Then the music changed, and I laughed.

"Save a Horse (Ride a Cowboy)" blasted through the speakers like the universe had a sense of humor. The crowd roared around me—cheering, whooping—but none of it touched me.

I was too focused on her.

As the bull slowed for a beat, prepping for its next jolt, I shifted my weight and flipped around, now riding backward. A collective gasp echoed from the crowd, just before the machine bucked again, hard. I leaned into it, pressing my back against the curve of the bull like I was daring it to throw me.

It did.

One brutal spin and I was airborne, landing hard on the mat with a thud that knocked the air right out of my lungs.

But hell, if it wasn't worth it.

Applause erupted around me, and cheering voices filled the

space. The rush still surged in my blood as I got to my feet, breath coming fast, heart slamming against my ribs. I threw my hands into the air and bowed, a slow grin spreading across my face.

I wasn't looking for cheers. I was only looking for *her.*

Penny was walking toward me with a smirk, radiating confidence.

Every step was deliberate, like she was stalking prey with that same deadly sway in her hips that drove me insane.

"You trying to prove something?" she asked, voice low and rough at the edges.

I grinned. "Depends. Did it work?"

Penny scoffed, but I caught the flicker of heat in her eyes before she could hide it. My hand came up, almost without thought, brushing along the curve of her jaw. If anyone was watching—which I knew they were—they'd know what I was saying without me having to spell it out.

Mine.

My chest rose and fell too fast, my breath still catching from the ride. But then I realized hers was, too. We were matched beat for beat, like the electricity between us had synced our pulse.

She stared up at me, pupils blown wide, and for one wild second, I thought this was it. I was going to kiss her, right there in front of everyone.

Claim her.

But she pulled back with a grin that was all teeth and challenge.

"I guess it's my turn."

Penny took a few slow steps back, her eyes not leaving mine. Then she turned, striding straight to the bull operator. She leaned over his table, both hands braced on the surface as she spoke.

My jaw slackened as I stared after her.

Her turn?

Was she really about to get on that bull?

I'd ridden it to prove something to her, to myself, to every bastard who looked at her like they had a shot. But Penny? She didn't have a damn thing to prove. She already had me. All of me.

My heart.

My soul.

My entire fucking existence rested in the palm of her hand.

With a flick of her wrist, she turned and walked toward the bull. Then, like she was born for it, she mounted the mechanical beast in one smooth, effortless motion, swinging her leg over and settling in as though she'd done it a hundred times before.

I left the mats, standing off to the side with my arms crossed, legs braced wide. My chest tightened as I watched her adjust in her seat. I peeled my gaze away for half a second and instantly regretted it.

Like flies to shit, men of every age lined the barrier now, leaning in with wide eyes and slack jaws. Their gazes glued to her—arched back, bare legs, the dangerous little smirk tugging at her lips.

I clenched my jaw, heat simmering beneath my skin like I was the one about to buck and throw someone across the bar. My gaze snapped back to her just as she gave a small nod to the operator.

The bull jolted to life, starting in a slow, taunting spin. Penny gripped the strap with one hand, her other arm raised in the air like she'd done it before.

Maybe she had because every eye, every breath, every beat of the music belonged to her now.

As the bull picked up speed, her hips began to roll, grinding in a motion that was all confidence and heat. She didn't just ride the bull; she commanded it. She moved in rhythm, like her body was built for this. For temptation.

I swallowed hard, throat dry, a thousand images flooding my brain. All of them of her riding me like that. That same rhythm. That same fire in her eyes.

Penny reached for her hat. With one smooth motion, she pulled it off, tossing her head back as her hair tumbled down her back in waves. She shook it out, wild and free, her smile dazzling and untamed. The kind of smile that made men stupid.

Including me.

The bull spun again, and she barely moved—solid, fierce, beautiful. Her chest puffed out, shoulders thrown back as she leaned forward and braced herself. The pathetic excuse for a shirt she wore clung to her, and when she arched, her breasts bounced in a way that nearly made my knees buckle.

I had to take a long, deep breath to keep from losing it completely.

If I glanced to the right, I knew what I'd see—those bastards drooling over her, eyes fixed where they didn't belong. While Penny might've been showing off, I was seconds from losing every ounce of self-control I had.

She was mine.

And the minute she hit that mat, I was done watching.

With one final jolt, the bull threw her. Penny flew, landing flat on her back, her laughter cutting through the roar of the crowd. She lay there for just a moment, breathless, grinning like she'd won.

She had won.

I was already moving.

Two long strides and I was at her side, bending down and scooping her up, flinging her over my shoulder like I'd just claimed my prize. The crowd erupted, louder than ever, and she threw her fists into the air like a champion.

And hell, she was.

My champion.

My temptation.

My undoing.

I carried her through the bar, past the stunned stares, the laughter, the hoots. Dudley gave me a mock salute, and somewhere in the background, Rhodes slid behind the bar and Aspen headed toward the crowd, like they'd been ready for this moment all night.

Penny didn't even try to fight me. She laughed—loud, full of joy—and clung to me like she knew exactly where this was headed.

Up the stairs.

To my apartment.

To *us.*

With one hard kick, I shoved the door open and stepped inside.

Then I slammed it shut behind us.

CHAPTER 36

The second the door slammed shut, I dropped Penny to her feet. She landed with a soft thud, barely catching her balance before her hands were in my hair and her mouth crashed into mine.

No words. No hesitation.

I devoured her like she was oxygen and I'd been suffocating. Our mouths met in a kiss that was starved and reckless, all tongue and teeth and desperation. It was the kind of kiss that tasted like everything we'd never said, like time lost and weeks wasted.

I gripped her waist, fingers digging in as if I could anchor her to me. One backward step and she dragged me with her, her palms cupping my jaw, keeping me close as she opened for me.

My tongue slid past her lips, finding hers like it belonged there because it *did*. We moved together like a melody we'd never forgotten, like the rhythm of us had never skipped a beat.

There was no fear. No doubt.

Just need.

Heavy, soul-deep, bone-shaking need.

The room filled with the sound of our ragged breathing, her body pressed so tightly to mine that I could feel the thump of her heartbeat echoing against my chest.

I slid my hands lower, palms coasting over the curve of her ass, lifting her in one swift motion. She jumped willingly, legs wrapping around my waist like second nature.

My whole body thrummed, electric with want. It coursed through me, thick and hot and endless.

Penny's lips moved against mine, her tongue tracing the edge of my bottom lip as I carried her across the room. Each step was a thud of boot on hardwood until I pressed her back against the wall. The force rattled the picture frame above her head, but she didn't flinch.

She smiled.

"You're my undoing, Pen," I muttered, my breath ragged against her mouth.

She gave a low hum of approval that vibrated straight through me.

I pulled back just enough to breathe, to look at her. Her chest rose and fell in sync with mine, her lips kiss-swollen and parted, cheeks flushed pink and trailing down her chest in the most distracting way. Her shirt clung to her curves, and the heat in her eyes nearly leveled me.

God, she was beautiful.

A wicked smirk tugged at my lips as I stepped back and gently set her on her feet. She wobbled slightly, and her eyes dropped—zeroing in on the thick press of my cock against my jeans.

"See what you do to me, Trouble?" I rasped, dragging my palm over the front of my jeans. "You on that damn bull..."

I shook my head, needing space but already hating the distance. "The way you rode it. All I could think about was you on top of me, moving like that."

Penny's jaw had slackened, those gorgeous brown eyes wide, glassy, like she was seeing me—really seeing me. Her mouth parted, but she didn't speak.

"And then," I growled, stepping back into her space, "watching every guy in that bar eye-fuck you like they wanted the same thing I did..."

I reached out and wrapped my hand gently but firmly around her throat, just enough to make sure her attention never strayed. Her pulse fluttered beneath my fingers, and her eyes darkened.

"Over. My. Dead. Fucking. Body."

That glimmer of challenge sparked in her gaze, lighting her up like a fuse. Her lids lowered, sultry and slow, and she bit her bottom lip hard enough that it made my cock twitch.

Then, with that slight head tilt that always drove me wild, she asked, voice breathy and full of defiance.

"And what makes you think I'm yours to claim like that?"

"In every fucking universe, every alternate dimension, you are *mine*, Penelope. My heart beats for *you*."

My soul was hers.

"You don't understand the effect you have on me," I murmured, leaning in until our lips brushed, just a whisper of contact, a promise of more.

Then I kissed her again—slow, deep, claiming. She melted into it, her body softening like she'd been holding her breath for weeks and finally exhaled.

Her fingers curled into my shirt. Her mouth opened beneath mine. And for a long, charged second, it felt like we were the only two people on earth.

She was the one who finally pulled back. My hand slid from her throat, giving her space even though every nerve in my body screamed to keep her close.

"I never had any intention of going home with anyone else," she confessed.

Those words hit me like a punch to the gut—and lower. My cock throbbed behind my zipper, already hard, already aching. She had no idea how deep that truth cut, or how badly I needed to hear it.

Or maybe she did.

Because in that moment, everything between us was left bare. No more pretending. No more slow burns. Just fire, about to rage out of control.

I snapped.

I was going to wreck her in the way she needed. In the way only *I* could.

"Take off your clothes," I ordered, voice gravel thick. "I need you naked and needy for my cock."

The softness in her eyes sharpened, turning devilish. She was all in.

She started with her boots, pulling them off with deliberate slowness, the heavy thud of them hitting the floor sounding like thunder in my veins.

Then, without breaking eye contact, she reached for the hem of her shirt and peeled it over her head. Her bra—black lace, nearly see-through—did nothing to hide the hard peaks of her nipples. The silver glint of her piercings teased me, mocked me. My mouth watered.

I leaned forward slightly, tongue running along my lower lip. *Jesus.*

She reached behind her to undo the clasp, but I raised a finger. "No. Leave it on. For me."

She dropped her hands with a smirk and moved to her shorts. Her fingers played at the button, then popped it open with a slow, sultry tease. She shimmied out of them, hips swaying, dragging the denim down inch by torturous inch before kicking them aside.

My girl.

Still in her bra and panties, Penny stood proud—powerful and fucking divine.

I turned the nearest dining chair, dropping into it like a king on a throne. Spreading my legs wide, I crooked a finger.

"Come here."

She walked over, stopping just short, waiting like a good girl for her next command.

God, I loved this game.

I'd loved being at her mercy, but this? *This* was different. This was her trusting me to take the lead. And the control, the power of it, rushed through my veins like lightning.

I tapped my thigh, watching the way her eyes darkened at the sound of a tap. "Come on, Pen," I said with a wicked grin. "Take a seat on Daddy's lap."

She rolled her eyes, a breathy laugh escaping her lips—but then she moved, stepping in close, straddling me.

Her thighs bracketed my hips, and she sank down, her center landing right on top of my cock with a pressure that made me groan. Through the thin barrier of our clothes, I could feel her heat, her slick arousal already soaking through her panties.

She rolled her hips once. Slow. Deliberate. My hands flexed against her, fingers digging into her skin.

"You're playing with fire," I warned, voice low and rough.

"Good," she whispered, leaning in to trail her lips along my jaw. "I want to burn."

Fuck me.

She kissed just below my ear, her breath hot, her hips moving in tight, lazy circles. I was seconds from combusting. Every grind sent a jolt of pleasure straight through my spine. I could feel the wet heat of her through my jeans.

"Penny..." I growled, my head falling back against the chair as she rocked her hips again, her lace-covered center dragging against my hard length. "You keep that up, and I'm going to come in my damn jeans like a teenager, *again*."

She gave a breathless laugh, but her eyes were molten.

"You think I haven't thought about this?" she said, nipping at my lip. "Thought about riding you like this? Making you beg?"

"Christ," I breathed, snapping my head forward and kissing her again. This time it was wild. Open-mouthed, tongues tangled, teeth clashing. Raw. Messy. Perfect.

My hands slid up her back, finding the clasp of her bra. "Last warning," I said, against her lips. "I take this off, I'm not stopping until you scream."

Penny's eyes flared, her lips curving. "Do it."

The clasp snapped open with one flick, and I pulled the lace from her shoulders, letting it fall between us. My breath caught.

Fuck, she was beautiful.

The piercings teased me, her nipples tight and begging for my mouth. I bent forward, wrapping one arm around her back while the other came up to cup her breast. My thumb brushed over the peak and she gasped, arching into my hand.

Then I sucked one into my mouth.

She let out a strangled moan, fingers threading through my hair, holding me close as I licked and sucked and flicked over the metal until she was panting, trembling against me.

I moved to the other, giving it the same attention, while my hand slid between us, trailing down her stomach, slipping beneath the waistband of her panties.

The moment my fingers touched her, I groaned. "So fucking wet, Pen."

"Only for you," she breathed, rocking into my hand.

I teased her, then pressed one finger inside her, watching her eyes flutter shut as she gasped. Her hips rolled against my hand, needing more.

"I could watch you like this forever," I said, adding a second finger, curling them just right. Her walls clenched, her breath coming faster, sweat breaking across her skin.

Her forehead fell to mine, lips brushing. "Mac..."

That whisper? That need in her voice? It undid me.

I stood, lifting her effortlessly in my arms, her legs still wrapped around my waist, and strode to the bed, leaving a trail of heat and urgency in our wake.

"I'm not stopping until you forget every man who's ever looked at you tonight," I said, pushing through the sliding door. "And until you remember exactly who you belong to."

She tightened her grip on me, lips at my ear, voice wrecked with desire.

"Then what are you waiting for?"

I tossed her onto the bed, and Penny let out a breathless, high-pitched laugh that sent a rush straight to my groin.

"Now it's your turn," she said, propping herself up on her elbows to watch me with those dark, wicked eyes.

It was my turn to strip for her.

I wasn't one for theatrics. No slow tease or dramatic flair like she'd given me. I kicked off my boots, then reached behind my neck and pulled my shirt over my head in one fluid motion.

Her eyes tracked every inch of me like she was memorizing it all over again—starting at my chest, lingering on the tattoos she'd traced so many nights before, until her gaze dropped lower.

With deliberate care, I undid my belt. The metal buckle clinked softly as I slid it free and let the leather glide through my belt loops. I held it in one hand, letting it dangle for a second, running my palm slowly along the worn strap.

A thought took shape.

Judging by the sly, knowing curl of Penny's lips, she knew exactly what I was thinking.

Without hesitation, she sat up straight and held her hands out in front of her. "Tie me up."

I chuckled, low and rough in my throat. "Not so fast."

If I were using this belt, there would be more to it than a simple binding.

Gripping it in one hand, I stalked toward her, stopping at the edge of the bed. I bent down until we were eye to eye. "Do you trust me?"

Her answer came without pause. She nodded and lowered her hands, her lips parted slightly with anticipation.

"Good. Then stand up," I ordered, stepping back. "Bend over the bedframe."

Penny rose and stepped off the bed, gliding toward the end where she folded at the waist, laying her upper body across the wooden frame. Her toes barely touched the ground, her ass raised perfectly in the air. She was an offering I didn't deserve but would take anyway.

"Good girl," I murmured, my voice thick as I approached her from behind.

My first order of business: get those damn panties off.

Looping the belt over my neck to free my hands, I slid my thumbs into the waistband and dragged them down her legs, slow and purposeful. When they pooled at her feet, I picked them up and tucked them into my back pocket.

For safekeeping, of course.

I dropped a trail of soft kisses along the curve of her backside. Her skin trembled under my mouth, goosebumps forming beneath each press of my lips. I knew her ass wouldn't be thanking me after what I had planned.

Straightening, I slid the belt from around my neck and wrapped it loosely in my hands.

"Now, Pen," I said, letting her name roll off my tongue like a promise. "There are rules."

She hummed in acknowledgment, already breathless.

"One, you don't move. If you sit up or try to stop me, there will be punishment." I ran my palm over the curve of her ass, circling gently, admiring the view. "Two, I want to hear you. Loud. No one else is here, I need you to scream for me."

"And if I don't?" she asked, her voice laced with that signature Penny sass.

I smirked. "You're a smart girl."

I grabbed her ass, watching the way it bounced beneath my hand, and let out a quiet growl of approval. "Three, if it's too much, you use our word. Do you remember it?"

Penny laughed, bold and unbothered. "Mercy."

"Good girl," I said, tracing the belt slowly along the dip of her lower back. "*Stop* won't work tonight. If you want mercy, you'll have to beg for it."

She was mine now—bent, waiting—and I planned to give her everything she didn't even know she craved.

I let the belt slide from my hand and rest it gently on her back in a warning, a promise, a weight she could feel.

"Count for me," I said, stepping in closer, my hand already twitching with anticipation.

She didn't look back. Just gave the smallest nod, bracing her forearms against the bed, her back arched beautifully.

I brought the belt down—firm, sharp, not cruel. The sound cracked through the room, followed by a soft gasp.

"One," she breathed.

I bit back a groan. Her voice, her body, and everything about her begged me to lose control. But not yet. I was going to make this last.

Another strike. Her skin warmed and bloomed with color.

"Two."

Each number made my blood roar louder in my ears. She was unraveling in front of me bit by bit, and I was the only one allowed to see her like this.

I gave her two more. I reached my hand down, soothing between each, letting her feel the contrast—pleasure, pain, worship.

"Three... four."

She was squirming now, her thighs pressing together, trying to relieve the pressure building between them.

"Pen," I warned, voice low.

"Sorry," she whispered, her hips stilling.

I smirked and gave her the fifth, just a little harder.

"Five," she moaned.

"Mm-hmm." I leaned over her, my chest brushing her back as I reached around and cupped one breast, teasing her nipples. "You sound so sweet when you're obedient."

She let out a whimper and pushed back against me, seeking more contact.

I tossed the belt to the floor. She'd had enough of that for now. My hand smoothed down her spine, slow and reverent, before slipping between her legs.

"Dripping," I murmured against the shell of her ear. "You like being my good girl, don't you?"

"Yes," she said without hesitation, breath shaky.

I slipped a finger inside her— slow, deep. She clenched around me instantly.

Then another.

And another.

She cried out as I worked her perfect pussy. I grinned, curling my fingers just right as I whispered, "That's it. Let go for me."

I worked her with deliberate rhythm, using my other hand to grip her hip and keep her steady. She was trembling beneath my body, still pressed against her back, every moan a drug that pushed me closer to my edge.

When she came, she shattered—back arched, voice echoing off the walls as her body clamped around my fingers.

"That's it, scream my name. Who's making you come, Penelope?"

"Fuck, Mac!"

With one more shove, her body collapsed.

I pulled out gently, licking her release from my knuckles as I stepped back.

"You're not done," I said. "Not even close."

With a light slap to her ass, I helped her stand, then lifted her.

Her legs dangled over my arms, her grip around my neck as her lips sought mine with a desperate hunger.

I carried her to the bed and laid her down in the center, spreading her out like a gift.

My knees hit the mattress, and I leaned over her, pressing a kiss to her lips, then her throat, between her breasts, down her stomach.

When I looked up, she was staring at me, pupils blown, lips parted, skin flushed and glistening.

"Ride or die, right?" I said, my voice rough.

"Every damn time," she whispered.

And then I showed her just how far I was willing to go.

I hooked my fingers into the waistband of my jeans, watching her eyes widen as I shoved them down, followed by my boxers. My cock sprang free, thick and painfully hard, already slick at the tip from how worked up she had me.

Penny's gaze locked on it, her tongue darting out to wet her lips like she was starving for me.

"You want this?" I asked, voice low, jaw clenched as I crawled over her.

Her legs parted on instinct, inviting me in.

"I always wanted you," she whispered, breathless. "Only you."

I groaned, positioning myself between her thighs, one hand braced by her head while the other guided me to her entrance. I dragged my tip through her wetness, just enough to tease, to make her squirm and curse under her breath.

"Mac," she warned, hips bucking.

I pushed in an inch, then pulled out.

Her eyes snapped open, pleading. "Please."

That word from her lips? Fuck.

With one thrust, I buried myself deep. Stretching her. Filling her completely.

We both gasped—like we'd just come up for air after drowning.

"Goddamn," I growled, holding still as her walls clenched around me. "You feel like heaven, Pen."

She clutched at my shoulders, nails digging into my skin as I pulled back and thrust again. Harder. Deeper. Setting a rhythm that had the bedframe knocking the wall behind us with every movement.

Penny met every thrust with a roll of her hips, her body clinging to mine like she was made to take me. Our breaths came out ragged, heavy, the room thick with heat and want.

"You're mine," I said through gritted teeth, eyes locked on hers.

"Yours," she panted, voice wrecked with need.

I lowered my mouth to her chest, pulling one pierced nipple into my mouth and sucking hard, feeling her shudder beneath me.

She was close. I could feel it in the way her thighs trembled, the way she held her breath before each moan escaped.

"Come for me again," I demanded, biting her gently before kissing up to her mouth. "Let go, Trouble."

She arched beneath me, body tensing. Her hands fisted in the sheets as her orgasm ripped through her, raw and beautiful. She cried out my name like a prayer and a curse all at once.

That did it.

I slammed into her once, twice more, before I came hard, growling into her neck as I spilled inside her, every muscle locked tight, holding onto her like I'd never let go.

We stayed tangled, skin to skin, our hearts thudding in perfect sync.

She cupped my cheek, brushing her thumb across the stubble there.

"I never stopped wanting you," she whispered.

My throat closed around the lump her words pulled up.

"Good," I murmured, pressing a kiss to her temple. "Because I've never once stopped being yours."

CHAPTER 37

Stretching my arms over my head, I arched my back with a soft sigh, the stiffness in my muscles easing just a little. The bed was warm, the blankets cocooning me like I was a butterfly about to emerge from a long slumber.

I felt recharged, clear-headed, and light in a way I hadn't felt in ages. I'd slept like the dead, blissfully unaware of anything beyond the heat of the man beside me.

After round one, Mac and I both passed out, tangled in each other's arms, laughter still clinging to the air. But somewhere in the middle of the night, I'd woken to the delicious feel of Mac's hard length pressed against my ass and just like that, round two had begun.

That second time... he'd wrecked me. Slow, deep, unrelenting.

Even now, my body hummed from the memory, muscles deliciously sore. I couldn't stop touching him, couldn't get enough, like we were clawing our way back to what we'd lost. But even with the hunger, there was something more I craved.

Mac's arms were wrapped around me, my back pressed snug against his chest. He wore nothing but his boxers, and I had on one of his old T-shirts. Sure, I still had a drawer here with some of my things, but I didn't want them. I wanted to wear something that smelled like him, something that felt like him.

Soft lips grazed the curve of my neck, just behind my ear, in a kiss I knew by heart. I let out a content hum, leaning into the tenderness.

"I don't think I have it in me to go again," I murmured, eyes still closed. "Between the bull ride and then you..."

Mac groaned, nuzzling deeper into my neck, his need clear in the way his body pressed to mine.

"You put the bull first on that list?" he teased, flipping me onto my back, hovering over me now with that crooked grin I could never resist.

"Your point?" I smirked, a slow wink sent his way.

But just as the air filled with our laughter, something unexpected tugged in my chest. A flicker of unease. A memory. The way things fell apart that morning not so long ago.

I swallowed hard, forcing the feeling back down. This wasn't that. This was now. Different. *New.*

His hand found my cheek, grounding me. My eyes fluttered open to find his warm brown gaze on mine, steady and soft. He knew. Somehow, he knew when I drifted too far.

I gave him a soft smile and cupped his face in both hands, lifting just enough to brush my lips against his.

"I hope you know," he murmured against my mouth, "I'm not giving this up. Now that I've had you in my bed again, you're never leaving."

My heart flipped at the rawness in his voice. I looped my arms around his neck, my legs wrapping around his waist like they belonged there.

I didn't want to leave. I wanted to stay right here, tangled up with him in the quiet afterglow like we were a picture frozen in time. But I couldn't say that. The words were true, but they felt too big, too heavy to give voice to.

So instead, I did what I always did when the truth got tangled in my chest. I kissed him again.

Mac parted his lips, letting me in, our tongues sliding together in a rhythm that made my pulse race all over again. Without breaking the kiss, he stood with me clinging to him, every inch of my skin glued to his as he carried us from the bed to the small kitchenette.

He set me down gently on the counter, and I grinned against his mouth.

"I had a thought," I said, breathless.

That made him pull back slightly, his hands braced on the counter, caging me in.

Mac quirked a brow, smirking. "And what's that, Penelope?"

"Where's Angus?"

Mac let out a laugh that shook his whole chest as he stepped back, arms crossing. "You're sitting half-naked on my counter, and *that's* what pulls your focus? My dog?"

I shrugged, legs swinging like I hadn't just derailed a hot moment. "I miss him."

"My guess? Our friends saw the writing on the wall last night and decided to intervene. I mean, did you see how fast Rhodes ducked behind the bar?" Mac chuckled, shaking his head in disbelief.

He turned to the fridge, and my eyes followed every move—the way his boxers hung low on his hips, the tousled mess of his hair, even messier now from our night together.

I bit back a smile and looked away, tucking the gesture away for just me as Mac poured orange juice into two glasses.

"I know," I said softly. "It's like he was waiting for that moment."

Mac nodded, handing me a glass and leaning against the counter beside me.

"Speaking of last night..." I took a sip of juice, pausing just long enough for effect. "I wouldn't be totally against doing it again."

Mac raised a brow, the corner of his mouth lifting. "Which part? The sex, or me spanking you with my belt?"

"Both," I replied with a wink.

He groaned, tipping his head back like he was already imagining round three. "Noted. Maybe next time, we find out what else we're willing to try."

He said it with confidence, but there was a flicker of something cautious in his expression—like he was testing the waters, trying to gauge how far I'd let him in. How much I still trusted him.

We'd already explored a lot together—bondage, spit, and my favorite, breath play. But none of it worked without trust. And once, Mac had been the only person I trusted enough to let take me that far.

It wasn't just anyone I'd let choke me to the edge and bring me back—again and again.

Perhaps I was willing to go deeper again.

"We'll see," I said, letting the words hang between us.

Mac smiled and kissed the tip of my nose before turning back to the counter. "What can I make you for breakfast? Waffles? They're the frozen kind, but still."

"Waffles sound amazing," I said. "Blueberry?"

He shot me a playful glare as he opened the freezer. "That's the only kind I keep."

As he got to work, I slipped down from the counter, juice in hand, and wandered toward his bookshelf. The library books he checked out a few weeks ago caught my eye.

Curious, I ran my fingers along the spines and smiled when I saw a familiar title.

I pulled it free and walked back toward the kitchen with the book in the air.

Curiosity gnawed at me. He didn't seem like the romance type, really the book type in general.

"Why did you check these out?"

Mac glanced over his shoulder, did a double-take, and then turned fully to face me. There was no smirk. No teasing glint in his eyes.

"For you, Pen," he said simply.

The book in my hand suddenly felt like it weighed ten pounds.

"I needed help, I needed to get into your head. And the best way to do that? Romance books," he said, his voice low but steady.

For a second, I couldn't quite process what was coming out of his mouth.

He'd gone to the library and checked out *romance* novels.

Because he didn't know what to do.

Because he wanted to understand *me*.

"Have you...read them?" I asked, gently setting the book down on the dining room table.

"Yup," he said with a nod. "Every single one."

Then he took a step toward me and pointed at the book in question. "That one? I read twice."

Fuck.

My heart did cartwheels in my chest, flipping and fluttering like it didn't know which way was up—followed by a warm wave that prickled across my skin, like my body couldn't decide whether to blush or break down.

The walls I'd so carefully rebuilt around my heart? Obliterated. Gone in a single, quiet confession.

This man—this complicated, maddening, big-hearted man—had rented out my favorite books. Not just read them, but studied them. Looking for clues, for answers, for ways to love me better.

No one had ever done that before.

No one had ever *listened* with such intent.

The groceries in my fridge.

The fresh roses.

My favorite books lined up neatly on his shelf.

And those damn blueberry waffles in his freezer.

Every single thing screamed, *I see you.*

And it was... too much.

Not in a bad way. But in the kind of way that made it hard to breathe through the swell of emotion gathering in my chest. I needed time. I needed space. I needed my best friends to help me make sense of this.

The pop of the toaster made both of us flinch. Mac turned toward the sound, pausing as he exhaled a shaky breath.

He didn't say anything, just focused on the waffles.

It was the perfect move because if he'd come any closer, if he'd touched me or looked at me with those warm brown eyes, I might have crumbled.

Right here in this tiny kitchen, I felt it happening.

I was falling in love with Mac Ridley. Again.

And I wasn't sure my heart was ready.

CHAPTER 38

Mac

Get the hell over here now

What? Omg is everything okay? I'm getting ready to go to Aspen's

Do you need me to swing by before?

Mac?

Mac

If you said any other plans besides going to Aspen's, I would've taken you up on that

So it isn't an emergency?

Mac

I'm starving... and I'm craving you

Mac and I were back at it—full steam ahead. We couldn't seem to keep our hands off each other. Ever since that night, my body craved him like a drug, my skin humming with the memory of his touch.

I wanted to imprint myself on him, sew us together so I could carry that feeling with me twenty-four-seven.

But real life didn't allow for that kind of constant closeness.

So tonight, I did the next best thing—I sought out my people. Not for the kind of soft, sugar-coated advice Sandy would give, but the raunchy, real talk I knew I'd get from my girls.

Ellie, Theo, and I were holed up at Aspen's cabin for a much-needed girls' night. The plan was simple: face masks, at-home spa treatments, too much wine, and board games we never finished because we talked too much. Right now, Theo and I were stretched out on the floor, heads resting in the laps of Ellie and Aspen while they brushed our hair like we were thirteen again.

Each of us wore a charcoal face mask, hoping it would bring our skin back to life. I silently wished mine could erase the sleepless nights I'd had—nights where Mac filled every dream, every toss and turn.

"This is my first full night leaving Frankie with just Rhodes," Theo sighed, her voice soft but laced with guilt.

"You know she's in good hands," Aspen said, leaning down to press a kiss to Theo's forehead.

"Yes!" I added, trying to turn toward her, only for Ellie to gently yank my head back into place. "Hard-working moms like you deserve a break, too."

Ellie smirked down at me. "You keep moving your head and this braid's going to come out crooked."

I winced and gave her a sheepish smile. "Noted."

She laughed, clearly not mad, just amused by my restlessness.

"Besides," Aspen continued, "it's good for both of you to have some time apart from her. If you're thinking about going back to work, this is a great warm-up."

Theo nodded. "I know, you're right."

"Have you thought more about it?" Ellie asked gently.

Theo had been offered an amazing gig—one she never would've hesitated to take before Frankie came along. A luxury ranching company wanted her to spend a month at a dude ranch out west, photographing the wildlife for a new campaign.

Theo was a gifted wildlife photographer with a stunning portfolio, and they were offering her great pay and a view to die for. But with a baby and Rhodes in the picture, she was torn.

"I think about it every day," she admitted. "At least twice a day, honestly. The money's incredible, and the photos the assistant sent me? Gorgeous. And who wouldn't want to spend a month in luxury?"

"Exactly," I said. "We've all got your back. We can help Rhodes with Frankie. If you're ever going to do it, now's the time before she gets too old and starts changing by the hour."

"You've got a whole village here," Aspen added. "Let us show up for you."

"You seem really excited about the job," Ellie said.

"I am," Theo admitted, her eyes shining with a mix of hope and nerves.

Ellie tapped me on the head, signaling my hair was done. I leaned forward and reached for the mirror on the coffee table. She'd styled it into two perfectly symmetrical Dutch-braided pigtails.

Theo sat up, too, once Aspen finished hers. Her fingers traced the edge of the blanket as she spoke, her voice lower now.

"Rhodes told me to go," she said, eyes on the floor. "He promised they'd be okay while I was gone, but... leaving them still doesn't feel right."

I reached out, resting my hand gently on her arm, grounding her with soft reassurance.

"You have to do what makes *you* happy," I said. "And whatever you decide, we're with you every step of the way."

Theo looked up at me with a small, grateful smile, then glanced around the circle to the others. Her face mask cracked slightly at the movement, the expression fighting the tight, drying clay. I couldn't help but laugh, and neither could anyone else. The awkward stretch of our masks had us all cracking up until we were doubled over on the floor like teenagers at a sleepover.

Aspen stood and disappeared into her tiny kitchen, only to return moments later with a bottle of red wine and four mismatched wine glasses.

"I feel like it's time to break this out," she declared, popping the cork with a loud *pop* that made us all jump. She poured generous servings and handed them around while we stayed sprawled across the floor in our spa-night chaos.

I grabbed the deck of cards beside me and shuffled. "All right, something easy. We all know once the wine kicks in, no one's going to remember the rules."

"Truth," Ellie agreed, settling in with her glass balanced on her knee.

"Okay," I said, fanning out the cards. "Who wants to go first?"

"I think Penny should," Theo said, fixing me with a look that immediately raised my suspicions.

I glanced around. "For the game?"

Aspen smirked, shaking her head. "Sure, but she didn't mean the game. You've got some explaining to do."

I stared down at my cards, pretending to focus on matching the color on the deck in the middle, but the flutter in my chest said otherwise.

"I don't know what you're talking about," I muttered, slipping a card onto the pile.

Total lie.

Why was I dodging this? I knew what they meant. I *knew*. Instinct told me to deflect—even though every part of me was screaming to just talk it through.

"Mm-hmm," Ellie hummed, eyeing me over her wine. "Nothing involving Mac and a certain recent... rendezvous?"

"Nothing about him throwing you over his shoulder like a rag doll?" Aspen added with a grin, slapping her card down like it was a mic drop.

I inhaled. Held it. Then exhaled, slow and not so steady.

"Fine," I said, tossing a card dramatically. "Mac and I had sex the night of the fundraiser."

Silence.

Not the surprised, gasping kind, but the eerie, synchronized blinking kind. Three pairs of eyes. No words. Just... blinking.

I threw my hands up. "Seriously? That's the reaction? Nothing?"

"Keep going," Ellie said calmly.

I sighed and leaned back on one hand, waving my other through the air. "And... it's been going on since roughly October," I mumbled. "With a month or so off."

That did it.

The three of them exchanged a single glance—one of those wordless, knowing glances only best friends could pull off—and then smiled. All of them. Matching, crooked little smirks.

I frowned.

Something was off.

I carefully set my cards face down on the carpet and moved to all fours, crawling forward into the center of our little circle like a lioness stalking her prey. My eyes narrowed.

They knew something.

I scanned each face slowly, deliberately, waiting for someone, anyone, to crack. I locked onto Theo first. Nothing. Just a cool, unbothered stare. Then to Ellie. Her poker face held strong, lips twitching at the corners but never betraying her.

Finally, I turned to Aspen. And there it was.

The eye twitch. The way her gaze flicked just a little too fast. Her wide-eyed panic.

Bingo.

"What do you know?" I asked, voice low and sharp.

Her face froze. Her body stilled like a kid caught sneaking cookies.

"N-n-nothing!" she squeaked.

Theo sighed beside me, unimpressed. "Really, Aspen? You think she's going to buy *that*?"

I leaned in even closer, until I was practically nose to nose with her.

I repeated myself, slow and deliberate. "What. Do. You. Know?"

Aspen groaned and flopped back onto the rug like a dying starfish. "Ugh. *Everything.*"

She peeked open one eye.

"We *all* know everything."

"You... what?" I asked, dropping back onto my heels, staring at my friends like they'd just confessed to hiding a body. My skin prickled, my throat tightened, and I could barely swallow.

"We know about the whole Mac thing," Theo said, her voice soft but sure.

"How?" I breathed, the disbelief in my tone laced with a touch of confusion.

"Mac told me," Aspen admitted.

"Then she told me," Theo added with a slight shrug.

I turned to Ellie, the only one who hadn't spoken yet. She hesitated before murmuring, "Logan told me."

"The guys know?" My voice pitched an octave higher. "You're telling me the guys know? Not only did you all keep this from me, but the guys knew too? And *they* acted like nothing was going on?"

Aspen winced. "I couldn't keep it from Boone."

I whipped my head toward Theo. "Let me guess, you don't hide anything from Rhodes."

Theo had the decency to look sheepish.

"And *he* told Logan, who told Ellie," I finished, gesturing toward her.

A breath escaped my chest in a long, deflating sigh, my shoulders sagging with it. I thought I'd be furious—righteously, explosively angry—but I wasn't. The heat drained out of me as laughter bubbled up instead. A deep, involuntary belly laugh took over, the kind that made my head fall back and my eyes water.

The fact that my mess of a love life had turned into a glorified game of telephone was honestly kind of hilarious. My friends were so entangled with each other that secrets didn't stand a chance. And the fact they'd managed to keep this quiet for so long? That was practically a miracle.

When I finally gathered myself, I looked back at them. None of them were laughing. They were sitting there, wide-eyed, watching me like I'd completely lost my mind.

"So... what? Mac came to you for help?" I asked Aspen, my voice finally steady again.

She gave a small nod. "To win you back."

"He came to *you*? Told you *everything*? Just to win me back?"

"He was a wreck," Aspen said, leaning forward. She grabbed my hands, her words spilling out fast, tripping over each other like she was still unsure how I'd react. "I—I know how much you liked him, and it was obvious he felt the same. If he didn't, he wouldn't have shown up at my house, practically begging for help. I thought I could do something. I thought it was the right thing."

"Aspen," I said gently, a smile tugging at the corners of my lips. "It's okay. I'm not mad. Honestly... I'm impressed."

I leaned back again, taking them all in. My wild, loyal, meddling friends.

"He really didn't want to lose you," Theo said softly.

I picked up my wine glass and took a generous sip before settling cross-legged on the floor. "Okay, spill it. How exactly did you all help him?"

"I told him about the romance books," Aspen offered with a proud little smile.

"I gave him a hard time for being a lying jackass," Theo said, raising her glass.

"I was... mostly moral support," Ellie said with a shrug, looking slightly guilty.

My heart swelled in a way I hadn't expected. These women, my best friends, had helped the man who hurt me because they believed he was worth it. Because they believed *we* were.

That bit of information hit me hard.

They all saw something in Mac. Something worth fighting for. Something worth giving a second chance.

The uncertainty I'd been clinging to started to dissolve, loosening its grip on my chest. I hadn't realized how badly I needed someone else to believe in him until now. They answered a question I hadn't even said out loud.

Was it okay to trust him again?

Was it okay to trust *myself*?

Yes. Because they saw it too.

I took another slow sip of my wine, the warmth spreading further than the alcohol could reach.

"Now that you know," Aspen said carefully, her eyes bright with mischief, "is there anything you want me to tell him? Maybe plant a little bug in his ear?"

I smiled, letting the thought roll around in my head before I spoke. "Between us," I said quietly, "I think I've fallen for him... again."

All three of them beamed, breaking into soft, knowing giggles that made my cheeks flush.

"But," I added quickly, holding up a finger. "I feel like I need more."

"Okay," Theo encouraged, leaning forward. "Keep talking."

I took a breath and let the words pour out. "Everything that happened between us, the secrets, the wife, the pretending like nothing happened, it broke something in me. It wasn't just a casual fling. I let myself fall for this guy in a way I haven't let myself feel in *years*. And he made me question all of it. I felt like I was the only one carrying the weight of what we were."

The room went still. No one interrupted. They just listened.

"It's hard to come back from that kind of heartbreak," I went on, my voice lower now, more vulnerable. "To go from being so one-sided to suddenly being told he wants to make things right. I want to believe him, I do, but it's like I keep waiting for the other shoe to drop."

"So, you need something big?" Aspen asked gently.

I nodded. "As much as I want to run straight into those tattooed arms and never look back, I need more. I need something real. Something that silences this back-and-forth battle in my head."

"What if I planted the seed?" Aspen grinned. "Put this poor man out of his misery?"

The rest of the girls burst into laughter, and I joined them, the tension melting away like fog in the sun.

Maybe I was ready. Ready to stop running from this thing between Mac and me. Ready to stop punishing him and myself for the past.

It was time. Time to write the ending to this messy, beautiful story.

And maybe, just maybe, fall into Mac for good.

CHAPTER 39

Aspen called me in a panic last night, said we needed an *emergency meeting* about this whole Penny thing. Her voice was sharp, clipped, like the kind of panic you don't fake.

She refused to say more, just that it had to be in person.

Since then, my brain had been spinning in endless fucking loops trying to figure out what the hell she meant. I didn't sleep. Not a damn wink. Smoked way too many cigarettes, which I was really starting to regret right now because I'd run out.

The bar was still closed, just me and the silence, doing my usual setup for the night. Then the door chimed, cutting through the quiet like a slap.

Finally.

I spun around, tense and more than a little strung out, desperate to hear whatever bomb Aspen was about to drop.

"It's about time," I grumbled, arms crossing over my chest. "You couldn't have shown up earlier? I've been up all damn night panicking."

Aspen raised a hand like I was a wild animal she didn't want to startle. "I had to get Ellie to cover for me so I could even come here. But I'm here now, okay?"

She slid onto the barstool with a loud exhale, folding her hands on the counter, and shot me a look that could cut steel.

"She knows."

I blinked. "What?"

"Penny," she said firmly. "She *knows*. She knows that we all know. She knows you came to me for help. She knows everything."

Her tone was tight, urgent, like she was trying to stop the bomb, aka me, from going off.

Penny knew?

Fuck.

My stomach dropped like I'd been sucker-punched. Of course she'd be mad. I'd gone behind her back, used our friends like chess pieces to win her over. It was another secret stacked on the pile I swore I was done building.

I'd had a plan. I was going to tell her when it was all said and done, lay it out in one big, grand gesture, be honest and open. No more hiding.

Well, so much for that.

I dragged a hand down my face, trying to wipe away the regret settling deep in my gut. "Well... fuck. Now what?"

Aspen shrugged like it wasn't her problem anymore.

"How'd she find out?"

"We had a girls' night," she said, wincing a little, "and it kind of... slipped out."

Of course it did. Aspen's as subtle as a damn megaphone.

"So she's mad?" I asked, bracing myself.

Aspen tilted a shoulder and said coolly, "No."

Just like that. Like it was nothing. The urgency in her voice from last night? Gone. Now she was calm, collected, and smirking even.

I narrowed my eyes. "You call me stating it's an emergency and now you're all *zen* about it?"

She rolled her eyes. "Okay, but I didn't tell her that I was going to tell you that I told her."

I squinted. "What? That sounded like complete gibberish."

Aspen sighed with sass. "I didn't tell *Penny* that I was going to tell *you* that she knew. Better?"

I shook my head. "Crystal clear."

She smirked. "So, I suggest you start planning the big guns. The finale. The go-big-or-go-home moment."

I stared at the counter, jaw tight, my bottom lip caught between my teeth.

The finale.

I already had something in the works... but it wasn't big enough. Not for *her.* Not for everything we'd been through. She deserved more. Something undeniable. Something that would stop her in her tracks.

I stood to my full height, arms crossing over my chest as I began pacing behind the bar. Aspen's eyes tracked me, back and forth, her curiosity barely contained. Moving helped me think. Helped the noise in my head organize into something real.

She didn't speak—just watched, waiting.

Then it hit me.

I stopped mid-step, a slow grin spreading across my face as the idea took full shape. Aspen mirrored my smile, leaning forward on her elbows, eyes bright with anticipation.

"Well?" she asked, practically buzzing.

So, I told her. The plan. The details. What I'd need from every one of our friends. Her eyes widened with every word, and before I could finish, she snatched a napkin off the bar and started scribbling furiously.

"This is good," she said, her pen flying across the paper. "Where the hell did you come up with this?"

I tapped my temple, grinning. "All up here, baby."

Aspen narrowed her eyes playfully. "Hmm. Sure. Let's pretend you didn't get it from one of Penny's romance books."

I laughed.

"We've got some time," I said, sobering just slightly. "But... there's something I need to do first. Before we pull the trigger on any of this."

She paused, mid-scribble. "And that is?"

I shook my head, the smile on my lips turning slow and sure. "Can't tell you. Not this one."

Aspen opened her mouth to protest, but then caught the look on my face and snapped it shut with a grin.

She pointed her pen at me like it was a weapon. “Say less.”

CHAPTER 40

"What the hell are we going to do?" Lizzie hovered over my shoulder as I sat at the desk, typing furiously on the computer. Our supplier emailed late last night, cutting us off. No more liquor deliveries.

In a place as tucked-away and stubbornly small as Faircloud, we didn't exactly have a long list of backup options.

I let out a low, frustrated sigh and scrubbed a hand down my face. "I don't know. I haven't gotten that far yet."

I'd come in early to knock out some office work, but as soon as I saw the message, I called Lizzie. To my surprise, she showed up almost immediately.

"We needed to place a new order today, too," she said, her tone sharp with urgency. "We're running low on half the inventory."

I nodded, eyes locked on the screen, willing a solution to appear. Thinking. Running through options. We could try the commission board for a new distributor, but even if we got a rush order approved, delivery could take forever out here. That's if a distributor was even willing to make the drive.

My phone buzzed on the desk, vibrating sharply against the wood. I didn't look at the caller ID. Just grabbed it and brought it to my ear with a brisk, "Yeah?"

"Mac."

Her voice. Penny's voice. Breathless. Tight with worry.

I snapped to attention, fingers lifting off the keyboard as a cold current of dread sliced through me.

"Pen?" I asked, heart already thudding in my chest. "What's wrong?"

"I—I don't know," she whispered. It sounded like she was moving, pacing maybe, her voice quiet like she didn't want to be overheard.

I leaned in instinctively, like that would somehow bring me closer to her. "Talk to me. What do you mean? Are you hurt?"

"No, I'm okay," she replied quickly. "But it's Sandy."

I froze.

Sandy. If it wasn't Penny, she was the next person I worried about most. I knew what that woman meant to her.

"What happened?"

"I had a patron stop by the library and they mentioned that Petal Pusher didn't open this morning." Her voice cracked slightly. "That's not like her, Mac. She's always there. Always opens on time."

"I'll go," I said instantly, already moving. My boots scuffed across the office floor. "I'll head over and check on her."

"I'm in a meeting with the board," Penny continued, her breath shaking. "I can't leave right now and I just—" She inhaled sharply. "I'm so worried."

Her voice broke something open inside me.

"I've got it," I promised, ready to storm out the door. "I'll call you as soon as I get there."

Ready and hell bent on making sure everything was okay, I hung up the phone. My sister caught my arm before I could storm out.

"Don't you dare try to stop me," I snapped, eyes blazing. If she thought now was the time to give me hell, she had another thing coming.

"I'm not," she said quickly, her voice steady but soft. "I was going to say, take your time. Go help her. We'll cover the bar."

I stilled. Gratitude flickered in my chest. Her expression was softer than usual, her features touched with worry.

"I know it was Penny," she added gently. "Go."

I gave her a firm nod and she released me.

Bursting out of the bar and onto the sidewalk, I broke into a jog toward the flower shop a few blocks away.

My heart pounded in my ears. Sweat gathered along my hairline. I wasn't a runner, and I was already regretting every cigarette I'd ever smoked because my lungs were on fire.

If anything happened to Sandy, Penny would be devastated. I didn't want to be the one to give her that kind of news.

Sandy never missed a day. Not once. The only time she ever closed Petal Pusher was when her husband, Hank, passed away—drastic measures.

When I reached the shop, I stepped into the vestibule and yanked on the front door. Nothing. Locked tight. The lights were off.

Pressing my face against the glass, I spotted a soft glow coming from the prep room in the back.

Her purse was on the counter. Her phone, too.

Shit.

Stepping back, I weighed my options. No spare key. No time to wait for emergency service.

I inhaled sharply, bracing myself. Then I raised my leg and kicked the door handle.

It rattled, but the lock held.

I kicked again, harder this time.

Still nothing.

"For fuck's sake," I muttered, setting my jaw and going for it one last time. I slammed my boot against the lock with everything I had.

Snap.

The lock gave way, and the door opened enough for me to shove my body through. I sprinted toward the back, bursting through the double black doors and into the prep room.

I found Sandy lying on the floor, completely still.

"Sandy," I called out, dropping to my knees beside her.

She groaned faintly, her eyes fluttering open before slipping closed again.

"Sandy," I repeated, gently lifting her head and leaning down to check her breathing. Her eyes opened again, unfocused.

"Mac?" she rasped, her voice thin and dry.

"I'm here." I scanned her quickly, looking for blood, a wound—anything—but I didn't see any.

She tried to sit up, grimacing in pain. I helped, but she immediately winced and sank back down.

"What hurts?"

"My hip... and my head," she murmured, her hand fumbling toward her temple.

"Okay, don't move," I said, cradling her gently and resting her head in my lap. I pulled out my phone and dialed the emergency number. "I'm calling someone."

She didn't respond. Her eyes drifted shut again.

"Hey," I said, tapping her cheek lightly. "Come on, Sandy. Stay with me. Penny would be pissed if anything happened to you on my watch."

A weak laugh escaped her lips, and her eyes cracked open again.

The phone rang in my ear, sharp and urgent, until a voice finally answered.

"Faircloud Emergency Service."

"I need help at Petal Pusher on Main," I said, forcing myself to stay calm as I looked down at Sandy. Her soft white hair was mussed, her head tilted to the side. Her eyes blinked slowly, unfocused.

"What's the situation?" The woman on the other end asked.

"I have Sandy here. She fell and seems pretty out of it. I don't see any blood."

I heard the rapid clack of keys, then a pause.

"Okay. I've dispatched someone to your location. They'll get her to the emergency clinic."

"Thank you," I said, the breath leaving my lungs in a rush of relief.

"ETA is five minutes. He's just down the road."

I stayed on the floor beside Sandy, gently brushing a hand over her arm to keep her alert.

She groaned softly, then cleared her throat. "Who called you?"

"Pen," I answered. "Someone came into the library and mentioned the shop didn't open this morning. She got worried."

Sandy shifted, like she wanted to sit up. I gently pressed my hand to her shoulder.

"Don't try to move. Just talk to me until help gets here."

I wasn't a medic, but I'd seen enough growing up—my dad on the floor too many nights after drinking himself into oblivion. You always had to be careful with head injuries. And since Sandy mentioned her hip, I could only assume she hit both on the way down.

"I've been down here way too long," she muttered, her voice thinned with pain.

"Just a little longer," I said, my tone soft. Steady.

"At least I'm lying on the lap of a handsome man." She tried to smile, even through the pain.

I huffed out a laugh, shaking my head. That was Sandy—trying to smooth the edges, even while broken.

"What happened?" I asked gently, needing to keep her talking.

"I don't know," she whispered. "One minute I was standing, the next... you were here."

I let out a low hum, but before I could say more, the sound of movement echoed from the front of the shop.

"In here!" I called out.

A tall, broad-shouldered man pushed through the doors, his gaze quickly finding us. He nodded and motioned to someone behind him.

A woman followed, wheeling in a gurney.

"Sandy?" the man asked, kneeling beside her.

"Oh, hi Buddy," she breathed, a tired smile forming on her lips.

Buddy and his partner worked quickly and efficiently, lifting Sandy off the floor with practiced care. I stepped back, heart tight, as they secured her onto the gurney and slipped an oxygen mask over her face.

"I'm coming with," I said firmly, leaving no room for argument.

Buddy and the woman exchanged a brief glance before nodding in silent agreement as they wheeled Sandy through the sleek black double doors. I stayed close behind, each step heavier than the last, a tight coil of dread twisting in my gut.

Someone had to tell Penny.

And that someone was *me*.

As we passed the front counter, I reached out and grabbed Sandy's purse and phone. The screen lit up in my hand—twenty missed calls from Penelope. My chest clenched. She must be beside herself.

I'd call her once we got Sandy settled, but right now, all I could manage was a message.

Climbing into the back of the ambulance, I sat beside Sandy as they secured her for transport. My fingers hovered over the phone screen for a beat before I began to type.

I'm with Sandy. She's conscious, but we're on our way to the clinic now. I'll call as soon as I can.

I hit send, the weight of those few words pressing down on me like a boulder.

Then I turned my attention back to Sandy, who was trying not to grimace through every bump in the road. I reached for her hand and held it gently in mine, anchoring both of us in the moment.

Because everything else, the bar, the liquor supply, the panic about the plan, none of it mattered right now.

CHAPTER 41

I ran through the sterile hallway of the emergency clinic, my shoes echoing on the linoleum floor. Each door I passed brought a fresh wave of dread. Room numbers blurred in my peripheral vision as I scanned them desperately, searching for hers.

As soon as my board meeting ended, I'd bolted from the library, barely remembering to grab my purse before sprinting to my car. The moment I'd overheard the conversation about Petal Pusher not opening, I knew. My gut had been right.

I hadn't even hesitated. I called the one person I trusted to handle it. The one person I was drawn to when everything inside me was unraveling. Mac picked up on the first ring, no questions asked.

Tears streaked down my cheeks, carving through what little makeup I'd bothered with this morning. I sniffled, slowing from a run to a brisk walk as I counted down the final doors. My heart was pounding, a chaotic drumbeat in my chest.

When I finally reached the room, I stopped cold.

Mac sat beside Sandy's bed, his large hand gently cradled in hers. She looked tired, worn, but she was smiling, soft and sweet.

The sight of her lying there—tubes of oxygen nestled in her nose, hair slightly mussed, wrapped in too-white hospital blankets—hit me like a punch to the chest. She looked so small. So fragile. And yet... still her. Still Sandy.

They both turned at once, as if sensing me.

"Oh, Penelope," Sandy breathed, her smile widening with warmth.

I laughed through a fresh surge of tears, my heart pulling tight in my chest. Relief nearly dropped me to the floor. I crossed the room quickly, ignoring the sting in my eyes and the wobble in my knees.

She meant everything to me. My mentor, my friend, the closest thing I'd ever had to a mother. Seeing her hooked up to monitors, her skin pale against the bright lights of the clinic, made something inside me crack.

I reached for her arm just as Mac stood, his chair scraping softly against the floor. He moved toward me and gently touched my waist, guiding me into the seat he'd been keeping warm.

"Sit," he murmured, his voice steady. "She's okay."

I sank into the chair, clutching Sandy's hand like I was afraid she might slip away if I let go.

"I'm gonna head out," Mac said, placing a strong hand on my shoulder. "But if you need anything, call me."

I looked up at him, meeting his eyes. That constant, grounding gaze. His touch was reassuring, his presence a balm to my frayed nerves. I nodded, too overwhelmed to speak.

He gave me one of those soft smiles that said more than words could, tapped Sandy's foot affectionately, and slipped out of the room.

The moment he left, I felt it. I was happy to be there with Sandy, knowing she was okay, but still, I wasn't content.

I had to go after him. I needed to thank him for showing up and stepping in for Sandy like he did.

Standing, I tapped Sandy's hand gently before turning and slipping out the door. She didn't say a word, didn't ask questions. She knew.

"Mac!" I called, jogging down the hospital hallway, my voice echoing slightly as I tried to catch him before he reached the stairs.

He turned at the sound of my voice, brows furrowed in

concern as his eyes locked on mine.

"What's wrong?" he asked, already moving toward me with urgency in every step.

"N-nothing," I said breathlessly as I slowed to a stop. We stepped to the side of the hallway, finding a quiet pocket between the chaos around us.

"Then why are you out here with me and not in there?" he asked.

I paused, taking a moment to simply look at him. *Really* look at him. The way his eyes always settled me. The familiar dip of his dimples when he smiled. The way his hair curled just slightly behind his ears, messy but deliberate.

God, I loved this stupid man.

My heart raced when he was near. My skin came alive, tingling with awareness. I felt safe, seen, *known*. As much as I'd tried to be angry with him all those weeks ago, here I was—full circle, back where it all began.

Back in the space where the only thing that made sense...was *us*.

I reached out and cupped his cheek, brushing my thumb lightly across his skin. He leaned into my touch, his hand covering mine in a quiet affirmation.

I rose on my toes and kissed him. Soft. Tender. Wordless. He kissed me back without hesitation, his lips meeting mine like they remembered the rhythm by heart.

I lingered there, suspended in that hospital hallway with him. For a few stolen seconds, the world outside of us was non-existent.

When I finally pulled back, he exhaled slowly, his eyes opening to meet mine, dark and steady.

"What was that for?" he asked, voice hushed.

"Thank you," I whispered, my hand still resting against his cheek.

"There's no need to thank me," he replied. "I meant what I said, Pen. I'd do anything for you. Roping the moon would be nothing if it meant being by your side."

"I just didn't know wha—" My voice faltered, the thought of losing Sandy choking off the words.

Mac pulled me into his arms before I could finish that sentence. I melted into his chest as the tears spilled over. His chin rested against the top of my head while his hand made slow, soothing circles along my back.

"I know," he murmured, and I felt his voice as much as I heard it as it rumbled through me.

I cried, and he didn't pull away. He didn't try to fix it. He just *stayed*. Solid. Steady. There.

I wasn't sure how long we stood there like that—me breaking, him holding.

Eventually, I leaned back, still wrapped in his arms.

"Do you need me to stay?" he asked gently.

I shook my head. "No. I'll be okay."

He studied me for a second before nodding.

"Call me the second you leave here, got it?"

"Got it," I replied.

Mac kissed me before slowly backing away. He walked until he reached the stairwell, where he paused, gave me a final wave, and disappeared.

I stood there for a few moments, arms crossed around my middle, holding the weight of everything.

Then I turned and made my way back into the room, where Sandy still lay.

"That one's special," Sandy rasped, her voice laced with affection despite the grogginess, the second I walked through the door.

"He is."

Retaking my seat, I leaned in, touching her hand on the bed.

"What happened?" I asked softly, studying her face as if I might find the answer written in the lines etched around her eyes.

"I don't know," Sandy admitted, her voice weak but steady. "One minute I was upright, the next I was... horizontal."

I tried to smile, but it faltered. Her version of the story

matched Mac's he'd sent over text—there were no answers, no clarity. Just an empty space where the truth should've been.

"You scared me," I whispered, my voice catching in my throat as I rubbed the back of her hand with my thumb. I couldn't meet her eyes, not with the emotion tightening my chest. A tear slipped free and dropped silently onto the stiff white hospital blanket.

Seeing her like this—fragile, tethered to oxygen, her strength dimmed—shattered something in me. My mind couldn't stop running through the what-ifs. What if Mac hadn't gone? What if she hadn't woken up? The thought alone gutted me.

"I'm okay, sweetie," Sandy murmured, giving my hand a light squeeze, pulling me back from the edge. "But I think it's time this old lady throws in the towel."

My head snapped up, brows pinching together. I couldn't imagine this town without that flower shop. Couldn't imagine Sandy without it.

I opened my mouth to argue, but she beat me to it.

"I don't think I can keep doing this on my own anymore," she said gently. "It's too much. Too much to manage at my age."

I pressed my lips together and nodded, even though it hurt to hear. I understood more than she probably realized. Running the store solo, barely getting help except during holidays, it had taken its toll. She'd kept the business, and herself, alive after losing her husband, pouring everything she had into it.

But even the strongest women have limits.

Even Sandy.

Her fall wasn't just a slip—it was a sign. A warning that it was time to let go of something she'd held onto for too long. And as much as it twisted my heart, I'd rather lose the flower shop than lose her.

"Our bodies need rest at some point," I said softly, brushing my thumb over her knuckles. "What does that mean for Petal Pusher?"

She sighed, her chest rising and falling in a slow inhale. "I don't know what the future looks like yet. But for now? I think it's okay to take a few days off."

I nodded again. That part, at least, we could agree on. She needed time to heal, to think, to just *be.*

And me?

I was just thankful she was still here. Still breathing. Still able to squeeze my hand and call me sweetie. Still able to look me in the eye with that quiet strength I'd always leaned on.

CHAPTER 42

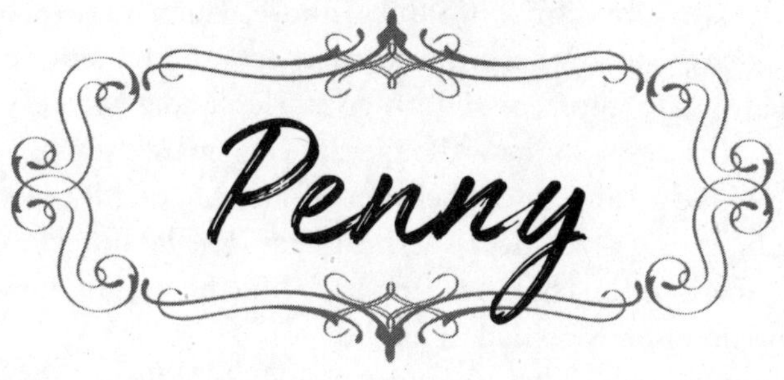

"Will you please quit it?" Sandy said with a half-laugh, half-groan as she pushed herself up from the couch. Her face twisted into a grimace, betraying just how much pain she was still in.

"This is exactly why I'm here," I said, rushing to her side before she could take another step on her own. "I'm here to help you. To make sure you get back on your feet *safely.* Do you not remember your fall literally two days ago?"

Typical Sandy. Always trying to tough it out, make it harder than it needed to be, just to prove she could. It had been forty-eight hours since she hit the floor of the flower shop, and here she was, limping around her house like it had never happened—or like she could will it out of existence. The stiffness in her steps and the small winces she tried to hide told a different story.

According to the doctors, she had a concussion and a badly bruised hip. Their best guess? She'd passed out from dehydration, collapsing hard and catching the edge of the prep table on her way down. No wonder her memory of it was a complete blank.

My mind kept spinning in circles, whispering what-ifs. What if she'd hit her head harder? What if no one had found her in time? What if I'd lost her?

The thoughts were sharp enough to draw tears. I sniffed, blinked them back, and kept moving—no use crumbling now.

I'd taken the last two days off from the library to be here. I couldn't stomach the idea of her being alone, not after everything. So here I was, camping out in Sandy's house, which was the picture-perfect image of southern grandma charm. Gingham patterns, antique wood furniture with its own stories, and a powdery floral perfume that clung to the wallpaper like a memory.

I slipped an arm under hers and guided her gently toward the dining table, our steps slow and measured. She let out a long sigh as she sank into the chair, leaning back like the weight of the past few days had finally settled in her bones.

"I remember perfectly fine, Penelope," she said with a stubborn little huff. "You have work to do. A job that needs you. Old me can manage just fine."

I rolled my eyes as I turned toward the kitchen. "Just bear with me, okay? You scared the crap out of me. And being here, taking care of you, is the only thing that's helping my brain calm down. I need to see you safe, not in a hospital bed, or..." I swallowed hard. "Worse."

I returned with her plate of breakfast and a mug of coffee, placing them gently in front of her before grabbing my own and sitting across the table. I gave her a soft, sad smile. She met it with a knowing smirk as she scooped up a forkful of eggs.

"Well," she said, chewing, "I guess it *is* kind of nice to have someone catering to me for a change."

"That's the spirit." I let out a small laugh and stared into my coffee, tracing the rim of the mug with my fingertip. The idea I'd been mulling over for the past twenty-four hours danced at the edge of my tongue.

"Sandy," I began carefully, "I've been thinking a lot about Petal Pusher. About its future. I want to run something by you."

She paused mid-bite, her fork lowering slowly to her plate. "Go on," she said, her voice a touch more serious now. "It's not like I can go anywhere."

I took a deep breath. "I can't imagine this town without that shop. And I know you've said it's too much now, too hard to manage on your own. But I might have a solution."

She tilted her head, interest flickering behind her tired eyes. "I'm listening."

"Ellie Cassidy," I said. "She loves flowers. She knows how to run a business. She's the one who got the farm stand up and running out at the ranch. And I know she's looking to move on, to start something new. What if that something... was Petal Pusher?"

Sandy paused for a long moment, her eyes distant as she considered my words. Finally, she nodded—slow and thoughtful, but certain.

"Have you spoken to her about it yet?"

I shook my head, fingers tightening around my coffee cup.

"Not yet. I didn't know where your head was at, and I didn't want to make offers I couldn't follow through on." I glanced up, searching her face. "I wanted to run it by you first."

Sandy picked up her fork again and took a bite of her breakfast, chewing with care. "I think that sounds lovely," she said finally. "If she's interested, I'd be more than happy to talk to her, work out some kind of arrangement."

Relief curled through my chest like warmth from a fire. "I'll talk to her. I'll tell her to come see you."

Sandy laughed softly, shaking her head. "Oh boy. I haven't had anyone on payroll—well, ever. It was always just me and Hank." Her voice softened as she said his name, a smile lifting her face, her eyes shimmering with memory. It was as if she were replaying a treasured home movie in her mind, golden and precious.

"What was he like?" I asked gently.

In all the time I'd known Sandy, she rarely talked about her husband. It never made me doubt how much she'd loved him—it just felt like maybe the loss was still too raw, the ache too deep to name aloud. I'd caught glimpses here and there—quick stories about the flower shop or their time in California, but never the full picture.

Maybe it was the rush of emotion from the last few days, or maybe something deeper, but I suddenly wanted to know more. I wanted a piece of her past to carry with me, something real and lasting.

She grew quiet, her gaze fixed on something far away, her expression soft with reflection.

"He was straight to the point," she said at last. "That man didn't sugarcoat a single thing." She gave a dry laugh, then added, "But somehow, he was still the gentlest soul I've ever known. He knew how to be soft when it mattered. He was patient. Kind. Compassionate."

A tender smile tugged at my lips as I listened—not just to her words, but to the way she said them, full of reverence and quiet love.

Without another word, Sandy stood. Instinctively, I moved to help her, but she waved me off with a look. Carefully, she walked to a wooden hutch in the corner of the room and returned with a photo frame in her hand.

Using the table for support, she extended the frame to me. I took it carefully.

Inside the glass was a portrait of a man—stocky, with a broad, easy smile that made him look instantly familiar. There was something teddy bear-like about him, a kind of gentle strength that radiated from his eyes. His hair was thick and dark, not a strand of gray in sight.

"He looks so cheerful," I said, unable to hide the smile spreading across my face.

Sandy let out a short laugh as she sank back into her chair. "Cheerful? Oh, not a chance. But kind? Always."

She let that hang in the air for a moment before speaking again. "Remember that story I told you the other day?" she asked.

Still holding the photo, I looked up and nodded.

"I've been thinking a lot about it lately. And then this whole fall..." Her voice drifted off, but her gaze didn't. She locked eyes with me, steady and clear, and reached out, placing her hand gently over mine.

"Don't take life for granted, Penelope. Not a single day. No matter how young or how old you are. Live with grace and with gratitude. For everything. Every heartbeat. Every breath."

Her words landed in my chest like a promise—one I wasn't sure I knew I needed until now.

There was a knock at the door, followed by the soft scrape of it dragging against the hardwood floors. My head snapped over my shoulder just in time to see Mac peek around the corner, his familiar frame filling the doorway to the kitchen.

"Mac?" I asked, confused. "What are you doing here?"

There was no reason for him to be at Sandy's this early. At least, not one I knew of.

He glanced at Sandy, then back at me, his mouth opening and closing as if trying to find the right words. Before he could sputter out an excuse, Sandy gave him some kind of look—one I couldn't interpret, but he could because he cleared his throat and stepped into the kitchen like he belonged there.

"I got a bat signal that someone needed rescuing," he said, flashing me a grin.

I turned sharply toward Sandy, my jaw dropping. "You did not," I gasped. "You called Mac to save you? From *me*?"

Sandy gave me a look so smug I could have screamed. "Penelope, sweetie, it's time for you to go home and take a shower." She pinched her nose dramatically and waved her hand in front of her face like I was some unwashed barn animal.

My eyes widened in mock horror. "I do *not* stink!" I pointed at her accusingly.

Laughter erupted from her and then from Mac, his deep, warm chuckle rolling in behind me as he stepped closer and gently grabbed my shoulders.

"Let's go, Pen. The truck's still running," he said, leaning in. He sniffed the air with exaggerated flair, then winced. "Oof. Okay, she's not wrong."

I gasped and smacked his chest with the back of my hand, earning another laugh from him. "You're both impossible," I muttered, spinning on my heel and stomping off toward the guest room with as much dignity as I could manage.

Behind me, their laughter echoed down the hall, bright and full of mischief. And just before I reached the door, I swear I heard it—*smack*—a perfectly crisp, unmistakable high five.

SANDY'S HOUSE WASN'T far from Petal Pusher, just on the outskirts of town, but the drive back to my apartment still took close to ten minutes, winding through quiet back roads as Mac's beat-up truck rumbled beneath us.

I sat in the passenger seat, arms crossed loosely, eyes flicking between the passing scenery and the man beside me. The silence was soft, companionable until I broke it.

"Do I really stink?" I asked, suddenly very self-conscious.

I'd always prided myself on smelling good. Perfume, lotions, hair products—it was one of my little passions, a personal ritual that made me feel put together.

Mac let out a low chuckle, cutting his eyes toward me for a beat. One hand rested on the wheel, the other draped lazily across the center console. "No," he said. "You don't stink. But we had to come up with something to get you to leave."

I huffed, turning to look out the window with a pout. "That's just mean."

He grinned. "You've been there two nights, Pen. It was time to get you home, rest, and shower. Maybe sleep in a real bed for once."

I wanted to argue, but the truth was, he wasn't wrong. Still, being near Sandy made the anxiety quiet, if only for a while. Watching her breathe, hearing her voice reminded me she was okay.

"I know you were scared," Mac said gently when I didn't respond right away. "But she's okay."

Something about hearing it from him—his steady, gravel-edged voice full of quiet reassurance—hit me harder than I expected. My throat tightened.

"I just... I can't lose her." I stared at the dashboard, eyes blurring. "It felt like a slap in the face. A reminder that it can all be gone in a blink. Anyone I love, just... gone."

The words came out raw, stripped down to their marrow.

I'd spent so much of my life not knowing what love and real affection looked like. And once I found it, once I let myself feel it, suddenly the idea of losing it felt like a kind of death. Like being abandoned all over again.

"She means a lot to you," Mac said, his voice low and understanding. He didn't try to fix it. Just sat with me in the grief of the moment, which somehow meant everything.

"She took a chance on me," I said. "Gave me a start when I had nothing and nowhere to go. When my mom packed up and left the day I turned eighteen, I had no idea what the hell to do. I saw the apartment above the flower shop was for rent, walked in, and offered Sandy every last dollar in my bank account from working at the library."

Mac reached for the radio, turning the volume down until it was just a whisper, giving me space to keep talking.

"She let me move in. Charged me almost nothing for rent in exchange for helping her on weekends. She supported me while I went to school online, while I worked at the library. She was the first person who really believed in me. Really *saw* me."

I paused, emotion rising fast. My voice cracked. "Without her... I don't know where I'd be. She's my family. This whole thing just reminded me how fragile life is. How stupid it is to waste time on grudges and bitterness."

Out of the corner of my eye, I saw Mac's jaw tighten, a flicker of something unspoken crossing his features. He nodded slowly, swallowing hard.

Even with my mom, I didn't carry hate anymore. But that didn't mean I had to let her stay in my life. Letting go didn't make me cruel—it made me free. I chose peace over resentment. I chose my own happiness.

She doesn't get to have that power over me anymore, and I'm better for it.

Mac's hand left the center console and searched for mine, his grip was commanding and consuming as he brought my hand to rest with his. Silence filled the rest of the drive until we pulled up to the store.

The broken door had been repaired, the lights inside Petal Pusher were off and a sign was hanging on the glass. *Be back soon.* Written in Mac's scratchy handwriting.

CHAPTER 43

I sat in my desk chair, one hand resting over my chest, the other hanging limp at my side. The room was still, and I stared blankly at the wall across from me, letting the quiet settle over me like a heavy blanket. I needed it—to think, to figure out how the hell to say what I needed to say.

Penny's words from yesterday echoed in my head. About permanence. About bitterness and resentment.

I dropped her off at her apartment and went home. I made it through another shift at the bar, but I wasn't really there. I kept thinking about everything that had happened over the last few months—not just with Penny, but with Lizzie.

As much as I hated to admit it, maybe I hadn't given my sister a fair shot. Sure, I had my reasons. I carried resentments I could practically name by date and time—bitter memories from a childhood that felt like walking barefoot over broken glass. But for all that damage, not all of it was her fault.

And if I was serious about growing, about taking accountability and not letting my past dictate my future, then maybe this was where I needed to start.

This morning, I called Lizzie and asked her to come by the bar. Told her it was important. I needed to talk. Really talk.

Now, I was just trying not to lose my nerve.

I shifted in the chair, leaning forward, elbows on my knees, head hanging low between my shoulders. Patience wasn't my strong suit, and waiting made every second feel like an hour.

Finally, the front door chimed, followed by the sound of it slamming shut. Footsteps echoed across the hardwood floor—quick and purposeful.

Lizzie appeared in the doorway, her stance guarded, arms crossed tight over her chest. Classic Lizzie—always braced for a fight.

"You said it was urgent," she said. "What's going on? You wouldn't tell me over the phone."

"I've been thinking," I said, meeting her gaze. "You and me—we've always been like cats and fucking dogs."

She nodded once. "It's just how it is between us."

"No," I countered, shaking my head. "It's how *we've* let it be. But I'm done with that. I'm tired, Lizzie. Tired of being angry. Tired of feeling bitter all the damn time. It's exhausting."

Her brows lifted slightly, surprise flickering across her face before she quickly masked it. Neutral. Detached. But I saw the shift.

"I've been holding onto this shit for years," I continued. "Toward Dad. Toward Mom. And yeah, toward you, too."

She studied me for a beat, suspicious. "Why now?"

I leaned back in the chair, letting it recline slightly, both feet planted on the ground. "A lot has happened. Lately, especially. It made me realize I've been dragging around stuff that I don't need to carry anymore."

I didn't expect some big, emotional breakthrough from her. This wasn't a Hallmark moment. But this was for me. For my own peace.

If she wanted to meet me halfway—great. If not, at least I know I tried.

"Me too," she said quietly. "I've spent so much of my life feeling that way. Angry. Bitter. Like that was the only way to survive in this family." She laughed, but it was a sad, broken sound. "Matching energy became too easy. It was the only way I knew how to live."

She meant living with Mom. I saw that. I felt that because that's how it was living with Dad, too.

I nodded, a crooked grin tugging at my mouth. "We're definitely products of our parents."

She took a breath, stepping further into the room and leaning against the desk. "I came here a bit heavy. Didn't really give you the space to explain yourself, talk about the bar. I'm sorry for that."

"You did," I said. "I really wish you had talked to me about what you knew."

Lizzie's gaze dropped for a second, then lifted again. "Yeah. Me too. I thought I was doing what was best for the bar."

"Why?" I asked. "Why do you care so much? Why not just let it all go to hell?"

She didn't flinch, didn't break eye contact. "Because of you. Some part of me knew if it all crumbled, everything *you'd* built would fall with it. And I didn't want that. Not really."

I blinked at her, stunned into stillness.

"I know you were the one holding this place together," she added. "Dad sure as hell didn't. I remember how things were when we were kids. It was always you and Mom cleaning up his messes. Me? I stayed in the background. Just watched."

I remembered being eight years old, helping Mom mop up spilled beer and rage while she cursed under her breath about Dad. About the bar. About how she couldn't keep living like this.

The divorce hadn't been vicious, at least not legally. But the wounds they left behind were deep and loud—clearly echoes that never quite faded.

"Lizzie," I said after a moment, my voice softer. "I don't want to fight with you anymore."

She nodded slowly. "Neither do I."

"Let's call a truce," I said, holding out my hand.

Lizzie hesitated only a second before slipping hers into mine. Her grip was firm, familiar. I gave her hand a squeeze, and she returned it without hesitation.

"Here's to growing up," she said with a smirk, "and not acting like such fucking children."

"Deal," I replied, matching her smile.

She pulled her hand back, the warmth of the moment lingering between us, but it didn't take long before she tilted her head and raised an eyebrow.

"Don't you have something to apologize for?" she asked, her tone deceptively light.

I tapped my index finger against my chin, pretending to think hard. "Hmm... smoking in the bar?"

"And?" she prodded.

"Giving my friends free drinks?"

"Go on."

"Being an ass?"

She stared at me, unimpressed, clearly waiting for more. I racked my brain but came up blank.

"I got nothing," I said with a shrug, grinning.

Lizzie rolled her eyes. "I just wanted to see what I could get you to own up to."

She pushed off the desk and turned to leave, her tone casual but her words sincere. "Apology accepted, by the way."

Then, just before she disappeared into the hallway, she tossed over her shoulder, "Also, get off your ass. The new liquor supplier will be here soon, and you've got work to do."

I flipped her off, grinning, and she stuck her tongue out in return before vanishing into the bar.

CHAPTER 44

Penny

If you ever say "yeehaw" during sex, I'm filing a police report.

So... Giddy up is okay?

Penny

Blocked. Reported. Arrested.

Be honest. Did you actually like that playlist I made for us?

Penny

It was 40% country breakup songs and 60% Shania Twain.

Is that a yes?

Penny

It felt like an emotional hostage situation.

But perfect to practice our dancing.

You up?

Penny

It's 10:42 PM, not 3 AM. The fact you sent me a you up text...

Cool. I'm coming over ;)

Penny

To do what, exactly?

Eat popcorn. Probably kiss you. Depends on your mood.

Penny

As tired as I am... I don't think I'd be able to deny the kissing part. Anything more than that I can't guarantee. But my freezer has ice cream. So come prepared for both!!!

Copy that. I'll bring a spoon and lower your sleepy defenses.

Penny

You're not allowed in unless you promise to behave.

Define behave. Like pants-on behave? Or just no setting the kitchen on fire behave?

Penny

Bare minimum, no fire.

Challenge accepted

If you're wearing my shirt again, I don't think I can stay respectable for long.

Penny

It's laundry day so I resorted to one of yours (;

I'm already in the truck.

How dare you send me a picture of your amazing meal like that and not invite me?

Penny

You really want to be sitting here with Theo, Aspen, and Ellie?

I don't hate their company

Penny

Well, Aspen was just telling us how her and Boone did the deed in his barn, would you like the details?

So they did it where we did? Nice

That barn sure does see a lot of action

CHAPTER 45

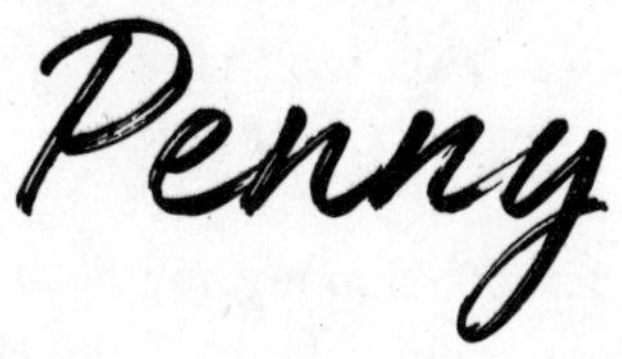

Mac

Meet me at the bar, 6:30 p.m. sharp. Not a minute later, Penelope.

Do you realize how hard that is for me to show up on time?

Mac

Trust me when I say, you're going to wanna try your hardest

This sounds... serious... I'll give it my best shot but no promises 😈

Perfect.

Six twenty-nine.

I made it on time. Honestly, I was a little impressed with myself. I was notoriously late for pretty much everything, but I wanted to at least *try*.

Still, I was a little out of breath as I reached the front door of The Tequila Cowboy.

A sign in Mac's familiar scrawl was taped across the tinted window:

BAR CLOSED.
COME BACK TOMORROW AT OPENING.
Y'ALL WILL LIVE.
— MANAGEMENT

I let out a soft scoff, shaking my head at the note before tugging on the handle. It didn't budge. I pulled again, harder this time, but the door stayed locked.

Peering inside was useless. The damn windows were too dark to see through.

Fumbling through my purse for my phone, I turned away from the door, ready to call Mac and demand he let me in. I was *on time*, and there was no way in hell I'd let him pretend otherwise. I deserved a gold star for this.

Just as I pulled up his contact and hovered over the call button, I felt a hand wrap around my mouth from behind.

A sharp gasp left my throat, muffled against the palm. My whole body jolted, heart kicking into high gear as arms wrapped around me and dragged me back.

Fight or flight surged in my veins. I was going to *fight*.

"Shhh..." a voice murmured close to my ear, deep and low.

My flailing slowed. I caught a glimpse of the tattooed arms holding me and felt the familiar shape of his chest against my back.

Mac.

"Quit putting up a fight," he whispered, his mouth grazing my ear.

Relief rushed in. My shoulders sagged even as my heart thudded wildly. I couldn't speak—not with his hand still over my mouth—but he filled the silence.

"Before I turn you around," Mac continued, his voice suddenly laced with something darker. Dangerous. It thrummed through me like an electric current, straight to my core. *God*, I knew that tone.

"I know you're gonna have questions. One, no one can see inside. Two, the bar is closed for the night. Yes, my sister knows. No, she doesn't care. And three...you can say no at any time."

The blood in my ears pulsed so loudly I almost missed the question that followed.

"Are you ready to see what I've planned for us?"

I nodded, barely breathing.

Slowly, Mac turned me around but didn't release me. His hand stayed on my mouth, his chest pressed tight to my back. His presence surrounded me, possessive, protective, and thrilling.

The bar was transformed.

The tables and chairs had been cleared, tucked away in the far corner. Rose petals littered the floor in scattered trails of crimson. Dozens of candles glowed softly from every surface, casting the room in a flickering, golden haze. The scent of wax and roses filled the air, and somewhere beneath it all, a soft hum of music played just above a whisper.

My eyes flicked toward the bar and caught.

Handcuffs.

A whip.

I squinted, my breath catching.

Was that... a vibrator?

Mac leaned in closer, his voice brushing the shell of my ear, thick with heat.

"Our very own red room, Pen," he murmured.

A shiver chased down my spine as goosebumps broke out across my skin.

Slowly, Mac lifted his hand from my mouth, and I took a step forward, creating just a sliver of space between us. His presence lingered behind me—grounding, intoxicating, safe in the most dangerous kind of way.

I let my gaze sweep the room again before turning back to him.

He stood casually, hands tucked in the front pockets of his

jeans, eyes locked on me with a gaze that pinned me in place. That crooked smirk curled at the edge of his mouth, dimples flashing just enough to make my knees weak.

God, those damn dimples were lethal.

I tipped my head slightly, a wicked smile tugging at my lips. My voice dropped to a sultry whisper as I ran my tongue slowly along the edge of my canine.

"You're lucky I was in such a rush... I forgot to put on panties."

Mac groaned, low and guttural, and closed the space between us in two strides. His hands gripped my hips, fingers flexing as if he needed to feel me—to make sure I was really there.

His palms slid upward, teasing along my sides, fingers brushing the strap of my dress. The light stroke against my skin made my breath catch.

He noticed.

He always noticed.

"It's about trust," Mac murmured, his voice rough and sincere. "I want you to know you can trust me, Pen. I'm here. I'm yours. *Forever.*"

Even through the heavy tension between us, his words landed softly in my chest, like a vow whispered into the soul. My heart fluttered at the confession, mixing with the storm of want brewing inside me.

"I do trust you," I said, and I meant it.

He lifted me in one seamless motion. My legs wrapped around his waist instinctively, arms falling around his neck.

"Let me continue to prove it to you. I'll never stop. Never again."

He carried me toward the bar, my body flush against his. I placed my lips to his, leaving a feather-light kiss, just one, before he set me down gently atop the bar.

I was nearly eye level with him. Still a little taller from my perch. Still held entirely in his control.

Our eyes locked.

Mac reached for the straps of my dress, sliding his fingers

beneath the fabric and drawing it down, slow and deliberate. My skin burned in the best way as cool air hit me, and my nipples peaked instantly, tightening in response.

Still, he didn't look away.

He undressed me like I was sacred—something to be revealed, not just taken. The dress slipped down to my waist, the fabric dragging goosebumps in its wake. I arched my hips slightly, lifting just enough for him to slide the rest off, his hands ghosting down my thighs as the fabric fell.

For a second, Mac glanced lower, confirming what I'd told him.

No panties.

A smirk tugged the corner of his mouth. One nod. One look of approval.

The dress hit the floor, forgotten, because now his attention was solely on *me*.

"Close your eyes, Trouble," Mac said, voice low and thick with promise.

Trust.

That's what this was. A test—for both of us. A leap I needed to take. My heart and my body wanted Mac. But now... now was when I'd see if my soul trusted him too.

Carefully, I closed my eyes.

Soft fabric brushed against my skin. A blindfold. He tied it snugly around my head, blocking out everything but the sound of his breath, the heat of his hands, the thundering beat of my own heart.

He placed his palms on my shoulders and gently guided me down until my back hit the cool surface of the bar. I followed his silent command.

Trust, I reminded myself again.

With my vision gone, everything was heightened. My skin buzzed. Each soft breath against my cheek, every shift of his weight, each brush of his fingertips—it all set my nerve endings ablaze.

One finger trailed slowly between my breasts, then down the center of my stomach to my navel. My body arched slightly beneath his touch, a soft whimper escaping my lips as I exhaled a shaky breath.

Then... nothing.

His hands vanished. The loss of his touch was maddening. I heard the sound of movement—Mac stepping behind the bar. Then something firm brushed against my lips.

It was cool. Smooth.

I darted my tongue out. It tasted sweet.

"Open up, baby."

I obeyed.

Mac dangled a cherry above my mouth. My lips wrapped around it, tongue swirling as I sucked it clean.

"Mmm," he hummed, low and satisfied. "That's good."

Another brush against my lips.

"Again."

This time, I played with it. My tongue curled around the fruit, teasing it. I let the cherry dangle as I licked it slowly, drawing it in before pulling the stem free with a soft pop.

Mac groaned—a deep, visceral sound that told me exactly how much he liked the show.

Then I felt his hand on my knee, sliding slowly down and coaxing my legs apart. He opened me completely, leaving me vulnerable and *aching*.

"This one's for me," he growled.

Something small and round traced the line of my sex. It was cold. My breath hitched, and I realized it was another cherry, this time slick from me.

The sensation was pulled away, and I heard Mac groan again.

"So fucking sweet," he muttered.

His hands returned, stronger this time, pulling me upright—but he left the blindfold on. The disorientation only fueled the fire roaring beneath my skin.

Then came the sound of metal. A soft clink. A scrape. My

breath caught.

The cuffs.

"I'm going to use the handcuffs, Pen," Mac said gently. "Then I want you to lie back with your head off the end of the bar. You'll feel a rush. If it's too much, use our word."

God, I could barely breathe. The anticipation pulsing through my veins was dizzying.

I swallowed hard. "Am I going to get to touch you at least? Because as much as I'm very much enjoying this... I'd love to taste your cock mixed with a little cherry."

Mac laughed—a dark, amused sound that slid over my skin like velvet.

The cold bite of metal touched my wrists, followed by the solid *click* of each loop locking into place. My pulse pounded at the base of my throat.

He grabbed my legs and shifted me, sliding my ass to the edge of the bar until I was perfectly positioned for him.

"Maybe," he purred, his breath hot against my lips. "We have all night. This is just round one."

His mouth crashed into mine, and one hand cupped my breast, fingers kneading before giving it a sharp smack. I gasped into his mouth, the sting blooming into pleasure.

He pulled back and pressed his hand to my shoulder, guiding me down again. I let myself fall.

My head dipped off the edge of the bar, neck arched. The blood would rush soon, dizzying me—but that would only make everything else feel even more intense.

"What should I use next?" Mac asked, his hands firm on my knees, holding me wide open beneath him.

I felt exposed. Vulnerable. But also completely safe—*seen*—with Mac looming above me, eyes locked on mine like I was his entire world.

"Surprise me," I said, breathless. Because honestly? Anything he chose would be perfect.

Mac's mouth descended, and when his tongue touched me, I

gasped—my body arching as a bolt of pleasure cracked down my spine. I lay there helplessly, wrists cuffed behind me, my weight pressing into my own hands. The pressure hurt more than I expected, but not enough to care.

I wanted to touch him. Desperately. To bury my hands in his hair, to hold him there while he devoured me, but I couldn't move. I was completely at his mercy.

And Mac didn't waste the power.

He feasted on me. His tongue traced circles around my clit, every flick both heaven and hell, a sinful torment that made my eyes roll back. I couldn't stop trembling, couldn't stop moaning as he licked and sucked with purpose.

There was *no way* Lizzie knew this was what Mac had in mind when he decided to close the bar.

"Fuck," I moaned, voice shaking.

He hummed against me, the vibration making my thighs quiver. His rhythm built, faster, deeper—then he stopped.

Just like that.

My body jerked in protest, aching with the loss of what had been so close. I whimpered, teetering on the edge of a denied orgasm, my core pulsing with frustration.

"Not yet," Mac said.

He leaned in again, running the tip of his tongue along my sex, back and forth as a tease before he pulled away again.

Then something new pressed against my clit—round, firm, slightly larger than the cherries he'd used earlier.

There was a *click*.

A sharp, sudden buzz filled the air, then my body. The vibrator came to life, sending shockwaves of sensation through me.

I gasped, every nerve igniting at once.

The pulse was steady, deliberate—too fucking good. My hips moved on instinct, grinding against the toy, desperate for friction.

"Ride it, Pen," Mac said, voice thick and low. "Look at you. So fucking needy."

Mac was the kind of man who'd talk you through your own

undoing.

I moaned—deep and raw—and then screamed, the sound ripped from my throat without thought.

His hand was suddenly over my mouth again, the sound muffled.

"People may not be able to *see* through the window," he murmured, "but it sure as hell isn't soundproof."

Then, cruelly, the vibrator was gone. His hand, too.

"Then turn up the fucking music," I hissed, frustration thick in my voice.

A beat of silence passed, and then music flooded the room, the bass pulsing hard enough to drown out anything else.

"What a good idea," Mac cooed, returning to me. "I should've thought of that sooner."

"I *still* haven't come," I snapped, irritation bleeding into desperation. He'd brought me to the brink twice, only to leave me aching, wild, and dizzy from the tension and blood rushing to my head.

"Say please," Mac said with a smirk I could hear in his voice.

I said nothing.

"Fine," he replied, and I heard the soft thud of the vibrator being set down on the bar top. A drawer slid open.

I lay there, wide open, blind and burning, my mind racing to guess what was coming next.

"When you finally say please," Mac said, smooth as silk, "then I'll stop."

Cold. *Ice-fucking-cold.*

I screamed as an ice cube touched between my legs, shocking and stinging as he held it there, pressed to my center. My hips jerked, trying to escape and seek it out all at once. The pain melted into pleasure as he dragged it slowly along my slit.

Water pooled beneath me as it melted, and then Mac's tongue returned—hot, wicked, soothing—only to be replaced by the ice again.

Over and over, the contrast drove me mad.

This wasn't the kind of pleasure that brought a quick release. It was the kind that built, layer by torturous layer, until the eventual fall would shatter me.

Each time Mac warmed me back up, the sting of the cold ice cube would bring me back again, edging the orgasm I desperately wanted to release.

"Do you want to come, Penelope?" Mac asked, his voice a low growl.

I nodded frantically, nearly shaking from the overwhelming switch between cold and heat.

"Please," I cried out, my voice cracking. "*Please.*"

"That's my girl," Mac said. "Begging for it."

The ice disappeared with a toss, landing somewhere across the bar. And then his fingers plunged into me, pumping deep and fast.

My blindfold came off, the sudden neon light stinging my eyes. I blinked against it, trying to focus through the haze of pleasure.

Mac hovered over me, his expression dark, intense—completely in control.

"Eyes on me," he ordered. "Scream my fucking name, Pen."

The hand that had removed the blindfold now circled my clit, rubbing hand and fast.

Stars exploded behind my eyes.

"Mac!"

My core tightened, the pressure unbearable.

I kept my gaze locked on his whiskey eyes as I fell, screaming his name again, my orgasm ripping through me like a tidal wave.

Everything else disappeared.

There was only Mac. Only the fire. Only the bliss of finally, *finally* falling apart in his hands.

CHAPTER 46

My cock was so hard I thought my zipper might snap under the pressure. Watching Penny come undone—watching her *scream* for me, *beg* for me—was my undoing. She was fucking perfect. Wild and stunning in every way.

Having her naked, sprawled out across my bar, flushed and glistening from the pleasure?

Nothing in my life had ever looked hotter.

I had no idea how I was going to work behind this bar again without getting hard at the memory of her body stretched out like that. She was wet, trembling, *mine*.

Penny didn't break eye contact as she came. I told her to keep her eyes on me, and she obeyed like the good girl she was. *My* girl.

And God, did she wear that title well.

"I need you inside me, Mac. I don't give a shit about first, second, third, or whatever fucking round," Penny hissed, her voice still shaking, thick with need.

If *me* was what she wanted, then that's what she would get.

I nodded once and helped her sit upright. Her hands were still cuffed behind her back, her hair tousled and wild from the blindfold, her lips red and kiss-swollen.

Reaching behind the bar, I grabbed a bottle of her favorite tequila. I cupped her jaw, gripping her cheeks firmly until her mouth opened, those glossy lips parting just the way I liked.

I tilted her head back and poured a slow stream of liquor straight into her mouth.

She let it pool there before swallowing, her throat working as the liquid slid down in a smooth line. I dragged my hand down, fingers wrapping gently around her throat, savoring the feel of her pulse thundering beneath my palm. I took a swig from the same bottle, then pulled her forward by the neck and spit the second shot into her mouth.

She drank it with no hesitation, tongue slipping out to lick her lips, a little bit dribbling from the corner of her mouth.

Fuck.

I couldn't hold back.

My mouth crashed into hers, messy and hungry and desperate. I reached behind her to release the cuffs, the metal clicking open just as she clung to me. Her fingers tangled in my hair, on my jaw—pulling me closer like she needed me to survive.

We kissed like we were trying to crawl inside each other, like nothing else mattered beyond this moment.

Still gripping her throat, I tore my mouth away to growl, "Get on your fucking knees."

Penny hopped down from the bar like a woman on a mission, her smile so bright it was almost wicked. She dropped to her knees in front of me with that spark in her eye—the one that always drove me wild.

I stroked the back of her head, threading my fingers through her hair as she looked up at me, wide-eyed and waiting. Her hands made quick work of my jeans, unbuttoning and pulling them down along with my briefs in one smooth motion.

My cock sprang free—aching and heavy.

She wrapped both hands around the shaft, slowly stroking, teasing me as her tongue flicked out to lick the tip. Just that first touch sent a bolt of heat shooting straight through me.

She lingered there, licking again before wrapping her lips around the head and sucking, slow and focused.

That *move*—the one where she pressed her tongue to the

underside of my cock while she sucked—that was the one that made my knees threaten to give out every time.

Penny took me deeper, working me inch by inch until I was fully in her throat.

No gag. No waiting. Just pure, practiced pleasure as I pounded against the back of her throat. Even then, she wasn't taking all of me.

Penny wasn't lying when she joked about not having a gag reflex.

"That's it," I grunted, placing a hand on the back of her head, guiding her deeper. "You like my cock, baby?"

She answered with a muffled *mmm*, pulling back with a wet *pop* as my cock sprang from her lips.

Her eyes locked on mine, filled with heat and mischief.

As much as I loved seeing Penny on her knees—lips swollen, eyes full of fire—I was desperate to be buried deep between her legs.

She opened her mouth to take me again, but I gripped a fistful of her hair and hauled her to her feet. I pinned her against the bar, my hand cupping her jaw as I kicked off my pants.

Then I kissed her hard. So hard it stole the breath from her lungs.

She gasped against my mouth, and I took full advantage, slipping my tongue between her lips, claiming every part of her she offered. She met me without hesitation, her body arching into mine, her hands threading through the hair at the nape of my neck like she couldn't get enough.

I lifted her effortlessly, guiding her onto the edge of the bar. Her back hit the cool surface, legs locking me in like she was made to take me.

Lining myself up, I shoved into her in one smooth, desperate stroke.

Her slick heat welcomed me, tight and pulsing around my cock like she'd been aching just as bad as I was.

"*Yes*," she panted against my lips as I buried myself deeper.

"Fuck, Mac, yes."

She was clenched so tight I had to grit my teeth. My hand slammed down on the bar for leverage as I drove into her again. Her heels dug into my ass, holding me to her like she never wanted me to leave.

"Choke me," she panted, grabbing my one hand with hers and bringing it up to her throat again.

The tattooed ink around her pretty neck stared back at me like it belonged in a fucking painting. She was a masterpiece.

"Touch yourself," I growled. "Show me how bad you want it."

Her hand flew between us, fingers finding her clit as I slowed my pace. I pulled out until only the tip of me remained inside her, then sank back in slowly, watching myself disappear inch by inch into her dripping heat.

"Faster," I ordered, my voice ragged.

She obeyed instantly, circling her clit faster, her moans growing louder, more desperate. I picked up speed to match her rhythm, thrusting hard, our bodies slamming together with every movement.

Penny's head fell back, her hair tumbling down her spine as she rode the edge of bliss. She rocked with me, matching every thrust, her whole body surrendering to the rhythm we'd built.

I was so fucking close.

Tension coiled tight at the base of my spine. Fire shot through my veins as the pressure peaked. I grunted, pulled out at the last second, and spilled across her stomach—hot, thick, and utterly spent.

My chest heaved as I leaned over her, panting, watching her body tremble beneath mine, still quivering with the aftershocks of pleasure.

We locked eyes, something unspoken and powerful passing between us. She reached up and touched my cheek—not with heat or urgency, but with something softer. Something deeper. Her fingertips brushed my skin in a gesture full of tenderness, and the faint smile on her lips held more meaning than a thousand words.

I loved her.

This—*this*—was what love truly felt like.

Penny Hudson wasn't simply someone I loved. She *was* love, made flesh. Bright. Gentle. Fierce in the quietest of ways. She didn't just take up space in my world—she was the world.

CHAPTER 47

"We have to get down to business!" Aspen called as she burst through the front door of the bar, her tote bag swinging from her shoulder. Ellie and Logan trailed close behind.

I looked up from the bottles I was counting, eyebrows raised. The three of them were headed straight for me, Aspen clearly on a mission. I spotted the corner of a laptop sticking out of her bag—she was serious. Dead serious.

The grand gesture was happening.

I texted Aspen right after the night in the bar with Penny.

The night that lived rent-free in my head.

The night that had ruined me in the best damn way.

Every dream, every stolen moment in the shower... it was all Penny.

Penny, laid out across this exact bar. Her voice, her gasps, the way her skin flushed. It haunted me in the most addictive way.

I'd been right, working here with a clear head afterward? Impossible. Every night I'd catch myself brushing my fingers along the spot where her body had been, chasing a ghost of warmth.

And I'd smirk.

Because no one knew.

Our secret. Ours alone.

A theme for us.

Yeah, I'd cleaned the hell out of that bar afterward. But some things don't wash away. And honestly? I didn't want them to.

I was ready to stop holding back.

I loved this woman.

Probably too much for my own good.

"What are you two doing here?" I asked, eyeing Ellie and Logan suspiciously as they settled near the bar.

"We're here as the friend representatives," Ellie said matter-of-factly. "The others couldn't make it, so we're gathering intel and reporting back."

"What intel?" I asked, leaning my forearms on the bar, my eyes narrowing slightly.

"This is going to be a group effort," Aspen announced, not even glancing up as she typed furiously into her laptop.

I shot Logan and Ellie a look. They both shrugged like *don't ask us*.

"I thought I was the one confessing my love to Penny," I said, pointing dramatically at myself. "Not you guys."

Finally, Aspen looked up. She placed a hand over her heart and sighed dreamily.

"Hearing you say you love my best friend makes me feel all warm and fuzzy inside."

"With what you've got planned," Logan chimed in, his tone unusually stern, "you're gonna need all the help you can get. So quit whining."

I raised my hands in mock surrender, lips twitching into a grin.

Fair enough.

"So," I said, glancing around at the small but determined group of co-conspirators. "Where do we want to start?"

"I'm going to order the things we need. Hopefully, I can get them delivered before the weekend," Aspen said, typing away on her laptop.

Ellie leaned over the polished surface, eyes curious. "Did you have any inspiration? Any visuals we can see to get the full picture of what you're planning?"

I hummed and pulled out my phone. Aspen had introduced me to Pinterest—more like, demanded I download it and start building what she called a *mood board*. It was a good tool to help us visualize everything we wanted for this grand plan.

Navigating to the shared board we'd been building, I turned the screen toward Ellie. Logan slid in beside her to get a look, though judging by the blank expression on his face, he had no idea what he was supposed to be looking for.

Aspen tapped Ellie's shoulder and took the phone, then passed it to Logan as she continued typing. He held the phone awkwardly, squinting at the images like they were a puzzle he didn't have the pieces for.

Then my phone dinged.

Once.

Twice.

A third time.

Logan handed it back quickly, as if sensing something was up. One glance at the screen, and I nearly groaned.

Penny

I can't stop thinking about your cock.

Penny

Please send me a photo... I'm about to get in the shower before work and I need more than just the memory of the other night.

Penny

I wonder what else we could do on the bar? 🤤

My fingers flew across the screen.

Dirty girl... but I'm busy right now.

Penny

Fine... I'll just have to use my imagination. And who knows who'll be there...

My jaw clenched.

Fuck no. Hold on.

Tucking the phone into my back pocket, I let out a low grunt and pulled my wallet from my jeans.

"Here," I said, tossing my credit card onto the bar like it was a grenade. "I'll be right back."

Aspen and Ellie were still fangirling over god-knows-what, and giving Aspen my credit card might have been a terrible idea—but right now, there were more pressing matters.

I darted down the hallway, slipped into my office, and shut the door behind me. Collapsing into my desk chair, I pulled out my phone and typed fast.

Prove you're in the shower.

A moment later, her response landed.

Penny

Is this enough proof?

The image made my breath hitch. Her breasts were covered in slick, glistening soap, one hand gripping herself while she bit her bottom lip. I could practically *feel* her through the screen.

I tilted my head, inspecting every detail. God, she was unreal. My cock stirred beneath my jeans, blood rushing fast.

I rubbed myself through the denim.

I think I still need convincing.

The typing bubbles popped up... then disappeared. My stomach twisted. *Shit. Did I go too far?* Maybe she just wanted something quick and playful, not—

Buzz.

A video.

I hit play.

At first, it was just her face. Smiling. Glorious. She dipped her head under the spray of water, then angled the camera to reveal her body, every inch of it slick with suds.

She ran the camera down, her hand following, tracing her curves until she reached between her legs. Her fingers moved with intention—teasing, rubbing, slipping inside. I swore the air left my lungs when she looked back up and whispered:

"How about now?"

"Fuck," I groaned, tipping my head back, a smile breaking through even as my zipper strained against the pressure.

I undid my jeans and freed myself, already hard and aching. My hand wrapped around the base, slow at first.

You're fucking perfect. I want that pussy on my face.

I opened my camera, angled it low, and took a shot—my hand wrapped around my cock, back arched in the chair.

Attached.

Sent.

Typing bubbles appeared almost immediately.

Penny

I wish you were here...

Me too. The things I'd do to you.

Penny
Like what?

I'd be on my knees, pinning you against the wall while you ride my face. You'd have all the control. I'd be there to worship you.

I groaned again, stroking harder at the fantasy. Just imagining her above me, wild and beautiful, had my thoughts unraveling.

You'd be screaming so damn loud, like I know you can, Trouble.

Another video landed in my inbox. I propped the phone against the base of my monitor and hit play.

Penny had her phone set at the edge of the shower, her fingers moving between her legs, her breath catching as she rubbed in tight circles. And then—

My name.

Over and over.

Moaned. Whimpered. Cried out as she tipped over the edge.

Her body trembled on screen as she came, her head thrown back, pleasure radiating through the phone like heat.

I watched it again. I had to. The way she used my photo as her source of release sent a jolt straight through my spine.

I closed my eyes, stroking myself harder, faster, as the sound of her voice echoed in my mind.

On a broken groan, I came, chest rising and falling, body spent.

Then—

A knock.

Panic struck. The chair rolled backward too fast and nearly took me with it. I scrambled, fumbling for a tissue and then with my jeans just as the door opened.

Logan stood in the doorway. Staring. Then, slowly, he looked up at the ceiling with the defeated expression of a man who'd seen too much.

"Why me?" he asked the heavens.

Still tucking myself away, I wiped my hand with a second tissue. No shame. None. Zero.

"Hey, man. Maybe one day, you'll get your revenge."

"For fuck's sake," he muttered. "Aspen needs your help."

CHAPTER 48

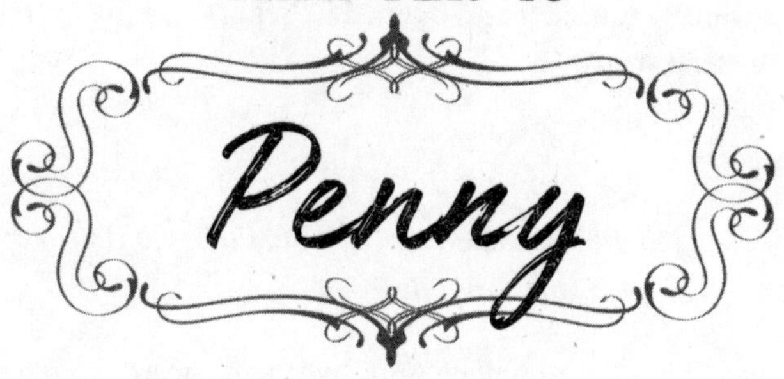

The day was finally over—thank God.

I collapsed into my desk chair with a sigh that came straight from my soul. Every muscle in my body went limp, my arms dangling over the sides like I'd just run a marathon instead of managing chaos for eight hours straight. My office was quiet, blessedly so, and I could finally breathe.

There had to be a full moon coming. Either that or the end-of-year madness had taken full control. School let out next week, and the kids were basically feral. One student tried to eat a crayon today. A *Macaroni and Cheese*-colored crayon, no less, because he thought it would taste like pasta. That was the final straw. I fled to my office before I said something I'd regret.

Outside, summer was settling in like a hot breath on the back of my neck. Spring was officially saying goodbye, and Texas wasn't wasting any time bringing the heat.

I sat up straighter, shaking off the exhaustion, when I noticed something resting across my keyboard.

A single red rose.

My breath caught.

I was so distracted by my thoughts that I didn't notice it until now.

I reached for it gently, twirling the stem between my fingers. Its petals were velvet-soft, a perfect bloom of deep red, so vibrant it almost didn't look real.

Attached to the stem with a piece of twine was a small folded note. I carefully untied it and opened it, heart skipping even before I read the first word.

Penelope,

I put together a scavenger hunt for you. I'll be waiting at the end. Read each clue carefully.

Your first stop: the place to go when you were having a rough day. They're always consistent and the only spot in Faircloud that has your favorite kind of this food.

—Mac

I pressed the note to my chest, a smile tugging at my lips, and let out a soft laugh. A scavenger hunt? For me? With Mac waiting at the end?

My heart swelled, full and warm. This was his Hail Mary. His big gesture.

Leaving everything behind except my phone and keys, I slipped out of my office and through the library, weaving past coworkers and curious glances without stopping. The front doors of the building opened to a golden horizon—the sun was setting, casting honey-colored light across the pavement—and the warmth wrapped around me like encouragement.

I already knew the answer to his first clue.

There was only one place in Faircloud that served my favorite comfort food. One place that never failed to lift my spirits when I was low.

The little Italian restaurant just a few doors down Main Street.

As I walked, I thought of the time Mac showed up at my place unannounced and filled my fridge with groceries and a container of chicken parmesan.

Thoughtful. Generous. Always paying attention.

That was Mac.

I reached the restaurant and pulled open the door, greeted instantly by the smell of roasted garlic, basil, and marinara. Soft Italian music floated through the air, and the lights inside were low, casting everything in a cozy, golden glow.

The hostess at the front counter smiled knowingly.

Without a word, she ducked behind the counter and came back up holding another red rose—and a white to-go container.

I smiled and offered a heartfelt "thank you" before stepping back out into the warm evening air. On the sidewalk, I paused to unfold the next note that was tucked beneath the rose's petals.

Penelope,

Go to the place where we danced for the first time. It's familiar. Completely you. It's also where you burned the breadsticks and tried to blame me...

—Mac

A laugh bubbled up in my chest.

My apartment.

That night had been an accidental kind of magic—music playing from the speaker on my counter, our impromptu dance in the living room, and, yes, the breadsticks that ended up charred because we were too wrapped up in each other to notice the timer.

I quickened my pace, passing the darkened windows of Petal Pusher, still closed. The stairwell to my apartment seemed steeper than usual, anticipation bubbling with each step.

I slipped inside, eyes scanning every surface for a flash of red.

Nothing in the entryway. Nothing on the coffee table or counters.

I placed the container in the fridge and continued my search, heart racing now.

Down the hallway, I wandered into my bedroom, and that's when I saw it lying across my bed.

A dress lay draped across the blanket, soft fabric rippling. A rose rested on top, as delicate and perfect as the others.

The dress was beautiful—long and flowing, with a thigh-high slit and cap sleeves. The soft pink floral pattern looked like it belonged in a garden of daydreams. My fingers skimmed the fabric, and something inside me fluttered.

I picked up the rose, then the note tucked beneath it, ready for the next clue.

Penelope,

Put on the dress with your favorite pair of boots and then head to the heart of Faircloud. After you find the next note, there will be a car waiting to take you to the next stop.

—Mac

The heart of Faircloud. That had to mean the Community Park—right in the center of town, the place where everything happened.

I slipped out of my clothes and stepped into the dress. The fabric hugged my hips as I pulled it up, fitting like it had been made just for me.

I walked over to the standing mirror and took myself in.

Every dip. Every curve.

The way the material clung to my skin made me feel like I wasn't just wearing a dress—I was wearing a memory. Mac knew my body better than anyone. He'd memorized it with his hands, with his eyes, with every glance that lingered too long and every touch that left me breathless.

Dropping to my hands and knees, I crawled into the back of my closet, fumbling for my favorite pair of boots—the exact ones

Mac always said made me look like trouble in the best possible way.

My heart pounded. Excitement bubbled hot in my chest. I didn't know what he had waiting at the end of this hunt, but every step closer made me feel like I was walking toward something that would change everything.

If I had the lungs for it, I'd have sprinted to the park. But I also knew my own stamina and, frankly, it wasn't going to get me far in this heat.

So, I walked. Briskly.

Down the stairs, back into the golden dusk of the Texas evening. I didn't bother with the crosswalk—just darted across the street and into the park, my boots clicking against the pavement.

Who was I looking for?

What was I even supposed to be looking for?

The winding sidewalk stretched out ahead of me, curving gently through the trees and flower beds. I let instinct lead, trying to think like Mac.

If I were Mac, where would I leave a clue in the heart of Faircloud?

Maybe... the heart of the park, too.

The pavilion.

The tall, white structure came into view just beyond a bend in the path. I felt my pulse kick. Someone was already standing beneath it.

Back turned.

But I knew that hair. That stance. That energy.

Sandy.

I slowed my steps and crept up behind her, but my boots gave me away. She turned, grinning as she held out another rose.

I blinked at her, smiling in disbelief. "He roped you into this?"

She shrugged, proud. "Of course he did. He's very persuasive and he sure as hell loves you."

Her words hit me square in the chest.

He loves you.

My throat tightened. I swallowed.

I'd known it, hadn't I? Felt it in every gesture, every look, every ridiculous thing he did to make me smile. But hearing it—*saying* it—was something else.

"I love him, too," I whispered, the words tumbling out like a prayer, light and sacred. It was the easiest truth I'd ever spoken.

Sandy smiled, eyes soft, and pulled me into a quick, warm hug. She planted a dramatic kiss on my cheek and pulled back, placing the rose in my hand with a wink.

"Go get him," she said gently.

I nodded, turning as she pressed the rose into my palm. Another note was tied around the stem with twine. My fingers trembled slightly as I unfolded it and read:

Penelope,

There's a truck waiting for you around the bend. Your driver's ready.

Your next destination is a place we'd go on the nights we needed to escape reality. The stars never shone quite as bright as you.

—Mac

I scanned the area, searching for a truck. Not that it helped much—this was small-town Texas, and *everyone* drove a truck. It was practically a requirement for residency.

But then, one stood out.

Leaning casually against the front bumper was Rhodes, his ankles crossed as he stared out at the fiery sunset sinking beneath the horizon.

"Rhodes?" I called, uncertainty lacing my voice.

He turned at the sound of my voice, that familiar, gentle smile blooming across his face. "Penny," he said softly. "You look lovely."

He was wearing a suit.

A damn *suit*.

Rhodes. The man who practically lived in jeans and a flannel. His hat was missing, too—his usually wild hair was brushed back neatly behind his ears. It was so unlike him, yet somehow still *him*.

Without a word, he walked around the truck and opened the passenger door, holding it open with quiet expectation. I hesitated, just for a second. Then I trusted my gut—and Mac—and slid inside with a soft smile.

He shut the door gently, like the moment was something sacred, and then circled around to the driver's seat.

"Sandy and now you?" I asked, turning slightly to face him. "Are you going to give me any hints about what he's planning?"

Rhodes tsked under his breath and gave a short shake of his head. "Not a chance." He glanced at me, his lips twitching. "So, where to?"

I pulled the note from my lap and read it again, this time with a little more weight.

"The overlook."

Rhodes nodded, shifted the truck into drive, and pulled onto the road. I doubted he didn't know where we were going; he was just asking for good measure.

Silence fell between us, but it wasn't uncomfortable.

"I know you knew the whole time," I finally said.

He gave me a sidelong glance. "It wasn't my place to say anything. But for what it's worth... he's really sorry, Penny. I've known Mac a long time. I've never seen him like this."

"I know," I whispered, looking down at the rose still in my lap. "I can see how hard he's trying. He's been trying for a while now."

The overlook wasn't far—just a few minutes from downtown Faircloud. As we got closer, my heart beat faster, nerves tangling with anticipation in the center of my chest.

"So," Rhodes began, "you two came here a lot?"

I smiled and turned to the window, my gaze drifting to the trees Mac and I parked beneath more than once.

"We did," I said softly. "Nights when we needed to breathe. When his place felt too small, mine too quiet."

I could still picture it. The two of us lying in the truck bed, the stars twinkling above us like our own private sky. We'd point out fake constellations and invent stories for them, laughing until our stomachs hurt. He'd wrap his arm around my shoulders, at first pretending it was just to stay warm or get comfortable.

But now? I knew better. It was always just an excuse to hold me closer.

The truck rolled to a stop, and I spotted a figure near the edge of the overlook.

Boone.

He stood with his back to me, the familiar shape of his cowboy hat outlined by the fading sun. He turned as I approached, his signature smirk already in place.

I didn't wait for Rhodes to open my door—I was already out and striding toward him.

"Oh my God," I said, laughing as I threw my hands up. "Did Mac recruit everyone for this?"

"Just about," Boone said, pulling me into a one-armed hug. "Took a lot of planning. He wanted it perfect."

"I can tell," I replied, my voice thick with emotion.

Boone's smile softened. "I'm sure Rhodes said something like this already, but I'm saying it, too. Mac really does love you, Penny."

The words landed deep in my chest. And not in a shocking way. No, they settled there like they'd always belonged.

And the fact that our friends saw it, believed in us enough to dress up and play along, to spend their night helping Mac...

It meant everything.

"Good thing I feel the same way about him."

Boone grinned and handed me the rose, letting it go only when he was sure I had it. A note was tied around the stem with twine.

I untied it with trembling fingers, heart racing, and read:

Penelope,

I can't wait to see you.

Your next and final stop is the place where we spent our first night together, surrounded by our friends. It was the night I knew I'd make you mine.

Boone is going to blindfold you. The next part is a surprise.

See you soon, Trouble.

—Mac

My breath caught.

This was really happening.

My attention snapped to Boone, who now held a black blindfold between his fingers, letting it dangle like a challenge.

"Time to get your man," he said with a grin, then stepped behind me and gently wrapped the fabric around my eyes. The world went dark.

Boone's hand found mine, firm and steady, guiding me toward a waiting truck. I didn't know if he or Rhodes would be driving, it didn't matter. My heart was pounding so loud I could hear it in my ears. As I sank into the passenger seat, one leg bounced uncontrollably with anticipation.

I stayed quiet for the entire ride, lost in thought, spinning through every possibility of what Mac was planning in the end. Boone didn't ask any questions. He knew exactly what this was, where we were going. That much was clear.

There was only one place that made sense.

Cassidy Ranch.

The first night I'd met Mac one-on-one had been at a bonfire there with Aspen and Theo. We'd flirted, joked, connected in a way that felt simple and magnetic. From that moment, it had been nothing but tension until the day we finally gave in.

And now here I was, blindfolded in a truck, following clues in a romantic scavenger hunt planned by the man I *loved.*

CHAPTER 49

I let out a breathy laugh, dropping my head between my shoulders and shaking it in disbelief.

The truck slowed, then came to a stop. A second later, the door opened and fresh air rushed in against my flushed skin. Two hands reached for mine and carefully helped me to the ground.

I followed blindly, one tentative step at a time, my pulse thrumming with every movement.

"Where are we?" I whispered.

"You'll see soon," Boone replied, his voice cryptic.

We walked for what felt like forever—boots on gravel, the rustling of grass underfoot, the smell of something sweet lingering in the air—until he stopped and gently let go of my hand.

In his place, a new warmth wrapped around me. Familiar. Immediate. I smiled before he even spoke.

"Hi," I breathed.

"Hi, Penelope," Mac said, and God... his voice. That low, husky rasp sent butterflies tumbling through my stomach.

He led me forward a few more steps before stopping.

"Ready?" he asked, his voice thick with emotion.

I nodded eagerly. "Yes," I laughed, barely able to contain myself.

Mac released my hand, then slipped his fingers beneath the blindfold. Slowly, he lifted it away—and the second my eyes adjusted, I froze.

I had been right. We were at Cassidy Ranch.

But not at the bonfire.

We stood in the doorway of the barn, and it'd been completely transformed.

Warm string lights hung from the rafters, bathing the space in a soft, golden glow. Rose petals had been scattered across the floor in the shape of a giant heart. It was intimate. Dreamlike.

I turned to Mac, my eyes pooling slightly with tears of pure joy.

My jaw might've hit the floor because he looked *devastatingly* good.

He stood proud in an all-black, sinfully tailored suit. His black dress shirt was unbuttoned just enough to reveal the edge of the tattoo on his chest. Cowboy boots grounded the look, but with everything else? He looked like temptation in fabric.

I bit my lip, unable to look away.

"You like what you see, Pen?" he asked, amusement dancing in his eyes.

I nodded slowly, dragging out my reply with a grin. "I do."

Just then, soft country music filtered through hidden speakers, the kind of song that tugged at your heartstrings and begged for slow dancing.

Mac reached for my hand and walked backward, leading me into the center of the rose petal heart.

His hands settled at my waist instinctively, like they belonged there. My arms draped around his neck as I tilted my head to look up at him.

"I was going to ask if you'd dance with me," he murmured, "but I guess it's second nature now."

"Is this our thing?" I asked quietly.

"I guess so," he said, smiling down at me. "We're not really dancers... but somehow, this is what we keep coming back to."

"Maybe because it gives us an excuse to touch each other?"

Mac chuckled, his voice a warm rumble against my chest.

"I'm always looking for a reason to be close to you."

"This was sweet," I whispered, my voice barely carrying over the soft hum of the music. "Everything you planned tonight."

Mac's lips curved, but there was something unreadable in his expression—something more. "It's not over," he said, his voice rough with emotion. "I've been working on something else."

I tilted my head, curiosity blooming like wildflowers in my chest.

Still swaying with me, Mac reached into the pocket of his suit jacket and pulled out his phone. He kept one arm looped around my waist as he glanced down at the screen. I followed his gaze and saw a long string of text in his notes app—paragraphs. Plural.

My eyes flicked back to his, breath catching.

"I'm gonna read something I wrote," he said, his voice low and nervous. "Because I didn't want to fuck this up."

I nodded, swallowing the lump forming in my throat, already blinking against the tears threatening to fall.

Mac cleared his throat.

"Penelope," he began, "these last few months have been the best months of my life. Getting to know you—your mind, your heart, and yes, your body." He paused, lifting his gaze to meet mine, and gave me a quick, teasing wink. "Has been time I'd relive a thousand times over.

"From the moment we sat around that bonfire last year, I knew I was going to make you mine. Whether it was just one night or multiple, I knew I'd have a piece of you. But deep down, I think I always knew... it was never just going to be one night. You were my undoing before you even said a damn word. Then you opened that beautiful mouth and my God..."

I laughed, the sound breaking free as I leaned forward and pressed my forehead to his chest for a second, my smile soaking into the fabric of his shirt.

Mac's voice softened, his tone shifting with regret. "Then I fucked it all up. I was stupid. Naive. I thought a woman as fierce, beautiful, and strong as you would just... come back to me. That

I'd be forgiven without doing the work. I waited. Hoped. Thought maybe I could coast and get back what we had."

He shook his head.

"But you didn't let me off that easily, and thank God you didn't. You showed me that love isn't easy. It's earned. You made me better, Pen. You made me *want* to be better. And you deserve that. You deserve all the attention, the intention. You deserve to be seen. Fought for. Worshipped."

He stopped reading then, locking his phone and slipping it back into his pocket with care, as if what he'd just said didn't even scratch the surface.

Mac's hands came up to cradle my face, and we stopped moving. The music faded in my ears as everything narrowed to just him. His touch. His gaze. His words.

"You're not just a part of my future, Penelope," he said, his voice raw, trembling with everything he felt. "You *are* my future. You're the reason I want to build something more. The reason behind every choice I'll make from here on out. You're my beginning and my end. My everything."

And that was it—the dam broke.

Tears spilled over, streaking my cheeks as I clutched at his jacket. His words were a balm and a wound all at once. Too much and still somehow not enough.

"I am so fucking in love with you, Penelope Hudson, that it hurts," he said, his eyes burning into mine. "I am a man wrecked because of it, because nothing will ever compare to you. I'm completely, irrevocably yours."

He lifted my hand, turned it palm-up, and pressed a kiss to the tip of my pinky finger.

"You have me wrapped around..."

He kissed the next finger. "Every."

Then the next. "Damn."

Another kiss. "One."

And another. "Of your..."

His lips pressed to my thumb, lingering there as he looked up at me with a tender smile that shattered the last of my composure.

"Fingers."

"Oh, Mac..." I breathed, my heart pounding so hard it echoed in my ears.

His eyes searched mine, warm and vulnerable, his voice barely above a whisper. "I hope I've done enough."

"You have," I said softly, a smile tugging at my lips. "I love you. I've loved you for far longer than I admitted. I never stopped. Not when everything fell apart, not even when I tried so hard to avoid you. I never lost this spark, the one that ignites every time I'm near you."

Mac exhaled, the breath of a man who'd been holding on, waiting. He pressed his forehead to mine, his touch gentle, grounding.

"You make me feel a way I never had," I confessed. Never once in my life have I experienced genuine, unconditional love like this before. Someone who spent weeks planning and plotting all on the hope that things would change.

"I meant it when I said I'd do anything for you, Penny," he murmured, voice rough with feeling.

I tilted my head and caught his lips in a kiss—urgent, aching, deep. It wasn't just a kiss. It was a declaration, a surrender, a promise sealed in the press of our mouths. It redefined every kiss that came before because this one... this one meant everything.

It was love.

It was forever.

A loud pop exploded behind us, startling me so much that I jumped back, clutching Mac's chest in surprise.

I spun around, only to find all our friends standing near the barn doors, each holding a confetti cannon, grinning like fools. Pink glitter rained down from the rafters in a sparkling, slow-motion storm of celebration.

"Oh my God," I gasped with a breathless laugh, my chest shaking as the confetti drifted around us like magic.

I looked up, spinning slowly in the glowing barn light, glitter clinging to my hair and shoulders. "*The pink glitter?*" I called, turning back to Mac with wide, amused eyes.

He was grinning, full and wide, as he gazed up at the shimmering sky of color. "How could I not? It was pretty iconic."

The barn erupted with cheers, whistles, and the unmistakable sound of love being celebrated by those who knew us best.

I looked around at the faces of our friends—beaming, laughing, holding up their phones and clapping like proud witnesses to something real.

Something right.

And then I looked at Mac.

My heart swelled so full it felt like it might burst, overflowing with gratitude and a joy that left me breathless.

I had my people.

I had *him*.

What did I ever do to deserve this kind of love?

Whatever it was, I'd do it again in a heartbeat.

CHAPTER 50

Penny trailed her finger slowly down the center of my chest, circling just above my belly button before sliding back up again. Over and over, she traced the same path, each stroke light as air, teasing and tickling in a way that lit up every nerve ending. I lay there beneath her touch, completely content, completely hers.

We'd spent the morning tangled in bed, the kind of lazy intimacy that didn't need to be defined. Just *us*. Just the quiet comfort of knowing the hardest part was behind us.

My girlfriend.

My *everything*.

I reached up and tucked a strand of her hair behind her ear, my fingers lingering at her jaw as I looked at her with a smile I couldn't contain. I must've looked like a lovesick idiot, but I didn't care. Not one bit.

We were here. Together. No secrets. No confusion. No more pretending we didn't want the life we kept dancing around.

Honesty was the new rule, so I decided to stop holding back.

"I've been thinking," I said softly.

Penny smirked, eyes twinkling. "I hope not too hard. Wouldn't want you hurting yourself."

I gave her a mock glare. "Fine. Forget it. I'm not telling you now."

She gasped dramatically and sat up, shifting to straddle my

hips, her thighs hugging my sides. The oversized shirt she wore slid off one shoulder, revealing a teasing flash of skin.

"Boo," she said, grinning. "Tell me."

I turned my head, feigning stubbornness, but she wasn't having it. She cupped my face, guiding my gaze back to hers.

"Mac," she whined, dragging my name out like it was a promise.

I sighed, hands finding her hips as I pulled her flush against me. My fingers dug in just enough to make her gasp as I began to roll her hips, guiding her to grind against me.

"I've been thinking," I murmured, "about how damn cute our babies will be."

Her eyes widened, her breath catching. "Babies?" she squeaked.

"Oh, Penny," I said with a wicked smile. "I'm going to get you pregnant. That's not up for debate."

Her lips parted, surprise written all over her face—and a flicker of something else, too. Something warm. Curious. Turned on.

"We have a lot of things to figure out first," she said, though her hips kept moving with mine, slow and sinfully sweet.

"Like what?" I asked, voice low, pulse kicking up.

"Well," she murmured, biting her lip, "we definitely can't raise a baby in either of our tiny apartments."

"Then let's get a house," I said instantly. "Let's move in together."

She blinked, stunned by how fast I answered—how sure I was.

I didn't flinch. Didn't hesitate.

Because I didn't need more time.

Didn't need more signs.

Penny Hudson was *it* for me.

"You're serious," she whispered.

"So fucking serious."

I sat up slightly, sliding my hands up her sides to cup her

breasts, thumbs brushing over the thin fabric of her shirt. She stilled for just a moment, then a slow, sultry smile spread across her face.

"Well," she said, her voice dipping into a sultry purr, "that could be kind of fun..."

Her lips found my neck, kissing, nibbling, teasing her way toward my ear. I groaned, letting the sensation roll through me like thunder.

"Think about all the places I'd get to fuck you," I murmured, my voice rough as I pictured her naked in every room of our future home—her body arched over countertops, knees on couch cushions, back against a shower wall.

The thought alone had my cock hard as stone. But it was the image of her, round with my child, glowing and soft and mine in every way, that nearly did me in.

Her grin widened as she ground down harder, rubbing along the length of me with a wicked giggle.

"Thinking about you, growing our baby..." I groaned, jaw tightening.

"You were *really* hot reading to the kids at the library," she teased.

I raised an eyebrow. "That's what you were thinking about while watching me?"

"Maybe," she sang, then leaned back, placing both hands on my chest with a satisfied smirk.

God help me, I was in so much trouble.

"Then let's do it. I'll get you pregnant right now."

I sat up, flipping Penny onto her back. She hit the mattress with a laugh, and her hair flew around her. I grabbed her wrists, pinning them above her head.

"We move in together first, then we talk about a potential baby," she said.

"Fine," I groaned, leaning down to press a trail of kisses along Penny's bare shoulder. "I'll start looking right after I'm done with you."

Just then, a knock sounded at the door—firm and relentless.

I sagged against her with a groan. "You've got to be kidding me."

Penny laughed, squirming beneath me. "Go see who it is and hurry back."

"I don't want to," I muttered, brushing another kiss to her shoulder before leaning in for one more. "I'd much rather stay right here."

Knock. Knock. Knock.

Whoever was on the other side of that damn door clearly wasn't taking a hint.

With a growl, I finally peeled myself off Penny and stalked toward the door in nothing but my boxers. I didn't care who saw me. This was my place, I wasn't promising modesty.

I flung the door open, ready to snap, only to find my sister standing there. Arms crossed, jaw tight, her sharp bob just brushing her shoulders like it was cut for battle.

"What?" I asked, my tone sharp, clearly irritated.

"Can I talk to you?" she asked coolly. "Downstairs."

I glanced over my shoulder at Penny, who gave me a playful wave of dismissal. I sighed, shutting the door softly and heading for my clothes.

After pulling on a pair of jeans and grabbing a T-shirt off the floor, I leaned down and gave Penny one last kiss. Then, reluctantly, I made my way downstairs to see what the hell Lizzie needed *now*, of all times—especially when Penny and I had just been talking about moving in together.

The hardwood felt cool beneath my socked feet as I padded into the bar. Lizzie sat perched on a barstool, waiting.

Naturally, I rounded the bar and stood behind it, leaning against the back wall. I crossed my ankles and folded my arms, giving her a look.

"So? What's so important it couldn't wait ten more damn minutes?"

She didn't flinch. "I want to give you the bar."

I blinked. "What?"

"You heard me."

"Why?" The word shot out before I could stop it.

She pulled a thick stack of papers from her tote bag and set them on the surface like a challenge.

"I never wanted it," she said quietly. "I thought I was doing you a favor by holding on to it. But after everything... I realize I was wrong."

My eyes flicked to the paperwork, then back to her face. She was unreadable, all business, no emotion.

"What's the catch?" I asked, skeptical.

She rolled her eyes. "You said you didn't want to keep fighting. We called a truce. This"—she nodded toward the documents—"is me honoring that."

I stepped forward, flipping through the pages. My name. Legal transfer. Ownership. It was all there.

The bar.

The woman of my dreams—half-naked in my bed upstairs.

Everything I wanted was within reach.

"What happens next?" I asked, my voice softer.

"We call the lawyer, sign those papers, and the bar is yours."

"No. I mean for you," I said, looking up at her again.

A flicker of surprise crossed her face. The guarded expression cracked just slightly.

Truth was, I *wanted* the bar. Always had. But now? After everything with Penny... after watching my friends rally for me, after Sandy and realizing what mattered, I wanted to change a lot about my life. That included Lizzie.

"I'm not sure," she admitted. "Maybe head back to the city. Find a new job. I haven't figured it out yet."

"Stay," I said.

She raised an eyebrow.

"Seriously. I'll take the bar, but I want you to stay in Faircloud."

Lizzie immediately shook her head. "I can't. My lease is up, and I don't have a reason to sign another because who knows how long it will be."

"Then move upstairs."

Her laugh burst out. "What? I cannot live in a one-bedroom with *you*. We barely survive an hour together."

"Not *with* me," I said, exasperated. "I won't be there much longer."

She blinked. "What the hell does that mean?"

"I'm looking for houses," I said with a shrug. "It's time I grow up."

Lizzie tilted her head, assessing me. A slow smirk curled her lips as realization dawned.

"This have something to do with the girl upstairs?"

"It's *because* of her," I said simply.

She hummed, nodding slowly. "I'm happy for you."

I reached behind the bar and grabbed the pack of cigarettes and lighter I kept stashed there. I lit one and took a long drag. Lizzie opened her mouth to protest, but I beat her to it.

"Hey," I said, tapping the stack of papers. "This is mine now. You can't say shit."

She snorted. "Not yet."

I exhaled slowly and looked her in the eye. "I really want you to stay, Lizzie. I want you in my life. I know things weren't always civil between us, but... I want to change that."

Her smile started small, but then it grew—bright, genuine, the kind I'd never seen from her before.

"I'll think about it," she said.

Lizzie slid off the barstool, reaching for her tote. "I won't keep you," she said softly. "Once you've signed the papers, let me know."

We exchanged a small smile, and I gave her a firm nod—the kind that said more than words ever could. Without another word, she turned and walked out the front door, leaving behind a stillness that settled deep into the room.

I sat there in the quiet, letting it wash over me.

Everything was changing.

And for the first time in a long damn while, it felt good.

I had the bar. I had my woman upstairs. I had a future that looked more like a dream than anything I ever thought I deserved.

The soft patter of bare feet came down the stairs, pulling my gaze upward. Penny stood at the base, wrapped in my oversized shirt, her hair tousled and wild from bed. Her eyes searched the room, cautious and curious.

"She's gone," I said, taking a slow drag from my cigarette. The smoke curled in the air between us as she relaxed, the tension falling from her shoulders.

Penny crossed the room and slipped behind the bar without hesitation, sliding against my body like she belonged there—and damn, she did. She wrapped her arms around my waist, resting her cheek against my chest.

"What's going on?" she murmured.

I let the cigarette hang between my lips as I wrapped her up in my arms, squeezing her tight, grounding myself in her warmth.

"She gave me the bar," I said into her hair.

Penny pulled back, her eyes wide with delight. "She did?"

"She did," I said with a grin. "As soon as I sign those papers, I'm officially the owner of The Tequila Cowboy."

Her whole face lit up. "Mac!" she squealed, grabbing my hands in hers. "That's amazing!"

I slipped my hands from her grasp, placed the cigarette into the ashtray, and then hooked my arms around her waist. With a playful grunt, I lifted her and settled her on top of the bar. She let out a surprised giggle, looping her arms around my neck like it was second nature.

"Now," I said, stepping between her legs and cupping her jaw with one hand, "I really have everything I could've ever wanted."

I kissed her then, slow and deep, letting every word I hadn't said fall into that kiss instead.

She kissed me back like she felt it, like she knew exactly what it meant.

I never thought of myself as a lucky man.

But with her in my arms, my name on the bar I'd built my

dreams around, and a life that finally felt like mine...

I couldn't imagine being anything but lucky.

THE END

EPILOGUE

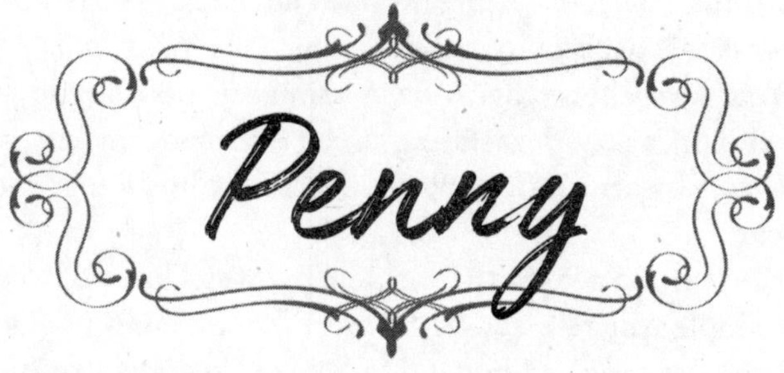

"Your sense of style is awful," I said, deadpan, as I yanked the thrifted Budweiser sign off the wall like it had personally offended me.

Mac turned around, all mock indignation and wounded pride. Hands on his hips, mouth already open to argue. "Excuse you, that is a work of *art*."

"It's a work of something," I muttered, tucking the frame under my arm, already making my way down the hall to the spare bedroom.

It took us two months to find a new home, which currently smelled faintly of paint and new beginnings. Mac moved into my apartment with me after his sister officially handed over the bar, and we spent a few chaotic weeks searching and arguing about backsplash tile, rug textures, and whether or not a vintage neon beer sign counted as "art."

Spoiler: It didn't.

Decorating with a man was not for the faint of heart. Especially not a man whose style leaned "college bar after last call." Meanwhile, mine could only be described as "cozy Pinterest board with a personality."

Still, somewhere between his chaos and my soft-girl aesthetic, we were finding a rhythm.

I was just shoving the sign into the corner of the closet when I felt him come up behind me. His arms wrapped around my waist, mouth grazing my neck in slow, strategic kisses.

"Mmm," I sighed, letting my head fall back. "You're not going to just kiss this decision out of me."

"You sure about that?" he murmured, his tongue teasing along my skin, a lazy, devastating sweep that made my knees weak.

"Mac," I warned, fighting a smile as his lips found the shell of my ear.

"I've learned a lot in the past few months," he said, voice low. "For example, you're a sucker for neck kisses... and books... and those lavender candles I pretend to hate but secretly like."

"You're very cocky for someone whose Budweiser art is about to die a lonely, dusty death in a closet."

He pulled back just enough to grin at me, that damn dimple softening his smirk. "You love my hands, Pen. Let me make you love my taste, too."

"Are we still talking about interior design?"

"Not even a little."

I turned in his arms and kissed him before he could say anything else.

He kissed me back like he always did, with both hands, all in. Like he wasn't just in this room, but in this life. With me. For good.

When we finally broke apart, I leaned my forehead against his chest. "Fine. You can keep the sign. In the garage. Behind the lawn mower."

"Fair," he said, pressing another kiss to my temple. "But I want it on record that you're limiting my creative freedom."

"I'm saving your reputation."

He grinned and dove back into silence with a kiss.

We spent the rest of the afternoon unpacking boxes and bantering over wall art and throw pillows. At one point, I caught him trying to sneak in Jack Daniel's bottles made into lights for the entryway.

He said it was "rustic." I said it was "tacky."

He lost.

Later, we ordered chicken parm, sat cross-legged on the floor of our new living room, and went through old photos we found while unpacking—ones from our high school years, blurry Polaroids of bonfires and bar nights, one of me on Boone's shoulders, laughing so hard I looked windblown.

And then there were the newer ones. Me and Mac. Our lives slowly merging like two puzzle pieces we didn't realize were always meant to fit.

At some point, as the sun dipped low and golden light filled the room, Mac leaned back against the couch and pulled me with him until I was sprawled across his lap, my head tucked beneath his chin.

He was quiet for a long time, his fingers running absently through my hair.

"You know," he said softly, "this house already feels like forever."

I smiled against his chest. "It does."

"And someday," he added, brushing a kiss to the top of my head, "when we've got a backyard full of dogs and maybe a couple of little monsters running around ruining your aesthetic..."

"You mean *our* aesthetic," I corrected.

He grinned. "Right. Our aesthetic. Even then, I'll still have that Budweiser sign. Somewhere."

"Only if I get my dream reading nook and floral wallpaper in the bathroom."

"Done deal."

We were building something here, something messy and sweet and real.

Something that felt like home.

I saw my life with him, clear as day. A future built on love, family, and the kind of traditions that stitched people together. I was ready. Because if there was anything the last year had taught me, it was that life could change in the blink of an eye.

I held Mac close, breathing in the scent of him—clean

laundry, a hint of cedar, and something warm that just felt safe. My mind flipped through images like a photo album: holidays with mismatched pajamas, our kids running through the house barefoot, late nights slow dancing in the kitchen.

"You know," I murmured, leaning back just enough to tuck a loose piece of hair behind his ear, "I'd marry you right now if you asked."

He let out a laugh, the kind that rumbled low in his chest, and tilted his head back like I'd just told him the wildest thing.

"Oh no," Mac said, still chuckling. "When I ask you to marry me, it's not going to be nonchalant. No way in hell."

I smirked. "I wouldn't be opposed to nonchalant."

He raised a brow.

"Well," I added, "maybe throw in a few fireworks."

Mac leaned in, his lips brushing mine in a soft, lingering kiss that made the room go quiet and the future feel so close I could taste it.

"Fireworks," he said against my mouth. "Got it."

ACKNOWLEDGMENTS

Four books written, and I'm so lucky to be able to have the same people to thank each time. The support I receive each time blows me away, and I know I say it a lot, but I truly mean it. To get to write stories people love truly is the best feeling in the world.

First and foremost, Nate—my wonderful fiancé. From the very beginning of my reading journey, you pushed me to take the leap, encouraging me to start a bookstagram. Did I ever think it would lead to writing four books? Absolutely not. And yet, here I am. Thank you for always believing in me, for your unwavering support, and for standing in my corner through it all. Thank you for spreading the word to anyone who can hear. I love you forever and always.

Keona—oh, my dearest Keona (the best PA a girl could ask for). I love you (so much it hurts). Thank you for being a constant source of strength, for talking me through doubts, impostor syndrome, and every "What am I even doing?" moment. Thank you for being my first phone call when I need to talk something through and being my sounding board. You remind me that my stories are worth telling, and I truly don't know where I'd be without you.

Vanesa, my ultimate hype girl—thank you for loving every MMC I write and for boosting my confidence with every new story. Your energy keeps me going. I can't thank you enough for being with me through this journey, coming along from the very beginning.

Mom and Dad—thank you for always believing in me and wanting to be a part of everything I do. I always know, no matter what adventure I embark on, you two will be there to support and help whatever dream become a reality. I love you both!

Mimi—my girl forever. Thank you for being a source of unconditional love and motivation through everything. If only you could see the inspiration you were to a character I wrote. One day, I'll have my book in audio so no one feels left behind.

Danie and Kayla—your insight, feedback, and guidance helped shape this book into what it was meant to be. Through voice memos, comments, and endless suggestions, you played a huge role in bringing this story to life, and I can't thank you enough.

Britt, Laura, Arthi, Olivia, Elise, and Carley—my second line of defense. You helped refine this story, offering your time, thoughts, and perspectives to make it the best it could be. I don't think I'll ever have enough words to express just how much I appreciate you.

And to the readers—three books officially published, and your support still blows me away. Thank you for shouting about my books from the rooftops, for recommending them to friends, family, and even your book clubs. I love you all more than words can say, and I only hope I continue to make you proud.

ABOUT THE AUTHOR

M. Hartley is a hopeless romantic with a soft spot for small-town charm and fictional cowboys with big hearts (and even bigger... you know). When she's not writing love stories over a glass of sweet red wine, she's spoiling her dog, Hank, or feeding her Swedish Fish addiction. Outside of writing, M. Hartley is a mental health advocate and therapist working in the community. She believes love has the power to heal, and that books are the perfect escape. Whether you're taking a mental vacation to a cozy small town or riding on the back of a dragon into battle, the possibilities are endless. M. Hartley writes romance because she believes there's nothing better than a love story that lingers long after the last page.

ALSO BY M. HARTLEY

Faircloud Series

The Story We Wrote

Where We Call Home

The Games We Play

Where We First Fell

Stone Ranch Series

Heart of Stone (Autumn 2026)

M. HARTLEY
WHERE WE FIRST Fell
A FAIRCLOUD NOVEL

Where We First Fell

After a betrayal that shattered her heart, Ellie Cassidy fled Faircloud, Texas, hoping time away would provide her the clarity she couldn't find in the confines of her small hometown. When the noise of the past finally quiets, she makes the hardest choice of all, to return.

Coming home means facing the whispers, the stares, and the weight of old wounds.

Faircloud has a way of testing her, and soon Ellie finds herself questioning everything all over again, especially her heart.

The only steady thing in her world? Logan Walker.

Her childhood best friend. Her fiercest protector. The boy who's quietly loved her for years and the man she's never stopped leaning on.

Logan has always stood by Ellie, even when it meant standing in the shadows. But when she needs an escape, he offers her more than just a shoulder—he offers a road trip, a chance to breathe, and maybe something she never dared hope for, a new chance at love.

As miles pass and secrets unravel, Ellie and Logan discover that sometimes, the love you've been searching for has been beside you all along, and the path back home leads straight into the arms you've always belonged in.